DORIS DAVIDSON

WATERS OF THE HEART

HarperCollins*Publishers*

F
653907

HarperCollins*Publishers*
77–85 Fulham Palace Road,
Hammersmith, London W6 8JB

Published by HarperCollins*Publishers* 1994
1 3 5 7 9 10 8 6 4 2

A catalogue record for this book is
available from the British Library

ISBN 0 00 224181 1

Set in Linotron Sabon by
Rowland Phototypesetting Ltd
Bury St Edmunds, Suffolk

Printed in Great Britain by
HarperCollinsManufacturing Glasgow

For the men in my life,
Jimmy, Alan, John and Bill
– not forgetting wee Matthew

PART ONE

Aberdeen

Chapter One

❖❖

1906

The screaming had stopped now, and seven-year-old Cissie McGregor was thankful that her sisters had slept through it. Not that they were old enough to know what was going on, but it would have terrified them, as she had been terrified last year, when Pat was born, until she had fitted all the pieces together in her mind.

The first thing she had noticed was the lump growing in Mam's belly, and it grew and grew for months before the new baby appeared in the kitchen bed, but it had taken her a long time to connect the baby with the lump. She still didn't know how a baby got inside her Mam, nor where it came out, but it must be terrible sore to make her scream the way she did.

'Why was Mam making noises like that?'

Marie's whisper recalled Cissie to her duty as eldest of the three girls. 'She's all right now, so go back to sleep.'

Reassured, Marie snuggled down again with her eyes closed, and Cissie wished that she could forget so easily, but it broke her heart to hear her mother in such pain. It suddenly occurred to her that when Pat was born he had started to cry not long after Mam stopped screaming, but there was no noise of any kind now. Maybe this one had been born sleeping.

A sudden clamour arising in the kitchen made her lift her head in an effort to discover what was happening now.

'No, Tam!' her mother was saying, sharply. 'I'll not let you do it.'

'How are you going to stop me?' Her father's voice

changed to coax his wife. 'It's the best way, Isa. I felt ashamed having to register the two dead bairns you had before, so I'll just . . .'

'It's a pity your shame didn't stop you from making any more,' Isa interrupted.

'The last two were all right,' he reminded her. 'Are you telling me you wouldn't have wanted them?'

'You've always got a way out, haven't you? Go on, then, take it away and do what you want with it.'

No more was said, but as Cissie listened to her father moving about, she tried to figure out what he meant to do. She had gathered that, during the three years between her sisters, there had been two babies born dead, so this one must be dead, too, and Da was going to get rid of it.

Hearing the landing door open and close quietly, she sat up on her knees to look out of the window and, after a few minutes, she saw him going down the hill with a bundle under his arm. Maybe they still took dead babies at hospitals, like they used to take bodies of men and women in the olden days to find out how they had died. She'd been interested when her teacher was telling them that, and when she'd said it was a cruel thing to do, Miss Deans had replied, 'Yes, it was quite barbaric, but it was the only way the doctors could learn.'

Her father safely out of the way, Cissie crept through to the kitchen and found her mother weeping bitterly in the bed in the recess. Her light brown hair was so damp that even the silvery threads through it, which always fascinated the little girl, were not shining like they usually did. 'Oh, Mam, don't cry,' she whispered.

'I can't help it, Cissie.'

'Are you sad because the baby died?'

'Yes, that's – oh, how did you know I'd had a baby?'

'I saw your belly getting fatter, so I knew weeks ago you were having another one, and I heard you screaming.'

'You shouldn't know about things like that at your age.'

Isa started another fit of sobbing then stopped to lift her head again, her blue-green eyes red-rimmed and swimming with tears. 'Don't worry your head about it, Cissie.'

'Has Da taken it away to the Children's Hospital at the Castlegate?'

'What makes you think that?'

'I thought he was taking the baby for the doctors to learn on. I know they used to cut up dead bodies to see why . . .'

'Oh, Cissie,' Isa shook her head. 'They're not allowed to do that nowadays. He's taking it to . . .' She stopped, shaking her head again. 'You'll have to promise me never to breathe a word of this, for a baby's birth has to be registered whether it's born alive or dead, but your father doesn't want people to know about this one. He's going to throw it in the docks.'

In Cissie's childish mind, this was no more barbaric than letting it be cut up by doctors, but she felt that she had to point out something her father must have overlooked. 'But what if somebody finds it?'

Isa's sigh ended in a sobbing hiccup. 'He was going to tie in a bit of the lead piping the plumbers left when they repaired the lavatories, so it would sink to the bottom and never come up.'

Satisfied that all was taken care of, Cissie was silent for a moment, then burst out, 'Mam, why do you keep having so many babies? Is us six not enough for you?'

'It's your father. He can't . . .' Isa broke off abruptly, having already said more than she should in her weakened state. 'Get back to your bed before he comes in, like a good lass, for he'll take it out on me if he sees you here.'

Cold and bewildered, the little girl had to shove her two sisters over before she could lie down again. She couldn't understand why Da would want more children. He was always on about the amount of food they ate and the clothes they all needed, though the younger girls wore what

5

she grew out of, and the two younger boys got Tommy's hand-me-downs. There would have been nine of them, if the other three had lived, so it was a good thing they hadn't, for there was hardly room for them all in the house as it was. Three in a bed was bad enough – it would be torture if there were more.

She had drifted into a troubled sleep when the click of the landing door brought her instantly alert, knowing that her father had come back. The sounds that filtered through made her strain her ears, but she couldn't hear what was being said until her parents raised their voices in anger.

'You'll have to stop it, Tam,' Isa said loudly. 'Even Cissie's noticed there's been a dead baby.'

'She's only a bairn herself, what does she know?'

'She knows they grow inside me, and it'll not be long till she understands how they get there. You're like an animal rutting every time you're at me.'

Tam gave a proud snigger. 'I'm a bull when I get going.'

'But the bairns are getting older. Do you want them to know the kind of man their father is, not able to leave a woman alone?'

'Ach, stop your whining! I'll not be able to touch you for a while.'

'Not for long enough. Before I know it, you'll have me in the family way again, and I'm not fit for it, Tam. If you'd stop drinking, that's all I ask. You'd be a good man but for that, for it's just when the drink's on you . . .'

'The drink kittles me up. Can you not understand how my body works, Isa? I can't help myself when I'm like that, and you're my wife. It's your duty.'

'I've done more than my duty to you, Tam, and my body'll not stand much more.'

'You're overtired just now.'

The voices died down to a murmur, and Cissie burrowed her head into the pillow. She loved her father as much as her mother, but Mam had made out the babies were his

6

fault, so how could he put Mam through so much pain? Surely he wasn't the fine man she thought he was?

Too sleepy to think any more, she cuddled up behind Marie and closed her eyes.

Chapter Two

❧❧

Marie gave her sister a sharp poke in the ribs. 'The kirk clock's struck seven, and Da's away ages ago.'

Struggling to make her body obey her, Cissie said, 'I'm just getting up.'

Two years younger, Marie was already broader than Cissie and almost as tall. Stretching her arms, she sat up to take out the rags she had put in the night before. Her straight fair hair was the bane of her life, and the rags, though they did help to put some body in it, didn't produce curls like Rosie's or deep waves like Cissie's. 'What was the noise in the middle of the night?' she enquired, running her fingers through her tousled mane.

'How should I know?' Cissie lowered her legs to the floor, wondering if they would take her weight when she stood up, for they felt as if they didn't belong to her. Waiting until two-year-old Rosie's eyes were open, she ordered, 'Out to the lavvy, you two.'

The normal weekday routine in the second-floor flat in Aberdeen's Schoolhill had begun. To avoid confusion, the girls went first to the lavatory at the far end of the back-yard, and it wasn't until they had washed themselves at the kitchen sink and gone back to their own room to dress that the boys got up.

As she ran the flannel over her face and neck, Cissie stole a quick glance at her mother and was shocked to see how ill she looked. Isa caught her eye and said, 'Will you manage to see to the breakfast, Cissie?'

'I'll manage. Hey, Rosie, you haven't washed your lugs – ears,' she corrected, for Mam didn't like them speaking the broad words they picked up from other children at school.

Isabel, always known as Isa, and Thomas McGregor, Big Tam to everyone, had been born in Inverness, where an almost perfect English was spoken, but had come to Aberdeen after they married so that Big Tam could get a better job. A tall, handsome man with an outgoing personality, he soon found employment in the railway goods yard at Waterloo. His wage, although not as high as he would have liked, was enough to rent the three-roomed tenement flat in time for his first child to be born, and even when five more arrived they lived quite comfortably, solely due to his wife's good management of the housekeeping money he gave her.

Big Tam was friendly with all their neighbours and could have a good laugh with the men in the bars he frequented, but Isa was more reserved, giving the impression that she felt she was a cut above the other wives. The only person who didn't seem to resent her lilting, genteel accent was Mrs Robertson on the first floor. Aggie was sixty-six, a tiny, white-haired woman with button-bright eyes twinkling out of a round pink face, and she had grown very fond of the frail little creature whose husband kept her in an almost permanent state of pregnancy.

When Cissie and her two sisters returned to the kitchen, Tommy had already washed and was drying Pat, and Joe was complaining that he was always last to get the towel. 'You should rise a bit earlier,' Tommy laughed.

'You'll have to stay at home today, Cissie,' Isa said from the bed. 'I'm not fit to watch the wee ones yet.'

'Yes, Mam.' Cissie was sorry that she wouldn't be going to school. She was the best reader in her class, and top at sums, so it wouldn't matter if she was just missing that, but Miss Deans gave them drawing lessons every Thursday, and that was what she liked most of all. Still, it couldn't be helped, for she could see that her mother was very weak.

At twenty minutes to nine, eight-year-old Tommy, Joe, six, and Marie, not long started school, left with their satchels over their shoulders, and Cissie began on the housework. It wasn't easy to do the cleaning and still keep an eye on Pat – at twelve months he was into everything and made the place a mess again as soon as she had tidied it – but she did her best and was thankful that Rosie was quiet.

At noon, Cissie heated the leek soup her mother had made the day before, and was ladling it out when Tommy, Joe and Marie came in from school. As usual, the bread vanished off the plate like magic, and she had to cut some more, her mother watching anxiously in case she cut herself, but her hand was as steady as a rock.

Their hunger satisfied, the scholars ran out, eager to have some time with their friends in the school playground, and Cissie made her mother a cup of tea. In the afternoon, she went to the butcher in George Street to buy mince for the supper. Their main meal was at seven, for Big Tam always had a few drinks before he came home from work, but his worst vice lay elsewhere, although Cissie was not old enough to recognise this.

When she came back, annoyed at Pat for being a nuisance in the shop, she found Aggie Robertson in the house and had to make another pot of tea. She didn't listen to the women's conversation intentionally, she couldn't help overhearing as she pared the potatoes.

'You can't go on like this every year, Isa,' Aggie said, in a stage whisper.

'Tam hits me if I refuse him.' Isa kept her voice low, but not quite low enough.

'He should see you're not fit to give him more bairns.'

'He says he can't help himself.' Isa's pale face flushed with embarrassment. 'He's very – you know.'

Aggie nodded in sympathy, some white hairs slipping free of her hairpins. 'Aye, there's some men like that, but my Jimmer wasn't, God rest his soul. It was every night when we were first wed, then it was once a month, like he felt he'd to put on a show, but he'd gi'en me Jim, that was enough.'

Aggie's son was forty-one and had been a tailor with the Northern Co-operative Society in the Gallowgate since he was sixteen, his back now hunched and his legs bowed as a result of sitting cross-legged on the floor six days a week for twenty-five years, but in spite of this, he was the apple of his mother's eye.

'Your Jim's a good son,' Isa murmured. 'It's a shame he never took a wife, but maybe he's made like your man was.'

'Jimmer was a good man to me,' Aggie observed with some pride. 'He left me a wee bit money when he died, and like I said, he never bothered me much when he was younger, and once he reached forty . . .' She stopped with a loud cackle. 'I think he forgot what it was for.'

A deep sigh escaped Isa. 'You were lucky! The minute Tam lies down beside me, he's at . . .'

'Ssh, little pitchers have big lugs.'

The intriguing subject was dropped, and Cissie was left wondering how Aggie's Jimmer had been different from Da. Whatever it was, it was something they did in bed, maybe that's why she'd heard the springs groaning every night, and Da grunting like a pig. She nearly turned round to ask what men did in bed, but had the sense to hold her tongue.

She was kept busy after Aggie left, with mince to cook, potatoes to boil, bread and jam to spread for her brothers and sister coming in at four. Then she had to listen to Joe and Marie doing their reading – Tommy was past that stage. When Big Tam came swaggering in at seven, ruddy face filthy, clothes greasy, reddish hair standing almost straight up, he was full of the bonhomie a couple of tots of whisky usually engendered in him, and made straight for his wife. 'Are you feeling better now, Isa lass?'

'I'm a good bit better. I kept Cissie off school, but I should manage to be up tomorrow.'

'Aye.' Crossing to the sink at the window, he pulled his flannel shirt over his head to wash himself, then sat down at the table where five of his children were already seated, eyeing the large dish of potatoes and waiting impatiently for Cissie to dish up the mince. Tam applied himself to the important business of feeding the inner man. 'You're nearly eight, aren't you?' he asked Cissie.

'In two months, Da.'

'You'll soon be a big help to your mother.'

'She's been a big help to me today,' Isa told him. 'She's done all the housework and looked after the wee ones.'

'I took up the coal when I came home from school,' Tommy protested, indignantly.

'So you did,' his mother smiled, then pretended to frown. 'You didn't wash your hands, though, and you've got black streaks down your face.'

He turned to his father. 'I can lift the full pail, now, and I just put it down once, on the Robertsons' landing.'

'Good for you.' Big Tam grinned and ruffled his son's hair, only slightly darker than his own, making it more untidy than ever. 'You'll soon be as strong as your Da.'

Cissie went to bed at eight o'clock like her brothers and sisters, but listened for her father going out, which he usually did in the weeks just before and after a baby was born. She had always supposed that he was going back to the pub, so she was surprised to hear her mother say, sharply, 'Can you not stay away from it for one night, Tam?'

'I need a woman!' her father snapped.

The door slammed then, and Cissie was left puzzling at the sound of her mother weeping. Why did he need a woman? He had a wife and three daughters already, weren't they enough for him? Recalling that her mother had told Aggie Robertson he hit her if she refused him, Cissie's suspicions intensified. Her father wasn't as good as he would have people believe.

Chapter Three

❧❧

1910

The blinds were raised for the first time in four days, but even the bright sunlight streaming in didn't cheer the young McGregors, and Cissie, eleven now, looked round the room at her brothers and sisters, still shining clean from the scrubbing she had given them after their dinner. Not Tommy. At twelve, he wouldn't have allowed her to shame him. Nevertheless she had forced him to dip the hairbrush in water, and his coppery hair had been plastered flat against his head for the funeral, making him look like a stunted old man, though it was as unruly as ever by this time.

Joe's hair had looked black from the soaking she'd given it, but was its normal reddish-brown now, matching the rims of his eyes, swollen from crying. Marie's face was white and pinched, her ribbon slipping off her long tresses, and Rosie had pulled hers off as soon as they came home. Pat, almost five, was sucking his thumb, as he always did when he was troubled. He was still the youngest, for another two had been born dead, though they had come during the day and Cissie would have known nothing about them if she hadn't heard Aggie giving Da a piece of her mind.

'It's bad enough making that poor wife of yours have a bairn every year, but covering up three deaths is something I'll never understand. You're no better than an animal, Tam McGregor, and I should get the bobbies to you.'

Cissie had waited for her father to erupt in anger, but

14

he had merely asked, over-politely, 'I hope you've bundled this one up for me?'

'It's under the bed like the last one,' Aggie had snapped, 'so your other bairns won't see it. You should think black, burning shame o' yourself, when your wife's lying through there at death's door.'

Cissie could find no compunction in her heart for her father, though he had been weeping ever since his wife died. Instead of getting the doctor in to see her, as he should have done, he had sat by the fire until the small hours of the morning, then crept out to get rid of the baby. On his return, he had come running through to her, his eyes wild in his pure white face.

'Your Mam's gone, Cissie,' he'd got out, like somebody was strangling him. 'She was all right when I took away – but she's – oh, my God, what'll I do?'

'Ssh!' she had whispered, more in control than he was. 'You'll waken Marie and Rosie with your carrying on. I'll come through to the kitchen in a minute.'

She had pulled her coat over her nightshift because it was cold, and had gone downstairs first to tell Mrs Robertson what had happened. It was Aggie, shivering in her winceyette nightdress, who instructed Tam what he had to do, and he'd run out without a word.

Aggie had looked at Cissie then. 'Will you be all right till I go down and dress myself? I'll be as quick as I can, but I can't be wandering about in my gownie when the doctor and the undertakers come.'

As soon as the door closed, Cissie had gone to the bed and looked down on her mother's face – so careworn in life and looking older than her years, but peaceful in death, as if she were glad to be leaving her worries behind. 'Oh, Mam,' she whispered, 'how will we manage without you?'

She had still been weeping silently when Aggie came back wearing her usual black dress which had seen better days. 'I think you'd better go back to your bed, lass,' she had said, gently. 'You can't do anything for your Mam now.'

Cissie had trailed away, but couldn't sleep for the noise of strange feet on the stairs. Then her attention was held by an angry voice saying, 'God Almighty! I should report you for that, Tam McGregor.'

'That's what I said, and all, doctor,' Aggie chimed in.

'If it wasn't that your wife was lying dead, I would,' the doctor had said. 'But perhaps that is your punishment.'

Cissie hadn't heard what her father mumbled, but Doctor Burr had gone on, 'You'd better get her laid out ready for the undertakers.'

Whoever he had been speaking to, it was Aggie who replied. 'I'll do it, Doctor.'

Cissie had no idea what was entailed in 'laying out', but she was sure that Aggie would see to it properly. Snuggling down, she had gone to sleep.

Mam had been buried in the Grove Cemetery, and the house seemed empty without her, though there were still seven of them there. Cissie tried to swallow the great lump in her throat. They would be lost without Mam – she'd always been ready with a kind word and a smile if they were upset, a smear of ointment and a bandage if they'd hurt themselves, a rub of wintergreen or a belladonna plaster on their chests if they had coughs.

Chancing a quick glance at her father, Cissie was amazed to see him standing up. 'I'm going out for an hour or so,' he said, catching her eye and looking away quickly. 'Make sure the young ones get to bed at the usual time, Cissie. It's up to you now.'

Nothing was said after he went out. Tommy rose to attend to his brothers and Cissie saw to her sisters, and it wasn't until they were settled that the two eldest McGregors sat down again in the kitchen.

'He's a dirty brute,' Tommy said, vehemently. 'He could

16

hardly wait till Mam was under the ground before he went to get another woman.'

This was Cissie's chance. 'Why does he need a woman?'

Tommy looked pityingly at her. 'Do you not know that yet? A man needs a woman to . . .' He stopped, drew a deep breath, then told her exactly why men needed women, in the frank, basic words he had learned from older school-fellows.

Cissie's eyes, the same bluey-green as her mother's, were popping out of their sockets by the time he finished, though she understood only part of what he said. 'I don't believe you,' she spat out, at last. 'Men aren't all like that. Mrs Robertson told Mam once that her Jimmer hardly ever . . .'

'Ach, Jimmer was an old man, and anyway, he's been dead donkey's years, he doesn't count.'

'He was still a man.' After a slight hesitation, Cissie said, 'Have you ever . . . ?'

Tommy flushed. 'No, I haven't, not yet, but I will as soon as I'm old enough.'

'How old have you to be?'

'It's nothing to do with age. It's when your . . .' Tommy sighed, then said, 'It's time we went to bed. If Da comes back and finds us still up, he'll go daft.'

Not wanting to disturb her sisters, Cissie undressed in the dark, mulling over Tommy's disclosure for a few minutes, but giving up because she found it disgusting. As she slid under the blankets, she let her mind go back to the funeral. Da had been crying so much that he hadn't thought of anybody but himself, and it had been Jim Robertson who had put his arms round her, while Tommy cuddled Joe and Pat, and Aggie was comforting Marie and Rosie. 'Your Mam's better away,' Jim had said, gently, squeezing her hand.

She had been shocked at his callousness at the time, but now she understood vaguely what he had meant. Jim had added, 'If you're ever in trouble, Cissie, come to me and I'll do my best to help you.'

She couldn't imagine being in any kind of trouble, but it was nice to know she had such a good friend downstairs.

It was the following evening before Cissie became aware of how much her mother's death would affect her. Big Tam came home at his usual time, ate his supper and sat down by the fire. 'You'll have to take your Mam's place, Cissie,' he told her. 'You're the only one who can look after the wee ones and keep the house going.'

'But I'll be at school all day . . .'

'You'll not be going back to school, Cissie. You'll soon be twelve, old enough to keep house for your poor old Da.'

He gave a slight smile at that, but it hadn't eased the ache in her heart. She loved school, she adored Miss Munro as much as she had adored Miss Deans, she couldn't stay away for ever — but if she disobeyed him, Da might take his belt to her like he sometimes did to Tommy for answering back.

*   *   *

It wasn't so bad. She'd got into the hang of it after three whole weeks, and with Pat at school now, she could get on with the housework in peace. She spent the whole of every Wednesday in the wash-house, though doing the laundry for seven took it out of her, and her knuckles were red-raw from rubbing the clothes on the washboard. She took her turn for cleaning the stairs and the two lobbies — one out to the backyard and the other out to the street. She planned the meals ahead and didn't have to run out at the last minute for things she'd forgotten. She could make soup and pastry (though her first efforts had been like cement), fry ham and eggs, stew rabbit or slices of shoulder steak. She could do everything Mam had done — but she still wished Mam was there.

Her brothers and sisters turned to her for comfort, and she felt quite grown up at times, but at other times, mostly when she was in bed, the tears came, tears of fatigue, of self-pity, of sorrow for her mother. Da went out every night and wasn't home before she fell asleep, but he seemed to be quite pleased with the way she kept house. He'd even started patting her head before he went out, like he would pat a dog for being good, and it felt nice to be appreciated.

Aggie Robertson had seemed surprised when Cissie told her that. 'He just pats your head? Well, maybe I was mistaken.'

Humphy Jim, as all the children called him, often stopped her on the stairs and said, 'Mind what I told you now,' and she always answered, 'Yes.'

Thinking it over as she sat down to have a glass of milk and a biscuit one afternoon, Cissie wondered why they were so concerned for her. She was managing fine, though she'd have to hurry and bake some oatcakes before suppertime, and there was still some ironing left over from yesterday.

Pat didn't usually come straight home from school, so Cissie was surprised that he was first in, but he spread a slice of bread with jam and ran outside again to play on the back green with Dougie Gibb from upstairs. Then Marie and Rosie appeared, with Joe just behind them.

'Where's Tommy?' Cissie asked, because he was never late.

'He's awa' to Greigie's . . .' Marie began.

'None of that playground words,' Cissie said sharply. 'You know Mam didn't like us speaking like that.'

'You're getting to be a right old grumph,' Marie pouted. 'He found a thruppenny bit lying on the pavement when we were going to school in the morning, and he went to Greig's candy shop in the Gallowgate to buy some sweets.'

'I hope he gets black-striped balls,' Rosie observed.

'I like clove rock best,' Marie put in.

'Soor plooms for me,' said Joe, looking defensively at Cissie. 'And you needn't scowl, for that's what they're called on the jar, so saying sour plums would be wrong.'

'He'll likely have eaten whatever he buys before he comes home,' Cissie said, dryly.

She was proved wrong in ten minutes. When Tommy came in, he had a large bag of assorted broken candies, so each of them got their favourite – Tommy's being horehound and Cissie's acid drops. They left a share of mixed pieces for Pat, who would eat anything, and who emptied the bag in seconds. As a result of indulging themselves, none of the children was able to eat very much at suppertime.

'What's wrong with you all tonight?' Big Tam surveyed them with a perplexed frown. 'I hope you're not sickening for something?'

The older children glanced at each other guiltily, but Pat, having no guile, gave the secret away. 'Tommy took home candy and we've eaten too much.'

Tam whipped round. 'Where did you get money to buy candy, Tommy? Did you steal it?'

Tommy's face turned an indignant red. 'No, I didn't steal it. I found a thruppenny bit on the pavement, and . . .'

'You should have left it where it was. Maybe some poor old woman went back to look for it and it wasn't there. Taking something that doesn't belong to you is stealing, no matter where you found it, and you know what I think of boys that steal.' Big Tam undid his belt. 'Take down your breeks and get over that chair.'

'Oh, but Da . . .'

'Get your breeks down!'

Mortified more than scared, Tommy opened his buttons and let his breeches drop to the floor, trying to cover his nakedness with his hands as best he could, because neither he nor his brothers ever wore drawers. He flinched but kept the tears back when he received three sharp strokes, and his shamed face was as red as the weals on his buttocks when he pulled his trousers up again.

When Tam finished his supper and went out, Tommy muttered, 'I'll pay him back for that, see if I don't.'

Cissie turned on Pat. 'It was your fault. You shouldn't have told Da about the candy.'

'Aye,' Marie sneered. 'You're just a tell-tale-tit.'

'I didn't know Tommy would get the belt.' The five-year-old had been horrified, and was aggrieved that nobody had told him to keep quiet about the sweets.

'Is it awful sore, Tommy?' Cissie asked, as she rose to clear the table. 'Will I put on some ointment for you?'

'And let you all see my backside again? No, thank you.'

To show their father what they thought of him, the young McGregors refused to talk to him for the next two days, but on the third evening, he shocked them by ushering in a woman of a kind they had never seen before. She was bold, painted, had yellowish blonde hair, and her silky blouse and straight skirt were so tight that her every curve was accentuated. If Cissie and Tommy had been older, they might have recognised her as belonging to the oldest profession in the world.

'Eh, Tam,' she simpered, as Cissie hastily set another place at the table, 'you didna tell me you'd six bairns. What a man you musta been.'

'What a man I still am,' he boasted, 'and I'd have had eleven if the rest had lived.'

'And what's your names?' the woman gushed, looking at Tommy first.

He hung his head, but little Pat made the introductions. 'I'm Pat, he's Tommy, Joe, Cissie, Marie and Rosie.'

'I'm Mina. Oh, Tam, your hoose looks real bonnie.'

Beaming, he said, 'Cissie's been a grand help to me since her mother died.'

Mina sat back as a plate was laid in front of her. 'So it's

you that's the housewife, Cissie? Well, I'm moving in, so you'll not have so much to do.'

'Moving in?' Cissie was aghast at this. 'But there's no room for you. Where'll you sleep?'

'Wi' your Da, of course.' Mina let out a raucous laugh. 'He said he needed a woman to keep him warm at nights.'

Later, hearing the springs of the kitchen bed groaning rhythmically once more, accompanied by groans from her father and delighted squeals from the awful woman, Cissie thought, with a grim satisfaction, that Mina would soon be suffering the same agonies of childbirth that Mam had gone through, and it would serve her right.

Next day, Cissie was feeling rather put out because her father's 'woman' was shifting things around and planning the evening meal, when Mina suddenly said, 'Should you not be at the school?'

'Da kept me at home to keep house.'

'There's not enough work here for two o' us. You can go back to the school the morrow if you want.'

Cissie's opinion of Mina underwent a swift change for the better. She wasn't a bit like Mam, but at least she had some heart. 'What'll Da say?'

'Leave your Da to me.'

Big Tam raised no objections when he was told, and Cissie went to school the following morning with her brothers and sisters. 'Mina's not so bad when you get to know her,' she told Tommy, whose only answer was a deep scowl.

A few mornings later, Mrs Robertson detained Cissie on the first-floor landing. 'I see your Da's got a bidie-in.'

'What's a bidie-in?'

This flustered Aggie. She hadn't remembered how young the girl was. 'Ach, me, it's . . . a woman a man takes into his bed when he hasn't got a wife.'

Cissie smiled now. 'Her name's Mina, and she's let me go back to school.'

'I don't know how long she'll last,' Aggie said, darkly. 'I used to see her standing at the foot of Market Street.'

'The foot of Market Street?' Cissie couldn't understand the significance of this.

'Where the notables stand to pick up a man. That's likely where your Da met her.'

Still uncomprehending, Cissie said, 'I don't know where he met her, but I'd better go or I'll be late.'

She carried on down the stairs thoughtfully, wondering why Aggie didn't approve of Mina standing at the foot of Market Street. Not that it mattered, anyway, for Tommy was the only one of the family who hadn't taken to her, and he was just being awkward. Da hadn't been out one night since she came, and he was always in a good humour, which made life easier for all of them.

Chapter Four

1913

There had been a succession of women looking after the McGregors at intervals since Mina had left. Like her, they normally lasted no more than three or four weeks, often not even that, but very few of them had been as willing to work as she had been. Most of them had left all the cleaning for Cissie to do at weekends, but she didn't really mind, not when they kept her father happy and let her go to school until they walked out – or were thrown out. She did worry that Rosie and Pat might be upset by so many strangers, but it didn't seem to bother them, and they didn't get attached to any of them.

The only woman they had been rather fond of was Mary, a rough diamond and one of the better ones, who had been with them for almost three months and had got her marching orders most recently. Her hair had been a deep red, and when Cissie had mentioned how blonde some of the others were, she had said, 'They'd likely peroxided their hair, but me, I use henna. It's more natural-looking.'

Mary's hair hadn't looked natural either, Cissie thought, but at least the woman hadn't let her do a hand's turn, and now she was having to do everything herself again.

Scrubbing the back lobby one morning, Cissie wondered why Tommy had been looking so pleased with himself lately. Ever since Mary left, he'd looked like a cat that had been at the cream. She still missed Mary at times, but hadn't been too upset about having to stay at home – she'd been due to leave school in a few weeks anyway – Pat and Rosie, however, had moped for days and Marie had been

24

unusually quiet. Worse still, Da was continually in a bad temper, and when he was angry, the whole family had to suffer. He'd skelped Pat's ear the day before yesterday for having wet shoes though it had been pouring rain the whole day, and he'd given Joe a thump on the back for sniggering. Things couldn't continue like this; she would have to ask Tommy what was going on. Fifteen now, he was working with a grain company at the harbour, almost next door to Waterloo Goods Station where their father worked, but he usually came home long before Da, and she'd surely manage to get him on his own.

At quarter past six, Cissie went out to the lavatory, and on her way back looked out on to the street to see if Tommy was coming. By good luck – or good timing – he was turning into Schoolhill out of St Nicholas Street and she waited in the front lobby for him. 'Had you anything to do with Mary going away?' she asked, coming straight to the point in case her father had decided to come straight home for a change.

Tommy puffed out his chest. 'Aye, I told Da I'd seen her going on a boat with a sailor one afternoon.'

Unwilling to believe this of Mary, Cissie said, a little accusingly, 'Did you really see her with a sailor?'

He laughed derisively. 'No, but Da believed me and that's what they fell out about. I said I'd get even with him for thrashing my bare backside that day.'

'But that was years ago.'

'It's something I'll never forget, and he'll not thrash me again. If he tries, I'll knock him flat on his back.'

'Oh, Tommy, could you not have let things be?'

'No, I couldn't, and if he takes home any more of his whores I'll get rid of them too. I just wish I'd thought of it when he took the first one home, for he shouldn't try to put anybody in Mam's place.'

Understanding now why he had never taken to any of the women, Cissie said no more and they went up to the

25

house, where there was a heated discussion going on.

'I know boys' feet are bigger than girls' feet,' Joe was saying, 'but that's because we've got bigger everything — bigger hearts, bigger legs, bigger hands, and . . .'

'Bigger mouths,' put in Rosie.

'And bigger brains,' Joe finished, triumphantly.

'Bigger heads, anyway,' Marie scoffed, 'but nothing much inside them.'

Nine-year-old Pat, feeling left out, made his own gleeful contribution. 'And I bet boys've got bigger willies than girls, and all.'

Unable to argue with this, his brothers and sisters were doubled up with laughter when Big Tam came in. 'What's so damned funny?' he demanded, but found it highly amusing, too, when they told him. Cissie dished up the supper and they all sat down, Pat still seething with resentment at being laughed at.

When they were supping their prunes and custard, Tam looked at Cissie. 'I'll be going out again tonight.'

This did not surprise her, for he had gone out every night since Mary left. 'Will you be late back?'

'No, and I'll maybe take somebody back with me, so I'd be obliged if you and Tommy went to your beds at the same time as the young ones.'

Before Cissie could prevent him, Tommy said, 'I suppose she's another whore?'

Tam stood up aggressively. 'Shut your filthy mouth!'

'I'm just speaking the truth,' his son said, quietly. 'You're the only filthy one in this house.'

Tam's hands went to his belt buckle. 'That's it! You've been asking for it for ages. Take down your breeks!'

'Take down your own breeks!' Tommy shouted, taking up a boxer's stance. 'I'm not a bairn now, and I'm not frightened of you any longer.'

'Da! Tommy!' Cissie pleaded. 'Stop it! You're carrying on like two fools in front of the little ones.'

The 'little ones' had been lapping it up, amazed at Tommy's bravado and wondering which of the protagonists would come off best, but their sister's words made them drop their eyes, and Tam turned abruptly from the table. 'I'll be back about nine, Cissie. And if your big brother's still in this house, I'll throw him down the stairs.' He stamped to the door and slammed it behind him, ignoring Cissie's cries of 'Oh, Da! Please!'

Tommy gave a bitter forced laugh. 'I was leaving anyway. I've been thinking of signing on a trawler to get away from him, for he just makes me sick with his women, and I can get a bed for a few nights from one of the storemen that works with me. His son got married a week ago.'

'Oh, Tommy, I don't want you to go.'

'He doesn't want me here, and I'll not stay where I'm not wanted. Don't worry, I can look out for myself.'

Tommy marched through to his room and emerged about three minutes later carrying a small bundle of clothes under his arm. 'I'm off now, Cissie.'

She saw that it was useless to argue. 'Will you write?'

'I'd better not.' He looked at her with smouldering eyes. 'I'll get even with Da for this as well, I swear, supposing I've to wait till his hair's pure white.'

There was a hushed silence after the door slammed again, but at last Cissie stood up. 'Rosie and Marie, you do the dishes, and Pat and Joe, get ready for your bed.'

'Where are you going?' Rosie asked tearfully.

'I'm going to have a word with the Humphy. I'll not be very long.' Cissie went out, but paused on the landing outside to gather her thoughts. Was this the trouble that Jim Robertson had foreseen after her mother died? He could do nothing about it, but she had to tell somebody. Lifting her shoulders resolutely, she carried on down the stairs, gave a light tap on the Robertsons' door and went in when a voice called, 'It's open.'

Sitting at the fireside with his boots off, Jim's jaded eyes lit up when he saw her, and his mother turned from the sink. 'What's up wi' you, lass?' she asked. 'You've a face on you as long as the day and the morrow.'

Cissie told them what had happened, then burst out, 'And Tommy's gone away, and he's going to sign on a trawler, and I don't know what Da'll say when he comes home.'

Jim's lined face relaxed into a reassuring smile. 'He wanted Tommy out, so what can he say?'

'Jim's right.' Aggie took a dish towel out of the press and started to dry the plates she had washed. 'And you've no need to worry about Tommy, for the trawlermen'll look after him. They're good like that.'

'Da's taking another woman home tonight, and it's a shame for Rosie and Pat.'

Aggie frowned. 'She'll maybe not bide, but if she does, you'll need to put up wi' her, the same as you'd to put up wi' the rest o' them. Your Da can't do without a woman, and if he can only get one off the streets, well, there's some of them have good enough hearts. They've come down in the world, that's all, and letting men pick them up's the only road they can make money.'

'Tommy said they were whores.'

'Aye, that's what they are, whores, but it's just a job like any other to them. Now, get up the stairs to your brothers and sisters. They depend on you, for you're the only steady body they've got.'

When Cissie trailed out, Jim said, 'I'm sorry for that poor lassie having Big Tam for a father. Surely he's had enough of women.'

'Some men never get enough.' Aggie hesitated, then said, 'Jim, do you never – you're near fifty and you've never bothered wi' lassies, maybe you're not like other men?'

His eyes regarded her sadly. 'I'm the same as other men, Ma, except for my back.'

'But your back wasn't always bowed.'

28

'Nobody round here now would remember me when I was young and straight, and what kind of woman would want to get into bed with a humph-back?'

Aggie shook her head, her heart too full of pity for her son to say anything. She was seventy-three now and she'd had a few queer turns lately, and what would happen to Jim when she passed on? He was that bent he sometimes couldn't rise in the mornings without her giving him a hand up. If only he had a wife to look after him, she could die happy. But like he said, who would take him?

When Big Tam led the woman into the empty kitchen, he said, 'Wait till I see if Tommy's still here.' Tiptoeing into the small lobby, he eased the boys' bedroom door open and peeped inside. 'Good! He's away. He's a troublemaker, that laddie, even if he is my son, for it's none of his business who I take into my house.'

'There's been other women before me, then?'

'Some, and it was through Tommy the last one left, though I was maybe a fool to believe what he said.'

Cissie, still shedding tears for her eldest brother, heard the usual sounds of her Da's pleasure, and burrowed her head into her pillow. She didn't know if this whore would be any better or worse than the rest, but for better or worse she was here to stay – until Big Tam fell out with her.

In the morning, she waited until she heard her father going out before she went through to the kitchen, and was relieved to find that the woman at the gas stove was quite different from any of the others. She was younger and her dark hair was piled neatly on top of her head. Her face had no powder or rouge on it, and it was smooth and unlined, not papery and wrinkled like most of her predecessors'. Her dark skirt and pale blue blouse were well-worn but modest, and spotlessly clean. 'You'll be Cissie?' she smiled. 'My name's Phoebe – Phoebe Garden.'

29

'Phoebe?' It was a strange name, but the girl was glad to see that the table was set and the porridge made.

'My mother saw it in a book,' the woman explained. 'She thought it was pronounced Fobe, but the minister corrected her when I was christened.' Her bright eyes dimmed a little. 'Your father was pleased your brother was away, but you must be very sad about it.'

'Yes, I am. He's going to sign on a boat, but he's never been away from home before, and I'm . . .' She broke off, not trusting herself to say anything more without crying.

Coming round the table, Phoebe placed an arm round the girl's shoulders. 'I'm sure he'll be all right.'

The lilting accent, so like Mam's, and the comfort of the soft body made Cissie want to bury her head on Phoebe's bosom, but she didn't give in to the weakness. There were still her younger brothers and sisters to see to.

When all the bustle was past and they were alone again, Phoebe said, 'I hope you don't mind, Cissie, but your Da asked me to come and live here with you.'

'It's nothing to do with me, but I don't mind. The only thing is, I'm fourteen now and I'm not at school. We'll likely get in each other's road all day.'

'Just what I was thinking. Maybe you should look for a job, for you don't want to end up like me.'

'What do you mean?'

Phoebe looked embarrassed. 'I was born in the Black Isle of very religious parents, and when I was sixteen, my father found me in one of his outhouses with a lad. We were only kissing and cuddling, but Father accused me of going against the teachings of the Bible by fornicating, and threw me out. I went to Inverness, but I'd never had to work before and I wasn't trained for anything, so I'd to go into service. I didn't like it, but I stuck it for about eight years, then I thought there must be more to life than that. I wanted to find a husband, have a family . . .'

'Have you been married, then?' Cissie interrupted, sure

that dozens of men must have fallen in love with this woman, she was so attractive.

Phoebe's lovely blue eyes clouded even more. 'I never met anyone I liked as much as Andrew, and I felt I'd soon be too old for love, so I came to Aberdeen, determined to make a fortune if I couldn't get a husband. I didn't find a husband and I didn't make a fortune because I couldn't get a proper job. I was ready to go back into service when I met a man who told me he was looking for a housekeeper, so I said I'd take it on.' She gave a dry, rueful laugh. 'It wasn't just a housekeeper he wanted, it was more a bed-companion, but I was so grateful for getting a decent place to live, I kept his house for him and slept with him till he tired of me.'

'Oh, Phoebe,' Cissie gasped. 'Did he put you out?'

The woman shrugged. 'I've been through it lots of times since, and I even started going into bars looking for a man for the night, for I discovered I could make more money that way. The thing is, I'm thirty now, and I'll soon lose my looks, so when your Da asked me to come and look after his children, I jumped at the chance.'

'But it'll be the same here. Da'll want you to sleep with him and he'll put you out when he feels like it.' Cissie did not want this nice woman to be under any misconceptions.

'I know, and I'm quite willing. I like your Da, Cissie, he reminds me a bit of Andrew, though he's a lot older.'

'Did you not mind . . . taking up with a lot of men?'

'Sometimes I didn't mind, and sometimes it was all I could do to let them get what they wanted, for they – no, no, you don't want to hear about that. But I'd like to have one man, somebody to care for me, to look after me for a change.'

Cissie felt drawn to her. She was really nice, and it would be almost as good as having Mam again if she were to live with them. 'I like you, Phoebe,' she murmured, self-consciously.

'And I like you, but go and find yourself a job, then if your Da ever puts you out, you'll be able to keep yourself.'

Before she left the tenement, Cissie called on Aggie, who listened, rather bemused, to what Phoebe had said. 'She sounds real nice, and if your Da likes her, he'll maybe wed her come time.'

'I hope he does,' Cissie breathed, 'but I'll have to find a job whatever happens, and I don't know where to look.'

'I could maybe help you. You know that wee dairy round the corner? Miss Birnie was telling me yesterday her assistant's leaving on Friday to get married. Go and ask her if she's got anybody else yet, and tell her it was me that sent you.'

'Oh, thank you, Aggie. I'll go right away.'

Cissie hurried down Schoolhill and turned left into George Street. Miss Birnie had been very pleasant to her any time she'd been in the little dairy, but working for her might be a different story. Still, it would be a job, if she was lucky and no one else had been taken on.

Ten minutes later, she opened the Robertsons' door and yelled, 'I got it, Aggie,' then raced up the next flight of stairs, startling Phoebe when she burst in. 'I start on Saturday morning at the dairy round the corner. Seven to half past four, for five bob a week.'

'Five bob? That's good. I don't suppose your da paid you anything for all the work you did in the house?'

'No, but I wonder what he'll say about me taking a job?'

'He should be pleased.'

When Tam was told, he frowned a little, but Phoebe stepped in before he could say anything. 'Cissie's a big girl now. She needs money to buy personal things, and she'll be able to pay something for her keep.'

In the face of Phoebe's calm logic and Cissie's obvious excitement, he had to make the best of it. 'Och, I suppose she should be working. She'll be fifteen next birthday.'

Cissie's excitement increased when Phoebe suggested

that she should hand over three shillings every week for her board. It meant that she would have two shillings to herself — twenty-four whole pence!

Having settled the household finances to the satisfaction of everyone concerned, Phoebe turned to Big Tam. 'Cissie was saying Tommy's to be signing on a trawler, so you won't have to worry about him.'

The man just grunted, but Joe's head jerked up. 'I'd like to sign on a boat when I leave school. I love the sea.'

'You can please yourself,' Big Tam said, as if he didn't care one way or the other, 'though I've no quarrel with you. You'll be leaving school at Easter, and it's up to you what kind of job you take.'

*   *   *

The leaves on the trees in St Nicholas Kirkyard had turned varying shades of red and gold — it was the season Cissie liked best because it fascinated her to see the beautiful autumn colours — and Phoebe Garden was still in the flat in Schoolhill, after nearly three months. Even Marie, who was envious of her lovely wavy hair, said that Phoebe was far nicer than any of their father's other women. She was always in the same happy mood, advising Rosie how to use her hairbrush so that the tangled curls didn't pull at her scalp, showing Marie the best way to put in her rags to have ringlets that stayed in all day, pinning up Cissie's golden-brown hair in the most becoming manner. She laughed as she stitched Pat's torn trousers, smiled while darning the elbows of Joe's jerseys, and sewed buttons galore on to shirts that had been hauled over heads still fastened.

Cissie often asked God in her prayers to let Phoebe Garden stay with them for ever, for her father was a different man nowadays, content to sit at home in the evenings and talk to his family. It was easy to see that he liked Phoebe, maybe even loved her, for his voice softened when he spoke to her, his eyes followed her as she moved around. He had stopped going to the pub before he came home from work, and his face was losing its blotchy redness.

'Wouldn't it be wonderful if Da married Phoebe?' Cissie asked Marie when they went to bed one night.

Marie pulled a face. 'It'd be all right for you, you're her pet.'

'I am not,' Cissie said, indignantly. 'She treats us all the same.' Nevertheless it gave her a warm glow to think Phoebe liked her best.

The months flew past, the trees shedding their leaves, the falling snow making a screen in front of the windows so that nothing could be seen until it stopped, then the lovely, Christmassy mantle of white lying over everything, until the thaw came and the streets were awash with grey slush.

Cissie pulled the collar of her coat up as she went to work, humming a little tune under her breath she was so happy. Miss Birnie had put up her wages, and Phoebe wouldn't take any more for her keep, so she had another one and six to herself. She would go up George Street as soon as she finished work next Saturday afternoon, for Isaac Benzie had a sale on, and she might see a blouse she could afford.

It was good to have a job, especially one she liked so much. She felt important standing at the marble counter and weighing out quarter-pounds of butter to make into round pats with the wooden boards. Then there was the measuring of half-pints of cream and putting them into little cardboard containers with lids – not that many women in the area could afford cream, only sometimes on a Saturday for the weekend. The milk itself was kept in large drums shaped like chessmen, and she had to use metal half-pint and pint jugs to pour it into whatever type of receptacles the women brought in. She had discovered the knack of judging exactly how much to cut off with the wire when anybody asked for a quarter or a half-pound of red cheese. The crowdie was weighed out beforehand and sold in small cartons.

Most of the customers were very friendly, passing on any gossip, especially if it involved a scandal, although they weren't malicious. Of course, there were some who wouldn't be pleased by anything anyone did for them, and Cissie took their grumbles philosophically. They probably had husbands who ill-treated them, or were widows with little money. She would remember what she was told about their families, and would ask if little Jackie had got over the measles, whether Jeannie had got a job yet, or if the twins' rickets was any better — the human touches which had prompted her employer to give her the increase in pay.

On Saturday at teatime, Marie looked jealous when Cissie brought home a new blouse. 'Wait till I start working,' she sneered. 'It won't be in a poky wee shop, that's one thing, so I'll be able to buy lots of new things.'

Seeing the older girl's sunny smile fading, Phoebe said, 'Cissie's happy in the dairy, and it's a beautiful blouse. Maybe she'll give you one of her old ones, and I can add a frill for you?'

'Yes, Marie, you can have the pink one, and Isaac Benzie had a lot of cheap lace in the sale.'

'I'll get some on Monday,' Phoebe smiled, 'and we can all have new-looking blouses.' This did the trick, and Marie forgot her jealousy, for the time being.

When Big Tam was shown Cissie's purchase and was told what they were planning, he said, 'I'll give you money to buy a blouse for yourself, Phoebe. You haven't had anything new since you came here.'

Her pleasure at this made Cissie's heart go out to her. The woman was utterly dependent on him for every ha'penny, but she didn't seem to mind.

'I'm tired hearing about girls' blouses,' Pat complained. 'What about our supper?'

35

At one time, Cissie thought, her father would have given Pat a wallop for speaking like that, but he just laughed. Having Phoebe Garden there had changed him, and hopefully, her last name wouldn't be Garden for much longer.

Chapter Five

❦

1914 was into its second day when Rosie complained that she didn't feel well, and Phoebe, thinking that the child had eaten too much rich food the day before, gave her a dose of castor oil that night. By the following morning, the effort of running up and down the stairs to the outside lavatory so many times had left the little girl pale and sweating, and she was put to bed with the instruction to use the chamber-pot if she had to.

Still on holiday from school, Marie screwed up her face in horror when Phoebe, preparing the midday meal, asked her to empty it. 'Somebody else's shit? Not me!'

So Phoebe carried out the unpleasant chore herself until Cissie took it over from her in the late afternoon. 'She's awful white,' she said, when she was scrubbing her hands.

Phoebe had also been alarmed by the nine-year-old's waxen skin. 'Should we send for the doctor?'

'It's maybe nothing. Bairns get over things quick.'

In the evening, Rosie's nose started to bleed, and Phoebe strung the cold door-key on a string and hung it down her back — her own mother's remedy for bleeding noses — which did make it stop for a short time.

Big Tam looked worried when he came through from seeing his youngest daughter. 'It's not like Rosie. She's always been quiet, but she's lying there like — she's given up.'

Unwilling to make the decision, Phoebe looked across at Cissie, who said, 'If she's not any better in the morning, Pat'll have to go for the doctor.'

Rosie had a restless night, but Marie made no complaints about being kept awake, and when Cissie saw that there was blood in the chamber-pot next morning, she was shocked and alarmed. Deciding that she had better not go to the dairy, she despatched Pat to ask the doctor to call as soon as he could. Big Tam also wanted to stay off work, but Phoebe reminded him that they couldn't afford to lose his wages.

After the doctor's visit, Cissie said, 'I've never heard of leukaemia, and what does fatal mean?'

Phoebe shook her head sadly. 'It means she — won't get better.' Marie bursting into tears at that, she went on, 'We'll have to keep cheery in front of her so she won't know how ill she is.'

For the rest of the day, they took it in turns to sit with Rosie, even when she was asleep, and each one went back to the kitchen in tears, it was so painfully clear that she was steadily weakening.

When Big Tam came home, he blanched when he was told what the doctor had diagnosed. 'Oh, God, not my wee Rosie?' he moaned, his hands clutching at his hair in his distress.

His children watched his torment uncomfortably, but Phoebe rose and put her arms round him. 'Don't let go, Tam,' she urged. 'You've your other bairns to think of.'

He straightened up then and took out his handkerchief to blow his nose. 'Aye, you're right, but I'd like to be with her this night; it might be her last.'

'No, Tam,' Phoebe said, gently. 'If she sees you, she'll know something's wrong.'

That night was not Rosie's last, and Phoebe made Cissie return to work the following day. 'She could linger on for a while yet,' she pointed out, 'and it's better we all carry on as usual.'

Phoebe attended to the little girl during the days that

followed, ignoring the housework and preparing quick meals when she got the chance, not that anyone felt like eating, but, as she said, 'We need to keep our strength up.'

Aggie Robertson, who had offered to sit with Rosie to let Phoebe do some shopping, and who had been a little offended when her offer was turned down, came up every morning to ask if she needed anything from the shops. The other neighbours came to enquire after the little girl, and so the days went by, with Rosie sinking lower and lower until, on the Sunday, with all her family around her, she slipped into a coma from which she never emerged.

She had always been so quiet as to be hardly noticeable, yet her passing left a far bigger gap in the household than even Tommy's departure had done, and it took a long time for them to come to terms with it. Phoebe, who had looked after her so lovingly, did her best to hide her own grief, and it was her calming influence that helped the others overcome theirs.

*   *   *

Just before Joe left school, Mr Morrice from the top floor, a welder with Hall the shipbuilders, told him there was an errand boy's job vacant. 'They always take the young lads on as apprentices when they're sixteen,' he added. 'It maybe wouldn't be as a welder, maybe a riveter or something else, but it would be a trade for you.'

Joe pulled a face. 'I wanted to go to sea.'

'Building ships is an important job, and you'd see them being launched when they're finished.'

Joe's eyes widened as this carrot was dangled. 'Tommy's on a trawler, would he ever get to see a launching?''

Mr Morrice laughed. 'No, nor your father, either. Not many folk see a launching.'

Joe went to the shipyard to apply for the job, and

with Mr Morrice's recommendation that he was a quiet, reliable boy, he was told to start on the Monday after he left school.

Big Tam smiled when he learned this. 'You're set for life now, Joe. Ships'll never go out of fashion.'

Phoebe took only half the boy's wages for his keep, and he confided to Cissie, some weeks after he started work, 'I know I'm only fourteen, but I feel like a man when I jingle money in my pocket.'

             *   *   *

The weather grew warmer and warmer, and by the beginning of August it was so hot that the grass in St Nicholas Kirkyard – which Cissie looked out on from her bedroom window – was turning yellow, and she was glad of the marble slab in the dairy to cool her constantly perspiring hands. Big Tam and Joe came home each night with their shirts sticking to their backs with sweat, and Pat went out to play in his bare feet, wearing only his breeches. Marie appeared one morning with the top two buttons of her blouse undone, but it was so immodest that Phoebe told her to fasten them before Pat saw her. Life in the McGregors' flat was more placid than it had ever been, and even the outbreak of war on the fourth had no adverse effect on them.

One forenoon in September, when Cissie turned to serve her next customer, she gave a cry of joy when she saw Tommy. 'It's my oldest brother,' she told Miss Birnie, who allowed her to go outside to talk to him for a few minutes.

'I'm going into the Merchant Navy,' he said, proudly. 'I thought I'd better let you know, for I'm putting you down as my next of kin in case anything happens to me.'

'Nothing's going to happen to you, Tommy.' Cissie's heart was fluttering wildly at the very thought.

'I didn't know you were working, and I went to the house first. That wouldn't have been the same whore Da was taking home the night he put me out, though?'

'It's the same woman,' Cissie said, carefully. 'Her name's Phoebe and she's awful nice.'

'Once a whore, always a whore,' Tommy retorted, then his expression changed. He had been impressed by Phoebe's appearance and gentle manner when she told him where Cissie was, and he added, grudgingly, 'Maybe not that one, though. Now, what's been happening since I've been away?'

Cissie gasped in dismay. 'Oh, Tommy, you won't know about Rosie. She wasn't well just after the New Year, and when we got the doctor, he said it was leukaemia.'

'Never heard of it. Is she all right now?'

'She died not long after.'

He shook his head, unable to believe it. 'Little Rosie? No, she can't be dead? Oh, Cissie!'

His stricken face made her stroke his cheek. 'I don't know what we'd have done if Phoebe hadn't been there. She nursed Rosie like she . . .' Cissie couldn't go on.

They looked at each other for some time, each drawing a little comfort from the other, then Tommy said, with a catch in his voice, 'I wish I could have seen her again. Next to you, it was Rosie I liked best.'

'I think Da liked her best, and all.'

Tommy's face hardened now. 'He's never liked anybody but himself, and he never will.'

'He likes Phoebe, he's been different since she came.'

'He'll never change, Cissie. Oh, maybe for a while, but he's got a wicked streak in him, and if she gets on his wrong side, he'll throw her out, the same as his own son. I still haven't forgotten that.'

To get his mind off it, and because she didn't want to think that their father would ever put Phoebe out, she said, 'Tommy, you'll come back to see me?'

'Maybe, but I'm not writing in case he sees the letters. You'd better get back to work now, Cissie.' He clasped her hand then walked away, his rolling gait suggesting that he was still unsure of solid ground under his feet.

Cissie returned sadly to her duties. Would she ever see Tommy again? He was her favourite brother, and if anything did happen to him, she would never forgive Da for making him leave home.

Chapter Six

❖

1915

Even before the end of the year, Phoebe had sensed a change in Big Tam. At first, she had put it down to the weather, for the icy coldness and the steadily falling snow were enough to make anyone depressed. On Hogmanay, she noticed that his face was strained, but it was another few days before it dawned on her what was troubling him. It was only natural for him to remember the death of his daughter, but he would consider it a weakness in himself, and she deemed it best not to say anything.

On the actual anniversary, it was Cissie who came out with it, when she rose to clear the supper dishes. 'It's a year today since Rosie died.'

Looking at Tam, Phoebe could see his tense mouth, his tortured eyes, and wasn't surprised when he jumped to his feet muttering, 'I'm going out.'

There was a short silence after he left, then Cissie said, 'I bet he's going to a bar. I shouldn't have reminded him.'

'He remembered himself, days ago,' Phoebe assured her.

Hours later, waiting for Tam to come home, Phoebe was indulging in her favourite dream: being a proper part of his family. She loved his children as much as she loved him, and was almost sure that he loved her, but she was still only an outsider. Oh, the bairns treated her as a mother, and Tam treated her as a wife, most of the time, but it wasn't the same as really being his wife. If only she were, she could face the neighbours without wondering if they were sneering at her behind her back. What was more, he wouldn't just walk out without telling her where he was going, though she could excuse him for it tonight.

When he came in, steady on his feet, he sat down to take off his boots. 'They're all in bed?'

'Ages ago,' she smiled. 'Tam, I didn't like to say it in case it upset you, but I know how sad you must be just now.'

'It's like it's happening again, tearing my heart out.'

She went over to him and laid her hand on his bowed head, wondering if this was the right time to say what was on her mind. She decided to risk it. 'Maybe you'd feel better if we got married. I'm willing, if you are.' She stepped back in surprise as his body jerked up and he looked at her coldly.

'I'll have no woman tell me what to do, especially one I picked up off the streets.'

Recoiling as if he had struck her, she murmured, 'Tam, I'm sorry. I didn't mean . . .'

'I can manage without you.'

'Are you — are you telling me to go?' she faltered.

'I'll leave it up to you.'

Phoebe's heart had slowed down when he reminded her of what she had been, but now she felt angry because he had thrown it in her face when she was trying to help him. She had thought he loved her, and she wouldn't demean herself by begging to him. 'I'll pack my things.'

Turning away, she thought that she could discern a flicker of dismay in his eyes, but she must have imagined it.

Cissie wished she knew what had happened. Last night Phoebe had said goodnight as usual and yet in the morning she'd been gone. Cissie had heard nothing, for her job made her so tired it would have taken a barrel of explosives to waken her, and she had puzzled over it all day.

She was pleased to find Phoebe waiting for her outside

44

the dairy at half past four. 'I had to see you, Cissie, to tell you why I left.'

'Has Da found somebody else?' Cissie's voice was flat – this was what she'd been dreading for some time.

'I don't think he has. It was my own fault. I suppose I was stupid, but I loved you all so much, your father, too, that I told him I'd be willing to marry him, only he wasn't willing to marry me.'

'Oh, Phoebe, I'm sorry. Did he throw you out?'

'As good as. I'm sorry, too, Cissie, but don't let him make you give up your job. Keep your independence, you might need it yet. Oh, Cissie, I'll never forget any of you.'

'We'll never forget you, either, Phoebe. Will you keep in touch with me and let me know where you are?'

'I don't think I should, but I'll tell you this – I'm finished with men. I'll find a proper job this time.' At the foot of Schoolhill, she said, 'This is goodbye, Cissie.' She kissed the girl's cheek and walked on into St Nicholas Street, her eyes streaming.

'Goodbye, Phoebe,' Cissie called after her. 'Good luck!'

Her spirits were so low that she did not look in any of the shop windows on her way up the hill, and, climbing the tenement stairs, she felt that the whole weight of the world was on her shoulders. She couldn't even face telling Aggie Robertson that Phoebe was gone, but she was determined never to give up her job, no matter how angry her father might be.

As it turned out, he didn't ask her to stop working, it was Marie he turned to. 'You'll soon be fourteen, and you don't like school, so you can stay at home and keep house.' He offered no explanation for Phoebe's absence, and Marie didn't ask.

Cissie was glad he wasn't going to take in another woman. She couldn't have stood it, because she would miss Phoebe, miss all their confidential chats. Still, she'd be sixteen in three months and could leave any time after that. She had a wage – and a mind – of her own.

When she rose at six o'clock the following morning, her father, already washed and dressed, was sitting at the table supping the porridge he had made, so she poured some hot water into the white enamel basin in the sink. Since she started working, she had washed in front of Phoebe and him – prior to that, he'd been out before she got up – but today she could feel his eyes on her and was conscious that her thin cotton nightshift did nothing to hide her swelling bosom. When she turned round, she shielded herself by crossing her arms over her chest.

'You needn't be shy in front of your Da,' he muttered, a thickness in his voice that alarmed her. 'I used to see you bare-naked when you were a wee girl.'

'I'm not a wee girl now,' she retorted, going round the opposite side of the table from him.

'No, that you're not.'

Glad to escape his penetrating gaze, she went into the bedroom wondering how to prevent a repeat of the situation, and came to the conclusion that Marie would have to rise at the same time as she did in future. Da surely wouldn't make any embarrassing remarks when there were two of them there. When she finished dressing, she woke her sister, but waited until she heard their father going out before she returned to the kitchen. Because she was later than usual, she had to gulp her breakfast, and ran out with her coat in her hand.

The dairy was extremely busy that day and, when she was left alone in the afternoon, she was so tired that it was all she could do to be pleasant to the queuing customers. It did ease off after four, and she had time to look at the clock. Only half an hour to go, thank goodness. At twenty to five, Miss Birnie not having appeared to relieve her, she was still in the shop when a young man came in. She hadn't seen him before, but when their eyes met, she felt a stirring of interest.

'A quarter of butter, please,' he said, shyly.

She opened a paper bag and slipped in one of the small pats she had made up earlier. 'Is that everything?'

'Yes, thank you.' He handed over the exact money, smiling to her as he held the door open for the shop-keeper, who came hurrying in.

'Oh, Cissie, I'm sorry I'm late,' Miss Birnie gasped. 'I was held up at Raggie Morrison's sale. They'd blankets going half-price, and ladies' underwear, coats and frocks reduced by twenty per cent, though I didn't have time to try anything on. But I got a good alarm clock for sixpence. Was that Hugh Phimister you were serving?'

'I don't know his name, but he looked a real nice lad.'

Her blush made Miss Birnie grin. 'The three Phimisters are all nice lads, and Hugh's only about a year older than you. His mother's the woman that gets the half-pint of buttermilk every Saturday.'

'Oh, aye, I know who you mean.'

'She must be ill, for I've never seen Hugh in here before. Well, away you go, Cissie.'

The girl was disappointed that she wouldn't see the young man again, and on her way home, she kept remembering the look in his eyes when she had served him. Maybe, if he was taken with her, he would come back.

Pat took her down to earth as soon as she entered the house. 'I've tore my school breeks, and Marie says she hasn't time to mend them.'

'Neither I have,' Marie pouted. 'I've been rushed off my feet all day with cleaning and cooking and everything else.'

Cissie sighed. 'Take them off and give them to me.'

The task presented no problem to her, for at school the sewing teacher had shown them how to make three-cornered rips almost invisible by using herring-bone stitch. 'What's for supper?' she asked, as she threaded a needle.

47

'Sausages from the butcher in the market,' Marie told her. 'They're better than Findlay's in George Street – his are all gristle and fat. And there's mashed tatties and peas.'

'Have you made a pudding?' Pat asked, not aware – or not caring – that his private parts were in full view.

'Semolina and jam.'

He grinned. 'I thought you'd been too busy to make any.'

When Big Tam came home, his sweating face was an unhealthy grey, and he sat down in his chair with a thump, as if his legs had given way. 'I've got a chill from that soaking I had on Monday,' he informed Cissie. 'I've been shivering since dinnertime.'

Cissie prayed that he hadn't caught a chill – he would get no pay if he was off work, and the money she and Joe took in wouldn't feed them all. 'I'll get a gill of whisky from the grocer to make some toddy for you.'

'You're a good lass, Cissie.' Digging his hand into his trouser pocket, he held out a half-crown.

He didn't touch the sausages and potatoes, but drank the toddy, shuddering as it went down. 'Ach, sweet whisky turns my stomach.'

'It'll do you more good than swigging it neat!' Cissie said, sharply.

As the evening wore on, she grew quite worried by his dry hacking cough, and even more concerned when she saw that his breathing was shallow and laboured. 'You should be in bed,' she ordered, when he leaned back with his hand on his chest after a prolonged bout of barking. She turned her head away hastily when he unbuttoned his spaver as unselfconsciously as eleven-year-old Pat had done earlier. Her father did wear drawers – she'd had to wash them when she was looking after the house – but still . . .

It was after ten o'clock before she went to bed, having first made a third cup of weak toddy for him using the dregs of the little bottle. Hearing him still coughing harshly,

48

she crossed her fingers that he would be better by morning.

Although she was anxious about her father, she still made Marie rise at the same time as she did. Big Tam, however, was too ill to be interested in either of his daughters' maturing figures. He looked so poorly that Cissie asked, 'Should I get Pat to run for the doctor, Da?'

'No, it's just a cough, but I'll take a day off work.'

'Do you want me to stay at home with you?'

His answer had to wait until he regained his breath after a renewed fit. 'No, Marie'll be here.'

'I'll get a mixture from Coutts the chemist before I go to the dairy. It's strong, and it should help you.'

When she returned with the bronchial expectorant, Cissie gave Marie whispered instructions to go for the doctor if Da got any worse, and, on her way downstairs again, she asked Aggie Robertson to check on him at dinnertime.

The girl was so concerned about her father that she didn't notice Hugh Phimister in the shop that afternoon until she served him, then was so flustered that she stammered, 'Is it b-butter you're wanting again?'

His dimpled smile made a thrilly tremble snake all through her. 'No. Half a pound of crowdie, please – loose.'

She weighed out the crumbly cheese and was wrapping it up in greaseproof paper when Miss Birnie came through from the room at the back. 'I thought it was your voice, Hugh. Is your mother well enough?'

The youth's cheeks took on a slight flush. 'She wasn't too well yesterday, though she's fine now. She's, eh, busy.'

Turning to the girl with a twinkle in her eye, Miss Birnie teased, 'I think Hugh's taken a fancy to you, Cissie.'

Hugh waited until they were alone again, then he said, 'Your name's Cissie, is it?'

'Aye, Cissie McGregor.'

He held out his hand. 'Pleased to meet you, Cissie.' His firm grasp sent tingles up her arm. 'What time d'you stop?'

'Half past four.'

49

'Would you like to come to the pictures with me tonight? We could go to the La Scala or the Picture House or the Electric, whatever you like.'

Her heart sank. She'd never been to the pictures, but she couldn't go out tonight. 'My father's ill.'

'Another time, then?'

'Aye, another time.' Cissie was afraid that he was only being polite and wouldn't ask her again. But when she went home, she was glad that she hadn't accepted his invitation, for her father's dark eyes were almost out of sight in his grey face as he lay propped up against his pillows.

'Mrs Robertson made me get the doctor in,' Marie told her. 'He says it's pulmonary something – to do with his lungs – and he's pretty bad. I'd to get tablets and a new mixture.'

Cissie went over to the bed. 'How do you feel, Da?'

'Not that good, Cissie, lass.'

'You'll be better in a day or two.' At least he didn't have what Rosie had, she thought, thankfully.

*   *   *

It was two weeks before Big Tam's breathing grew easier and his face lost its grey hue, though it was still very pale, and another week went by before the doctor allowed him to get up.

'My legs feel like rubber,' he said, as Cissie helped him to a chair.

'You've been real ill, you know.' She tucked a blanket round him as Marie stripped the bed. 'Five minutes the first time,' she warned.

He didn't argue, and seemed glad to get back into bed when the time came. 'Oh, Cissie,' he sighed, 'I'm terrible weak.'

'You'll not be fit to work for a while yet.'

With only Joe and Cissie contributing to the household funds, Pat needing a new pair of boots for his growing feet and the doctor's bills to be paid, the McGregors had been forced to live very frugally, and Marie had been complaining for days. 'I've never had to buy cheap meat, but I can hardly even afford that now, and I'm affronted to ask the butcher for just a bone to make soup.'

'You should have told him our Da was off his work.'

'That would be begging.'

'It's not begging when you pay for what you get.'

'Could I not dip into the rent money?'

At that, Big Tam said, feebly but firmly, 'You're not to touch the rent money, I'll go back to my work tomorrow.' But the effort of speaking so much made him clutch at his chest.

'See what you've done?' Cissie reprimanded her sister. 'No, Da, we'll manage. There's no shame in being short of money, and I'll give Marie all my wages till you're better, and I'll make Joe do the same.'

Joe agreed to this once he was convinced it would only be temporary, and Marie's pride was salved. She still had to buy cheap meat, but at least it was meat, and not just bones or scrapings off the counter.

The doctor said that Tam could start work in another two weeks if he took it easy, but Cissie told him to stay off for a further week to make sure he was really fit.

Four mornings later, Marie was washing herself at the sink after Cissie and Joe had left, whistling and splashing water all over the place, and her shift was soon soaked. It was clinging to her curves when she turned to get the towel, and her father murmured, 'Your chest's bigger than Cissie's.'

Not as modest as her sister, she ran her hands over her large bosom, so that her pink nipples shone through the thin fabric. 'It was bigger than all the girls in my class.'

Her pleasure in her body made him frown. 'You'd better watch yourself with the lads.'

'They liked it,' she laughed. 'Some of them tried to touch

me, and Jackie Main put his hand up under my blouse . . .'

'You'd better not let that happen again!'

'Och, Da, hold your water,' she grinned, impudently.

'That's enough, you cheeky besom, or I'll . . .'

'Or you'll what?' she demanded, knowing that he wasn't fit to hit her. 'Make me take down my drawers so you can belt my bare backside?' She gave her skimpy shift a defiant little twitch as she went back to her bedroom.

Fortunately for her own sake, she lost her bravado after Pat went to school and she was alone in the house with her father, and neither of them referred to the earlier episode.

*　　*　　*

Hugh Phimister had asked Cissie out twice, but had been very understanding when she told him how ill her father was. On the Saturday of Tam's first week back at work, she told Hugh that she could go out with him now, and he arranged to meet her at seven o'clock that night at the foot of Schoolhill. Her excitement was dulled by apprehension of her father's reaction to this, and she broke it to him nervously.

'You're not long sixteen,' he growled.

'I'm old enough to go out with lads.'

Her determined face stopped him from saying anything more, and Marie followed her from the room when she went to put on her Sunday clothes. 'What's he like?'

'Hugh? He's awful nice.'

'What does he look like?'

'He's about the same height as Da,' Cissie began, rather shyly, 'but he's not so broad. His hair's a kind of brown, not really dark but not really light, with a wave at the front, and his eyes are . . .'

Marie snorted at her dreamy expression. 'You've got it bad. What about his eyes?'

Fastening her skirt buttons, Cissie sighed. 'They're a funny colour, greeny-brown.'

52

'Greeny-brown? That sounds awful.'

'They're lovely and soft and smiley.'

'Eyes can't be smiley.'

'They look as if he's always smiling, then.' Cissie took one last glance in the mirror.

Tam frowned when his eldest daughter popped her head round the kitchen door. 'You're off, are you? Well, mind and don't let the lad get over-familiar with you.'

'I'll watch myself.'

'It's him you'll have to watch.'

Hugh was waiting for her although she was a minute early herself. 'Where do you want to go?' he asked.

'I don't care. Wherever you think.'

'The Picturedrome in Skene Terrace? It's nearest.'

While they strolled up Schoolhill, Hugh told her that he had still two years of his apprenticeship to do. 'Then I'll be a time-served joiner. Ma said my father was no use with his hands — he was a clerk in a shipping-office — so she made me and my brothers go in for trades. Ian's a painter and Callum's nearly finished his time as a plumber.'

Cissie told him proudly that Tommy was in the Merchant Navy and that Joe was working in Hall's, by which time they had reached the small cinema. When they went inside, she was disappointed that he didn't even hold her hand, but assumed that he was too shy at this stage. She couldn't get over the miracle of the cinematograph — moving pictures of real men and women in America acting out stories on a white screen, with printed words showing what they were saying. And even though she knew it was make-believe, she screamed when a train came hurtling towards her, and cried when the hero and heroine had a misunderstanding, though they made it up later.

After the show, they walked back slowly, neither wanting their time together to end. Crowds were spilling out of His Majesty's Theatre, for it was a live show that week rather than one of the occasional filmshows that had been introduced to compete with the new cinemas. 'I'd like to take you to the theatre,' Hugh said, 'but I can't even afford the pictures very often.' He looked sideways at her. 'Will you come out with me again?'

'If you let me pay for myself.'

'No, it's the man's place to pay. But maybe we could just go for a walk, if it's fine? What about next Saturday?'

'Aye, next Saturday.' Cissie wished he had made it sooner – it would be a whole week before she saw him again.

They walked past the Art Gallery and Robert Gordon's College without talking, and when they reached her door, she said, 'Here's my house. We're on the second floor.'

They were standing next to the opening into Wordie's stables, and Hugh, unable to think of anything else to say, remarked, 'I love watching the Clydesdales pulling the heavy loads on their carts. There's something about them that gets a hold of you.'

Having once had her feet drenched with urine while waiting at the kerb for one of the carting company's vehicles to pass, Cissie was not enamoured with horses, but she said, 'Yes, they're beautiful,' then wished she had been honest with him.

He held the lobby door open. 'Next Saturday,' he said, and gave her an embarrassed peck on the cheek.

When Cissie went in, her father said, 'Did he behave?'

'He didn't even hold my hand in the pictures.'

Her father relaxed. 'There's tea in the pot.'

Filling a cup, she asked, 'What did Mam and you do in Inverness when you were courting?'

'We went walking if it was fine, along the Ness, some-times up Tomnahurich – there's a good view from the top – or we climbed Castle Hill. If it was raining, we'd to sit in her parlour, with her mother glowering at me like I was trying to steal her daughter from under her nose.'

Cissie giggled. 'Is she still alive, Mam's mother?'

'She died before we were married, and your Mam's father had been dead for a long time. I never knew him – nor my own father, either, for he died when I was an infant.'

He had never told her anything about his early life and she wished he would always be like this. 'When did your mother die?'

'She died of consumption when I was sixteen, and it wasn't long after that I met your Ma and we started courting.' He stopped speaking then, looking into the embers of the fire as if he saw images of himself as a youth and his dead wife as the comely young girl she had been. Whatever memories they conjured up, he suddenly gave himself a shake. 'Are you to be courting this Hugh? What does he work at?'

'He's serving his time as a joiner. I don't know if he wants to court me, but I'm seeing him again next Saturday.'

A fit of coughing beset Big Tam then, but when it was over, he said, 'If he does start courting you, be careful. He was maybe biding his time tonight.'

'Biding his time?'

'Not letting you know what he's really after.'

'Och, Da!' Cissie was angry now. 'He's not like you.'

Tam's brows shot down. 'What do you mean by that?'

'I heard Mam getting on to you once for not being able to stay away from women, and you've had plenty of them here in this house, haven't you?'

He jumped up at that, his face an angry red. 'What chance have I had of being with a woman these past six weeks?' He paused, then said, hoarsely, 'What needs I go outside, any road, when I've a lassie at home ready for it?'

Some sixth sense made her jump out of his way before he lunged at her, and while he was still trying to regain his balance against the table, she made her escape. She was glad that her sister was asleep, for Marie would have seen that something was wrong. Her stomach heaved as she

55

undressed, and even hearing her father coughing for most of the night didn't make her any less angry at him. It was revolting to remember that his need for women made him take them off the streets, but it was a thousand times worse to think he was so desperate he would look to his own daughter.

Chapter Seven

Too ashamed to tell anyone, not even Aggie Robertson, what her father had said and done, Cissie made sure that she was never alone with him again, and, to safeguard Marie — whose large breasts seemed to be a source of pride to her and who didn't fully understand the danger she was in — she met Joe on the landing one night and asked him if he would mind not going out on Saturday evenings.

His mouth rose at one corner in the infuriating way it always did when he was puzzled. 'Why me? Marie's old enough now to see Pat goes to bed.'

'Eh, well,' Cissie hedged. 'He's still growing, and he needs all the sleep he can get, and Marie forgets the time once she gets her nose in a tuppenny horrible.'

This only half-satisfied him. 'But I can surely go out if Da's there with her, can't I?'

Cissie felt like screaming that this was exactly what she was trying to prevent, but she managed to smile. 'You know what he's like. He'll suddenly get tired of being in the house, and he'll just go out.'

Joe laughed. 'Aye, that's right, so he will.'

'Well, do you promise?'

'I promise.' He gave her an affectionate poke in the ribs as they went inside. 'You're a real old wife these days, do you know that? It's time you got married.'

Cissie thought sadly that she would give anything to marry Hugh Phimister if he ever asked her, but how could she leave Marie unprotected? She wouldn't be able to marry until her sister got married, and that would be years yet. She wished that Tommy was still at home. He knew what Da was like and he'd have soon sorted him out, but she hadn't seen Tommy since he joined the Merchant Navy. He must still be alive, though, for she'd have been notified if he wasn't. If only Phoebe hadn't left like she did. Da had been very fond of her, and would likely have married her if she hadn't gone and spoiled it by trying to hurry him.

An unexpected rush of longing for her mother made Cissie swallow hard. If Mam were still here, everything would be all right. Mam would have watched out for Marie and she, Cissie, would be free to live her own life, the way she wanted. Her thoughts wavered. She was selfish to wish Mam back to all that suffering, however much she missed her, and, in any case, it couldn't be. It might be best to tell Hugh on Saturday that they shouldn't see each other any more, that there was no future in it for him, that she was committed to looking after her brothers and sister – especially her sister.

By Saturday night, Cissie had more or less planned out what she would say to Hugh, but as soon as she saw him, his boyish face breaking into a warm smile when he caught sight of her, his long-lashed eyes crinkling, she knew that she couldn't hurt him. It wasn't that she hadn't the courage to say anything, she didn't want to say it. She loved him and it would break her heart if she couldn't see him again.

Taking her hand, Hugh said, 'It's been a long week.'

'Yes,' she breathed. 'I thought tonight would never come.'

'Would you like to take a walk to the Westburn Park? It's not too far for you, is it?'

'It's not all that far.' Cissie would have agreed to walk to John o' Groats and back just to be with him.

The long walk seemed to take no time at all, because Hugh told her of all the things he had been doing since he'd seen her, but as they went into the park, he said, 'You're very quiet, Cissie. Is anything wrong?'

This would have been her chance to tell him, but she just smiled. 'Nothing's wrong, I like listening to you.'

His laugh was somewhat self-conscious. 'I'd like to hear what you've been doing, and all. You must have had customers you were angry with, or had a laugh with?'

She related a few little incidents which had amused her, aware that his eyes hardly left her face the whole time. 'I can't remember anything else,' she said, at last. 'My job's not as interesting as yours.'

They had reached the West Burn, which ran through the park and gave it its name, and Hugh said, 'When I was little, my brothers used to let me paddle here, but I usually ended up falling in and going home soaking wet, and Ma gave them a telling off for not watching me properly.'

'You must have been like our Pat. He's always getting into trouble, and goodness knows how he'll get on when he leaves school. I pity the poor man that gives him a job.'

Grinning, Hugh flopped down on the grassy bank and pulled her down beside him. 'Might as well sit as stand.'

'It's lovely here.'

He looked at her for a moment, then murmured, 'So are you lovely. Your eyes are twinkling brighter than any star.'

'Oh, that's the nicest thing anybody's ever said to me.'

'It's true. I can hardly believe my luck to be sitting with you like this.'

Her heart leapt; he did like her. 'I'm lucky, and all.'

A light summer breeze ruffled their hair as he took her hand, but one strong gust suddenly billowed her skirt up. She was quite sure that Hugh couldn't have seen anything he shouldn't from where he was sitting, but she smoothed it down, looking at him in embarrassment, and without warning, his arms were round her. 'It's maybe too soon to be saying it, Cissie, but I wish we could be together all the time.'

Wishing that, too, she knew that it would not be possible for years. 'Some day we might be,' she said, gently.

'Aye, some day, but it'll be a long time before I could ask you to marry me. Not till after my time's out and I'm getting a journeyman's pay.'

It would have surprised him to know that this was balm to Cissie's troubled spirits. By the time Hugh was earning a tradesman's wage, Marie might not need her protection. 'I'm willing to wait,' she murmured, happily.

He held her away from him in astonishment. 'Are you? I've loved you since that day Ma ran out of butter, but I didn't dare to hope you . . .'

'I've loved you, too, from the very first minute.'

Both of them inexperienced, their first kiss was a quick meeting of unyielding lips, but their second was much more enjoyable, and it was some time later when Hugh broke away abruptly. 'I'll have to stop, Cissie, I can't trust myself any longer.'

Thankful that he could control his feelings, she was still disappointed that the kissing was over for the time being. 'It must be late, we'd better go home.'

Standing up, they brushed the grass off their clothes and Hugh gave her one last kiss before they set off. Their walk back was silent, charged with an intense awareness which had increased almost to flash point by the time they arrived at Cissie's door. Stopping, they looked at each other with a hungry longing, then Hugh said, hoarsely, 'Next Saturday?' and she was left, a bundle of raw nerve-ends.

She stood for several minutes inside the dark communal lobby until the fire inside her cooled down. When she felt calmer, she wondered if she would have let Hugh carry on in the park if he hadn't stopped when he did. Could she have let him do to her what her father did to his women? Hugh wasn't like Da, so it might have been all right. Oh, what was she thinking? Decent girls didn't think things like that.

When the clock in St Nicholas Kirk started to chime, she counted the strokes fearfully, but there were only ten – it wasn't so late. Heaving a sigh of relief, she went to the outside lavatory before going upstairs, and on her way up to the house, she met Joe coming down. 'Is Da in?' she asked.

'No, he went out about eight and he's not back.'

When Cissie went into the bedroom, Marie – disappointed that nothing had happened the week before – plied her with questions. 'Has Hugh kissed you yet? Has he said he loves you? Are you going steady now?'

'Yes, yes, and yes,' Cissie laughed.

'What's it like, being kissed?'

'You wouldn't understand.'

'Yes I would. I've read about it often enough.'

'I'd read about it myself, but, oh, Marie, it's just wonderful! Your heart thumps till you think it's going to jump out of your body altogether, your head goes round and round, tingly shivers go all over you . . .'

'Sounds like you need a doctor if you get kissed.'

'Don't be sarcastic. I knew you wouldn't understand.'

'How did he tell you he loves you?'

Cissie let out a long blissful sigh. 'He said he'd loved me since the day his mother sent him for butter.'

'Oh, that's real romantic,' Marie spluttered.

'It was the first time we met,' Cissie explained, huffily, annoyed at her sister for making fun of such a treasured moment. 'Go to sleep. I'm not telling you any more.'

She was still reliving the thrills of Hugh's kisses when she heard her father coming in, and pretended to be asleep when he eased the door open to see if she was home.

61

'Aye, Cissie's in,' she heard him say, and a female voice answered, 'So nobody'll interrupt us?'

Realising that he'd brought another woman home, Cissie felt her happiness ebbing away, and had to cover her ears in a few minutes to blot out the disgusting noises coming from the kitchen bed. She could definitely never let Hugh touch her if he made sounds like that – it made her flesh creep.

However much she had hated the idea that first night, Cissie had to admit that Sally's coming made life easier. She was brassy and common, but she kept Da satisfied, and he didn't need to look to his daughters for his pleasures. The only drawback was that she refused to take on any household duties, and Marie still had to do the cooking and cleaning. She complained every night to Cissie, who felt like saying it was their father she should be telling, but if Marie had told him, it would only have caused trouble.

'I wonder how long this one'll stay?' Marie said, one day.

'Till she gets fed up,' Cissie said, drily, 'or till Da gets fed up with her.'

'It's all right for you, you don't have to be in the house with her all day. She lies in her bed till dinnertime, and spends nearly the whole afternoon making up her mind what to wear. Then she paints her face, and she's sitting like a duchess by the time you come home. But you don't care about me, you're too busy thinking about your darling Hugh.'

Feeling guilty, Cissie said, 'I can't do anything about Sally, anyway.'

'I know. I just like to grouse.'

Unluckily for Cissie's dreams of another walk with Hugh, it was raining heavily on Saturday night, but he greeted her with his usual, heart-warming smile. 'Ma says I've to take you to our house.'

There would be no chance of him kissing or doing anything else to her now, she thought, uncertain whether to be glad or sorry. He took her arm and hurried her towards his home, a tenement a little way along George Street from the dairy. The Phimisters lived on the top floor and she was out of breath by the time Hugh rushed her up.

'Come in, Cissie,' his mother said, kindly. 'It's too wet a night to be walking about.'

One of the two young men seated at the side of the fire winked at the other. 'You don't notice the weather when you're in love,' he remarked.

'You're just jealous, Ian.' Hugh took her wet coat and hung it up in the tiny lobby. 'Cissie, you'll have gathered that that's my brother Ian, and that's Callum, and this,' he slid his arms round his mother's waist, 'is Ma.'

Mrs Phimister laughed. 'Never mind Ian, he's aye teasing Hughie. Sit down there, Cissie.' She turned to her youngest son again. 'I know Cissie from the dairy, but I hope we get to know each other better in a wee while.'

Her arch glance made Cissie blush, and Ian gave a great roar of laughter. 'We've a romance in the wind, have we?'

Callum, the eldest of the three, spoke for the first time. 'Wait till you take a girl home yourself, Ian, and you'll not think it's so funny to be tormented.'

'No girl would look at him twice,' Hugh laughed.

'They're always going on at each other like bairns,' their mother smiled, 'but you'll get used to them.'

Cissie returned the smile. They were a nice family, even if Hugh and his brothers did tease each other. They weren't alike – Ian being small and very dark and Callum rather stout with a florid face – but there was something about their foreheads, their eyes, that showed how closely they were related.

'Would you like a game of whist?' Ian asked, suddenly. 'Ma doesn't like playing, for she never wins.'

'I've never played whist before,' Cissie answered, shyly.

63

'We'll show you.' He took a pack of cards out of the table drawer. 'You and me against Hugh and Callum.' He shuffled, then dealt out as expertly as a professional gambler.

After a few hands, Cissie was enjoying the game. Her quick brain enabled her to remember which cards had already been played, and Ian was soon crying, 'Well done, partner!'

By the time Mrs Phimister told them to stop because she had made some tea, Hugh and Callum were down by over a hundred points and Ian was cock-a-hoop. 'Cissie, are you sure you haven't played before?'

'Beginner's luck,' laughed Callum.

'No, she's an absolute marvel,' Ian declared.

Stretching out, Hugh laid his hand on her shoulder. 'She is a marvel. The most marvellous girl in the world.'

She was saved further embarrassment by Mrs Phimister, who removed the deck of cards and whipped off the chenille table cover. 'Put on the tea cloth, Ian, and, Callum, you can help me to set the table.'

It was almost ten when Hugh said that it was time he saw her home. 'Don't bother to come out,' she told him. 'It's likely still raining and there's no point in you getting wet again when you don't need to.'

Twitching back the curtain to look out, Ian said, 'It's still bucketing down, but Hugh'll not shrink and, any road, what's a droppie rain when a man's in love?'

'I'll easily manage myself,' she assured Hugh, but was pleased when he insisted on accompanying her. 'Goodnight, everybody,' she murmured, 'and thank you for having me, Mrs Phimister. I've really enjoyed myself.'

'You're welcome, lass, any time.'

'They like you,' Hugh told her as they went downstairs. 'I knew they would, though.'

'And I like them – all of them.'

64

He gave her a quick kiss before he opened the street door, but when she saw the rain bouncing off the pavement and the water rushing along the gutter, she said, 'You can't come out in this, Hugh. You'll be soaked to the skin before you get home again.'

'As Ian said, I won't shrink,' he laughed.

Holding hands, they ran as fast as they could, but even in the short distance they had to go, they were both dripping wet by the time they reached Schoolhill. Cissie was hoping that he would come inside the lobby with her, but he tilted her head up with his finger and gave her a long kiss there on the pavement, the rain pelting on their faces and making their eyes blink.

'Oh, Cissie,' he laughed, softly, 'it's great to be young and daft, isn't it? But I'd better go. Next Saturday?'

Wet as she was, she stood and watched him until he turned the corner out of sight, and her heart was so filled with love that, when she went into the house, she burst into the kitchen without thinking. What she saw made her stand stock still, and she was unable to move for the sickness that rose inside her until her mouth was awash with bile. The sounds coming from the bed culminated in a great roar, and then the heaving mass stilled and separated.

Tam, still panting, turned round, his drink-glazed eyes leering at her from his beetroot-red face. 'So! You like watching it, do you? Maybe you and your lad have been at it, and all? Eh? Eh, Cissie?'

Sally's coarse giggles followed her as she turned and ran from the room, and Marie sat up with a start when she threw open the bedroom door. 'What's the matter with you, Cissie? Has Hugh Phimister been . . .'

'Hugh never touched me. Let me be.' The tears came now, and her harsh sobs made Marie understand.

'Did you go into the kitchen and see them? It's been bad enough listening to them, the filthy pigs.'

'Oh, Marie, it's . . .'

'Come to bed, Cissie,' Marie soothed. 'You're all strung up, and there's not a thing we can do about it.'

'That's what makes it worse. If you heard them, Pat must have heard them, too, and he's only twelve. What must he be thinking?'

'He'll be a man himself one day, and he'll do the same.'

'But I could never let a man do that to me, not the way they were carrying on. It was horrible! It made me want to vomit.' Her tears easing a little, Cissie began to undress. 'Marie, I never wanted to say anything, but watch yourself with Da. If he hasn't got a woman here, he could easily try to do something to you.'

'Has he tried with you?'

'Aye, but I was too quick for him.' Pulling her nightshift on over her head, Cissie lay down on the bed.

'I've just minded!' Marie exclaimed. 'When he was getting better of that pulmonary thing, I was washing myself at the sink, and he said my chest was bigger than yours, and he was looking at it like he never wanted to stop.'

'That's what I mean, so be careful.'

Marie gave a low giggle. 'My shift was soaking, so he must have got a right eyeful.'

'Oh, Marie.' Cissie shook her head, reprovingly. 'Don't let him see you like that again.'

'He liked it,' Marie laughed. 'I think he wanted to get hold of my titties.'

'Aye, no doubt he did, but if you carry on like that in front of him, it's not just your titties he'll touch. He'll end up doing the same to you as he was doing to Sally. Is that what you want?'

Shuddering, Marie said, 'No, and I'll not do it again.'

Marie was too proud of her perfectly-formed bosom, Cissie realised, and she'd been lucky Da hadn't been well when she flaunted it in front of him. If he had been, he'd have had her down on the bed before she knew what was happening. As long as Sally was there, she was safe, but after that . . .

Cissie shivered. She'd been afraid for her sister before, but it would be much worse after Sally left.

Chapter Eight

On her second week with the McGregors, Sally Johnston was on her way to the outside lavatory when she met Mrs Gibb from the floor above and took exception to her inquisitive stare. 'Who the hell d'you think you're lookin' at?' she shouted.

Bridling, the other woman answered, equally aggressively, 'One o' Big Tam's bidie-ins by the looks o' you, and you're the worst-looking I've seen yet.'

'You impudent bitch!' Fists at the ready, Sally made to follow Mrs Gibb as she ran upstairs, but as she explained to Marie later, 'I couldna wait, I was bursting for the lavvy.'

Marie couldn't help laughing, and rekindled Sally's anger by observing, 'She was right, though. You're no beauty.'

Sally was still seething from both insults when Tam came home, and couldn't wait to air her grievances. 'You'd better go up and gi'e that woman a bit o' your mind,' she ended. 'I'm not stoppin' here if I've to put up wi' the likes o' her and Marie.'

His scowl deepened. 'Nobody's forcing you to stay.'

'So that's the way o' it? Right, I'm off!'

Nobody was sorry when she packed her bag and marched out, her yellow hair straggling out beneath her flat hat, her painted lips set in a tight straight line. Cissie glanced across at Marie, who raised her eyebrows as if to say, 'Good riddance,' and even their father seemed to be relieved.

When he went out after supper, Marie said, 'Will he be

68

away to look for another one?' and Cissie shrugged. There was no telling what he would do.

They were all in bed when he came home, but he had no one with him, as far as Cissie could hear, and she knew she'd have to keep on the alert again, until he found somebody.

Cissie knew that Joe resented having to stay in on Saturday nights, but she had other worries on her mind. Over the past few weeks, Hugh's kisses had become more demanding, and the feel of his need against her made her own body cry out to be satisfied. She often wondered if she would have the will-power to stop him if he tried to do anything more, but he never did, and she went home each week glad that she hadn't been put to the test.

Marie surprised her one day by saying, in a voice tight with excitement, 'When I was in the butcher's this fore-noon, one of the lads asked me out, so I said I'd meet him at the Queen on Saturday at half past seven. I thought I'd better make it the same night as you go out with Hugh,' she added.

'That's good.' Cissie understood her reason for this and was grateful. 'What's his name?'

'I've heard them calling him Lewis, but I don't know his last name. I'll find out on Saturday.'

'Maybe Lewis is his last name,' Cissie suggested.

Marie looked thoughtful. 'I never thought about that.'

'You'd better not be late home, or Da'll go daft.'

'I haven't told him I'm going out, yet, and he'll likely go daft about that, and all.' Marie tossed her fair hair. 'Not that I'm caring. He can't keep me in.'

'Don't be too sure,' Cissie muttered.

It took all her powers of persuasion, backed by Joe's, to make Tam agree to let Marie go out with the young man, but eventually he said, 'All right, Marie, but I want you home by nine. That's late enough for a girl of fourteen.'

Marie cast a look of appeal at Cissie, who said, quietly, 'She's nearly fifteen. Make it ten.'

'Good God! Has a man no say in his own house?'

Joe chanced a smile. 'Not when there's so many females. Any road, Marie's got her head screwed on the right way, and she'll come to no harm.'

'She'd better not, or I'll break the laddie's neck.'

Cissie was making ready to meet Hugh on Saturday when a disturbing thought occurred to her. Marie looked grown up, yet she still had a child's mind and would be too easily – perhaps willingly – led astray. 'How old's Lewis?'

'About twenty, maybe more.'

'Does he know you're not fifteen yet?'

Marie shrugged. 'He never asked.'

'Don't let him do anything wrong.'

'I can let him kiss me, though, can't I?' Marie said, a little anxiously. 'You let your lad kiss you.'

'Hugh didn't kiss me the first time we were out. Anyway, he's a decent lad, and we don't know anything about Lewis.'

'He's decent, and all, Cissie. I'm sure he is.'

'Well, just one kiss, nothing more. Cheerio.'

As usual, Hugh was waiting. 'I'm taking you – home with me tonight again,' he told her, his faltering voice making her sure that he was nervous. Was he going to tell his family that they loved each other? He said nothing as they went along George Street, and she wondered if she had been over-optimistic. Maybe it was only a birthday party for one of his brothers? But he seemed too tense for that – not worried tense, more like he was nursing a wonderful secret. Could he be going to ask her to marry him, in front of his family?

When they reached his tenement, he stopped her before she climbed the stairs. 'I'd better tell you before we go up,

Cissie. You see, my mother's gone to see her sister and Ian and Callum are out, and all.'

'Are you telling me there's nobody in your house?'

'No – I mean yes, there's nobody in. We'll have the place to ourselves.' He regarded her hopefully. 'Please, Cissie?'

At first, she felt disappointed in him for not telling her before, then it occurred to her that he could easily have taken her into the empty house without telling her at all. She knew it would be dangerous to be alone with him for hours, but love swept away every iota of her common sense.

'Please, Cissie?' he repeated, and she nodded shyly.

While he was hanging up her coat, she was trembling with guilt at what might happen, and she realised, when he came to stand next to her, that he was trembling, too.

'I shouldn't have come,' she whispered. 'If you'd told me nobody was in when I met you first, I'd . . .'

'That's why I didn't tell you. I knew you wouldn't come, but I promise I won't do anything . . . Oh, Cissie, I love you.'

This was too much for her and she turned to him blindly. 'I love you, and all, Hugh.'

He pulled her onto the couch, and for the next fifteen minutes nothing mattered to her except the ecstasy of his lips against hers, the sensation that he was drawing her love into him. Her head was swimming, she ached for him when his hands began to explore her body, but suddenly she pushed him away. She had recognised the harsh breathing of a man in the heat of passion, a man who might behave like her father did with his women, and revulsion flooded up in her.

'Oh, God!' Hugh groaned. 'Please, Cissie, please?' His hands held her in a vice-like grip. 'You have to let me. I can't bear it.'

'No!' she screamed, struggling to get up. 'No! No, Hugh! You promised you wouldn't.'

He released her so abruptly that she was catapulted to the floor, but ignoring his outstretched hand, she scrambled to her feet. When she looked at him, the hurt bewilderment in his eyes almost made her sorry for refusing him, until she noticed that he was holding his crotch and felt sick again. 'I'm going home – by myself,' she said firmly.

He followed her when she went to get her coat. 'I'm sorry, Cissie, I couldn't help myself. I shouldn't have taken you up here, it was asking for trouble.'

Spurning his apology, she slammed the door and ran down the stairs. She should have known, she thought, angry at herself for trusting him. All men were tarred with the same brush. They only wanted a woman for one thing and didn't consider how the woman felt about it. Her hands fumbled with the outside doorknob in her haste to put as much distance between her and Hugh as she could, and she raced along George Street oblivious to the startled looks of the people who had to jump out of her way. She was in her own tenement lobby before she remembered that Hugh had given her the chance to refuse before he took her into his house, and she had let him believe that she wanted . . . But she had wanted it then. The truth made her stop in her tracks. She had known perfectly well what would happen and still she'd gone with him. She had only herself to blame.

Her feet dragged as she climbed the stairs. That was the last she would see of Hugh and she did love him. When she went into the kitchen, her father was sitting alone at the table with an empty bottle in front of him, his face flushed as it always was when he'd had too much to drink. He looked up in surprise. 'You're home early, Cissie.'

She tore off her coat and took her anger and frustration out on him. 'It's your fault. If I hadn't heard you making those awful noises with your whores, I'd have let Hugh . . .'

The abrupt halt, and her evident confusion, told him

what had happened. 'So you stopped your lad from taking his way with you, did you?'

Ashamed at having said so much, she turned to leave, but this time he was too quick for her – jumping up and pinning her arms to her sides. 'Come to your Da, Cissie, lass,' he crooned. 'I'll not take no for an answer like him.'

She was no match for his drunken, brute strength, and he swivelled her over to the bed and forced her down, despite her frantic struggles, one massive hand clamped over her mouth to stop her screams. The smell of whisky on his breath nauseated her and she thrashed her head from side to side trying to shake off his hand, not aware that his other hand was opening her buttons until his fingers squeezed her bare breast. His burning lips came down on hers, and not knowing that her bucking body was inflaming him even more, she kept fighting him when he hauled down her drawers and settled on top of her.

During the next few minutes, Cissie learned why her father made the revolting noises she had so often heard, and was certain that he would rip her apart before he was finished with her, but, at last, the final, strangled shout issued from him, and she could feel him pulsing inside her.

Breathing heavily, he remained on her for some time before he rolled off mumbling, 'I'd forgotten how good it is with a virgin.' His lascivious eyes hardened. 'If you ever tell a living soul about this, I'll swear you begged me for it because your lad wasn't man enough.'

She was past caring about anything except the excruciating pain in her innards, but she had to get away from him in case he took her again. With a great effort, she managed to swing her legs over the edge of the bed, but before she could pull her skirts down, his hand gripped her shoulder. 'Oh, Christ! I'm sorry, Cissie.'

With a violent movement, she freed herself and stood up, her legs almost giving way as they took her weight. 'I don't know what came over me,' Big Tam was muttering as she staggered into the lobby. 'It was you saying . . . I could picture what your lad . . .'

She didn't hear the rest, and when she went into her own room, she stood with her back against the door, thankful that Marie wasn't there to see the state she was in, and too full of shame to wonder why Pat and Joe hadn't heard anything. Realising that something was trickling down her legs, she took off her clothes to see what it was, and discovered that she was bleeding. Not ordinary blood like when she had her monthlies, but mixed with something sticky. Had some vital part of her been pierced? She couldn't go back to the kitchen to wash herself, so she made do with rubbing herself clean with a handkerchief.

When she felt calmer, she lay down, bitterly regretting having been so foolish as to tell her father what Hugh had tried to do. It must have sounded like an invitation, which he'd grasped before she realised what was on his mind.

Some fifteen minutes later, the lobby door opened, and when she heard the two voices, she realised that both her brothers must have been out. In the next minute, Pat came bouncing in to tell her where they had been.

'Da said you weren't feeling well, but I had to tell you. Joe said it was too fine to bide in, and he took me to the beach. He asked Da to come, but he said he was too tired.'

Not tired enough, Cissie thought, dully, but tried to show some interest. 'Did you enjoy yourselves?'

'Oh, yes, we walked along the sand for a while, and then we went back up to the prom and Joe took me on the Scenic Railway. I was a bit scared, and so was he, though he tried to make out he wasn't, but it was awful good fun.'

'It's time you were sleeping,' Cissie said, wishing that her brothers hadn't gone out, or that they'd come home half an hour earlier.

Marie came in on the dot at ten, and Cissie had to listen to her enthusing about the lad she had been out with. 'Lewis is his last name. His first name's Wilfie – Wilfred,

I suppose – and he took me to the Electric Theatre. You're awful quiet, Cissie. Have you fallen out with your Hugh?'

'Yes.' She left it at that. At least it made her sister stop chattering.

Marie soon fell asleep, but Cissie lay weeping silently for most of the night. When she heard her father coughing and moving about in the morning, she felt herself shrinking from having to face him. Giving Marie a push, she said, 'I've an awful sore head. I think I'll stay in bed.'

Assuming that she was still upset about quarrelling with Hugh, Marie looked at her sympathetically. 'It's my turn to cook the dinner this week, and your turn for the kirk, and Da'll not be pleased if you don't go.'

'He'll know why I'm not going.'

'You'll never believe this,' Marie burst out when she came in again after washing herself. 'Da wants to go to the kirk, but he doesn't want any of us with him. D'you think he's ill again, Cissie? He looks awful.'

Well may he look awful, Cissie thought, vindictively. It would be a blessing for all of them if the filthy pig died. But he was too wicked to die, worse luck.

When she heard him going out, she rose to help Marie with the dinner, and Pat, delighted at having a reprieve from the usual Sunday worship, turned to Joe. 'Has Da ever been at the kirk before?'

Joe made a face. 'Not that I can mind on. There must be something wrong with him, for he never said anything when I told him I was enlisting.'

Cissie whipped round. 'Was it last night you told him you were enlisting?' She was willing to believe that this was what had upset her father and led him to defile her, though she would never forgive him for it.

'Aye, I told him when we came back from the beach.'

So Da hadn't known before that, Cissie thought. 'Was he not angry?'

'He looked as if he didn't care one way or the other. It surprised me.'

It didn't surprise Cissie. Apart from anything else, Da must have known why Joe stayed in on Saturdays and would be pleased when he went away. Well, it didn't matter now. She wouldn't be going out with Hugh any more – and she'd go to bed at the same time as Pat when Marie was out.

Her stomach churned when she heard her father's feet on the stairs, but he didn't look at her when he came in. Maybe he was ashamed at what he had done, but it was too late. She wished that she had someone to confide in, to share the burden of what her father had done to her, but who could she tell? Miss Birnie was a kind, caring woman, but she was a spinster and would be shocked to the very depths of her being, and the only other person she could think of was Aggie Robertson, who was over seventy and must have heard worse things in her time – if anything could be worse. She couldn't speak about it yet, though. Maybe tomorrow.

Having half expected Hugh to come to the dairy on Monday, Cissie was quite relieved when he didn't. She had enough on her plate without coping with him, too, though she still loved him and it would have been comforting to know that he still felt the same about her.

The rain was lashing down when she finished work, yet she walked home slowly, trying to think how to tell Aggie what had happened, and her clothes were drenched when she reached Schoolhill. But she was desperate to talk to somebody.

'My, Cissie!' Mrs Robertson exclaimed when she opened the door. 'Come in and take off your coat, it's dripping wet.'

The girl followed her into the kitchen and sat down by the fire. 'I want to tell you something, but I don't know where to start.' Abandoning self-control, she burst into

76

tears. 'Oh, Aggie, Da did an awful thing to me on Saturday night.'

It was as though a huge hand wiped the smile off the old woman's face. 'That's what I've aye been feared for, lassie, kenning Big Tam.'

'He said it was better with a virgin,' the girl sobbed. 'Aggie, what's a virgin?'

'Something you'll never be again, that's one thing sure. It's a lassie that hasna been touched by a man – like your Da did to you.'

'If another man . . . would he know I wasn't a virgin?'

'Aye, lass, he would. Your maidenhead's broken now, and you wouldna bleed a second time.'

'Was that why I was bleeding? I thought my insides had got punctured . . .'

'My poor dearie. Well, it's done now and we'll just have to pray he hasna landed you wi' a bairn.'

'None of his whores landed with bairns.' Cissie had often wondered why they hadn't when her mother had had so many.

'They ken't how to prevent it.'

'What'll I do?' Cissie wailed. 'What'll folk say if I've a baby, and it would be worse if they knew Da was the father.'

Aggie looked grave. 'A bairn born oot o' incest sometimes turns out to be an imbecile, but we'll not let it get that far. I could sort you out if you tell me quick. You ken the signs?' At Cissie's slight nod, she went on, 'The longer you leave it, the worse it'll be to get rid o'.'

Cissie's eyes jerked wide in shock. 'Kill it, you mean?'

'Well, aye, but it's not really . . .'

'I couldn't let you kill an unborn baby.'

'It's the only way, in case it's not right in the head.'

'I don't care. I couldn't let you . . .' Cissie started to weep again.

After considering for a moment, Aggie said, 'Maybe

we're getting worked up for nothing, but for God's sake, never let him touch you again.'

Cissie sat down on the stairs to think before she went up to her own house. It hadn't crossed her mind that she might be in the family way, and she would have to wait in secret torture until her next show came . . . if it came. She wished now that she hadn't stopped Hugh on Saturday night. If she had let him do what he wanted and he had made her pregnant, they would have had to get married.

But he hadn't come to apologise – he likely didn't want to see her any more – and she didn't think she could face him again, in any case.

Chapter Nine

❧❧

Three weeks later, Cissie's mental agony had increased. She had prayed for a week that she was wrong, but she had never been this late before, had hardly ever been more than a day out. She couldn't bear to think about it, especially today, when Joe was leaving to join the Royal Navy.

At breakfast, Marie eyed her with concern. 'Is something wrong, Cissie? You've hardly said a word since you got up.'

'It's just . . . I'm going to miss Joe when he's away.' Cissie couldn't stop the tears from springing to her eyes, excusing them by saying to her brother, 'You'll be put on a boat when your training's finished, and you'll be . . .'

'I always wanted to go to sea,' he reminded her.

'A lot of boats have been sunk, Joe, and if you wanted to fight, you should have joined the army, it's safer.'

'I don't want to fight, I just want to go to sea. Any road, the army's not any safer than the navy. Look how many soldiers have been killed.'

'I don't want to lose you,' she sobbed, and ran through to her bedroom. Her own plight was bad enough without having to worry about two brothers instead of one.

When it was time for Joe to go, he shook hands with Marie and ruffled Pat's hair, then went to take his leave of his older sister. She had drawn the curtains and was lying in semi-darkness when he knocked and went in. 'Don't be upset for me, Cissie,' he said, sitting down on the bed. 'I want to go. Da's boiling mad at me now, so I'd better not come home again till I'm sure he's got over it.'

She fought down the nerve-ball that had gathered in her throat. 'I'll be praying for you, Joe.'

He laughed self-consciously. 'Oh well, I'll be all right, then. God'll answer your prayers, Cissie, for you've always been a good girl.'

If she had been capable of speech, she would have told him that she wasn't a good girl any longer, that she was in terrible trouble, but she could only shake the hand he held out. 'Goodbye, Cissie.'

It wasn't until fifteen minutes after he left that she was able to pull herself together, and she had to run because she was late for work. Somehow, Cissie got through the day, but when she left the dairy at half past four and saw Hugh Phimister waiting for her, she could have screamed.

'I wanted to come before this,' he said, quietly, 'but I was giving you time to get over what I did. I'm really sorry about it, Cissie, and I'll never do anything like that again. Please say you're not going to stop seeing me.'

She had let him go on until she regimented her thoughts, but now she tore her eyes away from his beseeching face. 'I can't go out with you any more.'

'Please, Cissie? I'll never put you in a situation like that again. I love you, and I thought you loved me.'

She loved him more than he would ever know, but it was impossible now. 'I'm sorry, Hugh.'

Grabbing her hand, he cried, 'You do love me, I can see it in your eyes. Why won't you come out with me?'

'I can't. Please, Hugh, leave it. There's a reason why.'

'Tell me, then. You owe me that.'

'I can't. It wasn't you, it's something I've done.'

His eyes darkened. 'Is there somebody else?'

She bit back the denial she longed to make; it was easier to leave him believing it. It would pain him for a while, but the truth would be even worse. 'Yes, there's somebody else. Now, just let me go home.'

'Is there no chance for me at all?'

'No.' She walked away, hot tears stinging her eyelids.

'I'll never forget you,' he called, softly, 'and if you ever change your mind, let me know.'

She walked as quickly, and as steadily, as she was able, but as she turned the corner into Schoolhill, she couldn't resist a backward glance. Hugh was still standing looking after her, a forlorn figure in the gathering dusk.

Cissie had finally accepted it. She had prayed it was the shock of her father's assault that had made her miss the first time, but there was no doubt now. In her torment, she went back to Aggie, who took one look at her woebegone face and said, 'So he did it? You should have come back before this, though. Will you let me get rid of it?'

'No, Aggie.' Cissie had turned it over and over in her mind and was still sure it wouldn't be right.

'Aye, well. I'll send my Jim up when he comes home, for he wants to ask you something.'

Hurt that Aggie had given her no sympathy, Cissie went up to her own house, where Marie, with a face like thunder, was rolling out pastry for a pie, and Pat was sitting with a huge smirk on his round face. 'Have you two been quarrelling again?' she sighed.

'Tell him to stop complaining about my cooking!' Marie burst out. 'If he helped a bit, it wouldn't be so bad.'

'I haven't the strength to help,' Pat grinned. 'I need proper food.'

Marie waved the rolling pin at him threateningly. 'What you need's a wallop with this.'

Cissie covered her ears and screamed. 'Stop it, the pair of you!'

Astonished, Marie laid down the rolling pin and went over to put her arm round her sister. 'I know something's been bothering you for a while. Can you not tell me?'

'There's nothing to tell. I'm tired, that's all, and I can't stand you two always fighting over nothing.'

'I'm sorry, I didn't think, but he drives me up the wall with his complaining.'

'It's only in fun,' Pat mumbled. 'Sorry, Cissie. I like to see her getting raised, but I won't do it again.'

She drew a deep breath. 'I'm sorry for shouting.'

Peace restored, Marie returned to her pastry-making, Pat took his jotters out of his satchel to do his homework and Cissie went to the sink to splash her hot face with cold water. She shouldn't have lost her temper – Pat and Marie were too alike in their natures and would always rub each other up the wrong way – but her nerves were nearly at breaking point.

When someone knocked at the door about an hour later, she said, 'It'll be the Humphy. I'll go.'

'Come out to the landing a minute,' Jim Robertson said, quietly, and when she shut the door behind her, he went on, 'Ma told me about the bairn, and I'm willing to marry you so it can have a name, and I swear nobody'll ever learn from me who its real father is.'

This was the last thing she had expected, and her legs wobbled dangerously. But he couldn't be serious? How could he think she would marry him? He was ancient, and his back – and his bandy legs? Oh, no!

Her silence made him persist. 'I'd look after you, and the bairn. I'm maybe not your idea of a husband, but it would save your face, and you'll not be able to bide in your own house once you start to show. If we get wed quick, folk'll think it's mine.'

Everything he said was true, Cissie could see that, and she had lost Hugh, anyway, but ... marrying Humphy Jim? Folk would laugh at her, and they'd think she'd let him ...

His rather sad eyes were regarding her seriously. 'I don't

know if it'll help you to make up your mind, lass, but I've loved you for years.'

'But I don't love you,' she whispered, sorry to hurt him, because he had always been so kind to her.

'I know that, I'm not stupid. Think about it, Cissie.'

Marie looked at her inquisitively when she went inside, and she flushed to the roots of her hair, but, thankfully, Pat kept talking until their father came home. Later, when Marie returned after an evening with Wilfie Lewis, she had forgotten her curiosity about Jim's visit and Cissie did not remind her. She wanted peace to think over what he had said.

All night, and all the following day, she considered his suggestion, and came to the conclusion that it was the only way out of the mess she was in. She would be away from her father, and she had always liked the Humphy, though not in the way a girl should think of her husband-to-be. Waiting until she knew that he would be home from work, she went downstairs and gave a small tap on the Robertsons' door. He opened it himself, his eyes, red-rimmed beneath his glasses from all the close work in the tailor's shop, filling with a radiant hope at her timid smile.

'I'll not come in,' she said, quickly. 'I just came to say yes, I'll marry you.'

He ran his hand across his thinning hair. 'Thank you, and you'll not regret it. I'll never do anything to you that you don't want me to.'

She had given some thought to this side of it, too, and murmured, 'No, Jim, when I'm your wife I'll let you do what you're entitled to do. It's only fair.'

Cissie waited until they were in bed before she told her sister, who was shocked into crying out, 'Oh, no! You can't marry the Humphy!'

'Whisht, you'll waken Pat,' Cissie murmured, 'and it's not a case of what I can or can't do. I have to.'

'You're not ... you haven't been ... not with him?'

Marie was even more horrified at this. 'I know you stopped going with Hugh Phimister, but carrying on with the . . . Oh! I know! It's Hugh's baby, and he'll not stand by you.'

'No, it's not Hugh's. I wish it was.'

Marie was silent for a few minutes, digesting the facets of the situation, but unable to believe that her sister had let Jim Robertson touch her. It was too distasteful to dwell on. 'Have you told Da yet?' she asked, at last.

'Not yet.'

'I wouldn't like to be you when you do.'

'I'm not telling him till the day before the wedding, so if he throws me out, I'll just go downstairs a day earlier than I meant to.'

Having been involved in her own troubles, Cissie had forgotten that her going would leave Marie in great danger, but it struck her now. 'You'll watch yourself with Da when I'm not here?'

Marie grinned. 'Oh, aye, I'll never let him touch me. It would be different if it was Wilfie.'

'Don't let him touch you, either.'

Giving a little giggle, Marie said, 'I let him feel my titties last week, and I could see he liked it as much as me, though he got all red and said he'd have to stop.'

'Oh, Marie, don't let him do it again, you maybe won't be able to stop him if he tries anything else.'

'I don't know if I'd want to stop him,' Marie laughed, and added, childishly, 'You didn't stop the Humphy, did you?'

Longing to say that it was their father she couldn't stop, and that Marie might land in the same boat with him or with Wilfie, Cissie kept quiet. Marie would not take her advice.

On the eve of her marriage, Cissie waited until her brother and sister went to bed before she told her father, 'I'm getting wed tomorrow.'

Big Tam's eyes, which had darkened as soon as Marie left the room, hardened now. 'Wed? For God's sake, that's a bit sudden, isn't it? But I suppose you're in the family way. Who's the father? Did that lad you went with manage to come to the boil after all?'

Cissie was amazed that he seemed to have forgotten what he had done. 'It's not Hugh I'm getting married to,' she said, carefully. 'It's Jim Robertson.'

His lower jaw dropping, he jumped to his feet and roared, 'Humphy Jim? You surely haven't let him . . .' He raised his hand to strike her, but her unflinching eyes made him pause long enough for the brutal truth to dawn, and groaning, he thumped back in his chair. 'Oh, Christ, Cissie, you're not telling me it's mine?'

'You're the only man that's ever been near me.'

'Does Jim Robertson know?'

'Aye, that's why he's marrying me, so folk'll not know the kind of father I've got.'

His anger flared again at this. 'You little bitch! Telling him about that when I couldn't help myself? Does his mother know, and all?'

'It was Aggie I told, for I had to tell somebody.' Cissie brought her courage to full pitch. 'One thing before we're finished, though. If you ever lay a finger on Marie after I leave the house, I'll get the bobbies on you. It's what I should have done before, if I'd had any sense. Remember, I'll just be down the stair, and I'll soon know.'

His face crumpled. 'Oh, Cissie, I'm sorry. I'd never have done it if I hadn't been drunk, and it was you saying your lad had tried it that got me going, but I swear to God I'll never touch your sister.'

He sat for a few minutes with his head bowed, then brought it up smartly, as if he had come to a great decision. 'Maybe you'll not believe this, but I've missed Phoebe something terrible since she went away, and I thought I would never see her again, but about three weeks ago

I went into a bar in King Street and there she was, behind the counter. I've asked her every night to come back to me, but she always refuses — not that I blame her — but maybe, if I ask her to marry me, she'll change her mind. I think an awful lot of her, and she'd be a good wife to me.'

Cissie covered her astonishment by saying, 'So she would.'

'But she'll not need to know about what I did to you. She wouldn't look at me again if she thought . . .'

'Don't worry, I'll not tell her. Once I leave this house, I'll never be back.'

Next day, three months pregnant, Cissie stood, trembling, in the registrar's office in her Sunday clothes, the blouse straining a little across her fuller bosom, the waistband of her skirt just a fraction too tight. Her light brown hair was drawn into a bun at the nape of her neck; it had lost its bounce and sheen now and wouldn't sit any other way. Her lips were almost as pale as her face, which made the dark circles round her eyes even more pronounced. Before the ceremony began, she glanced briefly at Jim, her heart aching when she thought how happy she would have been if Hugh had been standing at her side instead of this sweating stranger in a high stiff collar and a suit that had fitted him before he had a hump on his back. But she had chosen to do this for her child's sake, and she would go through with it.

In less than fifteen minutes, Mr and Mrs James Robertson walked back to Schoolhill, Cissie almost making the mistake of going past Aggie's door and carrying on up to the second floor, but she remembered just in time. Aggie shook hands with them both when they went in, but there was no rejoicing, no wedding jokes. The three of them sat quietly for hours after they had supper, until Aggie said, smiling a little, 'Will I have to throw the pair of you out? I'm that sleepy I'll need matchsticks to keep my eyes open.'

'Oh, I'm sorry,' Cissie gasped. 'I forgot you slept in the kitchen bed.'

Jim having told her to go to the outside lavatory first, she was undressed and under the blankets before he came into their room, and she averted her eyes as he took off his clothes, but her stomach churned when she felt him lying down beside her. She had primed herself to succumb to him, but now the moment had come, she wasn't sure that she could. All he did, however, was to lay his hand over hers for a moment before he turned away, and her heart filled with gratitude to him for his understanding.

Four weeks later, Tam McGregor married Phoebe Garden, who came back to live on the floor above, thus removing Cissie's fears for her sister – as far as their father was concerned, at least. Wilfie Lewis was a different matter, and she could do nothing about that.

Chapter Ten

❧❦

1917

His 'grandmother' was in sole attendance when young James Robertson was born, and she could see, as soon as he made his speedy entrance to the world, that her fears had been justified; his head was grossly misshapen, flopping like a rag-doll's, and even at this early stage, it was quite clear that he would never be like other children. 'It's a boy,' she murmured, tempted not to smack life into him, but Cissie's eyes were fixed on her in silent entreaty, and, in any case, he gave a weedy wail with no help from anyone.

'There's something wrong with him, isn't there?' the girl demanded. 'I know by the look on your face.'

'Aye,' Aggie sighed, 'he's not right.' It was on the tip of her tongue to say that it would have been better to do as she had suggested months before, but it was too late now.

'I hope Jim's not angry,' Cissie said, miserably.

'It'll not do any good if he is.'

Jim was not angry. His heart was sore for Cissie's sake, and he held the infant in his arms as if James were the most beautiful baby he had ever seen.

Phoebe, who had gone down to see Cissie every day since her own wedding, called in that afternoon. 'He's maybe not perfect, but babies like him bring love with them.'

This was true, as Cissie soon found out. She could not hate the slavering little thing, he was so dependent on her, and would be for much longer than a normal child, probably for as long as he lived, for bairns like him never grew to adulthood. They all doted on him – Jim, Aggie, Phoebe, Marie and even Pat – and there was not a more loved infant in the whole of Aberdeen. Big Tam did not come to see him – Cissie would have died if he had – but by scrimping drastically on her household expenses, Phoebe bought a lovely Moses basket which she said was from both of them, and from its luxurious depths, 'King' James ruled over his enslaved subjects. Of course, Phoebe had no idea that her husband was the actual father and imagined that Tam was angry at Cissie for getting pregnant to Jim Robertson, and the girl would never have dreamt of telling her otherwise.

She hadn't even told Phoebe about the two letters Joe had sent, in case her father got to hear about them, for the postman, who lived on the same landing as Aggie, had known to deliver them there. The first had been written when he joined the crew of an unnamed battleship after his training, and the other when he had returned to Britain after his first engagement with the enemy. It was this one which had upset her, for Joe had written like a disillusioned man, not like the eager boy he had been when she last saw him. She had written to him then, telling him that she was married and asking him to come and see her when he got the chance, but she realised that it might be some time before he could.

She worried more than ever about him now, and about Tommy, who was also on the high seas, likely running the gauntlet of German U-boats to deliver whatever cargo his ship was carrying. It wouldn't be so bad if she could only see them, to make sure that they were both all right, she thought, glad that she had a baby to take up her attention.

James was three months old when Aggie had her first 'turn'. Actually, she had had several warnings over the past six months but hadn't wanted to alarm Cissie by telling her. The girl, therefore, was all the more alarmed when the old lady reeled as she rose from the table. 'What's wrong, Aggie?'

Her mother-in-law collapsed into the nearest chair, and after laying the baby in the Moses basket, Cissie crossed the kitchen in two strides. 'Have you a pain?'

A slight movement of her head was as much as the old woman could give in confirmation, and Cissie couldn't think how to help her. The pain could be anywhere. Aggie's pink face was a ghastly grey now, her lips blue as she struggled to place her hand on her chest to show where it hurt. It could be indigestion, Cissie thought, or a bout of flatulence, but she soon realised that it was more than that. 'I'll go and get Phoebe,' she said, praying that her father's wife had not gone out shopping.

Fortunately, Phoebe was at home. Together they ran downstairs, both of them afraid of what they might find, but Aggie had recovered a little. 'You'd think the . . . devil was after the . . . pair o' you,' she gasped, as they burst in.

'Is the pain away?' Cissie puffed.

'Aye, I've had wee turns before, but that was the worst.'

Phoebe pursed her lips. 'It sounds like your heart. You'll have to take things easy. How old are you?'

'It's nobody's . . . business how old I am,' the old woman began, then common sense took over and she added, 'You're right, I'd better watch myself. I'm seventy-seven.'

Over the tea Cissie made, Aggie's cheeks slowly regained their natural colour and she found it easier to speak. 'I used to worry about Jim being left on his own, but he's got you now, Cissie, so he'll be all right when I go.'

Frowning, Cissie said, 'You're not going to die for a long time yet.'

Suspecting that it might not be as long as the girl hoped, Phoebe changed the subject. 'Is my wee James wakened?' He was a contented child and hardly ever cried, so she wasn't at all surprised to find his eyes wide open and his tiny fists waving. 'Come to your Grandma Phoebe, my wee lamb,' she crooned, lifting him out of the basket. 'You're not a bit like your Da, but I can see your Granda in you.'

If she had noticed the anxious glance that passed between the other two, she would have realised the truth, but she was planting light kisses on the baby's downy head, and Aggie let her breath out slowly. 'It's natural for there to be a family likeness, and he takes after his mother's side, not ours.'

'Aye,' Phoebe agreed. 'Well, I'd better be getting back, or Tam'll be in and no supper ready for him.' She handed the baby to his mother and went out.

'She doesn't know,' Aggie assured Cissie, 'not yet, any road, but it'll not be long till she puts two and two together, for I'm sure she must have got a shock to think you and my Jim . . .' She looked at the girl with her eyebrows raised. 'Have you let him . . .'

Opening her blouse to feed her child, Cissie could feel the heat creeping up her neck. She knew that Aggie's only reason for asking was her desire for a real grandchild – however much she loved little James, he was not of her flesh and blood – and she deserved an honest answer. 'I wouldn't refuse him if he asked, but he never makes a move.'

'Aye, well.' Aggie lay back and closed her eyes.

Not for the first time, a surge of deep affection for her husband welled up in Cissie. A bolster could be set between them every night, and she had sometimes felt like snuggling up to him, to let him know that his bowed back didn't revolt her any longer, but she wasn't sure if the tenderness he generated in her was pity or gratitude. It wasn't love.

Love was what she had felt for Hugh Phimister. She hadn't seen him since she broke off with him, and maybe it was just as well, for she couldn't have kept up the pretence of there being someone else. Miss Birnie would have told his mother that she was married, and he would be hurt to think that she had preferred a man so much older, a man with a hump on his back and bandy legs, when his own body was perfect.

Cissie jumped when a hand touched her arm. 'What are you thinking about, lass?' Aggie asked, gently.

Laying James over her shoulder to wind him, the girl said, 'Nothing, I was dozing. Are you all right now?'

'I'm fine. Eh, Cissie, are you sorry you married my Jim?'

'Why would I be sorry?'

'I'm sure he's not the kind of man you'd dreamt of.'

'He's a good man, none better, and I'll never be sorry I married him.' James giving a loud burp at that point, she changed him to her other breast.

'And you'll look after my Jim when I'm away?'

'You know I will, Aggie. You didn't need to ask.'

The old lady gave a long sigh. 'That's my mind at rest, any road. Now, when James is finished, gi'e him to me. I'll change him and you can get on wi' the supper.'

Cissie had to wait until she and Jim were in bed before she could tell him. 'Your mother had a funny turn today.'

He was all attention immediately. 'What kind o' turn?'

'Phoebe said it was her heart, but she got over it quick.'

'I'm glad you're here with her now. I never liked the idea of her being on her own all day at her age.'

'I'll always be here with her – and with you.'

She felt him turning towards her, still not touching her. 'You'll never want to leave me?'

'No, never. I . . . I like you an awful lot, Jim.'

His hand came over to brush her cheek. 'You know how I feel about you, but I never thought you'd . . .'

'I'm not saying I love you,' she interrupted, hastily, 'but I do like you, and if you want to . . . whenever you feel like it . . .'

'Not yet, Cissie. I want you to be sure.'

'I am sure.' She could feel his hardness against her side now, and suddenly remembered her father. Could she really let another man – could she bear that pain again?

As if he could read her thoughts, Jim moved away. 'I'd better wait, though I can tell you this, Cissie: it wouldn't be like your Da did to you, for I love you, and I'd never hurt you. But get some sleep now, like a good lass.'

Next morning, an irritated Aggie shrugged off her son's concern. 'Cissie shouldn't have said anything. It was just a wee turn, nothing to speak about. Get away to your work and stop fussing, you're like an old woman yourself.'

Cissie smiled as she handed him his dinner 'piece'. 'Off you go, Jim. I'll see she doesn't tire herself.'

When he went out, his mother looked at the girl. 'There's something different about him the day. I'm not being nosy, but . . . did you and him . . .'

Colouring, Cissie said, 'I told him I'd be happy to let him, if he wanted to, and he said he'd wait.'

'Aye, my Jim's a canny one. He wouldn't want you to give in to him out of pity. It'll take time, lass, for he knows it's not love you feel for him. Now, I'll see to the dishes and let you get to the butcher before the best beef's away.'

'But you shouldn't be . . .'

'None of your havers. Away you go, and don't hurry back.'

Even at eight o'clock in the morning, the sun was glinting on the quartz of the granite buildings and reflecting off the shop windows, and Cissie's spirits rose as she pushed the pram slowly down the hill, stopping to have a look at the display of ladies' underwear in Duncan Fraser's although it wasn't open for business yet. It was good to be out on such a lovely day, she thought, as she went past the chemist to turn the corner into George Street, and good for James to be getting the fresh air into his little lungs.

She smiled to everyone she met, and felt happier than she had done for a long time, even when one of her neighbours looked into the pram and said, 'Poor wee soul.' It didn't matter to Cissie what anyone thought. James was a darling, though he wasn't normal, and his brown eyes were darting all over the place, like he was curious about his surroundings. She left him outside the butcher's shop until she bought a ham shank to make lentil soup, but when she was passing the dairy on her way back, Miss Birnie ran out.

'Mrs Phimister told me yesterday her Hugh's been pining since you and him fell out, and he's joined the army – the Scottish Horse, I think. Maybe I shouldn't be telling you, and you married now, but I know you thought a lot of him.'

Aware that her ex-employer, like Hugh's mother, must have wondered what had gone wrong between them, Cissie could only say, 'Yes, I did think a lot of him, but it's all over. I'm happy with Jim, and there's the baby, now, and all.'

Her curiosity unsatisfied, Miss Birnie gave in gracefully. 'Let me see him.' Pulling the covers back, she gazed down at the gurgling infant for a moment, then said, sadly, 'Oh, I'm sorry for you, Cissie.'

'There's no need to be sorry for me, Miss Birnie. Jim's a good husband, and I wouldn't change James for all the tea in China.' As serenely as she could, Cissie rearranged the pram covers and walked on, in spite of the almost unbearable ache in her heart, an ache which was proof that she still loved Hugh as much as ever. Even remembering that his mother had said he'd pined for her did not help, and she was glad that he had joined the army, because there wasn't the slightest chance that they could ever be together again. The flashing reflections off the glass and the glittering quartz were lost on her as she plodded up Schoolhill. She did not look across at the clock in St Nicholas Kirk as she usually did, not even when the bells chimed the half-hour. In the last of the thirty minutes she had been out, she had been thrown completely off balance.

Leaving the pram in the back lobby, she carried her child

upstairs, the shopping basket slung over her arm. 'I hope I haven't been too long,' she began, then stopped in alarm. Aggie was stretched out on the floor, the upturned teapot lying beside her. Setting James down in the Moses basket, Cissie knelt down to attend to her mother-in-law, but got no response. She sat back on her heels to feel for a pulse, and could find nothing.

Her head spinning, she ran upstairs for Phoebe, but it was too late. 'She's gone,' her stepmother said, after a few moments. 'Poor Aggie, her heart's given out altogether this time. I'll stay here with James till you get the doctor to come and make out the death certificate. And you'd better go and tell Jim, so he can arrange the funeral.'

That night, for the very first time, Jim Robertson put his arms round his wife, who was weeping because she had been out when Aggie died. 'Don't upset yourself, lass. You likely couldn't have done anything.' Stroking her hair, he went on, 'I'm right glad I've got you now, Cissie.'

His lips were tender and compassionate as she turned to him – for her own consolation as much as his – but within seconds her stomach turned over, as she realised that her desperate kisses had aroused him beyond his control. She felt sick but she couldn't be so cruel as to refuse him when he had just lost his mother.

Gritting her teeth, she shook her head when he asked, very unsure of himself, 'You'll not be angry, Cissie?'

He was hesitant at first, but when his breathing quickened and she knew he was on the point of entering her, she had to grip herself tightly, waiting for the excruciating pain she was sure would come.

'D'you want me to stop?' His voice was thick, but gentle.

'No,' she forced out.

It wasn't as bad as she had feared. Jim had made no animal noises, nor had he hurt her, yet she still didn't like it. Maybe decent women weren't supposed to like it – only women like that Sally she had seen rolling about with her father. In a few minutes, instead of the frenzied thrusting and horrible roar she had expected, Jim withdrew at the crucial moment, and rubbed himself against her thigh.

When he was still, he groaned, 'I'm sorry, Cissie. I know you hated it, and I'll never do it again.'

'It's not your fault,' she whispered. 'I can't forget . . .'

'Aye, I know.'

Both Jim and Cissie took their own time to get over Aggie's sudden death, and although they slipped into a rather flat routine, it suited Cissie, who considered that she'd had more than her share of ups and downs – mostly downs – over the past year. Her life centred round her baby, and it felt good to be sitting quietly in the evenings, Jim reading the newspaper and she knitting little garments.

Phoebe came down most afternoons and pushed the pram when she and Cissie took James out for an airing. Marie, who was now working in George Street Woolworth's, usually called in on her way upstairs, not knowing that her little nephew was also her brother. Pat popped in and out at any odd time on the pretext of seeing the baby, but more probably because Cissie kept a good supply of sweets and biscuits.

When Jim offered to sleep in the kitchen, Cissie had told him not to be silly, so they still went to the same bed. She hadn't really expected him to lie beside her and not touch her, but he kept his promise and lay well apart from her. Sometimes, she wished that he would be more loving, and did put out a tentative hand to him one night, but when he moved towards her, she automatically drew back.

'I'm sorry,' he murmured, 'I thought you wanted . . .'

'I do, Jim, honest.'

'You're still not ready.'

'Will you put your arms round me, then? I feel lonely.'

After that, he held her every night, kissing her tenderly until she fell asleep, and although she could feel how much he wanted her, he did nothing else. She was grateful to him, for the holding and kissing was all she needed. Maybe some day she would forget her revulsion and respond to him as a wife should, but he was right. She wasn't ready yet.

Chapter Eleven

❖❖

Secure in her husband's self-sacrificing love, life for Cissie had regained a little flavour. She would never forget Hugh Phimister, would never love Jim in the same way, but she could sense the stirrings of something deeper than affection for him. She longed for more than platonic kisses, although she still wasn't sure if she could let him make love to her again. But he had been so patient and understanding that she was ashamed to have kept him hanging on for so long, and decided, late one afternoon, to tell him when they went to bed that she was ready for him at last. Surely it wouldn't be too difficult to feign enjoyment.

She was setting the table for supper when Phoebe ran in, her face chalk white. 'A telegram's just come,' she burst out. 'Joe's ship's been sunk and all hands lost.'

'Oh, my God!' Cissie held on to the nearest chair.

'Your Da'll be awful upset when he comes home, Cissie, and he's going to need you. It could be the time for you to make things up with him.'

Even weeping for her brother, Cissie's stomach cramped at the thought of talking to her father. Phoebe didn't know the real reason for her marriage to Jim, and must wonder why she was so bitter against her father, but she couldn't face him. 'I can't,' she sobbed. 'I can't, Phoebe! Honest, I can't.'

'Please?' Phoebe pleaded. 'For my sake?'

It wasn't fair, Cissie thought, resentfully. She couldn't disappoint this woman after all she had done, but it would be a terrible ordeal. 'All right,' she gulped, 'I'll come up after I give Jim his supper.'

'Thank you, Cissie. I'm sure it'll make your Da happy.'

Guessing that her father would be just as averse to the reunion as she was, Cissie doubted that very much.

When Jim came home and heard about Joe, he took his wife in his arms to comfort her, but when she nervously told him that she was going to see her father, he frowned. 'I don't want you to have anything to do with him, Cissie.'

'I'm doing it for Phoebe, Jim. She's been good to me, and James, and your mother, and all. I'd do anything rather than go, you should know that, but I couldn't say no to her.'

He sighed. 'Well, if it's for Phoebe . . .'

Cissie's feet trailed when she went upstairs after supper, her heart fluttered as she gave a timid knock on the door.

'You didn't need to knock,' Phoebe smiled, when she let her in. 'This is as much your home now as it ever was.'

'It was my home, but not now.' She went into the kitchen, where Big Tam was sitting so straight in his chair that it seemed an iron bar must be holding him upright. His face was pale, and his head was turned resolutely away from her. Her brother and sister, however, both gave her watery smiles.

It was Phoebe who spoke first. 'Marie, take Pat through to your room for a wee while.'

Marie looked perplexed as she got to her feet, but pushed her brother through the door and Phoebe went over to her husband. 'Tam, Cissie wants to speak to you.'

'I'm sorry about Joe,' Cissie murmured, unsure of what else to say.

'Aye.' It was almost a grunt.

'War's a terrible thing.'

'Aye.'

'I hope Tommy's all right.'

There was no answer, though a slight tic had started at the side of his jaw. Damn him, she thought, and had an urge to make him suffer for what he had done to her. 'My

James'll soon be six months old,' she said, deliberately.

The tic speeded up and Phoebe stepped in, to help things along, as she supposed. 'You should see him, Tam. He's very like you. He's even got your reddish hair.'

Seeing him look at his wife suspiciously, Cissie knew that he was wondering if she had told Phoebe the truth, and a touch of malice made her say, 'It's not surprising he's like you, is it, Da?'

His tortured eyes met hers briefly, in desperate appeal, but something drove her to turn the screw further. 'I'm his mother, after all, and you're . . .' she derived some pleasure from seeing him squirm in the pause she made, '. . . my father.'

Phoebe nodded vigorously. 'Aye, Tam, don't forget you're his grandfather, and he's such a wee pet, it's a shame he's not like other bairns.'

This reminder that the child was not normal was too much for him. 'I don't know why you came, Cissie,' he thundered, 'but if it was to rub it in about the bairn not being right, you shouldn't have bothered. It's been on my conscience day and night . . .' He stopped, aghast at what he was saying.

Comprehension dawning, Phoebe gave a horrified cry. 'He's yours! That's why you and Cissie . . . Oh, my God!'

'Phoebe, I'm sorry!' Cissie burst out. 'I didn't mean for you to find out. I didn't want to come, you know that.'

'I do know that, but I wish I'd known why.' Her voice was ice-laden. 'I thought you were my friend, but I see Tam's not the only one who's made a fool of me, and you'd better go – now!' She walked over and held the door open.

'I am your friend, Phoebe, that's why I couldn't tell you Da was James's father.' Cissie's desperate plea was ignored, and, sick at heart, she went out, weeping.

Jim looked up when she tottered in, and jumped to his

100

feet when he saw how distraught she was. 'I told you not to go. I knew it would just upset you.'

She ran to his outstretched arms, sobbing bitterly as she tried to blot out the sound of the harsh, angry voices from overhead. 'I should have listened to you. He wouldn't speak to me, and I did an awful thing. I couldn't help myself.'

He asked no questions, content to hold her until she was calmer, and at last, she said, 'I wanted to make him suffer for what he did to me, and I told him James was nearly six months. I was stupid, but I wanted to hurt him.'

'I can understand that,' Jim murmured, 'and you should try to forget about it. You'll only make yourself ill carrying on like this.'

'But you don't understand,' she sobbed. 'Phoebe said he wasn't like other bairns, and Da said it had been on his conscience, and . . . Oh, Jim, Phoebe knows now, and she's mad at me for not telling her before.'

'She'll get over it.'

'No, she won't! Just listen to them. Oh, God, I shouldn't have said anything about James. Da was upset about Joe and I made it a thousand times worse.'

'Whisht, whisht. It was bound to come out some time.'

'It would never have come out if I hadn't said that, and it was Phoebe I hurt more than him. She's so angry, she'll tell folk for spite, and they'll end up laughing at you.'

'Phoebe's not a spiteful woman,' Jim soothed, 'and folk have laughed at me for years, so it wouldn't matter to me if she told the whole of Aberdeen.'

At that moment, the noise upstairs rose to a crescendo, a door slammed and quick feet descended to the ground floor. Then the street door crashed with such ferocity that the dishes in Cissie's pantry rattled.

She looked at her husband in appalled dismay. 'I wonder which of them that was?'

Jim kept stroking her head. 'It wasn't heavy enough for Tam's feet, it must have been Phoebe.'

'Da's going to kill me if she's left him,' Cissie wailed.

'She'll come back when she cools down. She can't leave him for that, not when she used to be a . . .'

Cissie felt a little better until she realised that a man fathering his daughter's child was far worse than a woman earning a living by prostitution.

She was still trembling with repentance for what she had done in anger at her father and fear of what he might do in retribution, when Jim said, 'Give James his feed and we'll go to bed. Phoebe'll cool down and come back to your father in the morning and apologise to you, and it'll all be over.'

Not really believing this, Cissie sat down, but with her milk being affected by her agitation, James kept them awake all night – the night she had intended to be a proper wife to Jim for the first time, but which resolution she had completely forgotten.

Chapter Twelve

❧ ❧

Cissie had heard her father going to work at his usual time, halting long enough outside her door for her to panic, but he had carried on, and Jim had left shortly afterwards. She had placed all the footsteps going past, Mr Morrice and Mr Gibb from the top floor, then Pat's scamper, but no Marie; she must have been told to stay off work to look after the house. Cissie had wondered if she could chance going up to talk to her, but had decided that it wouldn't do any good, and it wasn't fair to involve her.

Jim had told her to keep the door locked after he went to work, which did make her feel safer. She had meant to make a stew for supper with a bit of spaul from the butcher, but she couldn't face going out, and he would have to be content with cheese pudding. Poor Jim, he had taken on more than he thought when he married her, but he hadn't complained.

Taking her son out of the basket, she sat down in front of the fire. As his little mouth fixed avidly on her, she pulled off his bootees to hold his tiny foot in her hand, such a well-formed foot, in contrast to the rather grotesque head lolling against her. What would his life be when he was older? He couldn't go to an ordinary school – other children would make fun of him, for bairns were cruel that way. She could remember jeering at a boy who had a club foot, and her mother had been angry with her when she found out.

'We're all God's children,' Mam had said, 'though we can't all be perfect.'

James wasn't perfect, Cissie mused, sadly, but she loved

him as much as if he had been, and that would never change. She would love him and look after him for as long as he needed her.

The cheese pudding was beautifully risen when her husband came in. 'I couldn't face going to the butcher,' she told him, 'so I hope you don't mind . . .'

'I love cheese pudding,' he smiled, chucking the baby under the chin before he sat down. 'How have you been?'

'I'm fine, and nothing else can happen, can it? Nothing bad? He'd have come last night if he'd been . . .'

'He's only got himself to blame,' Jim said, quietly. 'He should never have touched you. It wasn't your fault.'

Tears welled up in her eyes. 'You're so good, Jim.'

'What's good about marrying the girl I love?' he smiled.

'You know what I meant.'

'You look tired, Cissie. I'll do the dishes for you, and you can go to bed, for James didn't let you get much sleep last night. I'll take him through for his ten o'clock feed.'

It was hardly eight o'clock when she went through to the bedroom, and even when she lay down her brain wouldn't let her sleep. The previous evening's terrible scene kept coming back to her, her father's furious face glowering at her no matter whether her eyes were open or closed. Jumping to the floor, she went back to the kitchen in her nightshift.

'It's no use,' she said, her teeth chattering, 'I can't get it out of my head.'

Jim pulled her on to his knees. 'Cissie, it's all over. He can't do anything to you now.'

'I know, but when I'm on my own . . .'

'Lie down on Ma's bed, then.'

She went into the bed in the recess, and he came over to kiss her when she snuggled under the blankets. 'I love you, Cissie. Don't ever forget that.'

'I'll never forget, and I think I . . .'

'Watch yourself,' he cautioned, smiling ruefully. 'You're

in no state to make rash promises. I'll heat some milk . . .'

They both jumped at the sound of the street door being hurled back with tremendous force against the lobby wall, and Cissie grabbed her husband's arm. 'That's him!'

As the heavy feet came clumping up the stairs, Jim said, 'He'll not bother us. He'll go right up. Wait and see.'

Big Tam did not go right up. He stopped on their landing, found the door locked and bellowed, 'Open this bloody door or I'll break it down!'

'Don't let him in,' Cissie begged, gripping her husband's arm even tighter.

'He'll kick the door in if I don't. But don't worry, I'll not let him touch you.'

She had only time to think that he would be no match for her father when Big Tam staggered in. 'I hope you're pleased with yourself,' he shouted, making for the bed.

She cowered down, hauling the blankets up round her neck, but he dragged them off and pulled her on to the floor. 'I swear I'll make you sorry for what you've done. It's you I've to thank for Phoebe leaving me.' His hands rose to her throat, but Jim pulled at his jacket.

'Leave her be. It was all your own doing.'

Whipping round, Tam shoved him roughly away. 'My doing? Look at her standing there in her shift driving a man mad. It wasn't my doing, you humphy-backed bugger!'

Jim's fist shot out, and Cissie screamed, 'No, Jim! Don't fight with him, he's stronger than you.'

'No, Jim,' Tam mocked, in an exaggerated falsetto, 'you'd better not fight with me, you'll come off worst.' His voice deepened to a threat. 'Just stand there, like the Mam's boy you always were, and watch what I do to your wife.' Turning to Cissie again, he took hold of the neck of her shift and pulled hard, the buttons flying off to expose her breasts, full with the milk her baby would soon need.

Before he could go any further, he reeled from the blow Jim caught him on the side of the head. 'You little runt!'

he shouted, and knocked the smaller man down with one swipe of his huge fist.

Covering her bosom with her arms, Cissie tried to reach her husband, who lay gasping for breath on the floor, but Tam grabbed her and held her firm. 'That weakling's no use to you, Cissie.' He edged her towards the bed.

On his feet again, Jim looked round for something heavy to use as a weapon, and was picking up the brass poker when Tam saw him and let Cissie go. She watched in horror, unable to move, when her father wrested the poker from Jim and took it down on his head with such force that she heard his skull cracking, and he went down instantly.

'You've killed him,' she shrieked.

'Don't speak daft. It was just a wee tap on the head.' Tam dropped the poker on the mat and came towards her, his eyes wild with lust, and, sure that her husband was dead, she didn't even think of defending herself. With one sweeping movement, her father tore off her shift, threw her down on the bed, then ran his hands over her breasts and down her belly, moaning all the time.

Numb with shock, she put up no resistance when he lay on top of her. It was as if this was how it had to end, this was what fate meant for her. His wet lips came down on hers, his hands fumbled with his trouser buttons, and the stink of whisky on his breath made her retch. 'My own wee lassie,' he muttered, hoarsely, 'let your Da inside you.'

It was only when she felt his engorged organ against her thighs that she managed to scream, thrashing her legs about helplessly, for he was past hearing or caring what she did. But at that moment, little James, upset by the shouting and commotion, gave a loud cry. Without even looking round, Tam lashed out with his foot, and Cissie's horrified eyes could see the basket crashing to the floor, her infant, thrown out of the covers, hitting the fender and lying motionless.

Looking round in dismay at the result of his action, Big

Tam did not stop her when she heaved herself out from under him and ran to her child. Tam lay, dazed, for a few moments, watching as she lifted James up and cradled the lifeless little body in her arms, but it was her hopeless, keening cries that sobered him. Sitting up, he shook his head in disbelief, then held his arms out to her in some sort of supplication. 'Oh, Christ, Cissie,' he groaned, suddenly, 'what have I done?'

In her own world of grief, she paid no attention to him. She probably did not hear him as she lay down on the floor with her dead child in her arms, as naked as the day she was born.

Chapter Thirteen

❖❖

Phoebe McGregor had spent the night walking the streets, a horrible nausea gnawing at her innards. Tam was so rugged and handsome that it hadn't taken her long to fall in love with him, though trying to rush him into marriage had been a mistake; he wasn't the kind to be rushed into anything. She had been surprised when he asked her to go back to him, and had held out until he swore that he had missed her, that he loved her and wanted to marry her, after all.

Only two things had marred her happiness as his wife and mother to his family – the unexplained split between him and his elder daughter, and his flat refusal to go to see his grandchild. She had foolishly thought that he was angry at Cissie for letting the Humphy touch her, for it was hard to believe that she could be attracted to such an ill-shapen man, yet Jim was really a nice person when you got to know him, kind-hearted and considerate.

Oh, God, yes! He was so kind-hearted that he had made Cissie his wife, when he must have known that the child she was carrying was not his. Had he been told whose it was? Had he married her, not just to give the child a name, but to save her the shame of having it known publicly what kind of man her father was? And the rape had happened when she, Phoebe, had not been there to satisfy Tam.

As the day wore on, Phoebe's agonies lessened. She still loved him, whatever he had done, and he had been faithful to her since their marriage, she was sure of that. She could never go back to the sordid life she had led before, and there were Marie and Pat to think of; they needed a mother's guidance. Pat was at an awkward age, and it was patently obvious that Marie was ripe for sexual encounters. Wilfie Lewis wouldn't stand a chance if she made up her mind to be seduced – was it still called seduction when the girl was the instigator? In any case, she had to be told the facts of life – about the perverts she might come across – and who better to tell her than the stepmother who had first-hand experience? Only, would Tam take her back after the awful things she had said last night?

Realising that she'd had nothing to eat for twenty-four hours, Phoebe made her way to a seamen's café on the quay. A full stomach might help her to see things more clearly.

The proprietrix knew her, because she had gone there quite often at one time, and grinned when she went in. 'I haven't seen you for ages, Phoebe. I thought you was married.'

'I am married, but I'd a bit of a set-to with my man last night, you know how it is, and I've been wandering about all day trying to think what to do.'

'Ach, we all have set-tos at some time or other. When my Bill was alive, we wouldn't have known what was wrong with us if we didn't have a fight every week. You're better off now than you ever was, Phoebe, so why don't you just go back and say you're sorry. Maybe it wasn't your fault, but your man'll be pleased if you make out it was.'

Phoebe smiled at her perception of men's egos. 'I suppose I should. A cup of tea and a sandwich, please.'

Marie and Pat were playing Snap when they first heard the noise from downstairs. Their father had not come in at his usual time, though he had made Marie stay off work. 'It's up to you to keep house again now Phoebe's away,' he had said, that morning. She had resented that, because it was Cissie's fault that their stepmother had left, and she was even more resentful when he hadn't come home for his supper after she had bought sweetbreads for him at the butcher.

'That sounds like Da shouting,' Pat observed.

It did sound like him, and Marie, having listened at the kitchen door the previous night, hoped he was giving Cissie a good piece of his mind. It couldn't have been true what she said. Da couldn't be James's father. Jim Robertson was James's father, or, as Marie was more inclined to believe, Hugh Phimister. Fancy Cissie saying things like that about Da, especially in front of Phoebe.

The din in the Robertsons' flat increased even more, and Pat paused before he laid his next card. 'What d'you think's going on down there?'

'I don't know,' Marie said, firmly, 'and it's nothing to do with us.'

'Snap!' shouted Pat, triumphantly, taking advantage of his sister's wandering attention and scooping up the two stacks of cards. 'You'll soon have none left.'

A dull thud making the very walls reverberate, they looked at each other apprehensively. 'Da and Jim must be fighting,' Pat muttered. 'Maybe we should go down.'

'What could we do? Da's likely drunk.'

'I can fight boys twice my size.'

Well aware that they should be doing something, Marie just said, 'Don't be daft.'

'That's Cissie screaming.' Pat stood up. 'I'll have to go and help her.'

Marie's hand shot out and held him back. 'Wait.'

Another thud, clearer this time, followed in a few seconds by a strange wailing noise, made up Marie's mind. 'Go and look for a bobby, and I'll ask Mr Gibb upstairs to go and speak to Da, and I'd better get Mr Morrice, and all. Surely between them they'll get him calmed down.'

Pat was off before she got to her feet, and she ran up to the floor above, but neither Mr Gibb nor Mr Morrice would agree to accompany her to the Robertsons' house. They knew how aggressive Big Tam McGregor could be when he was drunk, they pointed out, and it was none of their business, anyway. In panic, Marie went back to her own landing.

Their next-door neighbour — a retired plumber, and always referred to behind his back as 'Cleekie' Coull, because the fingers of one of his hands were curled with arthritis into the shape of a hook — looked at her apologetically when she explained what she wanted of him. 'I'm sorry, Marie, but I try to keep out of family fights, and it's gone quiet now.'

Mrs Coull, having come out to see what was going on, said, 'It sounded like somebody was getting murdered down there.'

'Ach, you and your imagination,' her husband snapped. 'Big Tam and Cissie have just been having a row about something.'

She wasn't to be put off. 'I heard Cissie coming up to your house last night, Marie, and after she went back down, your father had a helluva row wi' his wife, so maybe it was something Cissie said about her. Then she slammed the door that hard and ran down the stair, I'm sure she's left him. Maybe he blames Cissie, and he's been taking it out on her the night, and Humphy Jim's likely tried to stick up for her and they've come to blows.'

Cleekie tutted in exasperation. 'Never heed her, Marie. Whatever it was, they've settled it now, and you'd better not go down, or you might start it up again. Leave well alone, that's what I always say.'

'Pat's away to get a bobby,' she whispered.

'Och well, he'll sort things out.'

Phoebe left the café much easier in her mind. All she needed to do was to say she was sorry, and Tam would welcome her back with open arms. She'd have to apologise to Cissie, too, but that could wait until tomorrow. She hurried up Market Street, across Union Street into St Nicholas Street and almost ran up Schoolhill in her desire to put things right. She was breathless by the time she reached the tenement, and when she passed the Robertsons' door, she noticed that it was half-open. This caused her some disquiet, for they never left their door unlocked at this time of night. She wondered whether to go in and see if anything was wrong.

Giving a light tap, she called, 'Cissie, it's only me.' There was no reply, no sound of any movement, just a deathly hush. Her heart in her mouth, she was hardly aware of taking the three steps which brought her round the corner of the tiny lobby to the wide-open kitchen door, but what she saw then made her clutch at the jamb.

They were all lying dead on the floor in a huge pool of blood, Jim in his shirtsleeves and Cissie with not a stitch on, the baby against her breast. The Moses basket was lying on its side and the poker was lying on the mat, stained red. 'Oh, sweet Jesus!' Phoebe whispered, her free hand going to her own breast. Surely Tam hadn't done this?

She stood, shaking, for some time, her ears pounding, her heart thumping, her brain numb with shock. At last, with a great effort, she turned to go for help, but a faint noise made her look round again at the gruesome tableau. One of the three must still be alive.

Cautiously, she moved forward and stretched out her hand to touch the infant, but the mother's arms tightened round him protectively. 'It's all right, Cissie,' Phoebe murmured, and the sound of the familiar voice made the girl loosen her grip enough to let Phoebe take the child. His gown was caked with blood and she had to smother a cry of anguish when she saw that his poor little malformed head was caved in at one side. There was no doubt that wee James was dead. Swivelling round, she righted the basket to lay him down, and only then saw the man on the bed. His eyes were blank and didn't see her, but his open spaver told her all she needed to know. The filthy devil had been trying to rape Cissie again.

Ignoring him, she laid James gently into the basket then ran through to the bedroom to get a blanket to cover Cissie, whose eyes were also blank in her white, blood-stained face, and who would obviously not be capable of telling her what had happened. All she could do was to find out if Jim was still alive, and then get someone to fetch a police-man and a doctor.

Moving across, she bent over to feel for a pulse in Jim's wrist, shuddering when she saw that the blood he was lying in had come from a gaping hole in his skull. He must have been trying to protect his wife, and Tam had hit him with the poker – and the baby, too? It was clearly too late to do anything for either of them, but before she could run for help, Pat came in with a policeman.

It was four o'clock in the morning before all the comings and goings stopped. The constable had sent Pat to Lodge Walk to fetch someone in authority, and he had returned with a sergeant and an inspector, who were followed fairly soon by the police surgeon and a photographer. Phoebe having told the inspector that she knew nothing, he had waited until the surgeon had examined Cissie and found no sign of rape before he started questioning her. He soon saw that it was useless, and agreed with Phoebe that she should be taken upstairs out of the way. He got nowhere with Tam either, and sent him off eventually in the Black Maria.

By this time, dozens of photographs had been taken and the surgeon had ended his scrutiny of the two bodies, so they, too, were removed. The inspector turned again to Phoebe, castigating her for moving James, then trying to find out if she had any ideas on what had taken place, and out of sheer exhaustion, she had told him what she thought.

'We'll be charging your husband with murdering his son-in-law and his grandson,' he had said, when she finished. 'I'll interview the young woman at Lodge Walk later, and I'll have to have a word with the neighbours.'

Sick with fatigue though she was, Phoebe could not sleep when she joined Cissie in bed. Marie had been told to sleep in the kitchen, because their stepmother hadn't wanted to put Cissie in her father's bed, and, to be quite honest, she didn't feel like going into it herself. For the next three hours, she lay with her eyes closed, picturing herself at the Robertsons' kitchen door again, seeing the three bodies on the floor, believing they were all dead. Then she would turn round slowly in her imagination, to see Big Tam sitting on top of the rumpled bedcovers, his shirt poking through his open spaver.

The whisky he must have drunk had made him desperate for a woman, and she had walked out on him. Did the two deaths lie at her door? He had blamed Cissie for making her leave, and that's likely why he'd gone to the Robertsons' house in the first place. With Cissie in her nightshift – it had been found in the bed ripped to ribbons – his lust had got the better of him, and when Jim tried to stop him, he had brought the poker down on his head without realising his own strength. What she couldn't understand was him doing it to the baby – unless he wanted to destroy the evidence of his previous rape. But he had been in a drunken stupor and his brain wouldn't have been clear enough to think like that.

It was seven o'clock when Phoebe heard the sharp intake of breath beside her and said, 'Don't be scared, Cissie. You're with me in your old bed at home. Are you all right?'

There was no answer for several seconds, then a hope-fully whispered, 'Was it a nightmare, Phoebe?'

Wishing with all her heart that she could say yes, Phoebe replied, 'No, my dearie, it wasn't.'

'They're both dead, aren't they? Jim and the baby?'

'Yes, and your father's been arrested for murdering them.'

After another long pause, Cissie said, 'He was mad drunk, Phoebe. He didn't mean to kill them.'

'Do you want to tell me about it? You'll have to tell the police at Lodge Walk, anyway.'

The story came out slowly, between many emotional breaks, and the sequence of events was just as Phoebe had suspected, except that the baby's head had been hurt when the basket fell over – at least Tam hadn't used the poker on James – but the brutality of the attack appalled her. The drink did terrible things to a man's brain, made him act worse than any animal, but, even though he was a lecher when he was intoxicated, he wasn't a deliberate murderer.

Having described the overturning of the basket and the infant's fall, Cissie came to a shuddering halt. What had happened after that was gone from her memory.

'I came in and found you,' Phoebe told her, 'and then the bobbies came.' If the girl ever did remember lying naked on the floor with her baby in her arms, she would tell her that she had covered her up and that no one else had seen.

Hearing movements in the kitchen, Phoebe swung her feet to the floor. 'I'm getting up now, Cissie. Do you feel like coming through with me?'

'Does Marie know what happened?'

'I'm afraid so, and Pat, for the police asked them what they'd heard – but they don't know the baby wasn't Jim's.'

'Thank God!'

Phoebe stretched across to stroke her cheek. 'Nobody ever needs to know that, Cissie. We'll keep it our secret, eh? You shouldn't even tell the inspector, for it's got nothing to do with what's happened.'

'Maybe he's been told already.'

'Your Da wouldn't have told him. He was awful ashamed of it, you know, and it was the drink that time, and all, but it was as much my fault last night as his. If I hadn't left him, he wouldn't have gone boozing, and . . .'

'You wouldn't have left him if I hadn't said things that made you realise . . .'

Heaving a long sigh, Phoebe fastened on her stays. 'Stop speaking about it, Cissie, and get dressed. You still have to go and speak to the inspector.'

Pat was washing at the sink when Phoebe went through to the kitchen. 'Don't ask Cissie anything,' she warned. 'She's still in a terrible state.'

'But I want to know why . . .'

'Never mind why. You're too young to understand, anyway.'

That night, both Cissie and Phoebe were reluctant to speak when they went to bed. The ordeal of telling the inspector what had taken place had been so traumatic for Cissie that she wished she, too, had been killed, and Phoebe was upset because she had overheard the constable saying that Big Tam deserved to be hanged. That had made her realise the penalty he would have to pay if he was found guilty of murder. She was glad, however, that she had remembered about the telegram her husband had received on the day before the 'incident', as the police called it. Learning that Tam's son had been lost at sea had seemed to make the Inspector take a more charitable view of what he had done – they believed it was why he had got drunk – and maybe it would affect the jury in the same way. It didn't excuse him, and she would never be able to live with him again, yet she didn't want him to hang for what was really an accident – two accidents. Was it too much to hope that he would only be charged with manslaughter, and be sent to prison?

'Phoebe.'

The quiet voice startled her. 'Yes?'

'I can't stay in Aberdeen after this. It's bound to be in the papers and everybody'll read about it.'

'Then they'll know your father wasn't the nice man they all thought he was.' Phoebe gave an angry snort. 'He was a monster through and through, though he fooled me, as well. Anyway, you can't go anywhere till after the trial. You'll have to give evidence.'

'Oh.' After a long pause, Cissie said, 'After that, then. I can't stay here with them all pointing at me and saying it was my fault.'

'They'll point at me, as well, and I wish I could go with you, but I'll have to stay here for Marie and Pat.'

'Marie's old enough to look after Pat.'

'It's my duty to look after them, I took it on when I married your father, and it's not fair to expect Marie to do it. She'll likely want to marry Wilfie in a year or two.'

It crossed both women's minds that Wilfie Lewis might not want to marry the daughter of a murderer, but neither of them mentioned it.

PART TWO

Dundee

Chapter Fourteen

❧❧

1918

Oblivious now to the eternal clatter of the machines that had driven her near to screaming pitch for the first week or two, Cissie could dwell on her own thoughts as the yarns sped through her nimble fingers. Most of the spinners, the weavers and the shifters had learned to lip-read so that they could mouth silently to each other as they worked, but she didn't want to become friendly with them. She would be expected to listen to their confidences in the short break in the middle of the day, and they would wonder why she didn't tell them anything about her own life. If she were to tell them, they wouldn't want to know her.

Her father was in Peterhead Prison serving a fifteen-year sentence for manslaughter, and, while she was glad that he had not been hanged for murder, she did worry sometimes about what would happen when he got out. It had been her evidence that had made the police reduce the charge against him — self-defence in Jim's case, and accidental death in the baby's — yet the venomous glare he had turned on her as he was led from the dock had let her know that he blamed her for his sorry predicament, and she was sure that he would come looking for her when he was freed.

That had strengthened her resolve to leave Aberdeen, but it was Phoebe who had suggested coming to Dundee. 'I read somewhere that the jute mills always need workers,' she had said. 'They're having to turn out thousands of sacks to make sandbags for the trenches, so we'll easily get a job.'

Cissie's heart filled once again with affection for her;

Phoebe had been a true friend, standing by her through all the troubles. Brushing a strand of hair out of her eyes, she lifted her head to look across at her stepmother, but Phoebe was too busy to notice. Surveying the factory floor, Cissie couldn't help feeling sorry for all the other women, they looked so tired. There were dozens of them, their ages ranging from over seventy to eleven, for parents would arrange half-time exemption from school so that their children could work either mornings or afternoons in the mills. Some of the older women looked fit to drop, their haggard faces set, their hands flying, for they could not risk being seen to slack. Even the young shifters – girls who put new bobbins on the spindles when the old ones were full – were concentrating desperately, and the constant shuffling of their feet told how badly their legs were aching.

'Hey, you!' The gruff voice startled Cissie, making her jump nervously and snap the yarn as the overseer's hand brushed her hip. 'What's up with you?' he demanded.

It wasn't the first time he had touched her like that, and she jerked away. 'Nothing's up with me, Mr Laidlaw.'

'You weren't paying attention to your job, and you've let the threads break.' Pretending to look over her shoulder, he rubbed his body against hers. 'I'd forget about it if you was nice to me,' he whispered, his stale breath making her stomach heave. 'If you meet me tonight, we could have a few drinks and then – well, you never know, do you?'

'I don't drink, Mr Laidlaw,' she said, primly, praying that he would go away, for she knew what he'd be after if he got her on her own.

'A wee drink would get you in the mood,' he persisted.

She felt like slapping his face, yelling at him to leave her alone, but he could make life difficult for her. He could even have her sacked. 'I'm sorry, I'm busy tonight.'

Not being a direct rebuff, this satisfied him, and to her great relief, he moved off. She could see Phoebe eyeing her with concern, so she smiled and bent her head to join the yarn, and to resume her thoughts.

It had seemed like another calamity when Marie had told them she was expecting Wilfie's baby, for she had barely turned sixteen, but she had gone on to say, 'He's going to marry me, though, so it's all right.'

Phoebe had looked relieved at that. 'Where are you going to live? With his mother?'

'She hasn't room, not with the baby coming.'

'We'll manage here. You and Wilfie can have the kitchen bed, and Cissie and me can have your room.'

'I'm going away as soon as the trial's over,' Cissie had reminded her.

Marie had looked a trifle uncomfortable then. 'Wilfie says he doesn't want to be in the same house as you, Phoebe, for you've made enough trouble for this family already, and he's willing for me to look after Pat. We don't want you here.'

Cissie still felt angry about that, after what Phoebe had done for them. Of course, Marie resented the love her young brother gave to their stepmother, and she had been pleased when Phoebe, too, had left the day after the trial ended.

They had found employment quite easily in Dundee, where the jute mills preferred women workers because they could pay them less than the men who, for one reason or another, were not in Europe fighting. Finding somewhere to live had proved much more difficult, however. One woman would have been welcome in several of the places they were told about, but no one was willing to take two, and they wanted to keep together. For two nights, they had slept in any corner that provided some shelter from the January gales that whistled through the wynds and closes, moving on whenever a policeman came across them.

For a few coppers, they could have had a bed in a lodging house, but they would have had to lie cheek by jowl with

123

the dregs of the drink-sodden prostitutes who no longer had the ability to attract men. It had been so cold outside that they would likely have had to resort to that, Cissie thought now, if the woman who worked next to her had not solved the problem for them. 'Where do you bide?' she had asked, when they were tidying up after their shift one night, more as something to say than out of any actual interest.

Cissie had grimaced. 'We haven't found a place yet.'

'Where've you been sleeping, then?'

Shrugging, Cissie had said, 'On the streets.'

Jen Millar had looked appalled. 'Oh, my God. Look, I've only got one room, and it's no palace, but you can come and share wi' me, if you like.'

'What about Phoebe? Is there room for her, and all?'

Cissie couldn't help smiling as she remembered Jen's frown. 'There's nothing funny going on between you two, is there?' she had asked, suspiciously.

'She's my stepmother.'

'I wondered why you were so close, but that's all right. We'll make room for her.'

Jen's single-end room was in a grim, blackened, tumble-down tenement behind the Overgate, and, as she had said herself, it was no palace. Cissie and Phoebe had been dismayed when they first saw it. A rickety, well-scrubbed table stood in the middle of the floor, a wobbly chair at one side of the fireplace, an equally unsteady three-legged stool at the other. Her dishes, chipped and cracked, and cooking pots were stored in an old orange box, and her complete wardrobe, a change of skirt and blouse, hung on a nail behind the door. Her spare set of underclothes was folded on top of another box, which they found out later held cleaning materials. Next to the fire, a third box held some coal and kindling sticks, with a chipped enamel basin perched on top. The window was screened by only a sheet of newspaper, almost brown from having been there so long, the whitewash on the ceiling was yellowing and the walls were red-ochred with the plaster falling off in places. The only saving grace was that the room was clean.

'There's no' a bed,' Jen observed, after hanging her shawl on the nail behind the door. 'I've just an old mattress on the floor, so we'll have to squeeze in. We'll no' be cold in the winter when there's three o' us cuddling up together.'

Having slept with her two sisters when she was younger, Cissie had thought nothing of this, but the mattress proved to be only three-quarter size, and she had found herself lying on the floorboards most of the time. Still, it was better than sleeping rough, she mused, and beggars couldn't be choosers. In any case, with three wages coming in over the months they'd been there, they'd been able to buy, second hand off a market stall, a pair of curtains which kept out the draught better than the old newspaper, and the old seats had been replaced by three chairs from a junk shop. Their next purchase was to be a single bed and some blankets for Jen, to let the other two have the mattress to themselves.

Cissie had often wondered what ill-fortune had brought Jen Millar so low in life, but she asked no questions of them, so they asked none of her. She was even-tempered and good-hearted, never harbouring a grudge, even when John Laidlaw, the overseer, took her to task unfairly. It was hard to put an age to her. Her hair was snow-white, and her pale, thin face, etched with lines, was always cheerful. Her body, too, was painfully thin, and her legs were like matchsticks. From her appearance, she could be in her sixties, but most of the workers looked older than they were; even the girls whom Cissie knew were only about thirteen or fourteen looked as old as she did, and she would be twenty on her birthday. Would she end up, in another year or so, looking as haggard as the rest?

There were very few men in the mill, just those who were not fit enough, or were too old, to be in the services, and most of them were friendly. Cissie would have been quite happy with her lot if it had not been for the overseer, who had hounded her from the day she started. At first, she had thought nothing of the reprimands — she was new to the job and it would take time to learn how to join the yarns again if she let them break — but nothing she did pleased him. Maybe he was hoping to wear her down into going out with him. If he was, he would be disappointed.

When the hooter sounded at six o'clock, twelve hours after she had begun work, she tidied her working area and joined the outgoing stream of women, most of them sullen-faced with exhaustion. The weavers were usually out first, classing themselves above the spinners and shifters, who were on a lower wage being unskilled, and not worth looking at. This had irked Cissie to begin with, for she considered herself as good as them, if not better, but she had realised that there was a hierarchy in every walk of life, and that she was on the bottom rung of the ladder here.

Once outside, she pulled up the collar of her coat to wait for her room-mates. The coats had made her, and Phoebe, the butt of many sarcastic jibes, for the other women wore shawls, but the jeering had only made them more determined to keep wearing their coats as long as they held together.

She saw Phoebe then, looking so different from the rest, her eyes still as bright a blue as ever, her brown hair still with a gloss on it, although it was only ever washed with yellow soap. 'I went to see Mr Dickson this afternoon,' she observed, as she linked arms with the girl.

'Mr Dickson?' Cissie gasped. 'Did Laidlaw know?'

'I said I was feeling sick and asked him if I could go to the WC, and he patted my bottom and said not to be all day.'

'And you went to Mr Dickson's office? What did you say?'

'I told him I wanted to learn to be a weaver.'

'You never.'

'He's very nice. He asked if I'd any experience, and I said I was willing to learn, and he said he would keep me in mind the first time there was a vacancy.'

Jen, who had joined them and heard most of the story, gave a rude snort. 'You'll never hear any more about it.'

'Oh, well,' Phoebe said, airily, 'you never get if you don't ask, and it was worth a try.'

'True enough,' agreed Jen, 'but you'd better not build up your hopes. Some spinners I know have been waiting years.'

Only a week later, Mr Laidlaw approached Phoebe with an odd expression on his crafty face. 'What have you been up to, Mrs McGregor? Mr Dickson wants to see you in his office.'

She gave him a sunny smile. 'He must have fallen for my girlish charms.'

When she returned, he was waiting for her. 'Well?'

'Well what?' She wanted to keep him in suspense for a moment or two yet, because he would get the shock of his life when she told him. She had nearly fainted herself.

'Why did Mr Dickson want to see you?'

'I told you: he's fallen for my girlish charms.'

'Don't be so bloody funny. What was it?'

'He said I'd to leave this job at the end of the week.'

His brows furrowing, the overseer said, 'You've got the sack? If somebody's complained about you, it wasn't me.'

'I haven't got the sack. I asked him last week if he'd let me learn to be a weaver.'

'You bitch! That must have been the day I let you go to the lavvy. And you say he's shifting you?'

'Yes, he's shifting me – into the office.'

His shock was every bit as great as she had hoped; his

127

pupils dilated, his mouth sagged. 'The office? Have you been doing him favours?'

'I've done him no favours,' Phoebe said, angrily. 'He just said one of the clerkesses was leaving and he wanted someone with a bit of go in them, someone who looked presentable and would be able to talk to people properly.'

'You've nerve enough for anything,' he muttered.

Phoebe watched him making straight for Cissie, and hoped that he wouldn't take his anger out on her.

Noticing him coming, Cissie was so nervous that her hands jerked the yarn and snapped it, and she was rejoining it when he reached her, but he had other things on his mind. 'Your friend's a fly one,' he growled. 'She's made up to Mr Dickson and got a job in the office.'

Unsure of what to say, Cissie wisely said nothing, and he went on, 'So you'll have to change your ways or I'll put a spoke in her wheel.'

A niggle of alarm running through her, Cissie murmured, 'I don't know what you mean.'

'I mean I can queer her pitch with the boss if you don't come out with me, and besides that, I can get him to give you both your books, and I could tell other overseers that you'd been sacked for stealing from your workmates, so no other mill would take you on.'

Knowing that he was quite capable of carrying out both threats, Cissie's heart sank. They couldn't afford to lose their jobs, so she would have to give in to this oily snake-in-the-grass, and she couldn't let Phoebe know.

'Eight o'clock tonight,' Laidlaw ordered. 'This end of the Wellgate, and you'd better be there or your friend'll not be working in any job, never mind an office.'

He strode away, swaggering a little now, and Cissie gulped back her tears. He was a vile man and she knew why he wanted to meet her that night, but how could she let him paw her with his sweaty hands, and let those horrible wet lips kiss her? She couldn't bear to think beyond that.

When the three women were walking home to the Overgate, Cissie professed to be as pleased as Jen about Phoebe's good fortune, then said, 'I'm meeting Johnny Keating at eight tonight. He's been asking me to go out with him for ages, and I kept putting him off.'

'Oh, I'm pleased for you,' Phoebe exclaimed. 'Johnny's a real nice laddie.'

'You've kept quiet about him,' Jen said, a little accusingly. 'There's many a one would have jumped at the chance of going out wi' him, he's so good-looking.'

Johnny Keating, employed as a cop-winder and about the same age as Cissie, was good-looking. His face was rugged, his hair almost blond, and though his light blue eyes were usually serious, she had noticed them softening when they fell on her. He was fairly tall, straight in the back and quite broad, and she'd often wished he would speak to her, so his was the first name that had come to her mind.

Jen insisted on cooking the supper – she had bought some herring from a Newhaven fishwife in the street – and Phoebe said she would lay the table to let Cissie fetch water from the tap in the backyard to wash herself, and the poor girl had to put on a show of excited anticipation of the evening in front of her. When she left the house, with cries of 'See and enjoy yourself' and 'Give Johnny our love' ringing in her ears, she made her way unhappily to the Wellgate, where John Laidlaw was waiting for her.

His sharp face brightened when he saw her, and he took her arm and walked her to the nearest public house, where he ordered a whisky for himself and a gin for her, but she shook her head when he laid the glass in front of her. 'I told you I didn't drink. I've seen what it can do to people.'

Eyes glittering even more, he said, 'One wee drink's not going to make you drunk, it'll just make you loosen up.'

Cissie realised that she would probably need the gin to help her endure the man's advances. 'That's it,' he smiled, as she raised the glass to her lips.

The clear liquid looked as harmless as water yet tasted foul, but her trembling had stopped by the time the glass was empty, so she did not demur when he gave her another and had two more whiskies himself. She felt lightheaded when he took her arm and led her out, and she put up no resistance when he said, 'My lodgings are just round the corner.'

It was another grimy tenement, the stench of urine in the close revolting her, and the smell of sweat in his bed was even more overpowering. For Phoebe's sake, she lay passively as the man sucked at her mouth, and let him open her buttons and fondle her breasts. She didn't even push his hands away when they went down to lift her skirts, she had been through it all before. His attempts at seduction, however, came to nothing, even with three whiskies inside him, and Cissie's spirits soared. John Laidlaw was just a pathetic creature who wanted to get pleasure from women but couldn't.

Shamefaced at first, his eyes narrowed suddenly. 'You'd better keep your mouth shut about this. If I ever learn you've told anybody, especially that high and mighty friend of yours, you'll be in big trouble.'

'I won't tell a soul,' she said, sure that he wouldn't bother her again after this fiasco.

Chapter Fifteen

'Why haven't you been out with Johnny Keating again?'

Having been sure that Phoebe would ask, Cissie was ready with her answer. 'We didn't get on as well as we thought.'

Her stepmother's mouth rose at one side. 'Did he try . . '

Cissie could not blacken the boy's character. 'No, he didn't, but I can't – he wouldn't want to go with me if he knew about me.'

Sighing, Phoebe said, 'Oh, Cissie, nothing that happened was your fault, and you're a widow now, so you're free to go with boys again, even get married if you want to.'

'I know that, but I don't think I'll ever want to.'

Jen, who had gone down to the outside standpipe for water, came puffing in then, so nothing more was said, but Phoebe had resolved to help Cissie.

With this in mind, she sought out Johnny Keating next day. 'Don't mind what Cissie said,' she told him, thinking that no preamble was necessary, 'she does want to see you again.'

He seemed a little taken aback, but his answer was only a split second slow. 'You're sure?'

'Quite sure. She'd trouble once with another man, and she's shy of making friends, but I do know she likes you.'

'That's good, for I like her, and all.'

'Ask her again, and don't take no for an answer.'

He didn't need a second telling.

On the following day, Cissie came home in high spirits. 'I'm going out with Johnny Keating tonight,' she announced. Then, remembering that she was supposed to have been out with him before, she added, hastily, 'Again.'

Phoebe looked suitably surprised. 'You changed your mind?'

'He changed it for me.'

'Don't spoil it this time, then.'

Knowing that she wouldn't spoil it herself, and hoping that nothing else would, Cissie went out to meet the young man. She had been astonished when he had come to her that afternoon and said, 'I'll be waiting for you at Draffen's at half past seven tonight, and don't say you won't turn up.'

Swivelling on his heel and leaving her, he hadn't given her time to say anything, but she couldn't get over the coincidence of it after the lie she'd told Phoebe and Jen.

It did not take her long to reach Draffen's department store in Whitehall Street, but being early, she had to wait a few minutes until he came hurrying towards her. 'It's not too cold for you to have a walk to Dudhope Park, is it?'

'No, that would be nice.'

She was shy with him as they started walking, and guessed that he felt the same, so when they passed the end of the Overgate, she said, 'That's where I live.'

'I'll meet you here next time, then.'

It was good to know that he meant there to be a next time, Cissie thought, and was pleased when he began to tell her about his family. 'My Da drives a horse and cart for James Wilson, the contractor. You know, he takes the bales of raw jute from the harbour to the mills, and takes what they've made back to the harbour. Mattresses sometimes, carpets, tarpaulins, ropes – and sacks, of course.'

Cissie laughed. 'Yes, sacks, of course.'

'Ma goes out cleaning and takes in washing, and I've two sisters still at school, so you see we're just an ordinary working family. Have you any brothers and sisters?'

'I'd three brothers and two sisters, but Rosie died and

Joe was lost at sea.' Not wanting to go into further detail about her family, Cissie said, 'Where do you live?'

'Hilltown, three floors up. You're from Aberdeen by the way you speak. What took you to Dundee?'

The dreaded question had come at last, as she had been afraid it must. 'Looking for a job. My sister, Marie, was getting married, and she said she would look after Pat, he's still at school. My oldest brother was on a trawler, but he went into the Merchant Navy when the war started.'

'I know your Ma's dead, for Phoebe told me she was your stepmother, but is your Da dead, and all?'

'Yes.'

'I'm sorry for asking, I can see it's upset you. You're not cold, are you?'

'No, I'm fine.'

He chattered on about his work as a cop-winder. 'That's why I'm in with the spinners and shifters, and it's not good wages, just thirteen shillings a week, but it's steady. I'm deaf in one ear, though it doesn't bother me, but that's why I didn't pass the medical for the army.'

When they reached Dudhope Park there were several people strolling about, some of them officers of the Black Watch, who, he told her, had occupied the Castle since the outbreak of the war. The weather being a little too cold to sit down, Johnny and Cissie kept walking, talking about this and that, and she soon learned that he had quite definite ideas as to how mills should be run.

'With this war on, the owners are making money hand over fist, but the workers should get a share in the profits. After all, if it wasn't for us, the bosses couldn't afford to live in their big, swanky houses and have servants to do everything for them. Take Dickson, now. He sent his son to a private school, with a fancy uniform, when his workers could hardly buy enough food.'

'But all bosses have more money than their workers,'

she said, a little surprised because she had never heard anyone saying things like this before.

'That's my point. Why should they have more money, when it's not them that do the work?'

'That's the way it's always been, and the way it always will be, I suppose.'

'That still doesn't make it right. Here's Bertram Dickson, never done a day's work in his life, yet he'll come back from the army and his father'll take him into the mill. He'll likely look down his nose at the likes of us, though if it wasn't for the hard graft we put in, there wouldn't be a mill to run. And when his father dies, Bertram'll fall heir to the lot, and he's never set a foot inside the place. He hasn't a clue what goes on. No, I don't agree with having one rule for the rich and one for the poor. Russia's got the right idea. They got rid of their Tsar and all his family.'

Cissie was shocked by his callousness. 'But that was in a revolution, and they didn't deserve to be killed. Does that mean you think our Royal family should be killed, and all?'

He had the grace to look ashamed. 'No, that's not what I mean, but workers get a better deal under the Communists, for the profits are shared out – according to their needs.'

'But surely you wouldn't want to be under Communist rule?'

He considered for a moment. 'I'm not so sure about that, I'm all for sharing profits. The way we are, Dickson and the other bosses keep their workers down too much.'

'Most people are happy to be getting a wage,' Cissie said, indignantly. 'They'd be a lot worse off if they didn't have a job, for they'd end up on the parish.'

Johnny gave a light laugh then. 'I'm sorry, Cissie. I don't know what you must think of me getting on my high horse, but I was at a meeting last night, and one speaker got folk all fired up about the unfairness of the present system.

That's the words he used. I shouldn't preach to you, though, or you'll maybe not come out with me again.'

Taking her arm, he gave it a squeeze. 'Are you annoyed?'

'No, I'm not annoyed.' She had been a little perturbed by his views, but he had only been repeating what he had heard.

'Good. I don't want to scare you off.'

Having walked around the park for almost an hour, they made their way back to the Overgate, and though she tried to make him leave her at the end of the street — she was ashamed to let him see the hovel she lived in — he kept holding her arm. They passed several shops, but when they came to the little pawnshop — deep in shadow because it was nowhere near a lamppost — he pushed her against the door's iron grille, laughing as it rattled loudly. 'Can I kiss you goodnight, Cissie?'

'If you like,' she murmured, praying that it would only be a kiss, or maybe more than one, not anything else.

It was only one, long and tender, and when he drew away, he breathed, 'I've been wanting to do that for a long time.'

'Before tonight, you mean?' she whispered, surprised.

'For weeks. I'd never have dared to ask you out, though, if it hadn't been for . . .' Not having meant to tell her about Phoebe's request, he stopped in dismay. 'I was wanting to,' he floundered, 'but I . . .'

'What made you, then? Oh, I bet Phoebe said something.'

'She thought we'd been out before, and she told me to ask you again and not take no for an answer.'

Feeling rather hurt now, she said, 'So you were forced into it?'

'No, Cissie, don't think that. I wanted to, and I was pleased when she . . .' He paused, then asked, 'Why did she think we'd been out before?'

It would be better to tell the truth, Cissie thought. It

would make no difference now. 'I went out with Mr Laidlaw, but I told her it was you, for she wouldn't have let me go if she knew it was him.'

His eyes had hardened at the mention of the overseer. 'Did he threaten you if you didn't go out with him?'

'He said he'd get Phoebe sacked and me, too, and he would make sure nobody else would hire us.'

'The bugger o' hell! I wish you'd come and told me, I'd have given him what-for. Did he do anything to you?'

'He tried to,' she gave a nervous little smile, 'but he couldn't – if you know what I mean.'

'He wasn't able to? God, that's a laugh, he makes out he's a great ladies' man.'

'Johnny, please don't tell anybody.' She was annoyed at having mentioned it, but it had just slipped out.

'Aye, he'd likely be after your blood if he thought you'd shown him up, but don't worry, I'll not tell anybody.'

'I'll have to go in now, it's getting late and we've an early morning, both of us.'

Her lips were still tingling from his last kiss when she went upstairs, her starry eyes making Phoebe and Jen look knowingly at each other and hold back the teasing remarks they had intended to make.

John Laidlaw kept away from Cissie over the next month, but she suspected that he was marking time until he could find some excuse to have her dismissed, so she worked carefully and diligently, determined not to give him one. She was meeting Johnny twice a week now at the end of the Overgate, walking with him to Baxter Park occasionally, sometimes back to Dudhope Park or strolling along the quayside at the docks and watching the lights from the merchant ships and whalers. One night, however, as soon as they met, he said, 'There's another meeting on tonight. Why don't you come with me? You'll see what I was meaning about the last one.'

She didn't want to go, but she could see that he did, so she accompanied him to the school hall where the meeting was being held. She was quite impressed by the first speaker, a tall man with a slight lisp who spoke in a down-to-earth manner, but the second one, the one everyone had come to hear, judging by the applause that greeted him, got too worked up for her liking, whipping the crowd into such a frenzy that they shouted encouragement and clapped their hands wildly every time he stopped for breath. Only one little man in a cloth cap and muffler, on Cissie's right, seemed less than happy. 'Bloody reds!' he muttered.

Cissie was inclined to agree. It had been advertised as a Labour meeting, but the sentiments being expressed were definitely communist. She turned her head to look at Johnny, but he was engrossed in a long diatribe against all capitalistic employers, nodding his head at the points that were being made. When at last the speaker came to an end – after fully seventy minutes – he waved his hand in acknowledgement of the standing ovation he was being given, and walked past his cheering audience to the door, smiling when a few men thumped his back to congratulate him.

'That was some speech, wasn't it, Cissie?' Johnny burst out triumphantly. 'God, it made you want to rise up against all the bosses and tell them what you think of them. See how they would get on if they had to stand for twelve hours at a time spinning jute on to spindles, or better still, shifting full spindles and putting on empty ones. They wouldn't like it if their fingers got caught in the machines, like some of the poor wee shifters, bairns most of them.'

Standing up, Cissie said, 'I'm sorry, Johnny, but I can't agree with what that man said. We need bosses to run the mills. What do the workers know about buying the raw jute? Or about getting orders and sending them all over the world? Could you work out how much it would cost to make a carpet, or to make a hundred sandbags? Oh, yes, the workers do the work, make the finished goods, and they're not paid well for it. Maybe the bosses are wrong about that, but there has to be somebody in charge or the work wouldn't be there for them to do.'

'Well,' Johnny gasped. 'You'd make a pretty good speaker yourself.'

Embarrassed now, she turned to go into the passage, but the little man in the muffler took her hand and shook it. 'That's the kind of talk I like, not that pudding-face of a man spouting things he doesn't live up to. Does he work in a mill or a factory? I'm bloody sure he doesna. He sits on his backside all day writing out speeches. You should go in for politics, lass. You'd make a better job than that lot.'

'I couldn't stand up in front of a lot of people,' she said, 'and I don't know the first thing about politics.'

'Neither do half of them,' growled the little man.

Cissie and Johnny were both laughing when they left the hall, and as he took her arm, he said, 'You've made one convert, any road.'

'He was converted long before that,' she told him. 'He called the speakers "bloody reds".'

'Och, well, everybody to their own opinion, I suppose. I shouldn't have taken you there tonight, for I'll never get you to see things my way.'

'And you'll never see things my way.'

He gave a loud laugh. 'We'd better leave politics out of it in future, eh?'

On November the eleventh, when the great news came that an armistice had been signed and the war had come to an end, Cissie and Johnny joined the celebrations at Magdalen Green, dancing and singing the night away along with the rest of the crowd. In this charged atmosphere, she felt the first stirrings of love for him, but when he, in the same highly emotional state, said on their way back to the Overgate that he loved her, she shied from telling him how she felt. If she did, he might ask her to marry him – she had told him that she was a widow – and it wasn't fair to lead him on, because she could never be his wife. He would expect to make love to her, and she was certain that she couldn't bear to let any man touch her in an intimate way ever again. The very thought of it was making her grip her insides as if she were about to be violated. Johnny wasn't an easy-going man like Jim Robertson had been, and though he had never tried anything, and might not try unless they were married, his body was so strong she could imagine the force of him when he did. He would be her father all over again, and she couldn't bear that.

As long as they were only walking out together, it would be all right, and she would stop seeing him at the first sign of him wanting anything else.

*　　*　　*

At Huntingdon, his large house on the Perth Road, Richard Dickson had been discussing the mill with his father. 'I am quite glad that I took Mrs McGregor into the office,' he observed, as he refilled their whisky glasses. 'She is very capable.'

Old Dick – as everyone knew him – gave a little cackle. 'I told you, didn't I? I ken't she must have guts to beard you in your den, so to speak, and I bet she's a good looker.'

'Oh, Father, what an old reprobate you are.'

'A reprobate, is it? What's wrong with having an eye for a pretty woman, even at my age?'

Richard had to laugh. 'I hope I'm as sprightly as you when I'm seventy.'

'I was thinking,' Old Dick said, smiling a trifle slyly, 'your secretary, that Miss Thingummy that looks as if she'd drop down dead if a man as much as looked twice at her, she should be retiring shortly, should she no'?'

139

'What's that got to do with anything?'

'It would kittle you up to have a bonnie woman beside you for a change.'

Richard frowned, but not at his father's turn of phrase, he was accustomed to that. Old Dick had just been a mill-hand before he worked his way to the top and bought the mill when the owner retired, and although he, too, had retired some time ago, he still took an interest in what went on. 'Are you saying I should make Mrs McGregor my secretary when Miss Lovie retires?'

'You could do worse. A working-class woman aye makes a go of whatever she tackles.'

'I get the impression that Mrs McGregor hasn't always been a spinner,' Richard said, thoughtfully. 'I am sure she has come down in the world.'

'I think you're smitten wi' her, and it's time you took another wife. Lydia's been dead for . . . how long is it?'

'Eight years.'

'That's a long time to be without a woman, Richard.'

'Oh, Father! I'm not like you.'

'I ken that, though my wenching days are done, I'm sorry to say. Mind you, I hope Bertram doesnae take after me when he comes out o' the army, for I'd like to see the day you hand over the mill to him. From my son to his son.'

His father's suggestion that he should make Mrs McGregor his secretary came back to Richard later. Perhaps it would not be such a preposterous idea, after all. She had warned him that she had never worked in an office before, but, in the ten weeks she had been there, she had mastered the book-keeping system, her handwriting in the ledgers was as neat a copperplate as he had ever seen, and in addition, she had learned to type. Everything she did was perfect, but there were times when he wished she would unbend a little with him. She was a widow, and, as his father suspected, he was strongly attracted to her.

He had discovered that she did not live in the Overgate

itself, the address she had given, but in one of the old, overcrowded tenements just behind. Moreover, she seemed inordinately close to the two spinners with whom she lived, especially the one she called Cissie. He had checked in his staff records, and had found that the girl's surname was Robertson, and this had given him cause to think. The names Cissie Robertson and Phoebe McGregor were vaguely familiar. He had heard them, or seen them, somewhere before – could it only have been when Laidlaw told him he had taken them on? Whatever it was, Cissie seemed to be quite a decent young woman, but the other spinner, Jen Millar, was much rougher, not the type of person he would associate with Phoebe. She may, of course, share with them because she couldn't afford to rent a house herself, so it might be wise to increase her salary to enable her to find somewhere better.

'Mr Dickson gave me a Christmas bonus,' Phoebe announced, as soon as Cissie and Jen came home, 'and he's putting up my wages starting from the second of January.' She looked at them proudly. 'It's a good thing he didn't make me learn to be a weaver, or I'd never have been so well off.'

The other two were grey-faced after their twelve hours on the spinning machines, but they cheered up at her news. She went on happily, 'We'll be able to look for a house now, somewhere a lot better than this.'

Cissie clapped her hands in delight, but Jen said, sadly, 'Aye, I suppose you want more room. It can't have been easy for you here. Well, when you go, I can throw out that old mattress seeing I've the single bed now. Or maybe you want to take the bed wi' you?'

'Of course we'll take it with us,' Phoebe exclaimed, not understanding, 'but we'll get two more single beds so we can have one each, and we'll get rid of that old flea-pit.'

'Oh!' Jen mulled this over for a moment, then said, 'If

you're meaning me to come wi' you, I can't. It's not that I'm ungrateful, but I'd not be happy anywhere else.'

'You can't stay here.' Phoebe let her eyes roam round the room, much more presentable than it had been but still not what anyone could call attractive.

Jen sighed. 'Me and Eddie was just seventeen when we wed, and that much in love we didna care where we bade.'

'I can understand that,' Phoebe declared, 'but Eddie isn't here with you now, so what . . .'

'He didna leave me, if that's what you think,' Jen burst out. 'I've never told anybody this, I couldna bear to mind about it, but he was labouring for a builder, and we made this room real nice – a double bed, a dresser over there, and . . .' She stopped, her voice wavering. 'We was that happy, and when I found I was expecting . . .'

In the short pause, Phoebe and Cissie exchanged glances, wondering what had happened to spoil Jen's idyll. 'I was seven months on when Eddie's boss came and said he'd fallen off a roof. I thought he'd been killed, and the shock made me miscarry, but he'd just been unconscious when they took him away in the ambulance. It might have been better if he'd been killed, though, for he lost both his legs.'

Phoebe's sympathetic gasp went unheeded. 'He took it hard about the bairn, and when he come hame, he hardly ate for weeks and sat without saying a word, till I wanted to scream at him. He did come round, but he was never the same. Then he took a cough, and I thought it was pneumonia . . .'

'Not much wonder in this place,' Phoebe muttered.

'. . . but it was consumption,' Jen continued. 'Well, I nursed him for over a year, and I'd to sell the furniture to buy food for him, and I'd to make do wi' boxes I got from the grocer, till the only thing left was the bed. After Eddie died, I'd to sell the bed to pay the rent, for I'd got behind, and I slept on that second-hand mattress for fifteen years – till you bought me the single bed.' Her eyes, misty while she recalled the past, suddenly filled with remorse. 'Ach, I dinna ken what made me tell you about Eddie, though maybe you'll see why I canna leave. My memories o' him are here.'

'Jen,' Phoebe murmured, 'you'll always have your memories wherever you are. If we got a house with two rooms, Cissie and I could share one, and you could have one to yourself.'

'It's awful good of you to think of me, but I'm stopping here. I've never been used to much, and it's no hardship.'

Jen was so resolute that Phoebe accepted defeat, but over the next few weeks, she and Cissie discovered that it was impossible to find a furnished house at a rent they were willing to pay, and they couldn't afford to buy furniture for the unfurnished flats which were much cheaper. They had almost given up hope when fate intervened.

Cissie was in the butcher's shop one Saturday afternoon when a woman happened to remark that her mother had died, and that she would have to clear everything out of the house before she gave it up. Scarcely daring to hope, Cissie said, 'I might buy your mother's furniture if you're not asking too much for it.'

The woman turned to her eagerly. 'She'd four rooms, so there's quite a lot, old but good. I'll let you see it, and we could maybe come to an agreement about the price.'

The house was on the second floor of a well-kept tenement in South Union Street, opposite a railway station, and the furniture was old-fashioned but solid, as the woman had said. 'What d'you think?' she asked. 'Is there too much? How many rooms were you wanting to furnish?'

Cissie shrugged. 'We haven't found a place yet, but we were thinking of somewhere with two rooms, so we wouldn't need all this. Maybe, if you were willing to sell some . . .'

'I'll tell you what. Come with me to the factor, and I'll tell him you're after the house, and maybe he'll let you have it. I know it wasn't a big rent, my mother couldn't have afforded it if it was, and he'll likely be glad to be saved the bother of looking for another tenant.'

An hour later, Cissie burst into Jen's room. 'Where have you been?' Phoebe demanded. 'We thought you'd got lost.'

'I've got a house and we can move in as soon as we like.' Cissie's explanation was a little incoherent at first, but she went over it again. 'And the woman was that pleased not to have to clear everything out, she let me have the whole lot for just two pounds.'

'What?' Phoebe gasped. 'For four rooms of furniture?'

'Yes, and dishes and pans and everything else. I told her it wasn't enough, but she wouldn't listen and I can still hardly believe it myself.'

'What's for the supper?' Jen asked, drily. 'I'm hungry.'

Having forgotten why she had gone to the butcher in the first place, Cissie was contrite. 'I'll go back.'

'Give me the money and I'll go myself.'

When Jen went out, Cissie said, 'I shouldn't have carried on about the house in front of her, but now she knows we've got four rooms, maybe she'll come with us after all.'

But Jen didn't change her mind, so Phoebe and Cissie moved out the next weekend. Having four rooms was like being in heaven, and they could hardly tear themselves away from the long casement windows. From the airy kitchen and the room that was Cissie's, they looked down on the River Tay, where ferryboats carried passengers across to Newport, and from the parlour and Phoebe's bedroom, they looked out on to the busy station and the bustling street. As Phoebe said on the day they took up residence, 'We'll never be bored, there's always something to look at.'

Cissie's mind was on more mundane matters. 'Thank goodness we've just to share the lavvy with one neighbour again, not a whole tenementful.'

*   *   *

Two weeks before Richard Dickson's secretary retired, he offered the post to Phoebe, who was so astonished that it was a full minute before she said, 'Oh, do you really think I'm up to it, Mr Dickson?'

'Of course you are up to it.'

'Well, I don't know what to say, but – oh, thank you, and I'll do my best not to let you down.'

She was turning to leave when the thought struck her. 'I hope you don't think I'm speaking out of turn, Mr Dickson, but you'll be looking for someone for my job, and Cissie's the very person.'

'Cissie? Cissie Robertson?' He sounded rather doubtful.

'She's my stepdaughter, a spinner like I was. We rented a house in South Union Street a month ago, so some extra money wouldn't go wrong. You won't regret it if you give her the job, for she's a good worker, and honest.'

'She has a good champion, anyway,' he smiled. 'I'll have to talk to her before I commit myself, however, so will you ask her to come to see me tomorrow?'

Cissie, of course, was thrilled when Phoebe gave her the message, and when, after talking to her for ten minutes, Mr Dickson told her that she had got the job, she was ecstatic. When Jen came to supper on Saturday, as she had done every week since they moved, she looked downcast when she heard about it. 'I'd better not come here again. It's not fitting for office ladies to mix with spinners.'

Cissie frowned. 'Don't be silly. Where would we have been if you hadn't taken us in when we came to Dundee?'

'No, it wouldn't do. It'll be all right as long as it's still new to you, but in a while you'll think yourselves better than me and you'll not want . . .'

'You're our dearest friend, Jen.' Phoebe was unhappily aware that it was the woman who would feel uncomfortable with them, not the other way round.

'And I'll always remember how good you were to me, but it's best I stop visiting. I'll not be on my own, for the lassie that came after Phoebe was put out o' her lodgings last Sunday and she's sharing wi' me now.'

'I feel awful about Jen,' Cissie observed, when their old friend had gone home. 'I hope she's not jealous of us having this house. She did get the chance to come with us.'

Phoebe shook her head. 'She's not jealous, and she's quite happy where she is. I'm glad she'll have company, though.'

When Cissie met Johnny Keating the following night, she burst out, 'I'm starting in the office two weeks tomorrow.'

A deep scowl crossed his face. 'So you're going over to the other side?'

'The other side?'

'The bosses' side. I've no more time for them in the office than I have for Dickson.'

'They're just workers, Johnny, the same as you.'

'White collar workers that never get their hands dirty,' he sneered.

Her hackles up now, she said, 'There's nothing wrong with that, and you can't blame me for trying to better myself.'

'Ha, so you admit it's a better job?'

'Of course it is. It's better pay, and shorter hours.'

'Once you're an office worker, you'll not want to be seen dead with the likes of me.'

'I'll still be the same, Johnny.'

'No, give it a couple of weeks and you'll be walking the other way when you see me coming.'

Angry now, Cissie snapped, 'The boot's on the other foot, if you ask me, and I'm taking that job whatever you say.'

'If I say I'll finish with you if you take it, will you give it up?'

'No, I won't give it up, and if you don't want to see me again, it's up to you.'

'Right, then, that's us finished.' He turned sharply away from her and stalked off.

She stood for a few moments, shaking with anger at him for being so pig-headed, then made her way home.

Phoebe was appalled when she was told. 'I'm sorry, Cissie. I wish I hadn't got you the job now.'

'It's not your fault. Johnny Keating's not worth bothering about. He's a Communist, and ignorant into the bargain.'

It did not take Cissie long – with some help from Phoebe – to understand the workings of the ledgers. She had worried about the typing, and her first two-fingered attempts had been so awful, and so slow, that she thought she would never learn, but she had persevered and was now quite competent.

She had been a clerkess for just over four months when the owner's son made his appearance. She knew, from what she had overheard, that Bertram Dickson, late Captain of the Scots Guards, was tall and good-looking, but she had not expected such a strikingly handsome six-footer. His lean figure was straight and lithe in the uniform he would be discarding shortly, his jaw was strong, his fair hair cropped short. His father, introducing him to the office staff he did not already know, came to her last. 'Our latest recruit, Cissie Robertson, Mrs McGregor's stepdaughter. She has not been with us long, but she's shaping up very well.'

It was when the young man looked directly at her that she got the full impact of his eyes. They were quite dark, not an ordinary brown or blue, but a startlingly deep violet, and they were looking at her with such intense admiration that she felt a flush creeping up her neck.

'Cissie?' he smiled, 'I'll remember that.'

Chapter Sixteen

❖❖

1920

When Phoebe told her that Bertram Dickson did not intend to take up work at the mill, Cissie's relief was tempered with disappointment at the thought of not seeing him again.

'He told his father he wanted to enjoy himself for a while before he started work of any kind,' Phoebe went on. 'I know Richard's disappointed, for he hoped he could hand over to his son some day, like his father did to him.'

Her use of the owner's first name made Cissie think. She had suspected for some time that there was an attraction between them, and wondered what her stepmother would say if Mr Dickson ever asked her to marry him.

The end of the war had meant a decrease in orders for the mill, and Cissie was glad to learn that Johnny Keating and Jen Millar were not among the workers who were paid off. She hardly ever saw either of them but was still interested in their welfare, and jobs were hard to come by.

Despite what he had told his father, Bertram turned up in the office every afternoon, and Cissie coloured nervously each time she saw him looking at her, afraid, yet half hoping, that he would come across and speak to her on his way to or from the little room Richard Dickson shared with Phoebe, and it was fully a month before he did.

Out of uniform now, he wore grey flannels with a Fair Isle slipover and a Harris tweed jacket, but he was as handsome as ever. His powerful violet eyes seemed to fix on her as soon as he came through the door, and when he said,

'Good morning, Cissie,' she answered, 'Good morning, Mr Dickson,' praying that her nervousness did not show.

Smiling, he murmured, 'The name's Bertram, Cissie.'

'Yes, I know, Mr Dickson,' she replied, not wishing to encourage him.

'You're a very pretty girl, you know.'

Her blush deepened. 'Thank you.'

'How about coming for a spin in my Sunbeam tonight?'

'No, thank you.' She wished that she could accept, but she couldn't possibly go out with the boss's son.

He pulled a wry face. 'Oh, Cissie, you've cut me to the quick. Look, I promise there won't be any funny business, I just want a companion. The girl I've been seeing has found someone else, and I'm at a loose end. Please take pity on an old soldier?'

His last sentence made her smile. He was nothing like the poor ex-servicemen who had to beg on the streets because they couldn't find work, and he had more than his share of charm. 'That's better,' he grinned, 'the sunshine of your smile has lifted the clouds from my heart.'

She suspected that his flattery was insincere, but she couldn't resist him any longer, and his eyes twinkled at her hesitation. 'You'll come?'

'Just this once.'

Phoebe scowled when Cissie told her that Bertram Dickson was calling for her in his car at half past seven. 'I'm sure he's a bit of a wolf, so watch yourself.'

'I'm just going out with him once, as an obligement.'

'I didn't like to say anything before, but Richard – Mr Dickson – has been asking me out, and I said yes today, too. I like him an awful lot, Cissie.'

'What if he gets serious about you?'

'I won't let it get that far.'

Phoebe had encouraged Cissie to buy one of the new, short-length dresses a few weeks before, and a pair of beige silk stockings to go with it, but she had never had the courage to wear either. Tonight, however, she slipped on the dress and asked, 'What d'you think? Is it too daring?'

The long straight bodice had a deep V-neck, which showed her slim throat to advantage, and the skirt, pleated from well below her waist, sat becomingly on her. 'No, it suits you,' Phoebe assured her, 'but wear the stockings, too. You want to cut a dash, don't you?'

'I want to look nice, not cheap.'

'You won't look cheap, it's all the rage.'

Running downstairs when Bertram sounded his horn, Cissie hoped he would approve and was pleased when he said, 'You look so stunning I'd better take you to Edinburgh.'

To make the journey shorter, he went across both the Tay and the Forth by ferry, but it still took them well over an hour to reach the capital, where he paid for seats for the second house of a variety show. Cissie enjoyed most of the turns, but the two comedians were so suggestive that she felt uncomfortable and was glad when their acts were over.

To round off the evening, and ignoring her protests that it was too late, Bertram took her to a cocktail bar, and gave her a martini. It wasn't as strong as gin, and tasted much nicer, but she refused a second, content to survey the other patrons, young men in evening suits and bow ties, and girls who sat with their legs crossed so that their skirts, shorter than hers, slid up to reveal their bare thighs. She glanced at Bertram to see if he was as shocked as she was, but his eyes were on her.

It was after one in the morning when they arrived back at South Union Street, and he gave her a quick hug before he let her out of the car. 'We'll have to do it again, Cissie.'

'Maybe,' she laughed, and ran inside.

Phoebe was in bed but not asleep. 'Come through and tell me how you got on,' she called.

After describing everything, Cissie asked, 'How did you get on with Mr Dickson?'

'He's a gentleman, Cissie. We had a meal in a restaurant, with wine, and he talked to me like I was a proper lady.'

'Did he ask you anything about yourself?'

'No, he didn't get personal at all.'

'Neither did Bertram, thank goodness.'

Phoebe was pensive for moment. 'I felt like I was cheating Richard, though. Maybe I should tell him the truth about me, but I don't want him to stop taking me out.'

'He did ask you out again? So did Bertram.'

'It's different with you, Cissie. You're free to do what you want, I'm not. Richard's not like any other man I've known, and I'm sure he likes me, but is it wrong for me to let him think I'm something I'm not?'

'Did you feel it was wrong?'

'Not at the time.'

'But you do now?' Cissie thought for a moment, then said, 'It's not wrong, Phoebe. If he asked you out again, he must have enjoyed your company, so you'd given him pleasure.'

'I suppose so.' Phoebe sighed, then gave a wry laugh. 'I didn't know I'd a conscience, but maybe I'll get over it.'

When she went to bed, Cissie couldn't help thinking that it was odd that she and Phoebe were going out with a father and son. The difference was, as her stepmother had pointed out, she was free to encourage Bertram if she wanted to, and Phoebe's conscience might prevent her from encouraging Mr Dickson, though they would make a perfect couple. Phoebe was tall, dark and elegant, but he was even taller and very distinguished. He had a neat moustache, almost black hair with just a little silver through it, and his skin was as fresh as a young boy's yet it seemed to fit in with the rest of his looks. He wasn't quite as handsome as Bertram, whose fairness must come from his mother, but she understood why Phoebe was drawn to him. His eyes were a definite blue, not violet like his son's, and they were kind eyes, serious, the eyes of a man you wouldn't be afraid to trust.

Could she trust Bertram? She had enjoyed being with him, and he done nothing wrong, but he wasn't like any other man she had known. Johnny Keating, of course, had turned out to be a Communist, but Hugh Phimister . . . She had practically forgotten Hugh since she came to Dundee, yet her love for him had gone much deeper than her feelings for Johnny. She hoped that he had come through the war — though if he had, he would be back in Aberdeen now and his mother would have told him about the trial. He would likely be thanking his lucky stars that she had broken off with him, and he'd never know what that had cost her.

She dragged her mind back to Bertram. He was a good man, just a little high-spirited, and of course she could trust him. What had she been thinking of to doubt him?

*　　*　　*

Bertram's thoughts kept returning to Cissie. The other girls he had taken out had let him fondle them, and in some cases, let him make love to them, but Cissie wasn't like that. She had said she was a widow, so she couldn't be as untouched as she looked, but he had the feeling she would turn on him if he tried anything, and he would have to go carefully.

He waited more than a week before asking her out again, and was quite surprised when she agreed. This time, he said he would take her to Perth, but when they came to a thickly wooded area, he drew the car off the road amongst the trees, to find out how she felt about him. He was delighted when she let him kiss her, but her lips kindled a fire inside him, and he had to restrain himself from caressing her. He didn't want to scare her, but she seemed to enjoy his kisses, and he was confident that, given time, she would respond to them in the way he was longing for.

The following morning, when he was on his way downstairs to breakfast, Bertram overhead something that made him stand still to listen. 'It's high time that lad of yours settled down to some work,' his grandfather was saying. 'He can't go through life sponging off you.'

'I've been thinking about that,' Richard replied, 'and I'm going to give him a choice. Either he does what we want and learns the workings of the mill from the bottom up, or he takes a job somewhere else.'

'If he doesn't?' This was Old Dick again.

'Then he gets nothing more from me.'

Bertram drew in a sharp breath, but they weren't finished yet. 'When I made my will,' his grandfather observed, 'I left him my share of the mill as well as half my money, but the way he's been gambling and carrying on with fast girls is making me have second thoughts. He needs somebody with her head screwed on, maybe a working lassie that would make him buckle to and settle down. If he doesn't see sense shortly, I'm going to cut him out altogether.'

Not waiting to hear any more, Bertram turned and tiptoed back to his room. Damn them both, he thought furiously, a man couldn't have any fun these days. When he'd suggested, a few weeks ago, that he'd be willing to go into the mill at management level, his father had said, 'You'll start at the bottom like I had to.' So what did they expect, for heaven's sake? He wasn't cut out to be a labourer, not even an overseer, and he would have to think of something before old Dick changed his will.

Taking Cissie home two nights later, he said, 'I've been considering starting up in business on my own. Not in jute, maybe something in the wholesale line – groceries or medical supplies, something everyone needs.'

'That's a good idea,' Cissie exclaimed. 'You shouldn't be frittering your life away like you've been doing.'

Her enthusiasm helped him to decide. 'Would you come and start up my books? You know about that sort of thing.'

'But wouldn't your father be angry if you took one of his clerkesses away?'

'He'll easily get another, and I want you.' This was true, in more senses than one.

'I haven't enough experience yet. I don't know anything about setting up books, just keeping them.'

Her eyes, looking up at him so earnestly, were driving him crazy, so he had to steel himself not to be angry. 'If you don't want to . . .'

'It's not that,' Cissie interrupted, hastily.

'You've got to say yes, Cissie.'

'I'll try, then.'

His childish pout vanished instantly. 'I knew you wouldn't let me down.' Turning to her again, he squeezed her, gave her a quick kiss and drove on before he lost his head.

Phoebe wasn't happy when Cissie told her what she'd agreed to do. 'You must know what he's after,' she said, heatedly, 'and it's not somebody to start a book-keeping system for him. You're mad to trust him.'

Cissie shook her head. 'He's serious about this business he wants to start.'

'Well, it's up to you, but be careful.'

As soon as his son came in, Richard Dickson launched into the grievance he had been nursing since that forenoon, when Phoebe passed on what Cissie had said. 'You might have told me you were going to start up in business, Bertram. I felt a complete fool when Phoebe – er, Mrs McGregor, told me.'

Bertram hoped that his father wasn't getting too friendly with the woman. He didn't want a stepmother coming between him and the Dickson cash, especially Phoebe, who would likely turn out to be interfering and money-grabbing. 'I've never had a chance to tell you. I thought maybe a wholesale grocery, that should be easy enough to run, and Cissie's going to do my books.'

'So Mrs McGregor said, and I am none too pleased about that, either. You should have had the decency to ask me if I could spare her.'

'I need her more, and I was going to tell you tomorrow.'

'And ask for money to start you off, I suppose?'

'Well, yes, but I'll pay you back once I get on my feet.'

'I can't see you making it pay; you've never done a day's work in your life. I don't know what your grandfather will say, he'd his heart set on you going into the mill.'

'He'll be pleased I'm settling down. Are you going to back me or not? Just a few thousand.'

'Just a few thousand?' Richard repeated, sarcastically.

'Mother would have let me have it.'

'Your mother spoiled you. If she had only let me knock you into shape when you were younger, you would be a better man today. I can't believe that the army has put some sense into you, but, all right, I'll finance you and I'll let you have Cissie to do your books. Perhaps she will be able to keep your nose to the grindstone and take your mind off all those flighty young girls you ran around with. I hear that you've been seeing quite a lot of her – is it too much to hope that you will stick to her? She could make a decent man of you.'

The inference that he wasn't a decent man stung Bertram – he could have taken Cissie any time he wanted and hadn't – but he merely said, 'Thanks for saying you'll help me out, Father. I'll be able to go ahead now.'

It took exactly four weeks for Bertram to apply to the council for the necessary permission, to find a suitable building to use as a warehouse, to buy the groceries he needed to stock it and to engage some staff. Then, on the Thursday before Dickson's Supplies was due to open, Cissie took her place in the small sectioned-off area he meant to use as an office, and started recording the invoices which had already piled up.

'This is the purchase ledger,' she explained to Bertram, 'and I'll start the sales ledger when you make some sales.'

'I knew you'd manage.' He dropped a kiss on her head.

'None of that,' she said. 'This is a business arrangement, and there's to be no nonsense.'

Bertram burst out laughing. 'Right, Mrs Robertson, we'll keep our relationship strictly formal during the day, but I can't guarantee anything about the evenings.'

Despite wanting her so badly that it hurt just to be with her, he did not rush her, wooing her gently by treating her to meals out, to shows in Dundee and Glasgow, to drives in the countryside on Sundays, and very slowly, he could tell that she was softening, coming round. But he had better make sure of her by professing to love her.

On Hogmanay, Bertram asked Cissie to Huntingdon, and she was dismayed to find that neither his father nor grandfather was at home. She recalled the time she had been alone with Hugh Phimister in an empty house. What a fool she had been to run out when she did that night. If she had given in to him, she would have been spared all the agony of what happened later.

'What are you thinking, Cissie?'

Bertram's quiet voice took her out of her reverie. 'Did you know there wouldn't be anybody in?' she asked.

He was stroking her hand as he might stroke a cat's paw. 'I knew Grandfather was going to see in the New Year with some friends, but I thought Father would be here. I swear I had nothing dishonourable in mind. You must know I love you, Cissie. It's hard for me not to take you in my arms in the office and let everyone see how I feel about you.'

She couldn't help smiling. The office window looked into the warehouse, and she could imagine what the storeman and the errand boy would say if they saw their boss kissing his book-keeper. 'Maybe we're together too much. You should go out with other girls.'

'I don't want any other girls. I've told you I love you, and I hoped you'd say you love me, too.'

'I can't, Bertram.' She didn't love him, not like she had loved Hugh. 'I think a lot of you, but . . .' She looked at him sadly. 'I suppose you won't want me to work for you now?'

He made a face. 'I seem to have made a fool of myself, but I'm not such a heel as to blame you. Your job is there for as long as you want it. Now, I'd better drive you home.'

In the car, she could tell by the stiff way he was sitting that he was hurt, and wondered if she had been foolish not to pretend that she loved him. She would be set for life if she married him, but she couldn't see herself letting him make love to her. In any case, he had said nothing about marriage.

Chapter Seventeen

❧❧

1921

Emerging – unsuccessful yet again – from a large store, Bertram was so frustrated that he gave his car tyre a hefty kick before he opened the door and sat inside. This touting for business was degrading, and he wasn't cut out for it. It wouldn't be so bad if he could get some decent orders, but it was nearly always the same story: 'I'm sorry, I've been dealing with my usual supplier for years.'

What if they'd been dealing with the same supplier since the bally flood, what difference did it make? He had tried to make them see he could give them better terms, he'd even pared his margin of profit practically to the bone, but only a few grocers had taken advantage of his offer, and even then, they hadn't been generous with their custom.

The engine gave an asthmatic wheeze when he tried to start it and, gritting his teeth, he tried again. This time, the motor coughed into life and he leaned back to continue his thoughts. He must be losing his touch. Had he been dealing with women, his charm would have won them round. Women couldn't refuse him anything – well, most women. Cissie was different. Even when he said he loved her – and that purely for the sake of getting round her – she had been unimpressed, damn and blast her! Well, he wasn't going down on his knees. She'd had her chance!

Driving off, he was hit by a flash of inspiration. He had been concentrating on the better type of stores, but there were dozens of tiny back-street shops run by women – old, maybe, but every bit as susceptible to flattery as young girls – mostly in working-class areas, where disorganised housewives ran in and out all day, every day. Little gold mines! Even if each order didn't amount to much, the sheer volume of them would mount up. Like Old Dick had once said when he was trying to make his grandson save a little of his pocket money every week, 'Mony a mickle maks a muckle.'

The trouble was, Bertram mused, he was running out of funds, and he would have to tap his father again. As well as the five thousand he had originally been given, he'd had to ask for the odd fifty quid over the past year — he'd been dashed unlucky with the horses — so he would likely have to suffer another lecture. Still, it was the only way to keep Dickson's Supplies going and his old man had plenty. It would all come to him in the end, anyway, so why shouldn't he get some now?

Taking no further time to consider, he changed direction and made for Huntingdon, and in a few minutes, he zoomed up the driveway and screeched to a halt outside the house. His breathing nervously unsteady, he asked the housekeeper if his father was home.

'No, not yet,' Mrs Frain told him, 'and your grandfather wasn't feeling well, so he went to bed early. That's a tray I'll have to carry up,' she ended hopefully, but Bertram did not rise to the bait.

Going into his father's study, he poured himself a glass of whisky from the crystal tantalus. He had better only have one to give him Dutch courage, he reflected — he'd need all his wits about him.

Richard was surprised to see his son already there when he walked into his study. 'You're home early, Bertram.'

'I'm in a bit of a tight spot, Father.'

Richard rolled his eyes to the ceiling. 'Again? How much?'

'It's not gambling debts, if that's what you think. It's the warehouse. The manufacturers are coming on a bit heavy, and I haven't been getting enough orders to pay them.'

'How much?' Richard repeated.

'About five hundred would stop the wolves baying.'

Sitting down at his leather-topped desk, Richard took his chequebook and pen from the top drawer. 'I'll give you four. You wouldn't take my advice before you went blindfold at this venture, but you had better listen to me now. Sell out and pay all your creditors in full, before you go bankrupt. You can come in with me if you like, but you will have to learn every facet of how the mill works, as I had to do with my father. If you ignore that advice, you are on your own.'

He blotted his signature and held out the slip of paper. 'I've made it out to Dickson's Supplies, not to you.'

'So you don't trust me,' Bertram sneered.

'You've never given me any reason to trust you. It's been one scrape after another ever since you were a boy. If your mother was still alive . . .'

'If Mother was alive she'd be more generous than you.' Bertram put the cheque in his breast pocket, then burst out, petulantly, 'I'll show you, though! I'll make a success of that warehouse if it kills me. There's money to be made out of groceries – look at Thomas Lipton.'

Standing up, Richard shook his head. 'Thomas Lipton had a head for business, and there's nothing in yours except women and horses. You should marry a nice girl and settle down.'

'Had you anybody particular in mind?'

'What's wrong with Cissie?'

'She's too sensible about everything.'

'That is the kind of girl you should marry, not someone who spends all her time buying fripperies, like your mother did. She had no thought of the hard work involved in making the money she wasted.' Richard took a step towards the door, then halted. 'Your grandfather didn't look too well this morning. Is he about?'

'Mrs Frain said he'd gone to bed early.'

'I hope it's nothing serious, but I'd better go up and see him. Just go through to the dining room, I won't be long.'

Bertram did not move after his father went out; he had some thinking to do. Not about his father threatening to stop coughing up – he could get round the pater any time he liked – it was his grandfather's illness that worried him. He hated the idea of giving up his bachelorhood, but if Old Dick was on the way out, it might be wise to take the plunge before he kicked the bucket, to fool the old boy into thinking his grandson had turned over a new leaf. But not with Cissie – he couldn't picture himself tied to her for life. Millie Winton? Bertram brightened at the thought of his old girlfriend, a ravishing redhead, full of fun and, with her father an MP, she could open doors for him. She'd never actually let him go all the way, though he could bet she knew a trick or two. He hadn't seen her around for quite a while, but he knew the places she usually hung out. He'd take her out a few times, pile on the love talk and then pop the question. She would likely agree to a speedy wedding if he convinced her he couldn't bear to wait.

Cissie was alarmed at the amount of demands piling up on Bertram's desk. His recent orders were better than they used to be, but they'd still to be paid, and how would he keep going when he couldn't pay his own bills? If he had still been taking her out, she might have said something to him, but he was treating her just as an employee now, and humble employees didn't interfere.

She was taken completely by surprise when Bertram came in and told her to write out cheques for all his creditors. 'I've had a stroke of luck,' he explained. 'I think I'm on my way up at last.'

'Oh, I'm glad,' she smiled. 'I was beginning to think . . .'

'You know what thought did. Seriously, Cissie, if things go on like this, all my worries will fly out the window.'

Wishing that it wasn't over between them, she gathered

up the red-lettered 'Final Notices' to make out the cheques to settle them.

When he arrived home that night, Bertram was overjoyed to find that both his father and grandfather – who had turned out to have only a bad cold – were out, and that there was no sign of Mrs Frain. She would likely have gone to bed long ago, and the way was clear for him to sneak a look at Old Dick's will to find out if he had got round to changing it. His heart pounded when he went into his grandfather's room, but it didn't deter him, and when he found a metal cash-box in the bottom drawer of the tall-boy, he guessed this was where important documents would be kept. Taking care to set them down so that he could replace them correctly, he took out yellowed receipts, some dating back to before he was born, letters from all over the world and, right at the bottom, a large brown envelope. Sitting down on the wicker chair, he withdrew the contents with trembling fingers.

Moments later, he was quivering with fury. The will had been changed, and what a devil the old boy was! There was a small legacy to Mrs Frain, another to an old friend, and his shares in the mill went to 'my son Richard Dickson, who will thus become sole shareholder.' Shorn of all legal jargon, it went on to say that his money should be put in trust for his first legitimate great-grandson. Should such a child not be born at the time of his death, his whole estate was to go to Richard.

This was a bad blow to Bertram, but what enraged him most was a note at the foot, in his grandfather's spindly, shaky handwriting. 'I wish I could bequeath my business acumen to my grandson, Bertram, who has inherited only his mother's selfishness and emptyheadedness. When he reads this, I hope he will understand why I have left him nothing.'

Taking great gulps of air to force down the bile that was

rising in his throat, Bertram put everything back in the cash-box, viciously hoping that Old Dick would rot in hell when he did pass on. Not only had he made a fool of his grandson, he had also cast a slur on said grandson's mother, a saintly woman who had devoted herself to her only child.

It was some time before Bertram could trust himself to go downstairs again, and the first thing he did was to knock back a couple of whiskies. Feeling calmer, he gave himself up to thought. Even though everything was to be put in trust for a child as yet unconceived, surely a father would have the right to draw on it when the time came? What was even more promising, the old man looked good for some years yet, long enough for his grandson to make a success of Dickson's Supplies; it was beginning to go like clockwork now. If he could prove that he had some business sense, Old Dick would probably relent.

Bertram poured himself another whisky. There was no hurry to find himself a wife. He would soon be raking in money hand over fist from his warehouse, through his own efforts, and he meant to enjoy it. As long as he could stay solvent, he could live it up.

Bertram was returning to the warehouse each afternoon with a pad filled with orders. 'It's easy as pie,' he exulted to Cissie. 'I've got all those old women eating out of my hand, and even some of the men are thawing to me.'

She was pleased for him. Business was booming, and he had even spoken of taking on a commercial traveller to canvass for orders, another storeman and a girl to help her in the office. He was his old charming self again, though he still hadn't recovered from her saying she didn't love him, which she regretted now. His dedication to the building up of Dickson's Supplies showed that he was not the playboy she had thought, and love had gradually crept up on her.

'Richard's surprised that Bertram's doing so well,' Phoebe remarked, one night.

'He was just unlucky before,' Cissie sighed. 'It wasn't his fault.'

'Nothing's ever his fault, according to him, so his father says. His mother spoilt him, you know. Richard doesn't speak about her much, and I don't think they got on very well.'

Cissie smiled. 'I think you get on with him pretty well.'

Blushing a little, Phoebe murmured, 'I like him.'

'Not too much, I hope.'

'If things were different, I could like him an awful lot. What about you and Bertram? What went wrong there? I thought he was quite keen on you.'

'He told me he loved me, and he was really hurt when I said I didn't love him.'

About to say that only his pride would have been hurt, her stepmother thought better of it. 'I think Richard hoped that you'd be the right one for Bertram, but I'm glad you had the sense to steer clear of him.'

'It's Bertram that steers clear. All we speak about nowadays is the warehouse, though I'm still glad I'm working for him.'

Her blush made Phoebe exclaim, 'You do love him!'

'Yes, I do, now.'

'I still don't care much for him, but if you want to patch things up, why don't you put out an olive branch?'

'We didn't quarrel.'

'He could be waiting for you to make the first move.'

'I don't want him to think I'm running after him. I'll wait a while yet, and see how I feel.'

*   *   *

Some weeks later, when Phoebe came home from being out with Richard, her eyes were so starry that Cissie said,

'What happened tonight? I can see you're excited about something.'

It was a moment before her stepmother answered. 'Richard took me to his house – and before you ask, he didn't do anything out of place. He took me into the drawing room, as he called it, and just looked at me for a minute, then he came right out and said he loved me.'

'Oh, Phoebe, what did you say?'

'I told him I loved him. It was out before I thought, so then I'd to tell him I wasn't a widow, in case he asked me to marry him. I couldn't tell him Tam was in prison, so I said we were separated, and I'd no idea where he was.'

'What did Richard say to that?'

'He said he was sorry I wasn't free, then he asked if I'd ever considered filing for divorce.'

'But can you do that when the man's in jail?

'It must be possible, or he wouldn't have said it – he knows the law better than I do – but how can I? If Tam was served divorce papers, he'd go raving mad. He might even break out of prison.'

'I believe he would.' Cissie shuddered at the thought of it. 'So that's that, is it?'

Phoebe cleared her throat nervously. 'Well, maybe this is going to sound awful, but I thought of telling Richard I had started a divorce case, then after a while, I'd say it had come through and we could go ahead and be married.'

Cissie's eyes were like saucers. 'Phoebe!' she cried. 'You can't do that! For one thing, it's not fair to Richard, and for another – oh, Phoebe, you'd be committing bigamy.'

They looked at each other uncertainly for a moment, then Phoebe, her shoulders drooping, said, 'I don't suppose I could have gone through with it, anyway. But just for a wee while, I thought – oh, I love him so much, and he treats me like no man ever treated me before. He makes me feel as though I'm really somebody, not just a tart he's picked up.'

Understanding for the first time how much Phoebe had hated the life she had led in Aberdeen, Cissie said, 'You'll still see him, though?'

'If he wants me to, but he might lose interest now.'

They said no more, but Cissie couldn't sleep for thinking. Phoebe deserved some happiness after all she'd been through, but it was unlikely that she would ever dare to divorce Tam.

Cruising round the streets looking for a promising young thing to pick up, Bertram was delighted to see Millie Winton striding along on her own. She'd been like the damned Elusive Pimpernel, and he'd given up hope of finding her. Stopping the car, he called, 'Hi, Millie, are you at a loose end?'

'Why?' she laughed, not stopping. 'Do you want to hitch on to me?'

'Why not?' He jumped out and took her arm.

'Where are we going?'

'To have something to eat, if you haven't eaten already?'

'No, I haven't, I was on my way home.'

He took her to the Caledonian Hotel, very expensive, but he considered it would be money well spent. Millie was good company, and to get her in a receptive mood he plied her with wine while they dined. Soon, her naturally flirtatious eyes were holding his across the table, her knees rubbing against his under the table, and he was sure that she would accept the proposal he meant to make later. He had the looks and the magnetism, hadn't he? He was waiting until he had her alone, so that he could try some gentle persuasion if necessary, but he didn't think it would be. She was the youngest daughter of a Member of the House of Commons and his father and grandfather would be impressed if he landed her.

Millie did not demur when Bertram suggested a late night spin, and he drove to his usual secluded spot. 'Ooh,' she giggled, as he drew up amongst the trees, 'I hope you're not after what I think you're after, Bertram.'

'Would you be annoyed if I was?' he parried, placing his mouth over hers so that she couldn't answer.

'Oh, Millie, my darling,' he breathed in a moment, letting his hands slip down to her breasts. She was kissing him so ardently that he wondered if he should wait until after he had done the necessary before he popped the question, but she had rebuffed him any time he went too far before. It would be better to let her know he was serious this time.

Her pelvis moving under him, she whispered, 'Oh, Bertram, your kisses were always so thrilling.'

'Millie, my angel, will you marry me?' His voice was thick with passion.

Her only reply was to pull him closer, and, believing that this signified acceptance, he squeezed her nipple with one hand and lifted her skirt with the other.

She struggled free. 'Don't get too worked up,' she said, in the supercilious tone which had put him off her before. 'I'm not one of the little tarts I'm told you dally with.'

'Who told you that?'

'Word gets around, you know.'

'But I asked you to marry me and you let me think you . . .'

She gave a little smirk at that. 'Yes, I did, didn't I?'

Recalling the incident the following forenoon, he thought ruefully that he should have known she was making a fool of him, but he had believed she was playing hard to get and had forced her down on her back to teach her a lesson. That was when her knee came up and caught him on the balls. She'd had to wait until he got over the pain before he could drive her home, and she'd actually laughed when she got out of the car. 'How did it feel to be at the receiving end for a change?'

He'd still been too sore to retaliate, and had driven away

seething. He was finished with girls – toffee-nosed girls like Millie Winton, anyway, who thought they could rule the world because their fathers were somebody and were filthy rich. His own father and grandfather had pots of money – though he wouldn't get his hands on any of it until the pair of them handed in their cards. He would be quite well off himself when he reached twenty-five and got the inheritance his mother had left him. As it was, he wouldn't be so bad if his income would only keep pace with his expenditure, but he'd had to take more and more out of his business lately to pay for his pleasures. He'd have to go easy for a while.

'Bertram, have you a minute?'

Oh, God, he thought. What was coming now? 'Yes, Cissie?'

'I was just going to say . . .' She stopped, then carried on, her cheeks reddening, 'Did you know your father and Phoebe love each other? Wouldn't it be great if they got married?'

He was not to know that Cissie was trying to turn his mind to marriage in the hope that he would consider her as a possible bride, nor had he the slightest idea that Phoebe's circumstances prevented her from marrying, so he was utterly horrified. Fighting back a wave of hysteria, he managed to stammer, 'I hadn't thought about it.'

He was glad when Cissie's head bent to her work again, for it gave him peace to think. He hadn't suspected that things were so serious between his father and Phoebe, and if they did marry, how would it affect him? Surely the bitch was too old to produce another heir to the Dickson wealth? How old did a woman have to be before her child-bearing days were over, for God's sake? He didn't even know when they started. He didn't know the first thing about the workings of the female body, though he had explored plenty of them. Christ, Cissie had dealt him a worse blow than Millie Winton!

Bertram took a deep breath to steady his jangling nerves. Even if Phoebe couldn't produce an heir, she would still be dangerous as his father's wife. He could sense that she didn't like him – the feeling was mutual – and once she started interfering, he could say goodbye to any more 'loans' from his father. But surely Pater wouldn't marry into the common herd, not when his first wife had been a Moncrieff and could trace her ancestry back to William the Conqueror? Of course, Old Dick's wife had been a weaver – 'Worth a dozen Lydias,' he was fond of saying – so he had likely encouraged their match. He seemed to have a penchant for the lower orders, who were all right in their place, but, Bertram thought viciously, should damn well stay there!

Chapter Eighteen

❖

1922

Since Richard Dickson put the idea of divorce into her head, Phoebe had thought of little else. As her husband, he could give her love and financial security and he would protect her if Tam broke out of jail to look for her. Nobody had ever escaped from Peterhead Prison and stayed free, but there was always a first time, and when Tam set his mind to something, nothing would stop him. Besides, there was Cissie to worry about; her father blamed her for having him locked away, and he would likely want to punish her, as well.

Having spent months agonising, she remembered that Tam would have no idea where his wife and daughter were. Even if he went to Schoolhill and asked Marie, she couldn't tell him, for she had only heard them say they might go to Dundee, and Dundee was a big city. They should be safe as houses – shouldn't they?

Phoebe came to a decision when she was getting ready to meet Richard one night. She would go through with the plan she'd outlined to Cissie: she would tell Richard she had applied for a divorce, wait a month or so and then say the decree had come through. That way he would marry her in all good faith, and Tam would be none the wiser. And even if Tam were to find out, under Richard's roof, not even he could harm her. The deceit would shock Cissie, but it wasn't Cissie's life that was being wasted.

Her stomach was churning when Richard opened his car door for her, and he looked surprised when she said, forcing the words out nervously, 'Would you mind just taking me back to Huntingdon tonight? I've something private to say to you.'

They were sitting down in his large drawing room before he said, smiling fondly at her, 'Now, my dear, what do you have to say that's so very private?'

She loved him so much that the lie almost stuck in her throat. 'I've . . . I've seen a solicitor about divorcing Tam.' It was out, though she was shaking like a leaf in a force nine gale.

Richard leaned forward eagerly. 'Oh, Phoebe, I'm so glad! Does he think there will be any difficulties? How long will it take? What did he ask you?'

Wishing miserably that she had some idea of the procedures involved, she stared hopelessly at him, then a tear trickled down her cheek. Seeing her distress, Richard jumped out of his high-backed leather chair and went to kneel by her side. 'Oh, my dearest,' he murmured, taking her hand and squeezing it. 'Don't be upset at breaking the marriage vows you made so long ago. Your husband broke his when he left you.'

Her tears gathered momentum, and in the next instant she burst out, unable to stop herself and sobbing as if her heart would break, 'It wasn't like that, Richard. You don't know the half of it.'

'Don't cry, my dear,' he said, compassionately. 'Tell me what's troubling you and perhaps I can help. I'd like to know about your life before you came to Dundee.'

Wordlessly, she shook her head, but he persisted, trying to make it sound jocular, 'Once you're my wife, you can't keep secrets from me, so you may as well tell me now.'

'You won't want me to be your wife after I tell you.'

'Phoebe, my dear, I'll still want to marry you whatever you tell me.'

Her shuddering sigh seemed to be dredged up from the very soles of her feet. 'You'd better sit down, Richard, it's a long, complicated story.'

Waiting until he had settled again, she said, unsteadily, 'I'll have to start when I was only seventeen, so you can understand better.' At his puzzled nod, she told him about her life in the Black Isle, and how her father had thrown her out.

'He must have been extremely narrow-minded,' Richard said, sadly. 'Couldn't you have convinced him . . .'

'He wouldn't listen, and in a way, I was glad, for he'd hardly ever let me out of his sight before.'

'Was that when you came to Dundee? I was sure there was something behind your working as a spinner.'

'Oh, no! There's a lot more, worse than that.' She continued with her story until she reached her arrival in Aberdeen, then she paused and looked at him in despair. 'I hadn't been brought up to earn my living, and I didn't know anything about life in a big city, and when I couldn't find a steady job, I . . .' her voice faltered, '. . . I found I could make money by . . . selling my body.'

Richard quickly smothered his gasp. 'You mean you turned to prostitution?'

She could tell by his expression how horrified he was and made a move to stand up and leave, but he gestured to her to remain where she was. His voice was harsh, however, when he said, 'Go on. You haven't told me about your marriage, nor why your husband left you. I take it that he found out what you had been doing?'

Shaking her head ruefully, she told him how she had met Big Tam. 'He knew all about me, that's why he asked me to go and keep house for him, but what he really wanted was to sleep with me. I didn't care, for I'd slept with other men, and I couldn't help liking him.'

While she was speaking, she recalled her promise never to tell anyone that Tam had been the father of Cissie's child, and not even to blacken his character and make things easier for herself could she break that promise. She cast around in her mind for something that would explain why Tam had been locked away. 'He didn't marry me till a long time after, and I was happy for a while, even though he'd an awful temper. When he'd had a few drinks, the least thing would start him fighting. Then he – he got a girl in trouble.'

She was floundering now, and the anguish on Richard's face was making it more difficult. 'Her – her father confronted him with it, and he lost his head altogether, Tam, I mean. He – I don't really know how it happened and I don't think he meant to kill the man.' She stopped, thankful that she had invented such a credible story, then ended in a rush. 'He was tried and found guilty of manslaughter and he's serving fifteen years in Peterhead Prison.'

Looking pensive, Richard said, 'I thought I'd seen or heard the names Cissie Robertson and Phoebe McGregor at some time before, and now I remember. There was quite a lot of publicity about the case at the time, and I followed reports of the trial in the newspapers. It was Cissie's husband he killed, wasn't it? And her child – his own grandson.'

Phoebe hung her head. At least the police, and the reporters, had never uncovered the whole truth. She waited for Richard to denounce her for being a liar as well as a prostitute, but he was sitting stone-faced, mulling over what had been said. This was much worse, for he wasn't giving her a chance to defend herself. Miserably, she rose to her feet and left the house quietly. It was all over between them, as she had known it would be when he learned about her past life.

Earlier that same night, Bertram had gone to meet Brenda, the girl Cissie had taken on three weeks before to help her. He had been pleasantly surprised when he saw her first, a fourteen-year-old blonde with wide, baby blue eyes and full lips. Not only that, she had a silhouette like an hourglass and his hands had itched to squeeze her swinging

173

breasts, so he could hardly believe his luck when Brenda gave him a blatant 'come-hither' look. When he found an opportunity, he arranged to meet her and had discovered her to be something of a man-eater. At first, he had enjoyed the novelty of a woman taking the lead, but she was beginning to bore him. He would have to think of a way to brush her off.

When he drew his new Riley up at the Royal Arch — erected in Dock Street many years before for a visit from Queen Victoria — Brenda was waiting, and, watching her as she stood looking down at the water, he cringed with embarrassment at the brevity of her skirt. She was a common little tart, and he should never have had anything to do with her.

She turned round then and came over to him, simpering as he held the door of the car open for her. Once inside, she said, 'I thought you weren't coming, Bertram.'

He nearly told her it would be the last time, but he may as well have his fun first. 'Sorry, my pet, I was held up.'

He kept his eyes away from the long expanse of silk-clad legs; time enough for that. 'I thought we'd have a wee run somewhere, since it's so warm.'

There was something different about her tonight, something that made him vaguely uneasy, but, telling himself that her peculiar half-smile only signified pride at being on such intimate terms with her boss, he drove up into the hills and stopped where no one would see or hear them. 'Out you get.'

She lay down on the old waterproof he kept in the boot for such eventualities, and he was about to kiss her when she pushed him away. 'My Dad wants to see you.'

He didn't have to ask why. Only a pregnancy would make a girl's father want to see the man she was involved with. 'How far on are you?' he muttered.

'I've missed twice, and Dad says you'll have to marry me all the sooner.'

'I never had any intention of marrying you, you little fool!' Bertram's insides were heaving, and he had difficulty in keeping his hands from her throat. This was a sickener, all right, but surely to God he would manage to wriggle out of it. He wanted an heir, but this teenage hussy would not be acceptable to his family as his wife.

Brenda's eyes filled with tears. 'I'd never have let you talk me into it if I'd known you weren't serious about me.'

'Me talk you into it? That's a laugh! You damned near had the trousers off me the first five minutes I was with you.'

'Oh, Bertram,' she wailed, 'I don't know how can you say a thing like that.'

'It's true, that's how! You've likely been at it with so many men you don't even know whose brat it is.'

'I haven't been with anybody else, honest I haven't.'

'Honest? You little bitch! You haven't an honest bone in your body. I bet you planned this from the start.'

'No, Bertram,' she sobbed, 'I never wanted this to happen, and my Dad says if you don't marry me, he'll have you up for interfering with an underage girl.'

Bertram cursed his own stupidity, but continued to brazen it out. 'I don't care what your father says. I'm damned sure I'm not the only one you've been messing with, you little tramp, and I'm not taking the rap for your bastard.' Her loud crying was getting on his nerves, so he snapped, 'Stop your bawling, for Christ's sake!'

'You're the only one,' she hiccuped. 'I swear it, and my Dad'll make you marry me.'

Knowing how pugilistic some working-class men were, he wondered feverishly how he could get out of this. 'Look, how about if I pay for an abortion? Would that satisfy him?'

Her tears stopped as if turned off at a mains. 'How much?'

He relaxed. Money always talked. 'Say five hundred?

That's a bloody sight more than it'll cost you to get the job done. On one condition. You have stopped working for me as from tonight. I don't want to see you again.'

She gave a sly smile. 'You'll have to see me to give me the money.'

Damn her! Bertram thought. If he could be sure she was setting him up, he'd tell her to go to hell, but she could be telling the truth. 'I'll need a couple of days, and you'd better phone in tomorrow and tell Cissie your mother's ill and you'll have to give up your job, or some excuse like that, otherwise she'll wonder why you haven't turned up.'

After he dropped Brenda – round the corner from her house in case her father really was on the warpath for him – he drove slowly home. He had got out of it rather neatly, but why had he been so stupid as to offer her so much? She would likely have been satisfied with one hundred, and his father wasn't going to be pleased about having to stump up another half grand.

Bertram was in luck, however. Richard had more worrying things on his mind that night, and wrote out a cheque for five hundred pounds without even asking why he needed it.

*   *   *

Having been certain that Richard would be so disgusted he would have nothing more to say to her except to tell her that she no longer had a job, Phoebe was astounded when he came to her the following morning and said, 'Will you come to dinner at Huntingdon tonight? We have a lot to thrash out and both my father and Bertram will be out.'

Her mind was not on her work that day, it was too occupied in wondering what they had to thrash out. He knew that she had once been a prostitute, and that Tam was in prison for manslaughter, so he wouldn't want to marry her now.

Richard kept her in suspense until they had eaten the

meal the housekeeper served, then, after saying that he wanted no interruptions, he led Phoebe to the drawing room. 'I expect you're wondering why I brought you here tonight,' he began, 'and, to be honest, I'm not too sure myself.'

Her heart plummeted. He must have regretted not telling her what he thought of her before. 'Go on then, Richard,' she said, quietly. 'I deserve all you're going to say.'

An expression of pain crossed his face. 'First of all, I must tell you that I understand why you lied about your husband's victims. You had not wanted to bring Cissie into it, and I admire you for that. However, as you no doubt gathered, I was struck dumb by the other things you told me, although I felt like taking you by the scruff of the neck and throwing you out. What did you hope to achieve by deceiving me? Did you expect me to marry you after you told me you were free? Did you plan to take all my money and then look for another fool to fleece?'

She had let him go on, her head bowed in acceptance of his anger, but now she looked up. 'It had nothing to do with your money, Richard. I love you.'

'Yet you didn't tell me the truth about your past life — not until I dragged it out of you.'

'I knew what would happen. I knew you wouldn't understand what despair and hopelessness can drive a woman to do, and you don't know what it's meant to me to have a man treat me so gently, so lovingly.' Wiping away a tear, she stood up. 'I'm sorry if you think I made a fool of you, because I didn't mean to. I know I've hurt you, and that's the last thing I wanted to do, so I'd better say goodbye and leave.' She was anxious to go before she lost control of herself altogether.

'Not yet!'

She waited reluctantly to hear what other accusations he had to fling at her, but he seemed to be struggling with his own emotions. At last he said, his voice so low that she had to strain to hear it, 'Oh, Phoebe, I'm torn apart. You have no idea what this is doing to me. I even considered suggesting that you be my wife in everything but name, but I couldn't insult you like that. Oh, I know you've done that kind of thing before,' he added as she opened her mouth, 'but I can't ask it of you. It is against my own morals.' He lapsed into silence again, as if searching for a compromise, and when he spoke, it was almost as if to himself. 'I wonder if it is possible for us to go on as before?'

Phoebe held her breath. Why was he prolonging her agony? He must be disgusted at what she had done, so why didn't he tell her straight out that he was finished with her? Or had he not made up his mind yet? Maybe it would be best if she made it up for him. 'I think I should leave, Richard,' she murmured. 'I should have told you before, and I know you'll never be able to forgive me for being what I was.'

'What you were,' he corrected her, 'and I don't condemn you, not now. I only feel pity that a woman as young as you were should have had to resort to prostitution.' He gazed at her mournfully for a moment, then said, 'I lay awake all last night trying to visualise my life without you, and I couldn't. Besides, it was as though you had been talking about another Phoebe, not the one I've grown to love with all my heart.' He stopped with a groan. ' Oh, my dear, you're a part of me now, a vital part. If I lost you, I wouldn't want to go on living. I'm pleading with you now to divorce your husband so that I can make you my wife.'

The entreaty in his eyes made her want to cry out, 'Yes, yes, Richard,' but she couldn't. 'I'm scared of what he'll do,' she whispered. 'I told you he'd a temper, and when he gets the papers telling him about the divorce, he'll want to kill me, and he'll break out of jail. He doesn't know where I am, but I'm sure he'll find me.'

'Your address would be on the notification.'

'Oh!' she gasped, in dismay. 'I can't chance it, then.'

With a low moan, Richard came across to her and took her in his arms. 'I'm not getting any younger, you know.'

'Neither am I. I'm thirty-nine.'

'And I'm fifty-six.'

He kissed her then, a kiss that told her far better than words how deeply he felt about her, and unable to hold out against him any longer, she said, 'All right, Richard, I will divorce him.'

He held her so tightly that she could hardly breathe. 'My darling, I'm so happy I could – oh, I just don't know what I could do. I'll give you my solicitor's name and address, and he'll make it as easy for you as he can.'

When Bertram came in, he frowned when he saw Phoebe. He had never liked her – he had the feeling she could see right through him.

'I'm glad you're home,' Richard smiled, 'so I can tell you our good news. Phoebe has done me the honour of promising to be my wife. You may not be aware that she isn't a widow, but I have persuaded her to divorce her husband, and we'll marry as soon as she is free, which should not be long.' He eyed his son quizzically. 'Aren't you going to congratulate us?'

Bertram's eyes were hard. 'Congratulate you?' he burst out. 'For letting a common spinner take my mother's place? If that woman's moving in here, I'm moving out.'

'You're a grown man, Bertram, don't act like a child,' Richard said, adding peremptorily, 'Apologise to Phoebe.'

'You've a hope! If you think I'll stay here and watch you making a fool of yourself with this – with this gold-digger, you're right up a gum tree. What Mother left me comes to me when I'm twenty-five, and that's only a couple of months away, so I can buy myself a house. I won't need you.'

His face now as suffused with anger as his son's, Richard said, 'What your Mother left you won't last long at the rate you spend. I can guarantee that within a few years you'll be crawling back here asking me to get you out of another fix. You're a waster. A complete waster.'

'Well,' Bertram sneered, 'it's good to know what my father thinks of me, but you haven't much room to speak, have you? You've been carrying on with this . . .' He turned to Phoebe and spat out, 'You trapped him into it, you bitch!'

When he slammed out, Phoebe burst into tears. 'I can't go through with it, Richard. Not if it means causing trouble between you and your son.'

'Please, Phoebe, don't change your mind because of him.'

'Your father'll likely think the same as Bertram.'

'My father thinks the world of you, my dear.'

At that moment, the door opened and Old Dick himself came in, hesitating when he saw Richard with his arms round the weeping Phoebe. 'Maybe I'd better go out again?'

'No, it's all right, Father. Bertram's been saying some rather nasty things about Phoebe and she's a bit upset.'

'That boy needs his arse kicked,' the old man declared, at which even Phoebe gave a tight little smile.

'We're going to be married as soon as she is divorced, and when I told Bertram, he said . . .'

The old man gave a snorting laugh. 'You don't need to tell me – he hates the idea of another woman taking his mother's place. Never mind, lass, you're a better person than Lydia ever was – her and her lah-di-dah family. She looked down her nose at me for calling a spade a spade, you know. Oh, I maybe go a wee bit far at times, but me and you'll get on fine. You'll not go into a fit of the vapours if I happen to let off some wind.'

She couldn't laugh, as he had no doubt expected, but he had certainly made her feel much better.

*   *   *

180

In his room, Bertram was pacing the floor in fury. So many weeks had passed since Cissie had scared the shit out of him by hinting this might happen that he'd come to think it had blown over. Taken by surprise, he hadn't been able to stop himself. Tonight's debacle had probably ruined any chance he had of getting a penny of the Dickson money. No man could have made a better job of doing himself out of his inheritance than he had.

It was too late now to do anything as far as his father was concerned. His old man knew him too well to believe any apologies he made, so that was out. And he would have to leave now he'd said he would; he wouldn't climb down over that. Still, if he kept to the straight and narrow long enough for Dickson's Supplies to show a whacking great profit, he might get round Old Dick, though giving up his women and gambling would be an awful sacrifice to make. He may as well be dead!

He perked up suddenly. Never say die! It would take time for Phoebe to get her divorce, maybe long enough to let him talk Cissie into marrying him. She was the only one of his acquaintances his grandfather would approve of, and she wasn't one of those clinging vine types. He could probably mould her into shape as a suitable wife for a successful businessman and a suitable mother for the heir to the family fortune. If that didn't send him soaring up in his father's – and his grandfather's – estimation, nothing would.

Lighting a Sobranie, Bertram stretched himself flat on the bed and tried to work out a plan of action. The first thing would be to find himself a place to live; not anything fancy because he'd only need it until his house was ready, the house he intended to have built with his mother's money. He would hire an architect to draw up plans to his specifications – a house worth calling a house, something that would outshine his father's or, at the very least, equal it.

He went straight to Cissie's desk the following morning.

'I don't know what you must think of me,' he said, trying to look ashamed. 'I've been acting like a spoiled brat. I was hurt because you said you didn't love me, and I've wasted so much time. Can you forgive me?'

'Yes, of course I can,' she smiled, her heart speeding up with joy.

'I realise now that people can't love to order.'

She looked at him shyly. 'I didn't say I could never love you, Bertram.'

His eyes lit up. 'You mean . . . you could?'

'I could,' she smiled.

So far, so good, he thought, picking up the telephone as soon as it rang. 'Dickson's Supplies . . . What? . . . Oh God! . . . How bad is it? . . . Yes, I'll come straight away.'

The blood had drained from his face when he laid down the receiver and turned to Cissie. 'My grandfather's been in an accident, and Father says it's very bad.'

'Oh, Bertram, I'm so sorry! Is there anything I can do?'

'I don't know how long I'll be at the hospital, and that's our date knocked on the head.'

'It doesn't matter. Off you go, I'll hold the fort here.'

A dishevelled and very anxious Richard met him in the hospital corridor. 'The doctors don't hold out much hope.'

'How did it happen?'

'As far as I can gather, he stepped off the pavement in front of a bus. I wish I'd paid someone to look after him during the day, he shouldn't have been out on his own. He was inclined to be doddery at times.'

Just then, the doctor came out of the private ward. 'I'm afraid there's nothing more we can do,' he said, sadly, 'it's just a matter of time. We've given him something to deaden the pain and you can go in for a few minutes.'

Bertram followed his father, not knowing what to expect, and the sight of the lacerated face and the head swathed in bandages made him feel ill. 'Bertram and I are both here, Father,' Richard said, gently.

The one uncovered eye swivelled round. 'Silly bugger,' the old man said, faintly.

For one awful moment, Bertram thought that his grandfather meant him, but the feeble voice went on, 'Never saw that – damn bus.'

Richard leaned forward. 'Don't try to talk, Father.'

'Not long . . . time's come . . . keep Phoebe . . . happy.'

'I intend to. Please rest now.'

The eye tried to focus on Bertram, but the effort was too much, and in the next second it had glazed over. The doctor who had been standing by stepped forward and lifted the old man's hand to check his pulse. 'He's gone, I'm afraid,' he said, sympathetically.

In something of a daze, Bertram walked into the corridor and waited for his father. 'What happens now?'

'I'll have to get the death certificate before I can arrange the funeral, but there's no need for you to wait.' Richard's voice broke suddenly. 'What an awful way to go. I know you didn't get on with him, Bertram, but I loved him. For all his faults, I loved him.'

It was the first time Bertram had ever seen a man weep, and without warning a huge lump came into his throat. 'I . . . loved him, too.' He was astonished at himself, but it was true. From the stories he had heard about his grandfather, they had been two of a kind, with an eye for a pretty woman, although the old boy probably hadn't been as bad as he was. Besides, Old Dick had been a widower for over thirty years, and no matter how many women he had been involved with, he had never neglected the mill or used the profits unwisely.

Richard gave him a little push. 'You'd better go, Bertram, I'll see to everything.'

Unable to face going back to the warehouse, he drove home, telling Mrs Frain the bad news before going to his father's study for a whisky. It was he who had been the silly bugger, he thought. If only he hadn't been so damned stubborn, he would have done as his father and grandfather expected. A few years of hard work in the mill and he'd have been in clover. He'd have got half his grandfather's money and been an equal shareholder with his father. Instead of which, he'd annoyed Old Dick so much that he'd left him nothing. Bertram Dickson, self-professed entrepreneur, had lost a fortune by his own stupidity.

Filling his glass again and draining it quickly, he felt better. All was not completely lost. His grandfather's money would pass to his father and would still be in the Dickson family, and even if Phoebe McGregor got half eventually, there would still be quite a considerable sum for him — if he shaped up to his father's ideal of what a good son should be. Marriage to Cissie was now a necessity — and a son to make doubly sure nothing went wrong. As her stepmother, Phoebe would make sure that Cissie's child inherited a hefty amount when the time came.

*   *   *

Cissie's heart went out to Bertram when he came back to work after the funeral. 'I'm truly sorry about your grandfather,' she murmured, awkwardly, and was surprised to see a muscle jumping at his jaw. She hadn't thought he had been so fond of the old man, but it seemed he was very upset.

'Yes, it's been a bit of a blow.' He cleared his throat. 'Any problems while I've been off?'

'No, everything's fine.'

'I don't know what I'd have done without you. Oh, what about that date I'd to cancel? Shall we make it tonight?'

Two days later, when they were checking over some figures together, he said, 'I've found myself a house, so I'll be moving out of Huntingdon tomorrow afternoon. I'd only be in the way there once my father marries.'

'Maybe it's best,' she said.

'I'll be packing some stuff tonight, so I won't see you,

184

nor tomorrow night, because I'll be arranging things in my new home.'

'That's all right. I understand.'

Once the move was made, Bertram saw Cissie every night for weeks, and although he never actually said he still loved her, she was sure that he did. When she shyly told him how much she loved him, he breathed, 'Thank God! I couldn't have borne it if you'd rejected me again.'

A few days later, while she was finishing work for the day, rather disappointed that he hadn't said he would call for her later, he came up behind her. 'I'm taking you home with me tonight, my darling. I've something to ask you.'

While she waited for him to lock up, she puzzled over what he might be going to ask her. Could he possibly be going to ask her to marry him? Was he taking her home with him to get her approval of the house they would be sharing?

In the car, she tried to picture what it would look like. A small cottage, perhaps, with a little garden front and back? A slightly larger house, but not as big as Huntingdon? She tried to imagine herself cooking in a modern kitchen on the latest model gas stove, then in her mind's eye, she saw an airy bedroom with a double bed covered by an eiderdown, and hastily turned her head away so that Bertram wouldn't see her blushes.

'Here we are,' he announced, breaking into her thoughts as he stopped outside a tenement in Lochee. Noticing that she looked disappointed, he added, 'This is only a stop-gap, and I took it furnished. It's not my style, but at least I'm on my own, that's why I brought you here.'

She followed him up to the top floor and found that the small flat was quite comfortably furnished, but when she sat down on the sofa, it wasn't as comfortable as it looked.

'I don't make any meals here,' he said, apologetically, 'so I can't offer you tea, but would you care for a sherry?'

'No thank you.'

'Do you mind if I have a drink? I'm building up my courage to say something I've never said in my life before.'

Sure now of what he was going to say, her heart hammered wildly, and she was happy to let him take his time over it.

He poured himself a small glass of whisky, then looked at her with his eyebrows raised. 'First, I must ask you this. Are you quite sure you love me now?'

'Completely sure,' she breathed.

Downing the spirits, he said, 'Will you marry me. Cissie?'

'Oh yes, Bertram,' she murmured. What did it matter that it wasn't the romantic proposal she had dreamt of?

A little smile flickered at the corner of his mouth as he laid his glass down and sat beside her, his arm round her shoulders. 'I'm not a churchgoer, and I'd hate to be a hypocrite by asking a clergyman to marry us, so how do you feel about a civil ceremony?'

'I don't care,' she laughed, almost swooning when his lips came down tenderly on hers. This – he – would be her future.

'Oh, Cissie,' he said, in a few minutes. 'You've made me very happy. Shall we go out for a meal to celebrate? I'll buy you an engagement ring tomorrow, then I'll show you the house I'm having built for us.'

'Were you so sure I'd accept you?' she smiled, quite glad that they wouldn't be living in the tenement, though she wouldn't really have minded wherever he wanted to live.

'Positive,' he grinned.

'Where have you been?' demanded Phoebe when Cissie went in some hours later. 'I waited supper for you, but when you weren't home by half past six, I took mine.'

'I've had mine, too,' Cissie smiled. 'Bertram treated me.'

'You're seeing an awful lot of him these days, I hope it's not serious.'

'So serious I'm going to marry him. He asked me tonight.'

Phoebe's eyebrows had shot down. 'I wasn't going to tell you this, Cissie, I didn't think it mattered, but he was boiling mad when Richard told him we were getting married.'

'He'd likely be jealous his father thinks so much of you, that's all. He's really nice, you know.'

'I know I encouraged you to patch things up with him, but I thought you'd soon see how shallow he was, and give him his marching orders. Oh. Cissie, he's not the man for you.'

'He is, Phoebe, he is. You're marrying the man you love, and surely you don't grudge me some happiness?'

'If only I could be sure he'd make you happy, Cissie, I'd be delighted.'

'He will make me happy, I know he will.'

*   *   *

Cissie would have been less sure if she had known that on his way home, her husband-to-be was congratulating himself on the way he had handled her. He had got her to say she'd marry him, yet he hadn't sinned his soul by saying again that he loved her. Not that he'd have worried about sinning his soul, he was quite an expert at it, but he didn't want to give her anything to hold over his head if he changed his plans – though he didn't think he would. Another thing, he wouldn't jeopardise his chances with her by indulging in any attempts at pre-marital hanky-panky with her, or with anyone else. Apart from Cissie's reaction if she were to find him out, she would tell Phoebe, who would tell his father – who was now in sole control of the entire Dickson fortune.

Chapter Nineteen

After admiring the huge diamond in Cissie's engagement ring, Phoebe tried one last time to make her stepdaughter see that it would be a mistake to marry Bertram. 'Are you sure?' she asked, with her eyebrows raised. 'Really sure?'

'Two hundred per cent sure.'

'He didn't threaten to fire you if you refused to marry him?'

Cissie tried not to show how much this pained her. She had never understood what Phoebe had against him. 'He'd never do a thing like that – he's decent – he hasn't done anything to me he shouldn't, not once.'

This astonished Phoebe, who had been sure Bertram was out for all he could get – with women and everything else. His father had hinted at it often enough. 'Do you really love him enough to marry him?'

'More than enough,' Cissie smiled, 'and he's even started building a house. He took me to see it after we came out of the jeweller's. It's not long started, but it's nearly as big as Huntingdon, and Bertram's waiting to see when it'll be ready before he fixes the date of the wedding.'

Phoebe stifled her doubts. Nothing she said would make any difference. 'Well, just remember, if you ever need me, you know where to find me.'

Cissie's smile disappeared. 'I'll never need anybody but Bertram, still I hope we'll stay friends, Phoebe.'

'I'll always be your friend, you know that, but Bertram doesn't like me.'

'Maybe he thinks you've turned his father against him, but when he sees you haven't, he'll come round.'

'I suppose so,' Phoebe sighed, certain in her own mind that he would never be friendly towards her, and not even sure that she wanted it.

As the weeks passed, so Phoebe's fear of what Tam would do when he got the solicitor's letter lessened. What could he do? He could never escape from Peterhead Prison and he still had eleven years to serve. When they released him, he would be an old man and would have got over his anger. She had been worrying for nothing, like Richard always said.

The beginning of 1923 brought storms which slowed down progress on the building of the new house. At times, when snow-laden gales swept round the site and made it dangerous for the men to be on the scaffolding, work stopped altogether. Bertram, of course, hounded the foreman, who turned on him one day. 'I've no control over the weather, Mr Dickson. You'll just need to have patience.'

Desperate though he was to be married before his father and Phoebe, Bertram could not argue with this logic, and tried to pacify the man. 'I can't set the date of my wedding till I know when the house is going to be ready.'

'Well, barring any more storms, we should have the roof on by next week, then it's plain sailing.'

'Could you give me any idea how much longer?'

Reluctant to commit himself, the foreman mumbled, 'Well, I'd say four or five weeks, maybe.'

'Four,' Bertram cajoled. 'I'll make it worth your while.'

'Right, four it is.'

That afternoon, Bertram went to the Registrar's Office and set the wedding for four weeks' time, gloating that he was beating his father to it. He was not to know that Phoebe had been notified some time ago that she had to appear in the divorce court in Edinburgh the following day – she had not told Cissie because she wanted Bertram to have the shock of his life when it was sprung on him after the event. She also guessed that he had not got over being left nothing in his grandfather's will, and hoped that his father's marriage might make him so angry that he would fall out with Cissie, who, hopefully, would break off that engagement. She deserved better than that rotter.

Driving Phoebe home, Richard said, 'How do you feel now, my dear? It wasn't such an ordeal as you feared.'

It had been more of an ordeal for her than he knew. While the case against Tam was being made – he had not contested it – Phoebe had prayed that Cissie's name would not be dragged through the mud again and she had almost collapsed with relief when the victims of the manslaughter remained unnamed. If Richard's solicitor had looked up the case, he had kept that information to himself. Remembering that she still hadn't answered Richard, she said, 'Everything went off better than I thought.'

The banns having been cried as soon as Phoebe had been given the date of the case, their wedding took place two weeks later, with only Cissie and a friend of Richard's present. Bertram had been asked, but no one was surprised that he preferred to stay away. 'He'll be ashamed of himself for the things he said,' Cissie excused him, and although Richard and Phoebe knew different, they did not disillusion her.

'I have made Phoebe give up her job,' Richard said, when he was driving Cissie home that evening, 'and I am putting a man in to manage the mill for me. Of course, I'll have to check up occasionally to make sure he's coping, but I want to spend as much time with my wife as I can.' He looked at Cissie quickly. 'I hope you don't think I am acting like a love-sick old fool?'

'I think Phoebe's very lucky to have a husband like you.'

'It is I who am the lucky one, Cissie.'

*   *   *

While the minister conducted the ceremony in Huntingdon, Bertram had been in his eyrie in Lochee trying to drown his anger that Phoebe had won the race, but, sober the following morning, he consoled himself that it was only by a couple of weeks, and he was practically sure that his father would be a non-starter in the fatherhood stakes. His spirits lifting, he took Cissie to see his new house that evening. The labourers had cleared the debris the builders had left, the plasterers had finished and painters had begun work on the inside. He took her through the rooms, telling her what they were. On each of the first and second floors there were three rooms and a bathroom; on the ground floor, a sitting room – 'Drawing rooms are out,' he had told her – a dining room, a lavatory, and a study for him.

'I've asked the electricians to put in as many sockets as they can,' Bertram said, 'and a light on the outside wall so that it shines into the garage. What do you think of it now? Some house, eh?'

He was like a child asking for praise, she thought fondly, but he deserved it. 'It's absolutely perfect, but isn't it a bit big for us?'

'You haven't seen it all yet.' Exultantly, he took her through a door at the end of the hall, where a flight of stairs led down to the basement. 'The kitchen's fitted with all the latest appliances,' he boasted, as they went into the large square room.

Since it was below ground, she was astonished that it had a window, but he explained that, because the house was built on a hill, the kitchen was on a level with the rear garden. 'There are steps at the side, so people can get round from the front, but deliveries will be made via the back gate. Now, this is the scullery, and there are two rooms which I haven't quite decided about yet. Maybe store rooms?'

'Oh, Bertram,' she burst out, 'I'll never be able to get round all the rooms every day, not even every week.'

191

'I don't expect you to do any housework, Cissie. All I ask is that you look fetching for me when I come home at nights. I have engaged a cook and two maids to start a couple of days before the wedding, that's when I will move in.'

In his car again, Cissie took one last awed look at her future home and couldn't get over how lucky she was. She had never dreamt, when she was lying on Jen's floor, that she would ever live in a house this size. And best of all, she would be Bertram's wife, with nothing to do except look fetching for him, as he had said. She would never again have to work, or go short of anything, in her life.

When Bertram drew up in South Union Street, he said, 'I've been wondering what to call the house — nothing as inane as Huntingdon.'

'What's wrong with Huntingdon?'

'It's so unimaginative — but you don't know the story behind it. My father had been searching for months for a suitable house, and Mother hadn't approved of anything he showed her — he didn't have her exquisite taste. When he found one she did like, he said, "Thank goodness, that's my hunting done," and that's what he called it.'

His expression of distaste made her laugh. 'I think it's quite sweet.'

His nose crinkled even more. 'Exactly! Sweet! Sickly! Like the awful Dunroamings and Chez Nouses you see everywhere. I want something with a ring to it, something with panache.'

'Panache? What's that?'

A fleeting look of exasperation crossed his face before he gave a gurgling laugh. 'It means verve, bravura. Yes, what better name could I find for my house?'

She couldn't think of anything much worse, but she only said, 'How do you spell it?'

'P-A-N-A-C-H-E.'

'People might think it's pronounced Panatchie.'

'Not educated people. I'll have a nameboard made and fixed to the gate.' Pleased with his own ingenuity, he slid his arms round her, and it was several minutes before he let her out of the car.

'Goodnight, darling,' she whispered, after the final kiss at the outside door of her tenement.

'You'd better go in and get some beauty sleep, my pet,' he smiled. 'You haven't many nights left to be on your own.'

Climbing the stairs to her flat, Cissie was assailed by misgivings. Bertram had always treated her gently, but what would she do when he wanted to make love to her? She hadn't been able to respond to poor Jim Robertson after Aggie died, but that had been different. Although she had liked him, she had never loved him, and surely her love for Bertram would overcome her fear of a wife's duties.

*   *   *

Bertram dropped Cissie at her flat at five past nine on the last night of his bachelorhood, but instead of going home to Panache, he drove down to the dock area to look for someone to satisfy the desire he'd had to deny with his fiancée – it would be the last time he would need a prostitute. He saw no sign of any as the car crawled along, and he supposed they had all been picked up by seafaring men, then it crossed his mind that some of them might not have started their night's work yet. He would hang around for a while.

Drawing up and pulling out his cigarette case and lighter, he leaned back to enjoy a quiet smoke, but when he rolled down the window some ten minutes later to dispose of the stub, he was accosted by a strident female voice. 'Was you waiting for somebody, dearie?'

A painted face leered in at him, so close that he could see the pock marks on the crepey skin, and he shuddered at the idea of even touching her. 'Well,' he began, 'I . . .'

'Only ten bob an hour, mister.'

'No thank you, I'm . . .'

'Sorry I've been so long,' came another voice, a pleasant musical voice, and the raddled hag moved away, muttering.

Bertram was astonished that this elegant, well-spoken woman was a complete stranger to him, but he was grateful that she had rid him of the embarrassment. 'I saw you were being pestered,' she said. 'I hope you didn't mind me butting in?'

'I'm glad you did. May I give you a lift?'

'That's very kind of you.' She walked round to the other door and got into the car.

When he stopped at the address she gave, she said, 'Would you like to come in for a drink?'

It was two o'clock in the morning when Bertram returned to Panache. Barbara Troup had told him she was a widow and things had progressed in a most agreeable manner. She had a decent figure and was quite good-looking, though he had seen, in the harsh light from the naked electric bulb in her room, that she was much older than he had first thought. Nevertheless, he had worked on her until they ended up in bed together, and he'd been delighted when she taught him some new tricks. She had amazed him further by asking for five pounds when he was leaving, because he had not dreamt that she, too, was a prostitute – a very high-class prostitute.

As he undressed, he knew that he wouldn't be satisfied with ordinary love-making again. Even when he was married, he would visit Barbara regularly, because he couldn't make Cissie do the things he wanted – not until she gave him his son. He was living for that wonderful day when he told his father he had a grandson and saw Phoebe's face when she knew her expectations had been halved.

The ecru linen suit Bertram had bought as part of her trousseau was perfect. Cissie wished that the full-length mirror in the old wardrobe was in a better condition, but even with bits of the silvering worn off, she could see that the long jacket and straight, almost hobble, skirt suited her, and when she pinned on the corsage of pink camellias he'd had a florist deliver – the same shade as her straw hat – she looked like a model in one of the fashion magazines. Her light brown hair, with a suggestion of gold in it, was sitting in a deep wave on her forehead, and the coil Phoebe had shown her how to pin was nestling under the wide brim of her hat. Her face was perhaps a little pale, but it made her blue-green eyes stand out more. Satisfied, she picked up her handbag and went down to the waiting taxi-cab Bertram had ordered for her.

Inside the drab room, she remembered her previous wedding. She'd just had her well-worn Sunday blouse and skirt to wear then, both a little tight although she had been only three months pregnant. She had stood beside Jim Robertson, who had seemed ill at ease in his high starched collar, her heart so sore that her responses were weak. But today, looking up at Bertram, so erectly smart and handsome in his tailored, navy suit, a white carnation in his buttonhole, she could feel her heart swelling with love and pride. Concentrating on the registrar's words now, she repeated them firmly and clearly, and at last they were husband and wife.

His kiss was only a peck – probably he was embarrassed in front of the witnesses – and he made up for it by squeezing her arm as they walked out to the car which was waiting to transport them to Panache. He had offered to take her on a honeymoon to Paris, but she had been horrified at the idea of him spending so much on her. She had always had to count the pennies, and it would take time to get accustomed to having plenty.

In the taxi, Bertram said, 'I'm glad that's over. How do you feel, Mrs Dickson?'

She let the unaccustomed name swirl round in her brain,

revelling in the sound of it on his lips. 'Marvellous,' she smiled, 'but I'm glad it's over, too.'

The cook had prepared a table fit for a king – for a whole court, Cissie thought, when she saw the amount of food set in front of them – and when they had eaten their fill, they went into the sitting room. The gleaming mahogany whatnot, laden with china ornaments, the octagonal occasional table, the upright chairs padded with delicately coloured patterned velvet and the low chesterfield suite in the same material, had all been chosen by Bertram, but she didn't really mind.

She smiled as he turned to her, expecting him to take her in his arms and give her his first real kiss as her husband, but he said, 'I think we'd be more comfortable if we got out of our wedding finery.'

Wondering, with a touch of alarm, if this was his way of getting her to bed as quickly as possible, she preceded him up the wide staircase, but once in their room, he crossed to the huge wardrobe and took out two silk dressing robes. 'We can't wear them now,' she protested, 'it's still the middle of the afternoon.'

He gave a loud laugh. 'Do you think it's decadent to sit around in a robe?'

She didn't know the meaning of the word, but shook her head. 'If you think it's all right . . .'

Timidly, she opened the buttons of her jacket and took it off, glancing at him to see if he was watching, but he was intent on removing his own jacket and shirt, so she stepped out of her skirt, embarrassed to be in only her camisole, stays and petticoat, and bending quickly to lift her robe from the bed where he had thrown it.

'You'd be more at ease if you took everything off,' he told her, and she saw that he had removed his trousers and was opening his knee-length drawers. 'Don't look so scared,' he smiled, 'I'm not going to jump on you. We'll have to get used to seeing each other with nothing on.'

196

Remembering the only time in her life that anyone had seen her with nothing on, Cissie began to tremble, but she let him open the laces of her corsets for her and take off her bodice. She was reassured when he held up her robe, and slipped into it thankfully.

'See? It didn't bother me.' Bertram was standing naked in front of her, but she couldn't help noticing that her nudity had bothered him, and was glad when he covered himself and they went downstairs again.

It was more comfortable with the robe on, she discovered, and settled back against the cushions of a wide armchair to listen to Bertram making ambitious plans for the future of his business. It was not what she had imagined the first hours of their married life would be, but it was quite nice to watch the muscles of his face rippling as he talked, to see the slight shadow on his upper lip – a little gingery – for she had never seen him before when he needed a shave, nor when his hair was all tousled like it was now. It was good to have time to study him like this, his violet eyes illuminated with enthusiasm, his hands expressing points he was trying to make, though she wasn't really taking in what he was saying.

Her attention was caught when he asked her opinion on the office expansion he was contemplating. 'You'd be as well to please yourself,' she answered, carefully. 'It won't affect me now you've got a new secretary.'

His smile was indulgent. 'I couldn't have my wife working for me, Cissie, it just isn't done, but I'm quite prepared for you to give me some advice. Do you think it would be viable to use a larger part of the warehouse?'

Pleased at being consulted, she said, 'You'd lose a lot of storage space. Wouldn't it be better to pull the partition down and build a new office outside the warehouse, at the side next the street? There's plenty of room, and it would be more businesslike to have your customers coming in by a proper door into a proper office, not a wee booth.'

He considered for a few minutes, trying to visualise it, and then nodded. 'Yes, I see what you mean, and it would probably be even better if I had two offices, one for the book-keeper and typist, and an inner sanctum for myself and my secretary.'

Cissie was glad that she had chosen a plain, middle-aged widow when she was interviewing for her replacement. If his secretary had been a presentable young girl, she'd have felt jealous of her being alone with Bertram all day. She had wondered if something was going on between him and Brenda at one time, but he hadn't been in the least upset when the girl left so suddenly because of her mother's illness.

When Elma, one of the maids, came to say that dinner was ready, she was very conscious of her deshabille, but the girl showed no surprise, and Cissie assumed that robes must be normal wear for rich people.

It was coming up for eight o'clock by the time dinner was over — a lengthy interval between each course to give them time to digest it, and coffee afterwards. 'Time we turned in,' Bertram said, nonchalantly, 'it's been a long day.'

It was going to be a long night, too, Cissie thought, but she was his wife now and rose obediently from the table. As she went upstairs, she hoped he would go the bathroom to give her time to get into the lovely nightdress he'd given her, though it was so sheer it would hide nothing, but he took it from her hand as soon as she picked it off the bed where Elma must have set it out.

'You won't need this,' he murmured, throwing it carelessly on the floor and pulling off her robe.

Discarding his own, he took her in his arms, his long tender kisses calming her fears, but when he guided her to the bed they came flooding back, and she lay in an agony of terror while he ran his hands slowly over her. It was all the worse because he hadn't switched off the electric light, and she closed her eyes to shut out the increasing desire she could see in his, but it made no difference. She could feel it against her and hear it in his breathing. It was all she could do now to keep from screaming and pushing him away before he went any further.

She was so tense that it was a few seconds before she was aware that Bertram had drawn away from her and had turned to the table beside the bed to light a cigarette. Why had he stopped? Would he start again when he finished smoking? She felt sick with relief when he pulled the cord hanging from the ceiling and plunged the room into darkness.

Sooner than she thought could be possible, he was asleep, but she was still wide awake. Had he been hurt by her lack of response? Would he be angry? What would she say if he asked what was wrong with her? He knew she'd been married before, and he would wonder why she was so afraid.

At last, Cissie fell into a deep sleep and woke in the small hours of the morning to find Bertram on top of her. She hadn't time to be scared and realised that her body was responding to the stimulus he must have begun while she was still asleep. It was nothing like she had feared. He was a tender lover and brought her slowly to a point where she would have pleaded with him to go on if he had stopped again, but he didn't. It was wonderful.

Some time later, Cissie lay beside her sleeping husband, blissfully knowing that she had given him, and herself, the greatest pleasure in the world.

Being alone all day with nothing to occupy her had soon palled on Cissie. Her only diversion was in working out a menu for the evening meal which the cook would have to prepare, and that did not take long. She had been nervous, the first day, with Mrs Gow — a stout, efficient person in a long, crackling white apron and a large cap covering her greying hair – but the woman's sneering attitude had given her the boost she needed. She could now give her orders in a firm authoritative voice, though she had the feeling that the cook was only pretending to respect her. The two maids – Elma, a well-built fifteen-year-old with rather sly eyes, and shy Georgie, fourteen and still flat in the chest – kept out of her way as much as possible, and Mrs Gow made sure that they did everything they were meant to do and had no time to chatter to each other.

Bored of doing little but reading, she went to Huntingdon to talk to Phoebe, but she had forgotten that Richard would also be there. Her stepmother, now also her mother-in-law, saw her disappointment. 'Why don't we meet every Wednesday afternoon? That's when Richard goes to the mill to see that everything's running smoothly.'

Grateful that she would have company on one afternoon a week, Cissie went home early, but she could not get over the change in Phoebe. She had always been an attractive woman, but she was absolutely beautiful now – her fair-skinned face aglow with love, her dark hair arranged fashionably on top of her head – and the expensive clothes she wore made her look like a high-born lady. Just the same, Cissie reflected, thankfully, she was still the frank, down-to-earth person she had always been.

To pass her time, Cissie went for long walks, sometimes passing the time of day with the old men who were also out for a stroll to fill the long hours of their retirement, but more often chatting to one or other of the nannies who were watching their charges in whichever park she happened to be visiting. She felt at ease with them, for she was still working class at heart, though she, like Phoebe, now wore clothes bought only in the most exclusive shops. Her spirits lifted when it was time for her to go home, to dress in one of the dinner gowns Bertram kept giving her, though she only had them on for an hour or so before he made her change into a robe. He was so thoughtful, she loved him more and more as time went on, and could scarcely wait for the end of the day when he would take her to bed and prove he loved her.

It was some months after her wedding before Cissie found a friend. She had been ambling aimlessly, annoyed by the smoke which belched out of the tall chimney stacks of the mills and hung like a pall over the city when there were no winds, but she decided to have a seat in Baxter Park. It was very hot for April, and her feet were sore in the strapped, high-heeled shoes Bertram liked her to wear. She sat down on a bench to ease them, and five minutes later, another young woman sat down beside her.

'I'm glad someone else has hot feet,' the stranger smiled, glancing down at the shoes under the seat.

'It's the pavements,' Cissie excused herself, shyly.

'Don't I know it. I'm tired of wandering about all day trying to fill in my time.'

'You, too? I thought nobody else would be like me.'

'Thank goodness I've found somebody young to talk to for a change. Most of the other wives have children to keep them occupied, and it's usually middle-aged matrons I sit down beside. You know the kind.' She adopted an exaggerated accent. ' "My eldest son is at Oxford. My daughter married a Lord." ' After a little giggle, she gave Cissie a hopeful look. 'Why don't we team up? I'm Dorothy Barclay, by the way, and I've been longing for decent company.'

'Cissie Dickson, and I'd be glad of your company, too.'

At first, she worried that she might inadvertently give away her humble origins, but she soon forgot that Dorothy had been born into a different background, and the girl made a tremendous difference to her life. They met at two every weekday except Wednesdays, and went for a walk, or into a tearoom, or ambled round Draffen's or D. M. Brown's, Dorothy buying what she called suitable clothes, although she often looked longingly at those she said were considered slightly 'fast'. She was a model of elegance, wearing dresses that complemented her slim figure and hats that framed her oval face but showed little of her hair. Only once, when they were sitting in one of the parks, did she remove her hat and reveal that her hair, swathed round her head, was a lovely, smooth, silky blonde.

When Cissie told Bertram about her friend, he didn't appear particularly interested, but after a few weeks of listening to her chattering about what they had done that day, he said, somewhat peevishly, 'Can't you talk about something else? I'm tired of hearing how wonderful this Dorothy is.'

'I'm sorry,' Cissie said, 'but I haven't anything else to speak about, and I'm glad to have somebody with me instead of walking about by myself.'

'I suppose she's one of the mill-workers' wives, is she? You'll have a lot in common with her.'

'That's not a very nice thing to say,' Cissie burst out, indignantly. 'And her husband's not a mill-worker. She said he owns some boats.'

Bertram's head jerked up. 'What's her surname?'

'Barclay, and she's just a year older than me.'

'Roland Barclay's wife?'

'Yes, I think she did say his name was Roland.'

'Good God, Cissie, haven't you ever heard of him? He owns a fleet of cargo ships.' Bertram rubbed his chin with his hand, reflectively. 'It wouldn't do me any harm to get to know Roland Barclay. I've been considering branching out and taking over one of the mills. I know several in financial difficulties.'

'I thought you didn't want to have anything to do with mills.' Cissie couldn't understand why he was looking so pleased with himself.

'I didn't want to work for my father, but I can see the

possibilities of having a mill of my own, especially now. Um, will you be seeing Dorothy Barclay tomorrow?'

'No, tomorrow's my day for meeting Phoebe, remember?'

'I'd rather you didn't see that woman at all. I'm sure she's a bad influence on you.'

Cissie gave a nervous laugh. 'She doesn't try to influence me on anything, and I won't stop seeing her. She's my friend as well as my stepmother. She's your stepmother, as well, come to think of it.'

'She's a fortune-hunter, after my father's money.'

Angry now, Cissie shouted, 'She's not a fortune-hunter! She loves your father as much as he loves her. She wouldn't care if he hadn't two ha'pennies to rub together.'

He tried to pacify her then. 'All right, have it your own way. In any case, it's the Barclays I'm interested in. Next time you meet your Dorothy, invite her and her husband to dinner – say, on Saturday of next week? You can write out a special menu, and give Mrs Gow time to prepare everything.'

In bed, Bertram tried to make up for being angry at his wife. 'I'm sorry for what I said about Phoebe. I just wanted to protect you from being hurt.'

'Phoebe would never dream of hurting me, and we love each other like a real mother and daughter – more than some real mothers and daughters.'

He hesitated briefly. 'Wouldn't you like to be a mother yourself, Cissie?'

Recalling how she had felt about wee James, she had to swallow her sorrow, and was glad that the darkness hid her. 'Yes, I'd quite like to have a little daughter.'

'I want a son, Cissie.'

'All right, a daughter for me and a son for you.'

'A son first.'

'We'll have to take what comes,' she laughed.

'I can't understand why there's been no sign yet.'

She couldn't understand that herself. They'd been married for fifteen months, and once had been enough with . . . no, she couldn't think about that.

She had no time to think at all, for in the next instant Bertram's gentle lips and hands were turning her body into a quivering, eager receptacle for his loving. It certainly was not his fault that she was not pregnant yet.

Chapter Twenty

The June dinner for the Barclays was a great success. With no idea what a special menu should be, Cissie had confessed her problem, somewhat diffidently, to Mrs Gow, who had eyed her with a trace of condescension. 'I hope you don't think I'm presuming, Mrs Dickson, but I've had years of experience at catering for the gentry, and I always found they're so tired of fancy dishes, they quite enjoy plainer fare for a change. Will I make out a menu for your approval?'

Cissie had taken care not to show her resentment at the inference that she wasn't gentry. 'Yes, thank you, Mrs Gow.'

The guests were loud in praise of the creamy barley soup, enthused over the thickly sliced pork with apple sauce, accompanied by roast and mashed potatoes, sweet young peas and carrots, and, surprisingly, a whole tender cabbage. When the main course was over, a mouth-watering chocolate mousse was brought in, and Cissie leaned back in some relief as her husband and the Barclays tucked into it. She hadn't been sure of the menu Mrs Gow had suggested, but it appeared that the cook had been right.

After the coffee, Dorothy patted her stomach. 'I'm so full I'll have to let out the laces of my stays tomorrow.'

Roland's glance held a slight warning, and she winked at Cissie who said, hastily, 'Are we all ready to go through to the sitting room?'

'You two ladies carry on.' Bertram said. 'Roland and I will join you once we've had our brandy and cigars.'

When Dorothy sat down in the other room, she said,

'Trust me to put my foot in it. You've learned my little secret now.'

'I don't understand.'

'I was only a shopgirl when I married Roland. I do try to behave like a lady, but I suppose ladies don't speak about their stays in company.' She gave a tiny chuckle. 'The old words come out in spite of me, and anyway, he can be a right stuffed shirt sometimes.'

Noticing Cissie's shocked expression and believing it to show disapproval, Dorothy looked stricken. 'I should have told you before. Now you won't want to be friends with me.'

Cissie burst out laughing. 'I was Bertram's secretary when he married me, but I used to be a spinner in his father's mill, and before that, at home in Aberdeen, I served in a little dairy.'

Clapping her hands, Dorothy cried, 'So we're both common shopgirls? I thought you'd been born a lady, but I always felt comfortable with you. I never dreamt you'd been playing a part, too, and I suppose we'd better keep it up in front of our husbands. I don't know about Bertram, but Roland would be absolutely mortified if he knew I'd told you about my murky past.'

Murky past? Cissie's heart contracted at the thought of her own past, murkier than anything Dorothy could dream of, but her friend was chattering on about the gaffes she had made in front of her cook and Cissie slowly relaxed. They were both laughing when the men joined them.

Roland beamed expansively at Cissie. 'I wish my wife was more like you. She cuts out all the fancy recipes she sees in magazines and makes our cook try them out, but they're too exotic for my taste. You can't beat good plain food.'

About to explain that her cook had been responsible for the menu, Cissie caught the mischievous twinkle in

Dorothy's eye and couldn't say anything in case she laughed.

After showing their guests out, Bertram returned smiling with satisfaction. 'That went off even better than I hoped. Roland's going to give me special terms for importing and exporting once I buy a mill, so all that remains is to find the right place. He even hinted he might invest in it.'

'I'm glad everything turned out well for you, and I'll tell Mrs Gow tomorrow how much they enjoyed the meal.'

Dorothy was waiting for her the following Monday, and took her arm as if they were old chums. 'I'm glad I don't have to worry about keeping up appearances any more, so would you like me to show you the shops I used to go to? I couldn't afford to buy anything in the department stores before I married Roland.'

Recalling the dismal stalls in the market on Dock Street where Jen had taken Phoebe and her to shop for second-hand clothes, where the stallholders kept up a running fusillade of jokes to make their hard-up customers part with a few more pence, Cissie had to smile, and they took the tramcar into the centre of the city. She had a moment of panic when Dorothy turned off High Street into Thorston Street, which connected with the Overgate. She didn't want Dorothy to know that she had once lived in one of the tumbledown tenements at the back, though her friend likely wouldn't care. What if they met any of the women who had known her before? Should she speak to them, or would they think she was patronising them now she had come up in the world? And if they didn't recognise her as the poor waif who used to live with Jen Millar, they'd be embarrassed at being spoken to by such a well-dressed lady.

Luckily, she saw no familiar faces, and Dorothy was too engrossed in describing the shops they passed to notice her disquiet. 'Do you see this grocer? You could buy a poke of broken biscuits there for a ha'penny, and bruised fruit cheap from the greengrocer, though you'd to watch what he put in the bottom of the bag wasn't rotten.'

Knowing all about this, Cissie just smiled, and her friend went on, 'The barber kept packets of you-knows under his counter for the men who didn't want to father any more kids, legitimate and otherwise.'

Laughing at this, Cissie thought that it was a pity more men hadn't bought 'you-knows' to stop their poor wives, legitimate or otherwise, having to give birth so often, but she didn't say so to Dorothy.

Carrying on into the Overgate itself, they walked slowly up the hill past Greenhill, the chemist. 'They sell a drink called Sarsparilla,' Dorothy informed Cissie, who had never had enough money to try it. There was more than one pawnshop – hocking her man's Sunday suit on a Monday and redeeming it when he got his wages on Saturday was a way of life for most wives in the area – and when they passed the three brass balls nearest to the close through to Jen's tenement, she wondered if poor Jen still lived there. Being after half past two, all the public houses were closed, but the street was still bustling with people, and Cissie knew that some of the characters who were staggering about drunkenly now would be lying in the gutter by nightfall.

'I love walking up here,' Dorothy observed, happily. 'You never know what you're going to see next.'

The familiar sights and smells were having a strange effect on Cissie – a nostalgia had risen in her for the old times with Phoebe and Jen. They had never had much money, but they had been as close as any three women could possibly be, and now they were separated by a chasm that could never be bridged. She saw Phoebe every Wednesday, but it wasn't the same – her stepmother still disapproved of Bertram – and she hadn't seen Jen for years.

'Are you getting tired?' Dorothy asked, suddenly.

'You're very quiet. Will we go in here and have a cup of tea, eh?'

They had come to a small tearoom, and because Cissie had never had occasion to go in before — it was so close to her old home — she followed her friend through the door with no fear of being recognised.

'I've really enjoyed myself today,' Dorothy said, when they were on their way out to the suburbs again.

'So have I,' Cissie said, and in a sense, it was true.

On Tuesday afternoon they went round the docks, Dorothy pointing out two of her husband's ships, and Cissie showing her the tenement in South Union Street where she and Phoebe had shared a flat. There was nothing to be ashamed of in having lived there.

'You're very fond of her, aren't you?' Dorothy observed as they walked back to get their tramcar.

'Yes, I am, but Bertram doesn't like her, and I don't know what he has against her.'

'Maybe he just doesn't like having a stepmother. Did you not resent her when your father married her?'

'No, I loved her from the day I met her.'

'When did your father die?'

'He isn't dead, but we don't know where he is.' For as close as she was to Dorothy now, Cissie couldn't tell her that he had been sent to prison over five years earlier. 'She divorced him for — deserting her.'

Phoebe had quite a surprise for her on Wednesday. 'I wrote to Marie on Sunday. Oh, don't worry,' she hurried on, as Cissie gasped with dismay, 'I didn't give her my address, or yours, I just sent some money to help her out. I've often wondered about her and Pat, and I've been saving some of what Richard gives me. I'm sure she'll be glad of the twenty pounds.'

Marie would consider twenty pounds a fortune, Cissie knew, as she would have done when she was in Schoolhill.

She, too, thought of her brother and sister occasionally — and of her other brother, Tommy — but it had never crossed her mind to make Marie's financial burden lighter. In any case, Bertram didn't give her much; he preferred to buy her clothes and to pay all the household expenses.

Changing the subject, Cissie told Phoebe about the dinner for the Barclays, and the invitation to their house in July. 'Dorothy says we should keep the dinners to once a month, so our cooks don't run out of ideas. We're great friends now,' she went on, 'and I see her nearly every day.'

Phoebe smiled. 'I'm glad you found somebody like that, and I bet Bertram's pleased you met her. He's the kind who would want to keep well in with men like Roland Barclay.'

Cissie decided to keep quiet about Bertram's intention to buy one of the mills. It would only make Phoebe think she was correct in her estimation of him, though he must have been thinking about it before he ever met Roland.

On her way home to Panache, Cissie was thankful that Phoebe had not given Marie their addresses. When her father came out of prison, the first thing he'd do would be to try and find her, and she felt much easier knowing that no one could tell him where to look.

When the clock struck midnight, heralding in the new year, Bertram raised his glass. 'Here's hoping 1924 will be as good a year for me as the last one. My profits have doubled over the past four months.'

Roland Barclay smiled as he drank the toast. 'Yes, we both seem to be doing very well. And here's to our lovely wives; we're two lucky men.'

Grinning at her friend, Dorothy said, 'We're lucky, too, aren't we, Cissie? Handsome husbands and beautiful houses we don't have to lift a finger to keep clean.'

Bertram, having had a few drinks already, sounded a

little sour when he remarked, 'All my dreams would come true if only I'd a son.'

Roland gave a roar of laughter. 'Dorothy knows it's not my fault we have no children.'

His wife's face tightened. 'No, he's told me often enough there's little Barclays scattered the length and breadth of France and Belgium.'

'Fathered before I met you,' he smiled. 'Didn't you sow any wild oats when you were in the Guards, Bertram?'

'Plenty, but I was never in any place long enough to find out if they germinated.'

The two men guffawed lewdly, although Cissie guessed that each had exaggerated in order to impress the other.

Cissie suspected that Bertram had impregnated her in the early hours of New Year's Day, but she waited until she was certain before she said anything. Sitting on the arm of his chair, she murmured, 'Bertram, I've something to tell you.'

His nose in the *Scotsman*, her husband murmured, 'Mm?'

'Will you listen, Bertram? This is important.'

Giving a little sigh, he laid the newspaper at the side of his chair and slid his arm round her. 'I'm all ears.'

'What do you want more than anything in the world?'

'A Rolls Royce. Is this some new kind of game?'

'It's not a game. It's something you've wanted for a long time. I wouldn't be surprised if it was the only reason you married me.' She grinned to let him see that she was only joking, then burst out laughing at his expression when he looked up at her. 'Has the penny dropped?'

Pulling her on to his lap, he said, 'I can't believe it! You're pregnant? Are you sure?'

'I wouldn't tell you unless I was sure. Are you pleased?'

'My darling, if I was a dog, I'd wag my tail off.'

After the kissing, they snuggled back in the chair, his

arm squeezing her waist, her arm round his neck. 'Do you know what I feel like doing right now?' he asked.

'Going to bed?' she smiled.

'That too, but I'd like to go out in the street and shout that I'm going to be a father at long last. You don't know how good I feel, Cissie. I couldn't feel better if I'd just been handed a million pounds.'

'A baby's going to cost you money,' she reminded him.

'I don't care what it costs. Oh, God, my leg's cramping. You'll have to get off.'

In another second, he was crippling around so comically that Cissie giggled, 'I didn't think I was that heavy.'

'You're not, you're as light as a feather. It was the way I was sitting.'

'I'll soon be all fat and horrible.'

'It won't matter to me,' he exclaimed. 'And I haven't thanked you yet, my darling. I'll be the happiest man alive when I hold my son in my arms.'

'Won't you be happy if it's a girl?'

'It's natural for a man to want a son.'

That night, Bertram was even more tender than usual. 'I want to be sure nothing goes wrong,' he told her, 'and when you're nearer your time, I'll stop altogether.'

'You know, Bertram,' Cissie said, blissfully. 'I think you must be the most considerate husband in the world.'

Next morning, Bertram said, 'I think I'll go to Huntingdon this afternoon to let Father know about his grandson.'

'Oh, let me tell Phoebe,' Cissie pleaded, 'and she'll tell him. I bet they'll both be pleased.'

Having wanted to see his arch enemy's face when she heard about the baby, Bertram felt cheated, but to humour his wife, he said, as cheerfully as he could, 'I don't suppose it matters who tells him.'

Bertram would have been bitterly disappointed in Phoebe's reaction. 'Oh,' she exclaimed, in great joy, when Cissie told her the good news, 'I'm so pleased for you. Maybe I was wrong about Bertram all along.' She was nearly sure she hadn't been, but marriage could have changed him.

Cissie chuckled. 'I always said you were wrong. He can hardly wait for the baby to be born. He wants a boy, of course, but I don't think he'll care if it's a girl.'

'Of course he won't,' Phoebe smiled, 'and Richard's going to be thrilled whatever it is. He's been champing at the bit waiting for a grandchild.' He had also expressed his sadness at not having fathered another child himself, and she longed to give him one, but her age was against her.

'Bertram wants to call him after his father,' Cissie was saying, 'but just think of the muddle we'll get in with two Richards in the family.'

Now Phoebe understood. Bertram hadn't changed. He had been afraid that his father would leave everything to her in his will, and he had married Cissie just to get a son. He would think that Richard would be so delighted to have a grandson he would divide his estate between his wife and the child, and was making sure by naming the boy after him – if it did turn out to be a boy. At first, she was amused at Bertram's transparency, then she felt sorry for Cissie, who hadn't the slightest suspicion of her husband's deviousness.

Conscious that her stepdaughter was regarding her anxiously, Phoebe gave a soft laugh. 'We'll easily sort them out – Big Richard and Little Richard?'

Cissie frowned. 'I hate hearing people say that.'

'It might be a girl, and whatever it is, I hope Bertram lets my Richard see it sometimes, or it'll break his heart. I don't care if he still won't be friends with me.'

'Wouldn't it be wonderful if the baby brings us all back together?'

Phoebe felt like saying it would be a miracle, but kept her sarcasm to herself. Cissie couldn't see past Bertram, and it was best to let it remain that way until he, himself, pulled the veil from her eyes, as his stepmother was sure he would, one day.

Bertram had told his wife before he left in the morning that he would have to stay late in the office that night, but, at half past five, he made his way to Barbara Troup's house, as he had done on all other occasions he had pleaded pressure of work for being late home. 'I've done it,' he crowed. 'I'd almost given up hope, but I've put a bun in Cissie's oven at long last. God, I was beginning to think she was barren.'

The prostitute grinned. 'Come to bed, my pet. I'll give you pleasure that wife of yours never could.'

Accepting her offer, Bertram thought gleefully that once his son was born, he would teach Cissie how to give him all the pleasure he needed, and he wouldn't have to pay five ruddy pounds a time for it.

Cissie had been afraid that Dorothy would be jealous about the baby, but her friend could not have been more pleased, and over the next seven months helped her to buy a complete layette – Bertram having been liberal for this good cause.

'I surely won't need five dozen terry nappies?' Cissie laughed one afternoon, about two weeks before the birth was due. 'I'm not having twins – I hope.'

'If it's wet weather, the nappies won't dry, and think how often a baby dirties them. And you'll need the same amount of Harrington squares, too.'

'Harrington squares? What are they?'

'They're like double muslin, and you use them next the baby's skin, so the towelling nappies don't get so dirty. I read it in a magazine.'

'With the amount of matinee jackets, day and night gowns, barracoats, vests and bootees I've got stacked away,

I could clothe a dozen babies. He – or she – will likely grow out of them long before I've got through half of them.'

'We've still to get the pram and a cot. No, the tiny thing would be lost in a cot, maybe you should get a Moses basket first.'

It was as if a well-aimed lance had pierced straight to the centre of Cissie's heart. This baby – looked for so long and conceived in love – would never lie in a basket. Every time she put it down or lifted it up, she wouldn't be able to hide her revulsion of the wicker bed, and Bertram would see that she was hiding something. He would demand to know, and in the state she would be in, she would blurt out the story of that night of hell. 'A cot's enough, Dorothy,' she murmured. 'A basket's extra expense for nothing.'

'Bertram won't mind the expense. He's so happy about this baby he'd buy the sun, moon and stars for it if he could.'

'I'm not having – a Moses basket!' Cissie spat out. 'I'll never – ever – let one come inside the house!'

Dorothy looked at her in amazement. 'Keep your shirt on! It was only a suggestion, it doesn't matter to me.'

'Oh, Dorothy, I'm sorry. It's not your fault. It's just . . . I once saw a Moses basket being knocked over and . . .'

Undeterred by the abrupt stop, Dorothy asked, 'Was the baby inside?' At Cissie's mute, miserable nod, she went on, 'Was it badly injured?'

'He – died.'

'Oh, poor little thing! The mother must have been out of her mind with grief.'

'Yes, she was out of her mind.' With grief, with shock, with anger, with fear, Cissie thought.

'I can see it upset you, too. Never mind, if Bertram wants a basket, I'll tell him they're out of fashion. Now, let me buy you a coffee to help you to forget about it.'

Following her gratefully to the restaurant of the store, Cissie knew that she would never forget. She had succeeded in pushing it as far to the back of her mind as she could – Bertram's love had helped – but another baby would remind her every day. And if it wasn't normal, would Bertram love it as much as Jim had loved wee James? Somehow, she didn't believe he would.

A hand on her arm made her look up. 'It was yours, wasn't it?' Dorothy asked, softly. 'It just dawned on me why you were so upset, but don't worry, your secret's safe with me.'

The bond between the two young women was cemented even more firmly, and Cissie knew that she could trust Dorothy never to bring up the subject again.

'Roland Barclay's been as jealous as hell since he learned about the baby,' Bertram gloated. 'He blames Dorothy, of course, for they've been married even longer than us, and it must be her, because he . . .'

'I know,' Cissie sighed, 'and I'm sorry for her. I know how I'd feel if I thought you'd done what he did during the war. You were only joking when you told him you'd sowed a lot of wild oats, weren't you?'

'Of course I was. I didn't want him to think I was a poor specimen of a man.' Recalling the number of oats he had sown during the war, and since he'd come home, he felt proud of how good a specimen of a man he was. For all he knew, he could have a dozen or more sons, but none legitimate. The coming one was the only one that would count.

He realised suddenly that he was fully aroused, probably with remembering his conquests, and he couldn't touch his wife when she was so near her time. Damn it all, what was he to do? He could hardly go out now – Cissie would ask where he was going. Wait a minute! What about Elma? He'd already been considering having a bit of fun with her, the only maid who lived in. She had never discouraged him when he gave her derriere the odd pinch, and she hadn't blinked an eyelid when he grasped her breast one night as he passed her in the hall. She had even licked her lips seductively, so he was sure she wouldn't turn him down.

When Elma went out after bringing in their night-time cocoa, Bertram hoped that his wife hadn't noticed the rather inviting look the girl gave him. 'You look a bit tired,' he said to Cissie. 'You should go to bed once you've finished your cocoa. I've got some paperwork to do, so it might be a while till I come up.'

He waited hopefully for some minutes after she left the room. Elma was untried ground, and that was always worth exploring. If everything went as planned tonight, she might even agree to sleep with him while Cissie was in hospital.

As he had hoped, the door opened again and the girl came in to collect the dirty cups, feigning surprise at finding him alone, although she must have heard Cissie go upstairs. There was no time for niceties – his wife might come down if he was too long – and, by the look of her, Elma was as ready for it as he was. Jumping up, he grabbed her round the waist and pushed her down on the sofa.

Chapter Twenty-one

As men often do, Tommy McGregor started talking to the stranger standing beside him at the bar, and was surprised to find that he was another Aberdonian, who said he had been working in Edinburgh for nearly four years.

'I'm in the Merchant Navy,' Tommy told him, 'and Leith's my home port, but I used to live in Schoolhill.'

'I used to go with a girl from Schoolhill,' the other man said, sadly. 'Cissie McGregor – do you know her?'

'She's my sister,' Tommy cried in astonishment. 'How long did you go with her?'

'We went steady for a good few months, then she . . . told me she'd found somebody else.'

Tommy sighed. 'I suppose she'll be married by this time. It's eleven years since my father threw me out, and I've only seen Cissie once since, just after the war started.'

'She was married, but . . .' The stranger toyed with his glass. 'You'll not have heard about your father?'

'Heard about him? What d'you mean?'

'Oh, Lord!' The man looked away uncomfortably. 'You're in for a shock, you'd better sit down.' As they made their way to a table, he added, 'My name's Hugh Phimister.'

'Tommy McGregor.'

When they were seated, Hugh cleared his throat. 'Cissie married the man downstairs from her, Robertson, I think.'

'Jim Robertson?' Tommy's mouth had dropped open. 'No, it couldn't be him. He'd a humphy back, and he must have been – oh, he was going on for fifty when I left.'

'That's him. Anyway, it turned out she was expecting his baby when she finished with me.'

Tommy's chin was practically resting on his chest now, his eyes wide with amazement. 'Cissie let the Humphy . . . God no, man, I can't believe that.'

'Neither could I when I learned about it, for I know she wasn't a girl like that. But it's true, and your father must have been that mad at Robertson, he got drunk one night and went to their house – I don't know the whole story, for it was my mother that told me when I came out of the army – but he accidentally killed Robertson and the baby, and now he's doing time in Peterhead for manslaughter. Hey, I'd better get you a whisky.'

Feeling as though a mule had given him a series of kicks in the stomach, Tommy watched Hugh making his way to the bar. Cissie and Jim Robertson? How could his little sister ever have got herself involved with the Humphy? He must have raped her – yet Jim had never struck him as a man who would harm a fly, let alone an innocent young girl. If it had been Big Tam, now, that would be a different thing. He would have raped his own grandmother and thought nothing about it. He'd been like a bull among cows when he got near women.

Tommy gave his head a shake. His father had always had a vile temper, especially when he was drunk, but what had made him kill the Humphy and the baby? Hugh Phimister had said it was an accident, but how could any man accidentally kill two other human beings? Maybe he'd gone downstairs to thrash Jim Robertson for landing Cissie in the family way, and he'd gone mad with rage and throttled him – but that didn't explain the baby's death. And it was nearly impossible to believe he'd waited till after the child was born before he took his anger out on the man who had fathered it.

'Here, drink this.' Hugh set a double whisky in front of him. 'I shouldn't have come out with it like that.'

After one good mouthful of the spirits, Tommy regained a little of his colour. 'Thank God you did, man, or else I'd never have known about it. Poor Cissie.'

'Aye, I was sick thinking what it must have done to her. Her father should have been strung up – oh . . .' He stopped, flustered. 'He's your father, and all, of course.'

Tommy gave a harsh laugh. 'He's not been my father since he threw me out, and I feel the same as you – worse. They should have hacked off his privates and then strung him up. Oh, I wish to God I'd known about it before. I'd have gone home at the double, for Cissie's sake.'

'Ma said she left Schoolhill right after the trial. I did go to the house, though, for I wanted to speak to her, but your other sister didn't know where she was. She'd gone away with your father's wife, so she's not on her own.'

This was another shock for Tommy. 'My father's wife? One of his bidie-ins, more like.' He took another swig of his whisky. 'How long is it since you spoke to Marie?'

'As soon as my mother told me what had happened – August 1919. I'd come home from the war determined to get Cissie back, for I was sure she loved me, and when I learned she was a widow I thought I was in luck, but I was too late. I hung around for a couple of months, but I didn't know where to start looking, and I came here to try to forget her.'

Finishing his drink in one gulp, Tommy stood up. 'I've to get back to the ship, I'm on watch in an hour, but thank God I met you.'

As he made his way down Leith Walk, he was so concerned about Cissie that he resolved to go to Schoolhill in the morning to see if Marie had heard from her since she left. He had to find her to make sure she was all right. He was walking up the gangway before he remembered that Hugh Phimister would likely want to know if he found her, and he'd forgotten to ask where he lived.

Walking out of Aberdeen's Joint Station the following

day, Tommy wondered what had happened to his other sister and his two brothers in the time he had been away. No doubt Marie would be married by now, likely Joe, as well, though Pat would still be a bit young for that. He'd had a few girls himself, but he had never taken a wife; a sailor needed to be free.

It struck him suddenly that he might be on a wild goose chase. His old home could be occupied by complete strangers now, people who would look at him with contempt for being Tam McGregor's son. His step faltered, then, squaring his shoulders resolutely, he carried on up Market Street. He'd come this far, and nothing ventured, nothing gained.

Crossing Union Street, he skidded on the icy tram rails and grinned as he steadied himself. He was nothing like as sure-footed on land as he was on deck. St Nicholas Street was even busier than he remembered, even a few motor cars now. There were still as many folk hurrying along the pavements, heads down against the blinding snow brought by the nor'easter, coat collars turned up. He never felt cold when he was ashore. He was accustomed to hundred-mile-an-hour gales at sea, howling round him as he clung to the rail making his way for'ard to the bridge in his oilskins. They had a constant battle with the elements in northern waters, it was easier round Gibraltar and the Mediterranean, then it was heat they had to contend with going through the Suez Canal on the way to India, but he wouldn't want to be anything other than a seaman.

Coming to the ladies' shop on the corner, he turned into Schoolhill and crossed to the far side, his heart beating a little quicker when he neared the tenement where he had been born. Neither of the names on the brass plates on the first floor was familiar to him, and he wished that he had looked at the nameplates in the street. One more flight. Damn! It was people called Lewis that were in his old home now, but he would be as well knocking since he was here.

While he waited for an answer, he glanced at the other door on the landing. Coull! So Cleekie was still living. He would try there if he had no luck at his first port of call. Turning hopefully as someone opened the door beside him, he began, 'Mrs Lewis?' then burst out, 'It's you, Marie? Thank the Lord for that.'

His sister, quite stout now, and with a toddler at each side, gaped at him for a moment, then her eyes filled with recognition. 'Tommy! It's never you, after all this time?'

'The bad penny always turns up again,' he laughed.

He followed her into the kitchen, still much the same as he remembered, though there was a sideboard in the recess instead of a bed, and some of the old ornaments were missing from the mantelpiece – broken, likely. Sitting down in what had once been his father's armchair gave him a weird sense of satisfaction, for he'd never been allowed to put his backside on it before. 'I might as well come straight to the point, Marie. What happened to Cissie?'

Marie looked at the floor. 'She went away with Phoebe, the woman Da married.'

'We'll come to that. What I want to know is why? I've been told a bit, but not enough.'

Heaving a long sigh, Marie said, 'I'd better make a pot of tea first, then I'll tell you everything.'

He was desperate to hear what she had to say, but knew she would be offended if he didn't accept her hospitality. 'Come to your Uncle Tommy,' he coaxed the two little boys holding on to their mother's skirts.

They let him lift them on to his knee, looking up at him with their innocent, round eyes, and he wondered if he'd been wrong not to take a wife and have children of his own. He passed the next few minutes by singing nursery rhymes to them, laughing as the elder boy joined in.

'How old are they?' he asked Marie as she poured the tea.

'Freddie's nearly four, Joey'll be two next month, and Isabel's five. She's at school.'

'You've been busy,' he smiled.

'I'm not having any more, though. I've told Wilfie he'll have to tie a knot in it. Come on, you two! Let your Uncle Tommy drink his tea.'

When her sons jumped down to play on the hearthrug with their blocks, she turned to her brother. 'I suppose you've heard Da's in prison?'

'Aye, I've been told that.'

'It wasn't his fault, Tommy. He didn't mean to kill Jim.'

'What led up to it? Did Cissie really marry the Humphy?'

'She had to. She was expecting his bairn.' Marie did not tell her brother what she had overheard on the eve of the dreadful quarrel; she had long since convinced herself that it wasn't true.

'Cissie would never have let Jim Robertson . . .'

'That's why Da was angry. He come home drunk one night . . .'

'When did he ever do anything else?'

Ignoring the interruption, Marie carried on, '. . . and he went into Cissie's house and fell out on Jim Robertson.'

She went over all she knew of the events on that terrible night, and when she came to an end, there were still gaps that he would have liked filled in, but it was clear that Marie could not tell him. Just the same, he had a strange feeling that she was keeping something back. 'So Cissie went away with Phoebe? Have you ever heard from her?'

'I've not heard from Cissie, but Phoebe sent some money a while ago.'

'You know where they are, then?'

'The envelope had a Dundee postmark, but there wasn't an address on the note. All she said was she hoped I could make use of the twenty pounds she was enclosing.'

Tommy whistled. 'Twenty pounds? She must have landed on her feet if she'd that much to give away.'

'That was when I remembered hearing them speaking about going to Dundee to look for a job in the jute mills. They wouldn't get big wages there.'

Tommy sat forward eagerly. 'The jute mills? Well, that's a start, any road.'

'But where would Phoebe get twenty pounds?'

Glancing at the two boys, Tommy lowered his voice. 'She was a whore, wasn't she? It wouldn't take her long to make twenty pounds. I've had to pay a couple of pounds a time in some of the places I've been.'

'Oh, Tommy!' Marie gave a shocked giggle. 'You never!'

'Mind, I don't often pay that much, and they're cleaner abroad than they are here.' His smile faded. 'I don't give a tinker's cuss about Phoebe, though. It's Cissie I want to find, and I won't have time to ask round the Dundee mills till after my next trip.'

His mind made up on this, he said, 'What about the rest of the family? Is Joe married?'

Marie's face fell. 'I forgot you wouldn't know. Joe was lost at sea in the war.'

'Oh, no! Poor Joe, he wasn't as lucky as me, then.' He sat for some time with his head bowed, remembering his younger brother – Joe, with his serious face, his thoughtful brown eyes. He never had much to say for himself, though he hadn't been as quiet as Rosie. Oh, God! Joe and Rosie. It was hard to think they were both gone.

At last, he shook his head and shrugged himself out of his depressing thoughts. 'What about Pat? How old's he now?'

'He's nineteen and as cheeky as ever. He sleeps in the same room as my three. Freddie's called after my man, Joey was after Joe, and Isabel's after Mam. Me and Wilfie sleep in the other bedroom, but we're thinking of shifting into the kitchen, to let Isabel get a room to herself.'

'I suppose Pat's working?'

'Aye, he got a job in one of the fish houses, and you

wouldn't believe the smell on him when he comes home. Not that he's bothered. He says it's attar of roses to him.'

Tommy laughed. 'That sounds like Pat.'

'He hasn't changed a bit, and him and Wilfie get on fine. You'll see them when they come home for their supper.'

'I'm sorry, Marie, but I'll not have time to wait. I've to be back in Leith for five.'

'Oh, Tommy.' Marie looked crestfallen.

'I'll be back, but maybe not for a while. I'd like to find Cissie first. We're sailing tomorrow for Calcutta, so I'll not be able to look for her till we come back.'

'Surely you'll have time for some dinner?' Marie pleaded. 'It's only second day's tattie soup but there's plenty, and I could make a tapioca pudding.'

'Second day's tattie soup was always best,' he chuckled, 'but I'll not sup with you unless you promise to put some jam on the pudding.'

'Jam on the pudding,' Freddie said, from the floor, and Joey, knocking down the tower they had made, looked up at his mother and his uncle, his eyes twinkling with mischief. 'Dam on de pudden,' he echoed.

Tommy roared with laughter. 'You've another Pat here.'

Chapter Twenty-two

❖

Cissie Dickson felt that Ricky was her reward for all the agonies she had gone through in her previous lives. Her son was perfect, his tiny face round and healthy, his chubby body firm and straight. His fair hair and violet eyes were so like Bertram's that she had to kiss him every time she picked him up. There had never been such a beautiful infant.

The whole household revolved around him, even Mrs Gow drooled over him, and the two maids had argued over whose turn it was to take him out in the pram when the nurse had an afternoon off. Bertram had wanted to engage a nanny, but what would have been the point of that when his mother had plenty of time to attend to him? And she was quite fit now, though the doctor had said she should take things easy for a while. She'd had no choice but to take things easy, anyway, for Nurse Valentine had never let her do a thing except feed her child. But the nurse, a proper tartar, had been engaged for only six weeks and had left the day before, and Cissie was determined to look after Ricky herself from now on.

She was pleased that Bertram hadn't made a scene when his father brought Phoebe to see the new baby, and though he hadn't exactly welcomed her with open arms, he would come round when he got to know her better.

He was in seventh heaven about having a son, and had been so overcome when he first held the child in his arms that Cissie had almost wept with joy. He hadn't missed visiting time once, and Cissie considered herself lucky to have such a devoted husband. And Ricky was the most beautiful, most darling baby in the world. What more could any woman want?

When she told Bertram that she was going to Huntingdon that afternoon with the pram, he looked at her anxiously. 'Are you sure you're fit enough to walk so far? I could drive you there before I go to work.'

'I can't go visiting so early in the morning. Besides, it's not very far, and it's quite a nice day for October.'

'I don't want you tiring yourself.'

'I'll take it easy,' she assured him, loving him all the more for his concern.

By the time she reached her destination, however, she was utterly exhausted, and was quite content to lie back in a chair and let Phoebe take the baby out of the pram to cuddle him. Richard stood behind his wife, looking down at the tiny face, but when she turned and put the infant in his arms, he seemed alarmed, though anyone with eyes could see how proud he was, Cissie thought. If only they could have a baby of their own, it would be the cherry on top of the icing on the cake for her.

When she rose to leave, Richard said, 'I think the walk here was a little too much for you, so I'll drive you home, and I'm sure Phoebe won't object to pushing the pram.'

Phoebe didn't object. 'Just give me ten minutes' start.'

After she went out, Richard looked enquiringly at his daughter-in-law. 'What does Bertram say about having a son?'

'He couldn't be happier,' she smiled. 'He wanted a son.'

'So he got his own way over that, like he got his own way over everything else in his life?'

'He couldn't have done anything if it hadn't been a boy,' she protested.

'He might have taken his displeasure out on you.'

'He's not like that. He's a very considerate husband.'

He laughed at this. 'I'm relieved to hear it. I'm glad I've got the chance to talk to you in private, Cissie. I want to tell you something I don't want Phoebe to hear. I made a new will last week, leaving Phoebe the house and the mill as before, and half the money – still a very substantial amount. The other half will go to Ricky. Bertram has always known how I felt about him, and he must have suspected that I would cut him out. I think that's why he was so determined to have a son – to provide me with another heir.'

'He wouldn't care if you left everything to Phoebe.'

Richard smiled benevolently. 'She'll still have more than enough to last her for the rest of her life. I must say at this point, that however disappointed I was in my son, his choice of wife had my full approval. Now, on to the other thing I wanted to discuss with you. I've been thinking of taking Phoebe to America for a holiday, for a year or perhaps two. Do you think she would like that?'

'Oh, I'm sure she would.'

'I thought it best to go before –' he paused. 'My doctor tells me I have only a few years to live – some obscure form of cancer. No, Cissie, don't say anything. I do not mean to tell Phoebe. I'd like us to see as much of America as possible. I shall make the arrangements tomorrow, then. Now, we'd better go. You'll want to be home before Phoebe gets there with Ricky.'

They drove home in silence, Cissie barely able to take in the dreadful news that soon she – and Phoebe – would lose this wonderful man.

Bertram did not pay much attention that evening to Cissie's account of her visit. 'You were right,' she said. 'It was a wee bit too far for me, but Phoebe pushed Ricky home in the pram and Richard took me in his car. He's going to take her to America for a long holiday.'

'Mm.'

'And he was speaking about his will. He said – Oh . . .' How could she keep Richard's illness from her husband?

228

She stopped in confusion. 'Maybe I shouldn't be saying anything, though he didn't tell me not to tell you.'

Bertram's head had jerked up. This was something he did want to know. 'You'd better go on now you've started.'

'He's been told he only has a few years to live, isn't that awful?'

This shook him for a moment, then his mind turned to what it meant to him, and he asked, curtly, 'What about his will?'

'Ricky gets half his money and Phoebe gets everything else.'

'I always said she was a gold-digger.'

'That's not fair, Bertram. She didn't ask him to do it, in fact she doesn't know anything about it. You surely don't mind? She is his wife.'

It could have been worse, Bertram thought. At least half the wealth would be within his grasp soon. 'No, I don't mind. I knew he wasn't pleased because I wouldn't go into the mill, the family business, and I guessed he'd cut me off without a penny, like my grandfather did.'

'I've often wondered about that. Was that the only reason your grandfather had?'

'Not exactly.' He decided to come clean, or half clean, at any rate. 'I was a fool when I came out of the army first, running around with lots of young things and spending all my money on them. Then Dickson's Supplies didn't get off the ground for such a long time, Father and Grandfather thought I was useless, not fit to inherit anything.'

'I see,' Cissie said, thoughtfully. 'And were you still running around with girls then?'

'God, no, Cissie! Once I started going with you, I never looked at another girl.'

'Why didn't you tell me about them before?'

'I wasn't sure how you'd feel, but it was just – oh, after what I'd seen in the war, I went off the rails a bit when I came home. Nothing to worry about, it's all over long ago.'

'Now I understand why your father said some of the things he did, but I told him you were the best husband ever.'

'As I shall continue to be, my darling.'

'Cissie,' Dorothy burst out, as soon as she went into her friend's house one wet day at the beginning of November. 'I'm near sure I'm expecting.'

'Oh, I can't tell you how glad I am, Dorothy. I sometimes wondered if you were jealous of me having Ricky.'

'Maybe I was, just a teeny bit, but, oh, I'll have a wee bundle of my own in another eight months.'

Cissie giggled. 'You wouldn't be so happy if you'd seen this one half an hour ago. I'd newly changed him when the wee monkey dirtied himself again, and it was all over his gowns and bootees and right up his back. I'd to strip him to the skin and give him another bath.'

Dorothy chuckled. 'Thanks for letting me know what's in front of me, but they say shit's lucky.'

'Have you told Roland yet?'

'I couldn't keep it to myself, though I'm still not really sure.' Dorothy paused, then looked at Cissie thoughtfully. 'Did Bertram stop making love when you were carrying?'

Cissie blushed. She was shy of discussing this, but her friend obviously had something on her mind. 'Not till I was about seven months on, and he hasn't touched me since.'

'Huh! As soon as I told Roland, he was on me like a ton of bricks, and you'd have thought he was trying to make another six babies the way he was going at it. I wish he would stop, for I'd love one whole night of peace.'

Cissie had smiled for a moment, then realised that Dorothy was in earnest. 'Once you're nearer your time he'll stop.'

'I doubt it.'

Waiting for Bertram to come home that evening, Cissie wished that he was more like Roland. He had stopped fussing over her like he did before Ricky was born; it was as if he didn't even like her now, for he hardly spent any time in the house. If only he would tell her occasionally that he loved her, like he used to. Her heart cramped suddenly, as it occurred to her that he had only once said that he loved her, and that had been long before their wedding, the night she had responded by saying she didn't love him.

Miserably, she tried to tell herself that she was wrong, that each time they made love he had said he loved her, yet she could only remember her own declarations, not his. But he did love her, of course he did. His kisses proved that – but there had been no kisses for a long time, either.

The baby had finished his last feed before Bertram came in, and Cissie, having been brooding for hours, could not help saying, 'I'm surprised you came home at all.'

As soon as it was out, she wished she hadn't said it, and could see that her sarcasm had angered him. 'What is there to come home for?' he snapped. 'A woman so tied up with her child that she doesn't bother to dress for her husband?'

So that was it, she thought, relief flooding through her. He was jealous of the baby, that was why he was so distant with her. 'I'm sorry, Bertram. I didn't want to spoil my lovely gowns when I'm still feeding Ricky.'

'And that's another thing. It disgusts me to see you flaunting your bare breasts the way you do. Why, you even did it one night in front of Roland Barclay, and he couldn't keep his eyes off them. You belong to me, and no other man has the right to see any part of you.'

'I'm sorry, I didn't think. When I lived in – when I came to Dundee first, it was nothing to see mothers standing on the pavements with babies at their bare breasts, and

231

nobody bothered, not even the men going past. It's quite natural.'

'Perhaps amongst the riff-raff, but not in my circles.'

'Oh, Bertram, stop being so silly. A change would upset the baby, and in any case, mother's milk is far better than any powdered stuff. I don't care what you say, I'm going to carry on breast feeding.'

Angry because he had lost the battle, he growled, 'Have it your own way, but not in front of the Barclays again. They must be as disgusted as I am.'

'Is that why you don't love me any more?' Cissie said, plaintively.

'Love!' he exploded. 'That's all a woman ever thinks of. Isn't it enough that I married you, and gave you a beautiful home and expensive clothes? I've made love to you . . .'

'Not since before Ricky was born.'

'Ha! Now it's out. You want me to start making love to you again, is that it? Why didn't you say? It hasn't been easy for me to keep my hands off you – it's been a long time.' His voice, and his eyes, softened now. 'All right, my dear, upstairs with you this minute.'

Presuming that the cruel things he had said had been the result of his long self-enforced celibacy, Cissie forgave him and followed him up to their bedroom.

Wishing that she had let well alone, Cissie sat in the dining room long after her husband went to his office in the morn-ing, her whole body aching from the terrible things he had done. Had that been the real Bertram? Had he held himself back before, or was she misjudging him? It was the first time in months for him, and who could blame him for being over-excited? It would be better tonight.

Sadly, Cissie was to discover that things did not improve. Bertram was like a crazy man every night, punching her, even biting her and drawing blood – in places where the marks would not be seen – working himself up into a frenzy before he rammed into her to satisfy himself fully, all the while shouting that he loved her, but not as if he meant it. At other times, he wanted her to be the brutal one, and made her do vile things to him in spite of her outraged protests. She dreaded going to bed with him and struggled against him with all her strength as soon as he touched her, but she was determined not to give him the satisfaction of hearing her screaming or pleading with him to stop.

It grew even worse when he started tearing off her clothes as soon as they went into the bedroom, forcing her down on her knees on the floor, pulling her arms up behind her until she thought they would be torn from their sockets.

'I'm your master!' he exulted, one night. 'Say I'm your master, damn you!'

She wouldn't say it. She wouldn't degrade herself – no man had the right to treat a woman like that, not even his wife – and he hauled her to her feet and threw her on the bed to do the foul things he seemed to revel in.

She knew the servants were speaking about her now. She had caught them in a huddle several times in the kitchen, and though they jumped apart, the way they looked at her showed they knew what was going on. Elma slept in the basement, two floors below, but could she have heard?

After some months of nights when she wished she were dead, she longed to confide in someone, to ask advice, to find out if other men behaved in the same way, but it was so shameful that she couldn't let anyone know, and there was no one to tell, anyway. Dorothy Barclay was so happy in her pregnancy that it would be wicked to upset her, and Phoebe had gone to America three months before.

The odd thing, Cissie thought one morning, was that at all other times Bertram was the perfect husband. He came home early, and sat with her in the sitting room after dinner, telling her what he had done during the day and asking about their son's progress. At these times, she loved him as much as ever, but the night-time Bertram was a stranger to her – a horrible stranger she loathed with all her being. She was tired of fighting him – maybe she should threaten to show Dorothy the marks he had left on her. That would surely make him stop. In any case, she didn't intend to let him do what he wanted without a murmur, and to do what he asked her to do to him. She must try to get the better of him.

Bertram was furious. Not only had Cissie threatened to show Dorothy Barclay what he had done to her, she had ended up by locking him out of their bedroom, after all he had done for her – a common spinner! He had provided her with a lovely home, good food, expensive clothes, and this was how she repaid him! He should have married a girl from his own class, or, preferably, a class above, but she'd been the only girl he could think of at the time who would fit the bill as far as his father was concerned. Granted, she had given him the son who would make it possible for him to get his hands on half the Dickson fortune in the not-too-distant future, but that didn't give her liberty to refuse him his rights.

Maybe it was time to move on to somebody new, for even Barbara Troup had palled on him before he stopped going to her. Elma had shaped up very well when she'd shared his bed during the two weeks Cissie was in the Maternity Hospital, and hadn't been disgusted by anything he did, but she was only a skivvy and he could do better than that.

Cissie had served her purpose, and he would have to think of some way to be free of her, but he'd better wait until Ricky was not so dependent on his mother. He would have to make her leave the boy behind, which would be a mammoth task, but it would have to be done. His son was the safeguard to his future. He had better not wait too

long, however. It must be done before his father and
Phoebe returned from America. His stepmother would be
livid when she found out, but it would be too late for her
to do anything.

Chapter Twenty-three

❖❖

1925

Cissie was thankful that Bertram's violent love-making had not resulted in the making of another child, although there had been times when she hoped it would, so that he would leave her alone for a few months. She had suffered agonising pain every night, even when she had been indisposed, but it was all over. Whatever had caused her husband's savagery – he must have had a brainstorm – it was over.

Their marriage had settled down again, and they were just an ordinary husband and wife now – no, not ordinary, because he never made love to her at all, but she preferred it that way. She didn't believe she would ever be able to let him touch her again. He stayed out late three or four times a week, but she didn't mind that. Several mills were having difficulties – some short-sighted engineers had exported textile machinery to Calcutta at one time, and India could now produce the goods cheaper than Dundee – and Bertram's would be no different. He probably hadn't wanted to burden her with his problems, and was sorting them out himself when the office was closed.

At almost a year old, Ricky was crawling about, a happy wee soul, babbling away unintelligibly. 'I think you must have taken up with a foreigner,' Dorothy teased, one day.

Cissie laughed, because her son was the very image of Bertram. 'What an imagination you've got. I believe you could write a book if you tried.'

'Write a book?' Dorothy scoffed. 'It takes me all my time to write my name, yet I still landed a rich husband.'

'How did you meet Roland? I've often wondered.'

'By accident, really. I went over my ankle one Sunday, and I was hanging on to a lamppost in agony when a car drew up and this handsome man asked what was wrong. It was love at first sight, and in a couple of months he'd bought a house and married me. Can you imagine it? Me, up to my ankles in Axminster when I was used to bare congoleum. Da didn't work half the time, and Ma was a cleaner. I think they starved themselves so I could get enough to eat, and I often wonder if that's why I was an only child. They couldn't have had the strength to – oops! I nearly said it. Roland would have a fit if he thought I knew words like that.'

Dorothy gave a rippling chuckle. 'It's a good thing we've got husbands like we have, though. It's good to know we'll be kept in luxury for the rest of our lives.'

For a moment, Cissie remembered how bleak the outlook was for all industry in Dundee. If the worst came to the worst, and Bertram had to close his mill, would there come a time when he couldn't keep her in luxury? But he still had his other business, and people would always need groceries. She would never be poor again, never have to suffer the hardship she'd had to put up with in Jen's squalid room.

She suddenly remembered what Richard had told her just after Ricky was born, and was glad that Phoebe was also set for life. Thinking about her stepmother led her to observe, 'I got another letter from Phoebe yesterday. They're still in New York, but Richard's hired a car, and they're going to drive across to California. She said it would take them days, though I can hardly imagine a country that size. I only hope he's not taxing his strength too much.'

Sitting in the drawing room one evening after a solitary dinner, Cissie was feeling neglected. Bertram never showed her any affection these days, and at breakfast he had said,

'I'm going to a conference in Glasgow today, and I've heard there's usually a booze-up afterwards. Most of the others live around there, so it won't matter to them, but I don't fancy driving home with a drink in. I'll have to spend the night in a hotel, and I'll go straight to the warehouse when I get back in the morning.'

'You've never been a whole night away from me before,' she had said, sadly.

'This may not be the only time. I'll have to start going all over the country to drum up business for the mill.'

She admired him for his determination, but hated having to be on her own overnight. Not that she was completely alone, though she couldn't count Ricky, and Elma was anything but friendly towards her.

Cissie looked up in surprise when the maid opened the door without knocking and said, 'A man's asking to see you.'

Frowning at her rudeness, Cissie wondered who it could be. The men Bertram dealt with should know to go to the mill or the warehouse in office hours. Before she could tell the girl to say that the master was not at home, the man walked in. 'I bet I'm the last person you expected to see.'

Giving a shriek of delight, she jumped up and threw her arms round her brother's neck. 'Tommy! Tommy!'

They hugged ecstatically, Tommy stroking her hair as he kissed her cheek, and neither of them noticed that the maid was watching them, her calculating eyes narrowing before she closed the door softly behind her.

Cissie was first to draw away. 'Sit down, Tommy, and tell me how you knew where I was.'

'It's a long story,' he warned.

'I want to know, supposing it takes all night.'

'To start at the beginning, I got speaking to an Aberdeen man in a pub in Edinburgh one night – oh, it must be about a year ago.' Tommy had given a great deal of thought to this after he learned that his sister had married a man who owned both a mill and a wholesale grocery company, and had decided that she wouldn't want to be reminded of Hugh Phimister, her old lad. There was no need to go into details. 'When I told him I used to live in Schoolhill, he asked if I knew you.'

'How could he have known me?'

'From reports of . . . the trial.'

Her face blanched 'Oh! You know about that?'

'Not till he told me, but I wish I'd been there at the time. I could have helped you through it.'

She looked at him miserably. 'It was awful, and knowing folk would be speaking about me made it worse. That's why I'd to get away, and Phoebe came to Dundee with me.'

'So Marie said.' He described his long, patient combing of every mill he could find. 'Nobody had ever heard of a Cissie McGregor. I'd only a few days at a time to look, for I'd always to go back to my ship for another trip, and I nearly gave up hope of ever finding you. But I made up my mind to keep at it, and I started going round them again, waiting at the gates for the workers to come out, and asking them if any of them knew you. As usual, I was getting nowhere last night when one old body said, "I ken't a Cissie Robertson once. She bade wi' me for a while.'

'Jen Millar!' Cissie exclaimed.

'I don't know her name, but I damn near kissed her. I'd forgotten your name would be Robertson. She told me you and Phoebe had moved to South Union Street, and you'd both got jobs in the office, then she'd lost touch with you.'

'I feel awful about that, I'll have to go and see her some time. But you still haven't said who told you where I was.'

'Hold your horses,' Tommy laughed, 'I'm nearly there. The office staff had all gone home, so I went back this morning and the manager said you'd married the boss's son, but he didn't know your address. I said I was desperate 'to find you, so he phoned your man's mill and got it. I didn't know if you'd be in during the day, so I waited till I thought you'd have had your supper.'

'We call it dinner in this house,' she smiled.

'Aye, I suppose you would. Anyway, that's it. My, Cissie, you look well. I needn't have worried about you, this place is like a blooming palace.'

'It's far too big, but it's what Bertram wanted. He's in Glasgow tonight, but you can meet him tomorrow. He should be home in the early evening.'

'We sail from Leith the morrow afternoon.'

'You can sleep here tonight. There's enough spare rooms to take the whole crew of your ship.' She leaned back in her seat and gave a sigh. 'Oh, Tommy, it's good to see you. Tell me about Marie and Pat. How are they?'

Knowing that he had plenty of time to hear about Cissie's tragedy, Tommy told her about Marie's children, about Pat's job in the fish-house, and they were telling each other what they had been doing since they left Aberdeen, when Elma came in. 'Will I make your cocoa now, Mrs Dickson?'

'Yes, Elma, and make enough for two.' She turned to her brother in dismay. 'I never asked if you'd had anything to eat. You could have had . . .'

'I got something in a pieshop.'

The maid withdrew, her face breaking into a broad smirk as she went down to the kitchen, and it was only a few minutes before she returned with the tray. 'Will that be all?'

'Yes, thank you, Elma, you can lock up now. Mr McGregor will be staying the night in the room across the passage from mine, so you had better put a hot water bottle in the bed to take off the chill.'

'Yes, Mrs Dickson.' Her face impassive, the girl went out, but her eyebrows shot up and her mouth pursed as she crossed the hall to lock the front door.

Tommy looked seriously at his sister. 'I think it's time you told me what happened that night, Cissie.'

She began long before the actual night, leaving nothing out and hushing him when he roared out in condemnation of their father for raping her. When she explained why she had gone upstairs on the evening Big Tam had got the telegram about Joe, she gulped, 'I only went to please Phoebe.'

His face grim, her brother listened while the rest of the tale unfolded, step by horrible step to the final, tragic denouement, by which time tears were flowing down Cissie's face and he was swallowing hard to keep his own tears back.

'Christ!' he groaned, when she came to a shuddering halt, 'I don't know how you came through that, Cissie.'

'Neither do I, now.'

Tommy looked at her compassionately until the long silence was broken by the musical chimes of the Westminster clock on the mantelpiece, the first ding-dong making Cissie look up. 'Oh, it's midnight! I'd no idea it was that late.'

'Aye, it's time we got some sleep. I'm glad I know the truth, Cissie, but if I ever meet up with that bugger when he comes out, I'll not be responsible for my actions.'

As they went upstairs, she whispered, 'His time's half in already, and I'm scared he'll come after me when he's out.'

'He'll never find you supposing he does,' he assured her. 'Look how long it took me, and he hasn't half my brains.'

She had a faint smile on her face as they went into their separate rooms.

Tommy held Ricky on his knee while they had breakfast, the boy gabbling to him even when his little mouth was full of scrambled egg. 'He's a bright one this,' he laughed.

Cissie beamed proudly, then said, sharply, 'Ricky, be careful. You nearly spilled your milk over Uncle Tommy.'

'Ommy,' her son said, looking pleased with himself.

'That's the first thing he's said that I've recognised,' Cissie exclaimed. 'He won't even try to say Dada or Mama, no matter how often I say it to him.'

Tommy grinned. 'It was likely a fluke. Say it again, son. Tommy?'

'Ommy,' Ricky obliged in his shrill voice, his violet eyes dancing with what seemed almost like devilment.

'You'd think he was just doing it to spite me,' Cissie said, ruefully. 'Say Mama now, Ricky, for me? Mama?'

'Ommy!' It was so decisive that the two adults couldn't help laughing.

Having been unable to persuade her brother to stay any longer, Cissie saw him out just after ten. 'I'm sorry you didn't get to meet Bertram, but you'll come back?'

'Try keeping me away now I've found you again. I'll make for Dundee every time the ship docks, for I want to see my nephew growing up.'

He took her in his arms. 'I'm glad you've got a decent man, Cissie. You deserve the very best after what you've been through.'

'Bertram is the very best,' she assured him, and as she watched him striding away, she was glad she had not told him about the long succession of nights when Bertram had been the worst husband any woman could have had.

When she returned to the sitting room, Ricky was standing in his playpen with his arms held out to her. 'No,' she told him firmly, 'you'll have to stay there. Mama has to sit down and think what we're going to have for dinner tonight.'

'Mama.'

Her heart filling with joy, she ran to lift him up, and the triumph on his face made her shake her head. 'You're a wee monkey. You knew how to get round me, didn't you, but that's it. One cuddle, that's all.'

'Mama,' he said, hopefully, when she bent to put him

back in the playpen, but when she didn't give in he settled down quite happily to play with his toys.

That afternoon, she had much to tell Dorothy Barclay, who was delighted that her friend was reunited with her brother, and amazed at Tommy's persistence in his search. Then Cissie told her why Tommy had left Aberdeen in the first place, but did not mention her own reason for leaving, and Dorothy – only waiting for her friend's story to end before imparting her own good news – did not notice the omission.

'And this morning,' Cissie went on, 'I said something to Ricky about Uncle Tommy, and he actually said "Ommy".'

Dorothy smiled. 'Now he's begun, he'll likely . . .'

'Yes, he said "Mama" just after Tommy went away.'

'Well, there you are. Um – Cissie, you'll never believe this, but after all the years we waited for Fenella, I'm going to have another one.'

'Oh, Dorothy, I'm pleased for you! There won't be long between them and they'll be company for each other.'

*   *   *

Bertram decided to go home for a bath before he went to the warehouse. He had been up half the night drinking, and it was almost noon before he surfaced with such a thumping head that he'd just had a wash and shave, and driving home had made him feel sweaty, so a change of clothes wouldn't go amiss, either. Knowing that Cissie would be out, he went straight upstairs to the bathroom to turn on the taps, and he had just taken off his collar and tie in the bedroom when Elma walked in. 'Don't you ever knock?' he asked, in some irritation. 'I might have been naked.'

'It wouldn't be the first time I've seen you naked,' she simpered. 'But I came to tell you something, Bertram.'

He was alarmed. 'Nothing's wrong with Ricky, I hope?'

'No, his mother's got him out in the pram. It's just – I

thought you'd like to know . . . a Mr McGregor turned up just after dinner last night, and Mrs Dickson ran and kissed him. Then, later on, she told me he was staying the night. He didn't leave until ten this morning.'

Bertram's face blanched, then turned magenta. 'What?' he bellowed. 'Are you telling me my wife slept with another man? The bitch! The Goddam bitch! The minute my back's turned! And her always pretending butter wouldn't melt in her mouth.'

'Bertram . . .'

Her interruption went unheeded as he began to pace the floor in his temper. 'No wonder she didn't want anything to do with me! She's had a bloody lover lined up, waiting for the first opportunity to get him into her bed!'

'Bertram, listen . . .'

'They've likely been carrying on for months, taking a room in some whorehouse for the afternoon – Christ! What a bloody fine wife she's turned out to be . . . Who is he? If I get my hands on him, I'll . . .'

Worried at the purple mottling on his face, Elma shouted, 'Calm down, Bertram. You'll give yourself a heart attack. I wouldn't have told you if I'd known you'd take it like this, but you're always saying you can't think how to get rid of her, and now's your chance. You flew off the handle before I got time to tell you they didn't sleep together, but I could say they did.'

His chest still heaving, he eyed her uncertainly. 'They didn't sleep together. Are you sure?

'He used one of the guest rooms.'

His unhealthy colour was receding. 'You'd be prepared to swear they used the same bed? But it would be your word against hers.'

'I changed the sheets and hid them so you can take them to the laundry, and nobody would be any the wiser. And Cook knows he was here for breakfast, and she believed me when I said they'd spent the night together.'

Looking at her admiringly, Bertram said, 'There's more in that head of yours than I thought.' He pulled his shirt off over his head, then smiled wickedly as he opened the top button of his trousers. 'Would you like to scrub my back?'

'Ooh, Bertram, what a man you are,' she giggled.

'Why don't we have a bath together? Tildy's not likely to come up, is she?'

'No, she's in the scullery cleaning the silver.' The eager light suddenly went out of her scheming eyes, and she said, regretfully, 'Mrs Gow would wonder why I was so long.'

'True, and I don't want anyone suspecting there's anything between us. Not yet. Not until after I throw my wife out, and that won't be easy. She'll likely kick up a fuss when I won't let her take Ricky.'

'Oh, Bertram!' Despite her dislike of her mistress, Elma couldn't stomach this. 'You're not keeping him from her, are you? That's cruel! And he needs his mother.'

'Come here, Elma.' He held out his arms, sure that a few sweet nothings would change her mind, and when she pressed against him, he murmured, 'I thought you'd be pleased to take her place, and he's only a year old. He'll soon forget her. Oh, Elma, my darling, think about it. A father needs his son.' He kissed her then, long, probing kisses that had her shivering with ecstasy.

He was running his hand down her back when she whispered, 'I'll look after him, I love him as much as you, anyway.'

Thankful that she had lost her scruples, he kissed her again and then said, as if he were sorry about it, 'You'd better go downstairs before I take you to bed.'

'We'll have plenty time for that,' she smiled, as she went out, walking as if she thought herself cock of the walk.

Dropping his trousers, Bertram gave a sneering grin. She had no idea that he was using her for his own ends. Once he got Cissie out of the way and things had settled down, he didn't intend to dally any more with Elma. She'd be Ricky's nurse or nanny, but not Bertram Dickson's mistress.

As he stepped into the bath, he gave a harsh laugh at the prospect of seeing Cissie's face when he barred her from the house. She had served her purpose by giving him the son who would fall heir to half the Dickson cash within a few years, and his father couldn't put any blame on him this time, because it was Cissie who had been unfaithful. He could still hardly credit what she had done, but she had played right into his hands. She would be home in another hour or so, little knowing what was in store for her, and he could hardly wait.

Cissie was humming softly as she walked up the drive, and smiled when Bertram came out to meet her. 'I'd have come back before this if I'd known you'd be home so early.'

There was no answering smile. 'It seems I did not come home early enough.'

His cold voice took her aback. 'What do you mean? Has something gone wrong at the mill? Or the warehouse?'

He wrenched the pram out of her hands. 'I'll take the baby inside and you can go wherever you like.'

'I don't understand. Why are you behaving like this?'

'You don't understand? Don't you think it is I who should be saying that? I go away for one night, and come home to find that my wife has had her lover in my house.'

'My lover?' It was a moment before the truth occurred to her. 'If you mean Tommy, he's my brother.'

'From what I have been told, no brother and sister would act the way you two did.'

Knowing that only one person could have told him anything, Cissie burst out, 'What's Elma been saying?'

'Can you deny that you threw your arms round him as soon as he came in, and that you kissed each other repeatedly?'

246

'What's wrong with that? We hadn't seen each other for years. Let me past, Bertram, we can't discuss this here.'

Blocking her way, he hissed, 'You will not set foot inside my house again. You cannot deny it, can you?'

'Of course I can't deny it. I did throw my arms round him, and we did kiss each other, but just like brother and sister, not like lovers.'

'That's not the way I heard it, and what is more, you even slept together.'

Cissie's legs were shaking now, but she did her best to keep calm. 'If Elma told you that, she's lying. She knew Tommy was going to sleep in the room across the passage from ours, she'd to put a hot water bottle in the bed, and the sheets would have been sent to the laundry. Ask her.'

'She has already told me that only one bed was slept in, and she has no reason to lie.' Wresting the pram from her, he wheeled it inside and slammed the door in her face.

Cissie leaned weakly against the wall. This couldn't be happening? He couldn't take her child away from her in retaliation for something she hadn't done? Anger suddenly replaced the self-pity. She wouldn't let her son go without a fight. Lifting the heavy brass knocker, she banged on the door. 'Bertram, let me speak to Elma!'

She kept pounding on the door, and at last the sitting room window was edged fractionally open by the new maid, who peered at her nervously then whispered, 'The master says I've not to let you in, Mrs Dickson.'

Tildy, just left school, was obviously terrified, but Cissie was past caring about anything except getting in to take her son. 'Open the door for me at once! I must get some clothes. He can't expect me to go with nothing but what I'm wearing.'

The white face disappeared but was back in a moment. 'The master says you should have thought of that before you . . .' She hesitated then repeated the words Bertram had flung at her, her face scarlet with embarrassment, '. . . before you started whoring in his house.'

A barked order from behind her made her close the window hastily, and Cissie was left standing, her small spark of rebellion fizzling out. What was she to do? Why had Elma told those lies? She knew that Tommy was her brother – but maybe she didn't! Cissie's heart sank as she recalled what she had told the maid about Tommy staying the night. She hadn't said 'my brother', she had said 'Mr McGregor', and Elma wouldn't have known that McGregor had been her maiden name. She hadn't connected them as brother and sister, but she had told a deliberate lie about the way they kissed, and worse, about them sleeping together. How could Bertram have believed that?

It was then that Cissie recalled the looks that she had seen passing between her husband and Elma at times, the kind of looks only lovers exchange. She had believed it was her imagination, had chided herself for being jealous, but she hadn't imagined it. When had it started? When had they had the opportunity? Of course! There had been ample opportunity when she was in hospital.

Turning round, Cissie kicked the door several times. 'Let me in, Bertram! I know you've been carrying on with Elma!'

He banged the window open. 'No one's going to believe a word you say after I tell them what you did.'

'Let me have Ricky,' she begged, 'and I'll go away, and you can sleep with whoever you want.'

His reply came at her like the voice of doom. 'If you do not leave this minute, I shall phone the police.'

Seeing him in his true colours at last, Cissie made her miserable way back to the street, her only thought being that her son was being kept from her on the other side of a locked door. But gradually, filtering through her numb anguish, came another thought. Where was she to go?

Chapter Twenty-four

❖❖

Fully clad, Jen Millar sank thankfully down on her bed. It was taking more and more out of her to keep working, but she needed the money and she was lucky to have a job at all. Her wheezing chest was beginning to alarm her. At first, she had only heard it in the silence of her own room, but she could hear the rasp of it now even over the clatter in the mill. Was she going to die, like hundreds of spinners before her, from breathing in the fibres of the jute she'd spun on to the bobbins for the past forty years?

She closed her eyes, recalling an old woman who had once worked beside her. Mary had been seventy, and shouldn't have been working at all, but it had been awful to listen to her hacking coughs, the fighting for breath, the whistling of her lungs. When her workmates told her to see a doctor, she had said, 'Some o' they poor's doctors would get rid o' the patient afore the cough.' She'd been forced to give up her job eventually, and hadn't lasted long after that, though whether it was her chest that killed her or not being able to afford food, nobody knew. The last time Jen had seen her, she'd been so thin she was like a skeleton, her parchment skin stretched taut over her cheek-bones, but her eyes had still twinkled in her skull-like face. 'I hope the good Lord doesnae object to hirstly chests,' she had gasped, smiling a little, 'though maybe it'll stop whistling in heaven.'

She had been dead the following day, and a woman who saw the corpse had said, 'I broke doon, I couldnae help it, for she looked that peaceful, and her wasted awa' to nothing.'

Shuddering at the thought of anyone seeing her when she was dead, Jen sat up with a jerk. She needed a cup of tea. She swung her feet to the floor, but the effort set up such a pain in her chest that she had to wait until it subsided before standing up. At that moment, someone knocked at her door, and she stood still until whoever it was went away. It was likely her from upstairs wanting to borrow something and there was nothing here except a spoonful of tea and a hard crust of loaf.

The knock came again, louder this time. 'Jen, it's Cissie – Robertson. You remember me, don't you?'

Aye, Jen thought, she remembered Cissie fine, but Cissie wouldn't be knocking at her door. It was a hallucination.

'Jen. I've got to speak to you. Let me in! Please?'

Slowly, the old woman went to the door to prove to herself there was nobody there, and moved back in alarm when a lady in an expensive coat and hat swept past her, a lady that reminded her of . . . 'Cissie! Is it really you?'

'I waited till you'd be home, but when you didn't answer the door, I thought . . . Jen, Bertram's locked me out.'

'Bertram? Your man?'

Sitting down on the nearest chair, Cissie said, 'You're the only one I could come to, Jen. Phoebe's in America . . .'

'Aye, I heard that.'

'And Dorothy Barclay's expecting another baby. I couldn't go upsetting her.'

Not knowing who Dorothy Barclay was, Jen said, 'I'll put a match to the sticks in the fire to boil the kettle for some tea. Tell me the time we're waiting.'

Cissie began with her surprise at Tommy's visit, and Jen said, 'So your brother did find you?'

'He got my address from Bertram's mill.'

Cissie carried on with her tearful account, and the frown on Jen's face deepened. 'But did you no' say it was your brother?'

'He wouldn't listen. He believed every word Elma told him, and it was all lies.'

'Had you fell oot wi' her? Got on to her aboot her work?'

'She's a good worker. They're all good workers, though Tildy hasn't been there long. Poor thing, she was scared stiff when she opened the window to speak to me.'

'Could you no' have climbed in the window?'

'Bertram was standing right behind her.'

Rising to pour the tea – the last she had – Jen said, 'I'd ask you to bide here the night, but you wouldnae want . . .'

'Could I, Jen? I've nowhere else to go.'

'It's a good thing I never threw out that old mattress after Gertie left, that was her that bade wi' me after you and Phoebe moved oot. I'll let you have the bed, though, for you'll be used to sleeping in . . .'

'I couldn't sleep, Jen. I'll just lie on the floor.'

In the ensuing short silence, Cissie realised that Jen was having difficulty in breathing. She had been too involved with her story to notice before, but her old friend's chest was heaving with every breath she took, loud rattly breaths that sent shivers up the back of Cissie's neck. 'Oh, Jen!' she exclaimed. 'You're ill. I shouldn't have bothered you.'

'It's just a wee wheeze. Cissie, would you go back to him, if he asked you?'

'Oh, Jen, I don't know. I don't know what to think. At first, I thought he'd been carrying on with Elma, and Tommy staying the night had given them an excuse to get me out of the way, but now I'm not so sure. He wouldn't take up with one of his maids, though why did he listen to her and ignore me? I wish I knew what to do!'

Wringing her hands in anguish, Cissie bowed her head for a moment, then looked at Jen again. 'I'm going to get my baby out of that house! Bertram can't keep him from me for ever.'

Jen stroked her chin. 'He's an influential man, mind, and

he could get a . . . what'sit? You ken, he could make it so you couldnae see the bairn again.'

Cissie's eyes filled with tears once more. 'An injunction, you mean? If I say Tommy's my brother, not my lover, they can't do that to me.'

Her lack-lustre eyes filling with pity, Jen murmured, 'He could make them believe what he wants them to believe. He'd tell them you were a mill-girl and they wouldnae listen to you. I'm sorry I'm no' giving you any hope, but you have to face up to it.'

'I was so happy to see Tommy again . . .' Cissie's sigh was almost a sob. 'He said he'd come to see me again, and he won't know where I am.'

'I've just thought. Wait till your man's at his work the morrow, then take your bairn, and whatever else you want, and get that Elma to admit to her lies.'

'She'd likely brazen it out, and even if I did get Ricky, Bertram would send the police to take him from me again.'

'They'll no' ken where to look for you. Now, you'll no' want to bring your son up in a place like this, and if I was you, I'd go right away from Dundee wi' him, and look for a job o' some kind.'

It crossed Cissie's mind that this would mean she was running away from her troubles a second time, but it seemed the only thing to do. 'Thanks, Jen, it's a good thing your brain's working properly, for mine's not. I'll pack as much as I can into the pram – it's deep enough to hold some of my clothes as well as Ricky's – and I'll take the ten pounds his grandfather gave him for his birthday. That should do us for a week or two till I find a job.'

Jen's watery eyes widened. Ten pounds was nearly half a year's wages to her, as Cissie would have remembered if she wasn't in such a state. It was funny how quick folk could forget poverty when they were living off the fat of the land. 'Aye, that should do you for a week or two.'

Although the repeated words held no sarcasm, they

jogged Cissie's memory. 'I'll pay you for letting me stay here,' she said, quickly. 'I've got some money in my purse, though Bertram never let me have much.'

'Indeed and you'll no'! The world would be in a sad state if a body couldnae help a friend.'

'I don't know what I'd have done if I hadn't had you to come to, Jen. But you can't have had any supper yet, so I'll go and get something from the pieshop, and you can boil the kettle for another pot of tea.'

Jen let her go without arguing — it would be stupid to let pride deprive her of her first decent meal for days — and went down to the back court for water. She had to stop every few steps to catch her breath on her way up again, but she was only concerned about the tea she was expected to make. A fine lady like Cissie would turn up her nose at using the same tea leaves twice as she had to do herself, more than twice, sometimes.

Her old friend, however, had seen her emptying the little packet into the pot and also brought back half a pound of tea and a box of biscuits. At the table, they recalled the days when they worked together, Cissie assuring Jen that she couldn't eat a thing and that it was a shame to waste that other pie.

At last, Jen said, 'I'd better get some sleep, or I'll no' be fit for my work in the morning.'

Not bothering to undress, Cissie stretched out on the old lumpy mattress on the floor, and pulled the dingy, motheaten blankets over her. She hadn't forgotten the icy draught that came in at the gap under the door.

In the morning, Jen had to leave in time to start work at six, but she told Cissie to stay for as long as she wanted. 'Just mind and lock the door behind you when you go, and put the key on the ledge above.'

'Thanks again, Jen, and I'll keep in touch with you.'

Left on her own, Cissie folded up the blankets, stacked the floppy mattress against the wall, then swept and dusted the tiny room. She would have to get used to doing house-work again, wherever she was. As she moved about, she wondered how long poor Jen would be able to work – she wasn't really fit for it now – and was thankful that she had thought of buying the tea and biscuits for her.

When she was putting on her hat and coat, she wished that she could do something more for Jen, and decided that money would be most welcome. There was only three pounds, fifteen shillings and thruppence three farthings in her purse, but she laid the three pound-notes on the table, keeping the rest in case things didn't go according to plan.

It was five to ten when she reached Panache and found the front door locked – Elma usually unlocked it as soon as she rose – but she lifted the knocker and rapped loudly several times. She was determined not to give the servants a chance to laugh at her by going round to the back.

When Tildy opened the door, her face paled then turned a deep crimson. 'Oh, Mrs Dickson, the master's away to his work and he said you wasn't to get in.'

Pushing past her, Cissie ran upstairs to the room she had shared with Bertram, her spirits sinking when she found Elma making the bed.

The maid was also taken aback. 'You shouldn't be here!'

Cissie's control snapped. 'How dare you speak to me like that! It's your fault all this happened, you and your lies! Maybe you didn't know Tommy was my brother, but you knew perfectly well we didn't sleep in the same bed, so why did you tell my husband we did?'

'I told the master the truth! He'd a right to know what his wife got up to when he was away.'

'You're a liar and a troublemaker!' Cissie shouted, then, regretting having let the girl see how rattled she was, she said, coldly, 'Pack your things, you'll be leaving tonight! I'll make my husband pay you to the end of the month, but I want you to tell him before you go that you lied to him.'

'The master won't make me leave,' Elma sneered. 'Him and me are – lovers!' She flung the word at Cissie triumphantly.

'You didn't know, did you? I was sleeping with him the whole two weeks you were in the maternity, and he's been wanting rid of you ever since. It's me he wants now.'

Cissie tried not to show her anger. Her first thoughts had been right, after all. To think that Bertram had been making love to this brazen-faced tramp! She felt like launching herself on the grinning creature, scratching her eyes out, tearing her hair out by the roots – only what good would it do? If she was what Bertram wanted, let him have her!

'Bertram said you hadn't to get in,' Elma went on, with great emphasis on his name, 'so you'd better go away again. You won't get him back, for he's mine!'

Gathering all her sickness, fury, disgust into one tight ball in her chest, Cissie said, very quietly, 'You have done me a good turn by letting me see the kind of man he really is, and I wouldn't come back to him though he was the last man on earth. Now, I'm going to get some of Ricky's clothes and mine, and you're not going to stop me. Do you hear me? Oh, for goodness sake, get out! Get out before I forget I'm a lady and kick you down the stairs!'

Elma left the room scowling darkly, and Cissie took some underwear out of the drawers and a few day dresses from the wardrobe, sighing over the lovely gowns she was having to leave behind. Then she went into Ricky's room and gathered as many of his clothes as she could pile on top of her own before going downstairs again. Her heart plunged when she saw that Elma had lined up reinforcements. The cook and the other maid were standing with her outside the sitting room, Mrs Gow looking rather uncomfortable, Tildy as nervous as a skittish colt, and Elma boldly defiant.

'Let me past, please,' Cissie said, firmly, though a lump

was throbbing in her throat and her whole body was quivering with anger. 'I want to get my son.'

Elma gave a sneering smile. 'The master gave us orders not to let you take him.'

'You can't keep him from me. I'm his mother.'

'I'm sorry, Ma'am,' Mrs Gow said, a little too politely, 'but we have our orders and it's more than our jobs are worth to disobey. Besides, you've given up your right to him by what you did two nights ago.' Her tone suggested that she had always been sure her mistress was less than honourable.

Preparing for battle, Cissie drew a deep breath. 'All I did two nights ago was to welcome my brother to my home. I hadn't seen him for over eleven years.'

Mrs Gow shook her head. 'A woman doesn't kiss her brother, and she certainly doesn't let him share her bed.'

Turning to Elma, Cissie said coldly, 'Tell them the truth, if you know the meaning of the word. You had to send the sheets my brother used to the laundry, hadn't you?'

The girl's eyes met hers unflinchingly. 'I don't know what you're meaning, Mrs Dickson. I sent no sheets to the laundry yesterday. I was shocked when I saw you'd slept with another man when the master was away, and I told Mrs Gow there would be trouble, didn't I, Mrs Gow?'

The cook nodded. 'Aye, that's what she said, and I could hardly believe the things she was telling me.'

Cissie raised her voice. 'Whatever she told you, it was a pack of lies.'

From behind the servants came a squeal of delight. 'Mama, mama,' and she appealed to Mrs Gow. 'Ricky's heard me. I swear to you Tommy's my brother, though I wish to God he'd never found me.'

Uncertainly, the cook glanced at Elma, who said, 'Don't believe her. If you'd seen the way they were carrying on, you'd know he wasn't her brother. It was disgusting, and her always making out she was something.'

Her eyes hardening, Mrs Gow said, 'I think you'd better leave, Mrs Dickson. If you want to get your son, you'll need to come back and have it out with the master.'

Another cry of 'Mama' made Cissie drop the clothes she was carrying and take a step forward. 'Get out of my way. I'm not leaving unless I take him with me.'

Poor Tildy's eyes were round with fear, but the other two closed ranks and grabbed Cissie's arms when she tried to pass between them. There followed a short, unequal struggle, both women being sturdier and stronger than Cissie, and at last she gave up. Turning away, she sobbed, 'I hope God punishes you for what you've done.'

Scarcely able to see through her tears, she trailed out, forcing one foot past the other and not caring where she went. It took her a little time to control herself and to be capable of logical thought. Why hadn't she gone straight in and taken Ricky without bothering about clothes? She could have been outside with him before any of them knew she was there, and now she had no clothes, no baby and nowhere to live. She couldn't go back to Jen, for the poor soul wasn't fit to cope with her in this state, and Dorothy wasn't fit to be saddled with her, either. If only Phoebe had been here, Cissie thought, distractedly, they would have gone to Panache together and taken Ricky, but Phoebe was thousands of miles away.

'Mrs Dickson!'

She turned round, hoping that her servants had relented, that they were going to let her go back for her son, but it was only young Tildy sprinting towards her, brandishing a carpet bag. 'Mrs Gow told me to pack your things for you,' she gasped, 'and I've been trying to catch up with you. I'm sorry, Mrs Dickson,' she added, as Cissie took the bag. 'I'd have let you take Ricky if it had been up to me, but Elma wouldn't . . .'

'I know, it's not your fault.'

'We'll look after him, so you won't need to worry. I'll

have to get back, though, or Cook'll give me whatfor.'

'Thank you, Tildy – and thank Mrs Gow for letting me have my clothes.'

The girl ran off, and Cissie walked on for a few hundred yards before stopping again. Some of Bertram's friends lived quite near, should she ask any of them for help, or advice? But it would likely get back to him and they would believe whatever he told them about her. And it would only make him more determined not to let her have Ricky.

The thought stirred her to action. She wasn't beaten yet. Changing direction, she headed down the hill towards the city, the rain, threatening for some time, now battering against her face. The shower did not last long, but she had hardly noticed its beginning nor its end, and when she came to the warehouse, she marched through the outer office into Bertram's inner sanctum and addressed him in ringing tones. 'You can't keep my son from me, Bertram!'

Embarrassed, his secretary left the room, and Bertram, who had jumped up at his wife's abrupt entry, came round his desk, looking at her with loathing. 'You know why I won't let you have him. You're not fit to be a mother.'

'I'm a fitter mother than you are a father!'

His top lip curled. 'How quaintly you express yourself, but what else could I expect from a woman of the lower classes? As for my fitness as a father, I have never taken a lover into my house.'

'You didn't need to take one in, you'd one there already, that's why you wanted rid of me. And Tommy isn't my lover! I told you, he's my brother. You must believe me! I can't bear to be separated from my son!'

'You will get accustomed to it.'

'I'll never get accustomed to it! I don't have to!' Cissie could feel her temper building up. 'If you won't let me have Ricky, I'll tell everybody about the awful things you used to do to me. God knows what got into you at that time, but I'm glad you did, for it's . . .'

'You think it has given you something to bargain with?' He looked at her contemptuously.

'I'll tell all your friends, and about Elma, too, and then they'll think as little of you as I do.'

'Who do you think is going to believe you? I am a pillar of society nowadays, and when I tell my associates that I picked you out of the gutter . . .'

Outraged, Cissie shouted, 'I wasn't in the gutter! I was working in your father's office when you first knew me.'

A cold smile played over his lips. 'And before that, you were only a spinner. No one will believe your fantasies.'

'I wish now I'd let Dorothy Barclay see all the marks and bruises you left on me. I should have taken Ricky and walked out then, but I loved you in spite of everything.'

The smile broadened. 'How unfortunate for you, because I have never loved you.'

'Why did you marry me?' she gasped.

'I needed a son to prevent my father from leaving all his wealth to our mutual stepmother.'

'But you didn't know he'd leave half to Ricky until after he was born.'

'I was sure a grandson would do the trick, and Ricky is my insurance for the future . . . the very near future, I hope.'

Cissie changed her tactics. 'You've plenty of money already, and I need my son. Please, please, Bertram. I'll do anything you want if you let me take him, anything.'

His violet eyes glittered with triumph. 'I never thought I'd hear you grovelling to me.'

'If you want me to grovel, I'll grovel. I'll go down on my knees to you, I'll kiss your feet, I'll do anything, just let me have my son!' Stepping forward, she grabbed his hand.

An evil smile spread across his face, as though he were considering what he would make her do, then, with a snort, he pulled his hand away. 'I was tired of you long ago, and nothing you can offer appeals to me.'

Pulling at the lapels of his jacket, she pleaded, 'Please, Bertram? I beg you, please let me have my baby. Then I'll go away and I'll never bother you again.'

'You'll never bother me again, in any case. I am keeping Ricky, and you are wasting my time as well as your own, so go now, before I have someone throw you out.' He prised her fingers open and strode to the door.

'Please, Bertram!' she cried, hysterically, as he held it open. 'Oh, please, please, please!'

Gripping her shoulder, he propelled her swiftly through the outer office, then with a last violent shove he sent her staggering out on to the tarred path and slammed the door behind her.

She stumbled along the wet streets, her last hope gone, not conscious of the people who stared in bemusement at such a well-dressed lady weeping bitterly in public. She was only conscious that Bertram would do everything in his power to keep Ricky from her. For some time, she walked blindly, not caring where she went, until her legs gave way and she was forced to slump against the harled wall of a building she was passing.

Ten full minutes passed before her body came anywhere near being alive again and she was capable of thought. Levering herself away from the wall, she started to walk, a little steadier now. She had to find a place where she could sit down to gather her senses. Looking around to see where she was, she was astonished to find that she was in Thorston Street, a stone's throw from the Overgate! Her feet had led her back to her old haunts.

Sitting at a wobbly table in a tiny cafe, Cissie allowed the hot tea to revive her further before she tried to think what to do next. Should she do as Jen had advised and leave Dundee? It was admitting defeat, but what else could she do in the face of what Bertram had said? And could she bear to stay in the same city as the son she would never see again? Was it possible for her to begin a new life somewhere else? It seemed to be the only thing left for her.

Where should she go? Her insides gave a sudden jolt. In her distress, she had forgotten about money. When she went to Panache, she had intended taking the ten pounds Richard had given Ricky, and events had put it right out of her head. In hindsight, what she should have done was look for the money she knew Bertram kept in the house, but it hadn't occurred to her, and, apart from the clothes in the carpet bag, all she had to her name was the fifteen and thruppence three farthings in her purse. There was more likelihood of her getting a job in a city, but she couldn't afford to go far away. Perth was too near, and Bertram sometimes went to Glasgow on business – it would have to be Edinburgh. Nobody would ever think of looking for her there.

Getting to her feet, she walked out of the teashop and made her way to the bus station. Travelling by bus should be cheaper than going by rail.

Cissie looked at her watch and couldn't believe that it was only ten past six – it seemed like days since she had left Jen's room. She had been through two hells, and she still hadn't got her baby. She couldn't have been sitting in this freezing bus shelter for more than an hour or two, but her feet felt as if they didn't belong to her. Would she ever feel whole again? Her heart was bleeding with the longing to hold her son in her arms again. She couldn't possibly leave Dundee without Ricky!

Lifting the bag by her side, she got up wearily, unsure of what to do but knowing that she must do something. When she went out into the street, she stood uncertainly, wondering which direction to take. She couldn't burden Jen again, and that left only the Barclays. She hated the idea of upsetting Dorothy, but she had no option, and her friend would be hurt if she didn't ask for help at this time.

When she reached the Barclays' house, she was so tired that her feet were dragging, but that was nothing compared with the agony inside her. Trailing up the short driveway, she rang the bell and waited, her heart palpitating at the thought of what would happen when Roland went to Panache to demand that Bertram give up his child. It probably wouldn't end in a fight, though, because Bertram would want to keep on the right sight of the man who had invested so much in his mill. He would probably hand over the baby.

When the little maid answered the door, Cissie said, 'Can I speak to Mrs Barclay, please?'

She was expecting the maid to come back and take her in, but it was Roland who appeared. 'I have forbidden my wife to see you again,' he said, abruptly.

Her whole body quivered with bitter disappointment. 'Did Bertram phone you?' she whispered.

'He didn't phone. He came to the house late last night, and I've never seen anyone in such a state. He was a broken man, and I was glad Dorothy was in bed and didn't see him. He told me exactly what had happened, and I don't know how you have the nerve to show your face here.'

'He won't let me have Ricky! I didn't do anything, Roland! Tommy isn't my lover, he's my brother! Ask Dorothy, I told her about him.'

'Please don't involve my wife in your affairs. She is in a delicate condition and I'll do everything I can to prevent her being distressed. I have no more to say to you.'

The door closing with a bang, Cissie turned away. If only she had come straight to Dorothy when Bertram took Ricky away from her, she thought, miserably, he wouldn't have had time to tell Roland. But what could Dorothy have done except sympathise? It was really Roland she had been depending on. She should have gone to his office yesterday afternoon. Her long walk had been all for nothing. She had been sure Roland would be on her side, and he thought the worst of her, too. And Bertram would make sure that no one else believed her, either.

Plodding down the hill again, she prayed that whoever was looking after Ricky was feeding him properly. He had been seven months old before she weaned him, and even now his little stomach couldn't cope with anything stronger than milk puddings, mashed boiled eggs and bland foods like that. If he had colic, would they know what to do? And he would be crying for her, he needed his mother. Oh, God! She had to go back to the house and try again!

Tears were streaming down her cheeks when she arrived at Panache, but she didn't care who saw them. She banged on the door several times, waited a few seconds and banged again and again. No one answered her urgent summons, so she moved along to the sitting room window and kept knocking on it until her arms were sore. At last, unable to bear it any longer, she shouted, as loudly as she could, 'I know you're there, Bertram! Let me in, before I take a stone and break this glass!'

Her throat was so tight now that she was having difficulty breathing, yet she was determined not to give up, not as long as there was breath left in her body. She scanned the path but could see no stone large enough to do any damage, and it suddenly occurred to her that she could appeal to Mrs Gow. An older woman would surely understand the torture she was going through.

Waiting for a moment to gather strength, Cissie went round the side of the house and down the basement steps, but in spite of the repeated knocking on the back door, it also remained firmly closed — and locked, she discovered.

'Mrs Gow,' she called, 'please let me speak to you. Elma was lying, I did nothing wrong.'

There was absolute silence, as if there were no one in the house, yet she knew that wasn't the case. They were all in there, all against her. Elma had spread the poison, and Mrs Gow had never liked her anyway, she had always sensed that, and wee Tildy would be too scared of them to voice her own opinion.

Utterly drained, emotionally and physically, Cissie leaned back against the wall at the side of the door, then her legs refusing to take her weight any longer, she slid slowly to the ground.

Inside, Mrs Gow was saying, 'She must be away, though I didn't hear her feet going round the side again.'

'Will I go out and have a look?'

'Aye, Tildy, we'd be as well making sure.'

The girl went into the scullery and unlocked the heavy door, and when she saw no sign of anyone, she crept along and went up the steps to look round the front of the house. There was no one there, either, so, letting out a little breath of relief, she turned and came back. Her mouth fell open when her eyes, accustomed now to the darkness, spied her mistress slumped between the back door and the wall of the garage – she hadn't thought of looking to that side when she came out – and ran over to see if she was all right.

Mustering a little energy from somewhere, Cissie put her finger to her lips. Tildy on her own was one thing, Tildy joined by an unfeeling Mrs Gow was another.

'Are you ill, Mrs Dickson?' the girl whispered, anxiously.

'Just very tired,' Cissie whispered back. 'Please, Tildy, will you help me to get Ricky back?'

Terrified that the cook would come out to see why she was taking so long, Tildy hodged from one foot to the other. 'I – I'd like to, Mrs Dickson, but . . .'

'Is Elma in the kitchen with Mrs Gow?'

'No, there's just me and Cook. Elma went with the master, to look after the baby when he took him away.'

This was something Cissie had never envisaged. 'He took Ricky away?' she said, faintly. 'Do you know where?'

'No, I only heard him saying they'd wouldn't be back for

a while. Cook thinks he'll stay away till you stop making a nuisance of yourself. That's what she said,' she added.

'Oh, God!' Cissie moaned. 'What am I going to do?'

'I'll have to go in, or Cook'll be wondering . . .'

'Yes, I don't want you to get into trouble because of me.'

'Will I help you up, Mrs Dickson?

'No, I'll be all right. I'll just sit here for a while.'

'I don't believe what they said about you!' Tildy burst out suddenly. 'I'm sure Elma's got her eye on the master and wants to get him for herself, but Cook can't see it.'

A tiny ray of warmth came into Cissie's frozen body. 'Thank you, Tildy. It's good to know one person sees through her.'

'Cheerio, Mrs Dickson, and I hope . . .' The girl hesitated, then said, 'You must be heartbroken. I'm sorry.'

Left alone again, Cissie felt that her heart was not just broken, it was smashed to smithereens by what Tildy had told her. How could she ever hope to get her son back when she didn't know where he was? She kept sitting with her back against the wall for a few more minutes before she rose groggily to her feet. Then, lifting the bag, she made her way silently round to the front of the house and down the drive.

She was beyond tears as she staggered on, beyond hoping. She was beyond anything except getting as far from Panache as she could. When she reached the Nethergate, she felt an urge to carry on to the pier and jump into the Tay, but Ricky's darling little face came into her head. Alive, there was always a chance that she would get him back; dead, she would have abandoned him to his father and that awful girl.

Her senses suddenly reminded her that she wasn't far from the Overgate and the friend who would stand by her, and with a gulping sigh, she made for Jen's room. 'Oh, my

God!' the old woman exclaimed, when she opened the door warily and saw the bedraggled figure. 'What a state you're in, Cissie!'

'I haven't got Ricky back,' Cissie said, unnecessarily. 'Bertram's taken him and Elma away.'

'Have you had anything to eat since I saw you last?'

'I couldn't eat, I'm not hungry.'

'You'll no' be fit for anything if you starve yourself. Look, I bought a tin o' ham wi' that money you left, and a loaf and margarine, and a bag o' coal, and there's still plenty o' the tea you took in. Sit down at the fire and heat yourself till I get things ready.'

'What'll I do, Jen?' Cissie sobbed, as Jen bustled about.

'What did you try the day?'

After Cissie told of all her unsuccessful attempts to get her son, Jen sat down to wait until the tea infused. 'Can you no' think on anybody else that could stand up to him?'

'Dorothy Barclay was my only real friend, and Roland, that's her husband, wouldn't let me speak to her. Bertram had told him the same as he'll tell all the people we know, and nobody's going to believe me.'

'Aye, I can see how you're placed.' Jen thought for some time, then said, 'You wouldnae think on going to the bobbies yourself? Your man's kidnapped the bairn . . .'

'He'll tell them the same as he'll tell everybody else, and they'll believe him. Who's going to think a businessman like him would get rid of his wife because he was taking up with one of his own maids? Elma admitted that.'

Jen stood up to move the teapot farther away from the fire in case it came to the boil. 'It lets you see gentry's no' better than working men. Come and eat something, Cissie. You'll feel better for it.'

When they were seated at the small table, the old woman said, 'I heard your man's told all the mills not to take you on, so you'd not get a job at any of them.'

Cissie gave a tearful sigh. 'I might have known.'

'Maybe you should get away from Dundee, like I said last night. Let things cool down for maybe a year or so . . .'

'A whole year?' Cissie was aghast at this.

'He'd think you was away for good, and you could catch him and that lassie off their guard. He cannae bide away from his businesses, he's bound to come home sometime. You could just go and take the bairn. Think on it, Cissie.'

Lying on the old mattress, Cissie gave much consideration to Jen's solution, and came to the conclusion that it might work. She would go to Edinburgh and take a job, then she'd go back to Panache in a year, and take Ricky when Bertram was at his office. Tildy would help, if she was still there, and it would be two against two, not three against one as it had been before.

At quarter to six the next morning, Cissie said goodbye to her old friend. 'Thank God I had you to come to, Jen, and thank you for putting up with me.'

'Ach, Cissie, I'm glad I was able to help you a wee bit, and mind, let me ken when you get your bairn back.'

'I promise.' Cissie was pleased that Jen had said 'when' and not 'if'. It made what she had seen as the impossible seem possible, after all.

PART THREE

Leith, Edinburgh

Chapter Twenty-five

❧❧

1925—26

Still jobless after two whole weeks in Edinburgh, Cissie was at her wits' end. At each place she tried – offices first, then shops – they had looked at her expensive clothes and told her she wasn't suitable. When, in desperation, she had gone round the factories, more than one overseer had eyed her up and down and laughed in her face. But maybe it hadn't been just the way she was dressed. Her experiences over her last two days in Dundee had left their mark. The pain in her heart, still almost unendurable, made her nervous and jumpy, her hands had developed a permanent shake. That would put any employer off, and, besides, she had no references to show, no one to vouch for her. To get money for food, she'd had to sell her engagement ring for three pounds, less than a hundredth of what it was worth, but it was all any jeweller would give.

Her well-cut clothes had been an advantage in only one respect. When she was looking for a place to live, on the day she arrived, she could have had her pick of a dozen rooms, but she had chosen the cheapest, in a house in Pilrig Street, off Leith Walk. The landlady had been surprised when she said she would take it, and no wonder, Cissie thought, looking round the room. The only items of furniture apart from the bed were a wooden chair and a green-baize-covered card table, pock-marked with cigarette burns, though there was a shallow cupboard with hooks for her clothes, and, fixed to the fireplace wall, a shelf holding one cup and saucer, two plates and a pan. The linoleum was worn down to the jute backing in places, and there were big jagged tears sticking up ready to trip her.

She had discovered that the mattress had holes in it where the prickly horse-hairs poked through, and the two blankets were so threadbare that she would freeze to death in winter. The little gas fire in the chimney breast and the single gas ring standing on the tiled hearth, her only means of heating and cooking, gobbled up the shillings. Tonight she had no money left to feed the meter nor herself, and she was glad that she hadn't Ricky with her, after all. She couldn't have let him go hungry.

As usual when she thought of her son, she was assailed by the acute agony of losing him. It was bad enough during the days, but nights were worse, when she woke a dozen times, her eyes streaming because she had been dreaming of Ricky, her innards aching at being so far away from him. It was only a matter of fifty miles or so, but it might as well be hundreds. But her baby would be properly cared for, Cissie assured herself; Bertram would make sure of that, because Ricky was his insurance for the future.

Jen had told her to wait a year before she tried to snatch him back, and surely by then she would be in a position to provide for him. He would be completely on solids by then, and they would sit together at a table and . . . oh why couldn't she stop building castles in the air and face reality? Her stomach was rumbling emptily, and she would willingly have taken cheese from a mousetrap if there had been such a luxury in the room. She couldn't carry on like this, and her landlady would be expecting her to pay two weeks' rent in the morning. The stylish clothes had stopped her from asking anything in advance, though she had looked dubious when her new lodger had said she would settle at the end of every fortnight.

What was she to do? Cissie wondered, hopelessly. If only Phoebe hadn't been in America . . . Phoebe? When she had been in the same financial straits, she had kept the wolf from the door by selling herself to men. Cissie pondered over this. Could she possibly bring herself to do that? If it was the only way . . .

She lifted her handbag and went over to the cracked mirror above the mantelpiece. Taking out the garish lipstick she had bought for fun when she was out with Dorothy Barclay one day, she was about to apply it to her mouth when her hand halted. She couldn't do it. She couldn't let a stranger paw at her, not even to get money to pay her rent and buy food. Flinging the metal container from her in disgust at herself for even thinking of painting her face to get a man, she flopped down on the bed and gave way to tears. She couldn't live with herself if she turned prostitute. She would have to tell her landlady in the morning that she couldn't pay for the room, and she'd likely be thrown out on the street. That would be the end of her, for there was no Jen here.

She sobbed until she was exhausted, then, out of the blue, she remembered her brother. Tommy's ship was based in Leith! Why hadn't she thought of it before? It was over two weeks since she had seen him, though, and he would be on the high seas again by this time. She'd be wasting her time trying to look for him. No! Anything was worth trying, in her present predicament.

Rising unsteadily to her feet, Cissie took her coat and hat from the cupboard and crept down the stairs. As she turned out of Pilrig Street into Leith Walk, she realised that the docks would be full of ships, and she had no idea which one to look for.

There had been a problem with the loading – the dockers asking for extra money for handling asbestos and the owners flatly refusing to negotiate – so the ship had been held up for well over a fortnight. First Mate McGregor had been angry when the captain went home to Grimsby to see his wife, for it meant that he was left in charge and didn't have time to visit Cissie again. He'd let the skeleton crew take turns to go ashore in the evenings, but he had only left the ship once, and it was time he had some more time off.

He was whistling as he swung down the gangway in his go-ashore clothes with two of his shipmates, and grinned when one of them gave a low whistle. 'Look at that dame! I fancy my chances with her.'

They all looked at the woman who was walking towards them, head down, and the other man said, 'Ach, she's dolled up to the nines. I wonder where she got that frock? It must have cost some poor bugger a pretty penny.'

Tommy let out a roar of laughter. 'The buggers that take up with dames like that can't be poor, and she wouldn't look at the likes of you two. This is a job for an officer.'

Swaggering in front of them, he wished he could see her face. He hadn't planned on having a woman tonight, just a couple of pints, but this was no ordinary pro. She had a lovely body, and he didn't care what she looked like. 'Are you looking for me, gorgeous?' he asked.

Her head snapped up. 'Oh, Tommy!' she cried, and started to weep noisily.

'Cissie?' he gasped, taking hold of her elbow.

'I've been all round the docks looking for you,' she sobbed, collapsing against him, and he waited until his two smirking shipmates were well out of earshot before he turned her round to face him. 'I don't know what's wrong with you, or why you're here, but I'd better get you to the station to catch a train back to Dundee. You can tell me what's wrong the time we're waiting.'

'I've left Dundee. I'm living here.'

With the intention of taking her to the hotel he presumed she was staying in, he hailed a taxi which had just dropped off two staggering sailors, and his spirits hit rock bottom when he saw where Cissie told the driver to stop. The other terraced houses in the street looked quite respectable, but this one hadn't seen a lick of paint since the year oatcake, and the wooden door was chattered at the foot as if mice had been at it. This was no hotel! He let her go in first, and she had only put her foot on the first step of the stairs when a middle-aged woman came out of a side room, sleeves rolled up, mouth pursed, eyes flashing.

'No men visitors allowed,' she ordered, folding her arms.

'He's my brother,' Cissie gulped.

'I've heard that one before.'

'Aye, and you're hearing it again!' declared Tommy, his narrowed eyes daring her to say anything else.

They carried on up, and as soon as Cissie took him into her room, he sat down with her on the bed. 'Let's hear it.'

Her voice was hopeless as she told him why she was no longer living at Panache, and when he learned that Bertram had believed the lies Elma had concocted, he thumped his fist against the wall. 'By God, if I had him here, I'd break his bloody neck! I've a good mind to go to Dundee tomorrow . . .'

She grabbed his arm. 'No, no, Tommy! You'd only make it worse, and he's not there anyway. He's taken Ricky away – with her! And I don't know where they are.'

'You mean – he's keeping Ricky from you? But he can't do that, Cissie.'

Swallowing painfully, she said, 'He took the pram from me and locked me out. I went back the next morning but Elma and Mrs Gow wouldn't let me take my baby, and Bertram laughed at me when I went to his office.'

'Could you not have got Phoebe to help you?'

'She's in America with Richard, and Bertram had told his friends not to have anything to do with me. Jen Millar was the only person I could go to. I don't know what I'd have done if she hadn't taken me in.'

'Oh, God!' Tommy groaned. 'I'm sorry I caused you all that trouble, Cissie.'

'It had nothing to do with you,' she sighed. 'He wanted rid of me anyway, and you staying the night was just the chance he was waiting for. If it hadn't been that, he'd have found something else. Jen told me to leave Dundee, and I couldn't get a job, and I wouldn't be able to look after Ricky even if I had him here with me.'

Looking round him with an expression of distaste, Tommy said, 'Is this the only place you could get?'

'It's the cheapest I could get, and I've no money, and I went down to the docks on the chance your ship was still . . .'

'Didn't you think what could happen to you down there?' Tommy said, grimly. 'It's a good thing it was me that picked you up. God almighty, you're surely not as desperate as to go looking for trouble?'

'I couldn't be more desperate. I've had nothing to eat for two whole days, and two weeks' rent's due in the morning. I was scared I'd be thrown onto the street again. I did think of trying to get a man to pick me up, but I couldn't face it, and I was just looking for you. I was going round and round, and two men did try to – but I got away from them.'

He gathered her in his arms when she gave a low moan, and rocked her for several moments until her heart-rending sobs stopped. 'Look, Cissie, will you be all right till I go out and buy something to eat?'

He returned in ten minutes with two bundles of fish and chips and a bottle of lemonade. 'I was thinking the time I was waiting to be served,' he said, as they opened out the newspaper wrappings. 'I could maybe get you a job, and a place to live, and all.'

Her tear-ravaged face brightened. 'Could you, Tommy?'

He tore a piece of fish off with his fingers. 'Mind, I'm not promising, but whatever happens, you're not staying here another night. When I finish this, I'm going out to see an old friend of mine, and I'll maybe be a wee while, but I'll definitely be back. I'll get you out of here, and I'll pay off that bitch down the stair and tell her what I think of her for taking money from you for a shit-house like this.'

She smiled a little at that and they stopped talking until they had eaten every last crumb, then she was left alone, wondering what her brother had up his sleeve, but knowing that she could depend on him to come back.

It was only half an hour later when he came bursting in. 'Right, then. Get your things packed. It's all fixed.'

Within five minutes he was carrying the carpet bag down to the taxi he had waiting outside, but when it turned down Leith Walk, she looked at him fearfully. 'We're not going back to the docks, are we?'

'Wait and see.'

She was almost sure they were, and was puzzled when the cab turned into Duke Street and drew up a little way along. Tommy led the way into a small sweet-shop, where a thin, grey-haired woman smiled at him then eyed Cissie a trifle doubtfully. 'This is your sister, is it, Tommy?'

He gave a chuckle. 'Aye, Mrs Barbour, she really is my sister and she usually looks a bit better than this.'

Having forgotten that her face would be puffed up with weeping, her eyes red, Cissie gave a gasp of dismay, but Mrs Barbour took her through the back shop — which she clearly used as a store, though there was a sink, a chair and a gas ring in it — and up a flight of stairs outside. 'This is my house,' she explained, 'and this'll be your room. If you want to wash your face, the bathroom's on the left. You'll start tomorrow in the shop, so I'll leave you to unpack your bag. Come down when you're ready.'

Too choked to speak, Cissie nodded gratefully, and went into the bathroom before she did anything else. It was so good to be able to wash properly that she laved her face with water over and over again, and lingered over drying it because the fluffy towel felt so soft after the board-hard bits of things she'd had in Pilrig Street. She felt much better when she went into her room to hang her four dresses in the wardrobe and to lay her silk underclothes neatly in the chest of drawers. Then she stood at the mirror – a crinoline lady in an olde-worlde garden painted along the bottom – to comb her hair, not so difficult to keep since Dorothy Barclay had persuaded her to have it bobbed.

When she went down to the shop again, Mrs Barbour looked at her with approval. 'That's better. I can see you're a bonnie lass now.'

Tommy hooted. 'If I hadn't come across her earlier on, she wouldn't be so bonnie.'

Mortified, Cissie blushed and hung her head, but the woman said, 'It's all right, lass. Tommy's told me.'

When Mrs Barbour was serving in the shop, Cissie looked sadly at her brother. 'Did you have to tell her?'

'Even if you had been trying to pick up a man she'd not hold it against you. I've known her for years, and she's the best woman I've ever met.'

'How did you get her to give me a job?'

He smiled reassuringly. 'I told her my sister was needing a job and a place to sleep, and she said, "I'll have her here." I knew she would, she's the salt of the earth.'

At half past nine, when Tommy said he should have been back on board ages ago, Mrs Barbour smiled, 'Aye, and it's time I closed up.'

After making sure that the shop door was securely locked, she took Cissie upstairs. 'I hope you'll not mind me saying this,' she began, making Cissie wonder what was coming, 'but you can hardly serve behind a counter in that frock. It's more suited for an afternoon tea party. If you've nothing suitable, I think I've a couple of skirts and blouses that might fit you.'

'I'd be very grateful for them,' Cissie murmured. 'You see, I didn't think when I left – my house . . .'

'No, no, I don't want to hear about it. I can see you've come through some trouble, and I'm glad I can help you. Now, I open the shop in the mornings at half past six for the dockers, so I rise at five, but I'm not expecting you . . .'

'I'll manage,' Cissie smiled. 'It's not the first time in my life I've had to get up at five.'

'I'll say goodnight, then. I hope you get a good night's sleep, for you look as though you're needing it.'

Although Cissie was sure she wouldn't sleep after all that had happened, the warm white blankets and eider-down were so comfortable that she soon dropped off, and she didn't move until Mrs Barbour tapped at her door at half past five the following morning.

'Breakfast's ready.' she said. 'It's pouring rain outside, but it'll make no difference to us, for the workers still need their fags.'

'You sell cigarettes, too?'

'And pipe tobacco and matches. I'm really a confectioner and tobacconist, but there's not room for that on my sign, and, anyway, everybody just calls it the sweetie shop.'

Over the porridge and toast, Mrs Barbour told her new assistant about the most popular sweets. 'I can guarantee, as soon as I get a new jar, the clove rock will go down before you can wink, and it's not just the bairns that like it. Liquorice allsorts, now, they don't go so quick, a lot of folk don't like them, but I'm kept busy making tablet.'

'Tablet?'

'Sugar and condensed milk and butter, and a wee drop of vanilla essence, all boiled together till it sets when it's cold – not as hard as candy, but not as soft as fudge, and it melts in your mouth.'

'We called that toffee in Aberdeen.'

'Well, you'll know it's toffee they're needing when they ask for tablet,' Mrs Barbour laughed. 'I get the fags and most of my sweeties from the wholesalers, but I make the tablet and the fudge myself before I go to bed, though now I've got you, I can do it any time I like. I was thinking about getting somebody in, anyway, for I'm not as able as

I used to be. It's a long day to be standing on my feet, and my legs swell up by night.'

Remembering how tired she had been after a day in the mill, Cissie hoped that her legs would stand up to it now.

'Mind you,' Mrs Barbour observed, 'we can each have half an hour off for our dinner and our supper, so it'll not be so bad.'

Cissie offered to clear up the dishes to let her employer open the shop because it was half past six already, and when she was finished, she smoothed down the skirt she had been given and checked that the buttons on the blouse were all properly fastened. Satisfied that she looked respectable, she went downstairs.

After only a week, Cissie felt that she had always been serving sweets and cigarettes. Her brother had looked in for a few minutes on her first day, and had smiled encouragingly as she weighed out some boilings for a schoolboy and handed a twenty of Capstan Full Strength to a docker with what Mrs Barbour called a 'kirkyard' cough and who shouldn't be smoking at all, never mind anything as strong as that, but Tommy's ship had sailed the following day, the stevedores having climbed down over the extra pay. The best thing about her job was that she got on so well with her employer. As long as there were no customers, they talked while they dusted the big jars, and chatted companionably in the kitchen for a while after the shop closed at nine thirty. As Mrs Barbour had said, it was a long day, although they had two separate half-hours off for meals, Cissie having her dinner from half past twelve to one, her supper from five to half past, and her employer taking her breaks immediately after.

Never having had pocket money when she was a little girl, Cissie was intrigued by the items in the children's section. Sherbet fountains and dabs; lucky bags holding tiny trinkets as well as several sweets; lucky tatties, cinnamon-covered candy that sometimes had a ha'penny inside so the fortunate purchaser could buy another; liquorice shoelaces and pipes; gobstoppers that changed colour as they were sucked; tiger nuts; bullseyes; locust beans; 'cow' candy, the brown cow on the wrapper being the maker's trademark; and many others.

She had been surprised at how long Mrs Barbour waited for the boys and girls to decide what to buy with their pennies and ha'pennies, and when she mentioned it, her employer had smiled. 'They're still customers, supposing they've only a bawbee to spend.'

With the adults, boiled sweets sold best, probably because they lasted longest; candies, plain and flavoured; chocolate violets, chocolate-covered fondant with a tiny iced flower on top; coconut rolls. Mrs Barbour's home-made fudge and tablet, of course, were steady favourites, but the most popular on Saturday nights, when people bought them to suck in church on Sunday morning, were what were marked on the jar as 'Mint Imperials' and were known as 'Pandrops' or 'Granny's Sookers', which looked like thick white buttons but were peppermint all the way through.

Mrs Barbour did stock a few boxes of chocolates, but they were only bought by young men out to impress a sweetheart, or by older men trying to sweeten their wives the day after they'd had a night on the booze or upset them in some other way. Cissie was amused by their hang-dog expressions when they pointed to the highest shelf and muttered, 'A half-pound' or 'a pound' – and very occasion-ally, 'two pounds' – depending on how badly they had misbehaved.

Two more weeks had passed when Mrs Barbour said, 'It can't be much fun for you being stuck here day and night with an old woman. You should go out on your half-days.'

'I'm quite happy,' Cissie assured her. As happy as she

could be, she thought, with her son God alone knew where.

'There'll come a time when you'll wish you'd seen a bit more of life.'

'I've seen more than I want to see already.'

'It would do you good to take a walk to Princes Street and have a look at the big stores. I used to spend hours there at one time, but I need my rest nowadays.'

Cissie would have been quite glad to have a rest every Wednesday afternoon, too, but she went out after that to please the old lady. She didn't visit the large stores in Princes Street – going round the different departments didn't appeal to her when Dorothy wasn't at her side – but there were many interesting places to see, and she learned more about the history of Scotland by exploring Edinburgh's old town than she had ever done at school. Even the things she remembered were brought vividly to life by seeing the actual places where they had happened.

The Royal Mile – running parallel to Princes Street and separated from it by centuries as well as by the railway line – made her feel as if she were in a different world. At the top of the hill stood the Castle, its dark outline in keeping with the dark deeds which had been enacted within its walls. Before going inside, she stood reverently in the tiny chapel built by Queen Margaret, wife of Malcolm III, where there was room for only a handful of people. In the Castle itself, she wandered from chamber to chamber, coming eventually to the room where Mary, Queen of Scots gave birth to the son who would be the first king to rule over Scotland and England. This visit was enough for one expedition.

On the following week, she started at the other end of the Royal Mile and steeped herself in the atmosphere of the Palace of Holyrood House as she made her way through the corridors. It made her flesh creep to look down at the spot where David Rizzio, the Queen's ill-fated Italian musician, was murdered at the instigation of her jealous husband, Lord Darnley, and she couldn't help thinking that no matter how turbulent her life had been, it was as nothing compared to the sufferings of this woman of history.

On another day, she passed her free afternoon by looking in the windows of the little shops which lined the famous street, and ended up by going into St Giles Cathedral, which was halfway between the two royal residences. After walking round the old building, she sat down in one of the wooden pews, picturing the outraged Jenny Geddes throwing a stool at John Knox – a strong opponent of the young Queen Mary – because he was preaching against her beliefs.

It was on this occasion, not having taken so long as she had done on her other visits, that she went over the Bridges and had a walk along Princes Street Gardens, where she took a seat beside the Scott Monument. Unfortunately, the peace which had seeped right into her in the cathedral was ousted by thoughts of her son, and she wondered if she would ever feel completely serene again. The anguish of the separation was still gnawing at her innards, and it would never go away until she held Ricky in her arms once more. The pain in her heart becoming unbearable, she went up the steps on to the street, crossed over and took a tram back to Duke Street.

That evening, having often wondered how her brother had come to be on such good terms with Mrs Barbour, she said, 'Have you known Tommy for a long time?'

'Aye, I've known him for a good few years now,' the old lady smiled. 'He comes in here at least once every time he's in port, and him and me have had some great arguments, not quarrelling, just in fun. He's not like the other seamen that come in, and I've aye had a soft spot for him.'

'He said you were the best woman he'd ever met.'

Mrs Barbour looked pleased at this. 'You're a lot like

your brother, Cissie, and I'm going to tell you something I haven't spoken about for years. You see, Tommy reminds me of my son in a lot of ways. He's got the same nature, for never a thing bothered my Jack, always in a good humour and he could make jokes of anything – just like Tommy. Well, at the beginning of the war, Jack said he wanted to enlist. I wasn't happy about it, but he didn't have a father to advise him – my man had died just a year before – so he took his own road and joined the Royal Scots.'

Noticing that her employer's eyes had filled, Cissie said, 'Was he killed in France or Belgium?' It was out before she thought how insensitive the question was.

Mrs Barbour shook her head sadly. 'He never got out of Scotland – well, just across the border. He was stationed at Larbert, but his regiment was ordered to Gallipoli, and they were put on a troop train for Liverpool. It got as far as a wee place called Quintishill, not far from Gretna Junction, when . . .' She broke off, her voice wavering, then sighed and went on, 'There was some mix-up with the signals – the men hadn't been told soon enough it was coming through – and it ran into a local train sitting on the same track.'

'Oh, Mrs Barbour!' Cissie exclaimed. 'That was awful.'

'That wasn't the worst. They were still trying to get the bodies and the injured out, when the Glasgow express from London ploughed into the wreckage, for the signals had been forgotten with all the commotion. Over two hundred soldiers were killed, most of them from Leith like my Jack, and near as many seriously injured.'

The two women sat in silence for some time, Mrs Barbour reliving the time of the tragedy, and Cissie trying to imagine it, then the old lady said, 'There's a memorial to the disaster in Rosebank Cemetery, that's where a lot of the dead were buried.'

'That's the cemetery beside Pilrig Street, isn't it? I'll have to go and look at the memorial some time.'

'I don't often go, for I can remember my Jack without it, especially when Tommy comes to see me. Speaking about your Tommy, Cissie, I'm sure it wasn't chance that stopped you turning to prostitution the night you met him at the docks.'

'I'd changed my mind about that, I couldn't do it. I just went to look for Tommy.'

'If you hadn't found him, you'd maybe have changed your mind again.'

She was probably right, Cissie thought, but all she said was, 'I still don't understand what you meant when you said it wasn't chance that stopped me.'

'I'm not a religious woman, but I still believe there's a greater power than us that shapes our destiny. You weren't meant to be a prostitute, and He stopped you from making a big mistake.'

'He didn't stop all the other bad things that happened to me,' Cissie burst out.

Mrs Barbour sighed. 'We've all to suffer so much, that's what makes us the people we are. If we went through life without coming up against an adversity, we'd end up having no thought for anybody but ourselves.'

'I've met people like that,' Cissie muttered, and added, bitterly, 'I married one.' She was silent for a moment, then said, 'Mrs Barbour, can I tell you about it? I'd like you to know what happened.'

'I'm not forcing you tell me, lass. I'm not one for poking my nose in where it's not wanted.'

'I want you to know.'

Cissie began at the point when she had first met Bertram – her life before that had no bearing on her later problems – and when she finally explained why she had been on her own in an awful room with no money, Mrs Barbour murmured, 'Aye, I can see now what brought you so low.

Poor lass, you must miss your son, but have you never thought on divorcing your man and getting custody of the bairn?'

Not having thought of this before, Cissie gave it her full consideration for several minutes, then the hope left her eyes. 'They'd believe whatever Bertram told them, and he'll not give Ricky up without a fight.'

'You'll never know unless you try.'

'I can't afford to pay a solicitor, anyway.'

Mrs Barbour leaned forward. 'Look, lass, would you let me see to that side of it? I've no family now except a sister in Grangemouth, and though I've only known you for a wee while, I feel closer to you than I've felt with anybody else since my Jack died. I want to help you. Make an appointment with my solicitor for next Wednesday afternoon, and see how it goes from there. It's worth a try, isn't it?'

Too excited to sleep over the next week, Cissie was in such a state of nerves when she went to consult James Latimer at 2.30 on Wednesday that she was sure she would not be able to talk to him at all, but when she was shown into his small office, she was soothed by his friendly smile. He asked her to tell him about Bertram, nodding encouragingly when she stumbled over describing the nights of brutality. And when she stopped, he said, 'Did you tell anyone about this, show the bruises and marks to your friends?'

'I was too ashamed to tell anybody.'

Mr Latimer's smile vanished. 'So it would be your word against his; that makes things more difficult. Let us press on, however. I take it that was when you left him?'

'Oh, no.' She told him the rest, aware before she reached the end that he was looking at her suspiciously.

'I see,' he muttered, looking down at the notes he had been making. 'You cannot prove that the man concerned was your brother, and there is an independent witness who swears you slept with him, so it is not just your word against your husband's this time. I am afraid, Mrs Dickson, that, in view of this – and his position in the world of business – I can hold out no hope of success if you took this to the divorce court. I am sorry, and I wish you good afternoon.'

Dismissed, Cissie stood up and walked out. Why had she let Mrs Barbour talk her into it? she thought dismally. She had known it would be useless.

When she returned to Duke Street, the old lady eyed her sorrowfully. 'I can see it was no good. I'm sorry I raised your hopes, lass.'

'You did it for the best,' Cissie gulped. 'I thought I'd get Ricky back, and now – oh, I wish . . .'

'If wishes were horses, we'd all be running stables. But, Cissie, look at it like this. If you'd your son here, you'd be torn between giving attention to him and to the shop, and when all's said and done, he's better off where he is. I'm not being cruel, lass, for his father's a rich man and can give him a lot more than you. Be grateful for that.'

'It's the only way I can bear it. Um, Mrs Barbour, do you think I'd be silly to go to Dundee, just to see him for a minute? I'd keep out of sight of the house, and maybe his nanny would come past with the pram. I wouldn't let him see me, in case he got upset.'

After thinking deeply for a moment, the old lady murmured, 'Would it not break your heart to be so near him and not be able to touch him?'

'My heart was broken the day he was taken from me. I know it'll be difficult for me, but I have to know if he's all right, if he looks well and happy.'

'You've your mind made up on it, I can see that, and I'll not try to stop you.'

'I'll go next Wednesday.'

Mrs Barbour stood up. 'It's time we got some sleep, but mind, lass, any time things get the better of you, when your heart's sore for your son, come and tell me. Even speaking about your troubles sometimes helps.'

Cissie didn't like to say that her heart was always sore for Ricky. She had thought it was the end of the world when she lost her first son the way she did, and it had taken her a long time to come to terms with it, but to lose her second when he was still alive seemed even worse. She would never come to terms with that.

Chapter Twenty-six

❧❧

On the way to Dundee, doubts began to arise in Cissie's mind. If Bertram had come back to Panache and she was lucky enough to catch a glimpse of Ricky, could she remain silent and do nothing? Common sense told her that an attempt to snatch him in the street would ring the death knell on any hope of ever getting him back for good, but would common sense prevail when she saw him?

As she sat on the tram taking her to the outskirts of the city, she reminded herself that she was still in no position to look after him. She couldn't have him with her in the shop from morning to night, and she couldn't leave him in her room upstairs on his own. If she could find a job where there would be facilities for a child it would be different, but until such time, it was best to leave him where he was.

On legs that wanted to run, she forced herself to walk from the tram terminus towards Panache, vacillating between hoping that she would see Ricky, and that she wouldn't, in case it might be too much for her. She took up her position beside some bushes at the corner of the street, at a spot where she could see the front door. She had been there for about forty-five minutes when she happened to look away from the house and spotted someone pushing a pram up the hill. Her heart tightened when she recognised who it was. It was late afternoon, of course, so Elma would be on her way home with Ricky after his outing.

Cissie drew back as the pram came nearer, yet she felt like jumping from behind the bushes to shove the girl aside and run off with the baby. It took all her will power to keep still, and she had to hold her breath when the pram went past. Only when Elma's back was towards her did she step out and crane her neck to see her son. Thankfully, he was fast asleep, otherwise he might have seen her and cried out. His chubby face was flushed, his mittened hands were lying over the covers, and he was the picture of health.

Although relieved that he looked so well, she felt as if her heartstrings had been riven asunder, and it was several minutes until she pulled herself together and walked back to catch the tram into town, reluctantly admitting to herself that, whatever else Elma was, she could not be faulted on the way she had looked after Ricky.

The trauma of seeing her son and not being able to touch him had been so great that Cissie went to Dundee only once every four weeks. She was extremely grateful that Mrs Barbour did not expect her to talk about it when she came back, because there were times when she couldn't bear to describe how she had felt, but sometimes she did tell her how sturdy Ricky was growing, how he was sitting up in his pram and laughing.

Only once did the old woman say, 'Has it got any easier for you, just seeing him for less than a minute?'

'Not really,' she answered, honestly. 'He seems fond of Elma and she thinks the world of him, it's just . . .'

'I know. You must want to hug him, and play with him.'

'It's when I think of what I'm missing,' Cissie gulped. 'He'd just said "Mama" for the first time when . . . when I lost him, and he must be speaking a lot now.'

One warm afternoon in April, when she was later than usual in arriving at Panache, Cissie was delighted to see Ricky playing in the garden at the back, and took up her stance a little farther along to have a better view. He was crawling crablike at first, then, to her amazement, he took hold of the wooden bench and pulled himself to his feet. Her heart was in her mouth when he stepped forward, but she gathered that it wasn't the first time he had walked. He was rather unsteady, but obviously determined, and he was more than halfway across the lawn before he thumped down. Elma ran into sight and picked him up, and although Cissie could hear nothing, she sensed that the girl was murmuring endearments as she hugged him. Laughing, the little boy slid his arms round her neck, but it wasn't long until he was struggling to be set down again, and the minute he was, he toddled back towards the bench.

It was another half-hour before Elma took him by the hand and led him inside, and Cissie turned away, glad that she had seen how much progress he was making, but sad that she hadn't shared in it. It occurred to her that Richard and Phoebe had been in America for well over a year — they had left when Ricky was only three months old, and he was a year and a half now — and she decided to go to Huntingdon. There was always the chance that they were home. Richard would make short work of Elma's lies and force Bertram to hand Ricky over, and maybe he would let his daughter-in-law and grandson live with them until she could provide a home.

Filled with hope, she marched up the long drive and rang the doorbell, but it echoed so eerily that she was sure the house was empty. She had thought that one of the servants might have been kept on to look after it — the housekeeper having left when Phoebe moved in, Richard had employed a cook to replace her, and there had already been two maids — but it appeared that no one was here. After trying twice more, she walked away dejectedly.

Her gloom was lightened that night when Tommy came to see her, his second visit since she came to Duke Street. When she told him of her trips to Dundee, he said, 'I wish you'd let me go and get Ricky back for you. I'm pretty handy with my fists, and I'd knock Bertram's block off if he gave me any trouble.'

'Where would that get us?' Cissie sighed. 'He'd have you locked up, and he can be so charming when he likes, the police would take everything he says as gospel. We can't prove we're brother and sister without birth certificates, and I didn't even think of taking mine with me when I left Schoolhill.'

'Me, neither, but you can't go on like this. Couldn't you sneak into the house some time and grab Ricky when your man wasn't there?'

'It's not as easy as that. Elma's with him every hour of the day, and she wouldn't give him up. If there was a row, he'd be upset, and I couldn't do that to him. I'll have to wait till Phoebe and Richard come back from America.'

'How long will that be?'

'I don't know. Richard said they'd be away for a year or more, and it's fifteen months now.' A sudden horrible thought struck her — what if Richard had been taken seriously ill?

Mrs Barbour, who had gone down to tidy her store to allow them to talk, came in at that point, and no more was said on the subject, but when Cissie saw Tommy off at the shop door, he said, 'We're off to Valparaiso in the morning, and we'll likely pick up a cargo there, so I'll not be back for a good few months. Maybe you'll have the bairn back by the time I see you again.'

'Oh, Tommy, I hope so!'

When she next went to Dundee, Cissie made for Huntingdon first, with the same result as before. Phoebe had surely written to say where they were, but the letters would have gone to Panache and Bertram would undoubtedly have destroyed them.

*   *   *

292

Cissie had noticed that Mrs Barbour was easily tired and was leaving most of the serving to her, yet it came as a shock when the old lady announced that she was going to retire. 'I've been thinking about it for a while,' Mrs Barbour went on, 'for I'll be seventy-five this year. My brain's not up to keeping track of what I need to order, and I'm forever worrying if I've paid all the bills.'

'I could do the ordering for you,' Cissie suggested.

'I know you could, you're as smart a lass as I've ever come across, and that's why I've made my mind up. My sister in Grangemouth's been at me for years to sell up and go and live with her, and that's what I'm going to do. Well, I'm not selling up, I'm leaving you in charge, for I know I can trust you not to lose any of my customers.'

It was a minute before Cissie could find her voice, then she gasped, 'Are you sure? If you sold up, you'd have money to keep you in your retirement.'

'Do you not want to take on the shop?'

'Of course I want to, but I was thinking of you.'

'I've looked at it from every angle, Cissie, and it's best I go to my sister's, for if I retire and stop on here, you'd think I was criticising, though that's something I'd never do. Besides, Bessie needs me – she's three years older and doesn't keep well – and her house is all on one floor, so I wouldn't have any stairs to climb. I'll not leave for at least a month, to give you time to get used to the ordering, and you can ask me anything you're not sure of, though I think you know the business as well as I do now.' She half turned away, then added, 'Oh, I near forgot. You'll have the run of the house, and all, once I go.'

Cissie felt she had to protest about this. 'You could let it, and I could get a room somewhere close. I can afford it, for you've never let me pay a penny in rent since I came.'

Shaking her head, the old lady said, 'I'm not needing any extra money. I'll still have the profit from the shop, not that it's a fortune, but I've always got by on it. Anyway, I'd rather have you in my house than strangers, and before you say it, I'm still not taking rent from you. The use of the house'll be part of your wages, the same as the room's been, and you'll get a bit extra for being manageress.'

'Oh, but Mrs Barbour . . .'

'You'll take out what I've been giving you plus another ten shillings, before you bank the takings every week. I'll arrange with them to let you sign all the cheques, and I'll show you how I do the books, but you'll manage that, seeing you used to work in an office. As long as you don't run me into debt, it'll work out dandy.'

Over the next four weeks, Cissie kept her mind resolutely off her son so that she could concentrate on absorbing what she needed to know about running the little shop, and she felt quite confident when the day came for her employer to leave. Her only regret was that she was losing a friend, a woman who had become very dear to her, and when the taxi arrived to take the old lady to the bus station, she had to fight back her tears.

'Goodbye, lass,' Mrs Barbour gulped. 'I'll miss you.'

This was too much for Cissie, who could only clasp the hand held out to her, and she was left snivelling into her handkerchief as she watched the taxi moving away with the old lady in the back seat also wiping her eyes.

Cissie was so upset that she couldn't eat that Sunday, and spent the night worrying about the responsibility she had taken on. Would she be up to it? Would the trade go down through blunders she made? Would she remember to pay the bills on time and notice when the stock of some particular item was wearing down? She fell asleep from sheer weariness, and dreamt that, because she had forgotten to order in time, she was fending off irate customers who were demanding to know why they couldn't get their usual brand of cigarettes and their favourite sweets.

In the morning, she laughed at her fears. She had a good memory and wouldn't forget anything, but just to make sure, she had better keep a notebook handy to write down all the things she needed to remember. The paying of the bills should be easy enough, because the wholesalers sent in accounts at the start of every month, listing the invoices for every delivery, and they gave a discount if the accounts were settled within seven days, so all she had to do was to write the cheques out as soon as they came in. The books for the shop were much the same as those she had kept before – Richard had called it the double-entry system – and she had to make sure that the money she paid into the bank and the cheques she wrote were recorded in the cash book.

At the end of her first week, Cissie was pleased when she totted up her takings. She had drawn in a little more than Mrs Barbour usually did, but she had also had to order more, so it might not look so good at the end of the month. She was also getting to know the customers better than ever before. Instead of unloading their troubles on Mrs Barbour as they had been wont to do before, the women were telling her about their husbands' faults, children's illnesses, cats being sick on the hearthrug, dogs peeing on a newly washed floor. There was the other side of the coin, too. They told her when a husband got promotion, when a child did well at school, when a baby was on the way. She was genuinely glad or sorry for them, and could soon put names to husbands and children, even pets.

She laughed at the jokes cracked by the men who came in for cigarettes, asked after their wives or girlfriends, listened without arguing while they ranted on about the government or their boss, and dealt with them carefully if they came in after a few drinks and were too familiar.

She was even experimenting every night making different flavours of tablet, candy and fudge; her coconut ice took an instant trick with the women, her rum-and-raisin fudge with the men, the puff candy with the children. She relished the challenge of managing the shop, and the only time she felt sad was when she saw a boy who would be about the same age as Ricky would be. That was when her heart turned over and she had to discipline her thoughts so as not to wonder how he was, and if he would still remember her.

With the books to write up, delivery notes to check with invoices, all her time was fully occupied, even Wednesday afternoons and Sundays, but she had managed to scribble a short note to Phoebe at Huntingdon. As yet, there had been no reply, but surely it wouldn't be long, she thought as she tumbled, heavy with fatigue, into bed one night. She had also written to Dorothy Barclay, but that letter, too, had gone unanswered.

She was dusting the last of the jars on the middle shelf one day when a young man came in. He was a stranger to her, but there was something about him that reminded her of Hugh Phimister, and her heart contracted. She had tried not to think of Hugh, of the might-have-been she would never know now, but she had never forgotten him. 'Yes?' she asked, in her usual bright way. 'Have you made up your mind, or would you like time to have a look?'

His eyes had the same earnestness as Hugh's, crinkling in the same way when he smiled. 'A quarter of pandrops, please. It's for my mother, she's ill and I wanted to cheer her up a wee bit.'

'I hope it's nothing serious,' Cissie said, as she lifted the big jar down and unscrewed the lid.

His timid smile vanished. 'The doctor says it's cancer.'

'Oh, no.' Cissie held the jar over the scales and shook out enough sweets to weigh almost double the four ounces he had asked for. 'Maybe he's wrong. They're not infallible.' She put the jar back on the shelf and opened a paper bag, wondering why the man had told her. Cancer was something people didn't normally talk about, for they considered it a taint, something to be ashamed of – some even thought it was infectious – but maybe he felt he had to tell somebody. She gave the top of the bag the usual twist and held it out.

'There's a lot more than a quarter in there,' he observed, digging into his trouser pocket.

'A wee bit,' she smiled. 'From me to your mother.'

He held out a half-crown, and when she had counted out his change into his hand, she said, 'I hope her doctor's wrong.'

'Thanks, so do I.'

His eyes were so mournful when he turned to go out that Cissie couldn't get him out of her mind all day, and she hoped he would come back to let her know how his mother was.

He did not appear again, however, and after a few weeks, Cissie came to the sad conclusion that the woman had died. She was disappointed that he had not come to tell her, but he was maybe too shy to make friends with her, and perhaps it was all for the best. Did she really want his friendship? Friendship between a man and woman could turn all too easily into something deeper, and she had no desire to tread the stony path of love again. Never!

Besides, she had only felt drawn to him because he had reminded her of Hugh Phimister.

She had been so busy one Friday evening – the day most of her customers were paid their week's wages – that she went upstairs thankful to sit down and have some peace. Not that she had any worries about the shop, for it was doing even better than when Mrs Barbour was there. Her employer was happy living with her sister, and sent weekly letters of praise to Cissie, had even given her a five shillings' rise in appreciation for all her hard work, yet there were times, like tonight, when she couldn't help thinking of Ricky, of Hugh, of Phoebe. Why hadn't her stepmother answered her letter? She must be home by this time. Had Bertram actually turned Richard and Phoebe against her?

When she felt her eyelids drooping, she fought against it for a few minutes, then smiled to herself. She should be in bed, not sitting in a chair remembering people from her past, people she would never see again. She levered herself to her feet, staggering a little as she went across to the sink, on legs that were already half asleep, to fill the kettle for a last cup of tea. Waiting for it to come to the boil, she picked up the evening paper she hadn't had time to read. There was hardly ever anything interesting in it, and she turned the pages half-heartedly. She was folding it up when her eye caught a familiar name in the Stop Press column.

The police have issued the following bulletin: A prisoner from Peterhead has not reported in since he was released on parole three weeks ago. Thomas McGregor, from Aberdeen, was arrested for murder in 1917, but the charge was changed to manslaughter. McGregor, fifty-eight years of age, has greying reddish hair and is over six feet tall. He is not considered dangerous. Anyone with any information is asked to contact their nearest police station.

With no thought now of tea or sleep, Cissie sat staring into space, her heart pounding with fear. Her father was out! Already! And he wasn't considered dangerous! What did the police know? He would be searching for her, and when he found her . . . She had known he would be released when he had served his sentence, but she had always believed that he would be out in 1933, maybe 1932, not 1927. Oh, God, what was she to do? He had been free for three weeks already and she would never feel safe now.

Gradually, her panic abated. How on earth could he find her here? Even if he traced her to Dundee, to Panache, he would come to a dead end. Bertram didn't know where she was – nobody knew. She had nothing to fear. Nothing!

Standing up to turn off the gas under the kettle – on the verge of boiling dry – she remembered the letter she had written some time ago to Dorothy Barclay and her blood ran cold again. Roland would have told Bertram where she was, and if her father did trace her to Panache, Bertram would give him her address. Thinking of that letter reminded Cissie that she had also written to Phoebe, and it dawned on her that her stepmother was now in as much danger as she was herself. Tam McGregor would be after her, too, for having the nerve to divorce him. It didn't matter that she must have believed the lies Bertram told, she must be warned about this.

Not wanting to alarm Phoebe too much, Cissie tried to keep her own fear out of the note she wrote, merely stating that Tam was out of prison earlier than expected. Although she was still hurt that her previous letter had been ignored, she did not refer to it. Ending with just plain 'Cissie', she addressed an envelope and went out to the postbox.

Chapter Twenty-seven

❧❦❧

Unable to eat or sleep, Cissie was looking wan and haggard, her eyes dark-ringed and sunk far into their sockets. Every time the shop bell tinkled, she sagged with relief when she recognised a friendly, familiar face, or even a complete stranger. Tommy had appeared three days after she read the awful news, but although she craved reassurance more than anything, she couldn't tell him. Remembering their father's temper, he would know that she was right to be afraid, and he would have gone back to sea as worried as she was. Worse, he might have thrown up his job so that he could stay with her, to protect her. She couldn't let him jeopardise his future. He, too, was quick to be roused to anger, and if the two men ever did meet again, it could result in another murder — whose would depend on which of them struck first.

Tommy had known something was bothering her, of course, and had done his best to winkle it out of her, but she had managed to take his mind off it by telling him that his old friend had retired, and he had left believing that it was the responsibility of managing the shop that had got her down.

She went to bed every night thankful that another day had passed safely, and that Ricky was in no danger. Even if her father did turn up at Panache, Bertram — and Elma — would make sure he did nothing to harm his grandson.

The weeks crawled past for Cissie, stretching into months, and still nothing had happened. The razor-sharp edge of her terror gradually blunted, until, at last, there came a day when she woke one morning feeling as if she had come out of a long, dark tunnel, and she laughed at herself for having been in such a state of mindless terror.

*   *   *

As Tommy made his way to the sweetshop, he hoped that Cissie would be happier than the last time he saw her, for she had been in a dashed strange mood, as if she was scared stiff. When he tried to find out what was wrong, she had hinted that she was having a struggle to keep the shop on her own, but he hadn't been fooled. Still, whatever it had been, surely she would have got over it by this time.

On reaching the shop, Tommy knocked three times on the locked door and followed this by the warbling whistle he always gave to let Cissie know who it was. In a minute, she was letting him in, and he was glad that she looked better. 'How's things?' he asked, following her up the back stairs.

'Fine. I'm sorry about last time you were here. I was off balance a bit.'

'Aye, I could see that.'

While she filled the kettle in the kitchen, she remarked, 'I thought you might have come back before you sailed.'

'We'd a few problems, as always, and I couldn't get away.'

'Tell me where you were this time,' she urged. 'I love hearing about all the exotic places you go.'

'Not so exotic this trip.' He told her a little about the busy port of Hamburg first, and went on, 'We'd another load to discharge at Bremerhaven and a whole cargo to pick up at Rotterdam. You know, it's funny, but I never feel easy with the Germans, I suppose it's a hangover from the war. I get along great with the Dutch. They're much friendlier.'

Cissie smiled. 'You'd get along fine with anybody, but I don't think I'd like to go abroad among foreigners. How do you manage to speak to them?'

301

'Most of them speak English, and if they don't, I get by with signs. You know me, I'm never stuck. Now, what about you, Cissie? Have you heard from old Mrs Barbour lately?'

'I'd a letter last week. Her sister's housebound now and needs constant attention. I think she likes being needed, though, for it's given her a purpose in life again. She asked about you.'

'Give her my best wishes when you write. She was a nice old body. We always got on like a house on fire, though I don't know what made her take to me in the first place.'

'She told me you reminded her of her son.' Cissie related the tragedy of the troop train, then went on, 'But she liked you for yourself, as well. You're a really nice man, Tommy, and I'm not saying that just because you're my brother.'

Turning pink, her brother gave a self-conscious laugh. 'Ach, Cissie, you're not so bad yourself.'

'Have you to go on watch tonight, or can you stay?'

'I've not to be on board till tomorrow, but are you not scared for your reputation?' His grin vanished. 'I'm sorry, I shouldn't have said that.' He hadn't meant to remind her of the only other time he had spent a night in her home.

She raised her shoulders briefly. 'It doesn't bother me now, Tommy. It was better for me to find out what Bertram was like, but I wish I could see Ricky again, or even just find out how he is.'

'You should write to – Phoebe, wasn't it? She'd tell you. Or your friend.'

'I've written to both of them, and they've just ignored my letters. Bertram's likely turned them against me, and I'm glad he doesn't know where I am.'

'He can't do anything to you.'

'I'd feel safer if he didn't know where to find me.'

'Have you given up the idea of getting your boy back?'

'I'll never stop hoping, but I can't do anything. Anyway, how could I look after him when I'm tied to the shop all day, and all evening? Oh God, Tommy, he'll soon be three, and he wouldn't know me supposing he saw me.'

'Aye, it must be hard to bear, but us McGregors can face up to anything.' He looked at her with his eyebrows raised. 'Cissie, don't you ever feel life's slipping you by?'

'What d'you mean? I've got a good job, a good house and lots of friends . . .'

'Customers? Are they really your friends?'

She considered for a moment. 'I'd say most of my regulars are friends, like you were with Mrs Barbour.'

'Is that enough? A woman your age – you're only twenty-eight, you should have a man about the place.'

'Are you thinking of giving up the sea and coming to help me?' she teased.

He frowned. 'I'm serious, Cissie. You've been married, you must miss having a man in your bed?'

Recalling Bertram's sadism, her eyes darkened. 'I prefer being by myself, and anyway, I'm still married.'

'That doesn't stop some women taking another man.'

'I don't want another man!'

'All right, don't fly off the handle at me.'

'What about you? You're a year older than me, isn't it time you were thinking of taking a wife?'

Tommy gave a deep sigh. 'I'd like fine to have a wife and bairns, but what girl would want to marry a man she'd only see three or four times a year?'

'Have you ever had a girlfriend?'

'A few, but nobody special.'

'You'll meet the right one some day, Tommy, and when you do, don't let happiness slip through your fingers. Ask her if she's willing to marry a seagoing man, and if she loves you enough, she will.'

'You're good at handing out advice,' he laughed, 'but not so good at taking it.'

They went to bed when they'd had a cup of tea, and Cissie lay thinking over what her brother had said. If she'd been completely honest, she would have told him that there were times when she wished she had someone to love, someone to love her; not for the physical side – she didn't think she could face that again – just to know he was there for her to turn to. Apart from the man whose mother had cancer, she had met no one she really liked, and she had only been attracted to him because he reminded her of Hugh Phimister.

In the morning, Tommy had the porridge made before she got up, and insisted on drying the dishes for her afterwards. 'I'm practising for when I'm married,' he joked.

'I meant what I said last night, so just remember.'

'Yes, ma'am. I'll put a notice on my chest, "Wife wanted for this lonely sailor", and thousands'll be knocked down in the rush.'

'Och, you.'

'I'll not have time to come back before we sail, and we're bound for New Zealand this time, so it'll be a good while before I see you again.'

Tommy left when Cissie opened the shop, and she was still smiling at the picture of him with a placard on his chest asking for a wife. In spite of all his joking, he would make some girl a very good husband.

*   *   *

It surprised Cissie how quickly the weeks sped past. It seemed that she had no sooner written out one lot of cheques than it was time to write another, and 1928 was on her before she knew where she was. Her sales of sweets had gone down a little since some of the factory workers and dockers had been paid off, they couldn't afford lux-uries now, but the tobacco side was still much the same. The men wouldn't do without their cigarettes even if their wives went short of housekeeping money. Since it was cheaper, some of them had taken to making their own, so she always had to have a good supply of the packets of papers and the little roller machines that they needed.

When a large van drew up outside one forenoon, she heaved a sigh of relief, because she had almost run out of fives of Woodbines, the best sellers of all. 'The usual place,' she told the driver without looking round from tidying a shelf, for he knew she kept her extra stocks in the back shop. When she realised that he hadn't moved, she turned to ask him if anything was wrong, but the words dried up in her mouth. It wasn't the usual delivery man, it was the last person on earth she had ever expected to see.

Their eyes locked, man and woman stood motionless for a moment though it seemed like an eternity to her, then he set the carton down on the floor. 'I never thought I'd see you again, Cissie.'

'Hugh!' It was all she could say, but she turned away with reluctance when her next-door neighbour walked in, and she was in so much of a daze that she did not take in what was asked of her.

'Ten Craven A, please,' the young wife repeated, adding, with a laugh, 'Have you gone deaf this morning, Cissie?'

'Oh, I'm sorry, Betty.' Conscious of her burning cheeks, she turned to the shelf, lifted one of the red-and-black packets and laid it down on top of an advertisement for Fox's Glacier Mints.

Handing over the exact money, the other woman stole a glance at the handsome man who was looking at Cissie as if he were afraid to take his eyes off her. 'Did I interrupt something?' she asked, archly, winking as she went out.

After dropping the coins in her till, Cissie lifted the flap and came out from behind the counter. 'I'll show you where to put that,' she murmured, recalling the last time she had spoken to him and feeling awkward and shy.

He picked up the carton and, walking in front of him

on trembling legs, she pointed to where it should go. 'You look well, Cissie,' he said, after depositing it.

'So do you.' They were mundane words, and she guessed that he, too, was unable to express his emotions. 'Did you ever get married, Hugh?' she asked – the only thing she could think of – then wished she hadn't. If he had, he would feel uncomfortable telling her, after all they had once been to each other, and if he hadn't, he might think she was hoping they would get back together.

'Aye, Cissie, I did, but it didn't last long. I met her a year after I came to Edinburgh, and we never quite hit it off. I wanted a family and she liked a good time, so we agreed to separate after about three years.'

She was acutely conscious that they were standing less than a yard apart and prayed that he wouldn't try to take her in his arms. Too many years had gone past, too much had happened for them to pick up where they had left off, and once he learned the truth about her, he wouldn't want to. Besides, she wasn't free.

The doorbell tinkled, and she tore herself away from his yearning eyes and went to attend to her business, her hands shaking as she handed two gobstoppers to the small boy and dropped his ha'penny in the till. When she returned to the back shop, she said, 'We have to talk, Hugh. Can you come back tonight at half past nine? That's when I close, and we can go upstairs to the house.'

'I'll be here, Cissie.'

As she watched him driving away, she hoped that he had not misinterpreted her invitation, and memories of being alone with him in his mother's house came flooding back. If she hadn't run away from him that night and gone home to find her drunken father on his own . . . Dear God, if only she had her life to live over again.

Back behind the counter, she tried not to think of the consequences of that night, but another unwelcome memory came, the awful look on her father's face as he was led away after the trial, the glare which had told her he blamed her for everything and meant to punish her when he was set free. It was as vivid as though it had happened yesterday, yet it would be eleven years in March. But he'd been out for months and he hadn't found her, she reassured herself, and she had other things to think about now.

Her heart had almost stopped when she saw Hugh, but it had been a pleasant shock, a welcome shock. He hadn't changed much, just a little broader and more serious. What could she say to him when he came back tonight? He would want to know why she had left Aberdeen, and she couldn't tell him that.

She was very distracted all day, and by eight o'clock, her excitement was at fever pitch. She kept checking her watch until, at half past, she realised that she must have looked at it a dozen times in the past ten minutes and steeled herself to stop.

Luckily, there was the usual rush in her last hour, and she was taken by surprise when her visitor arrived, pale-faced and looking as nervous as she felt. Pulling down the blind and locking the door behind him, she took him up to her kitchen.

They stood, each intensely aware of the other, until Hugh said, 'I can hardly believe this. I didn't think I'd ever see you again.'

'No more did I,' Cissie murmured. 'Will you not sit down?'

He took a chair at the fire and waited until she was seated in the other one. 'I was a bit annoyed this morning when another driver went off sick and I'd to take on his round as well as my own, but if it hadn't been for that, I'd never have found you.'

She smiled nervously, not really sure how she felt about him yet. She had always believed that she had never stopped loving him, but it was a different thing now that they were face to face. She was glad to see him, but she wanted no more complications in her life. 'You didn't take up joinery again when you came out of the army?'

'I'd been used to working with horses all the time I was in France, and I got quite attached to them, so when I came to Edinburgh I got a delivery job, driving a cart. Then the boss bought motor vans and I learned to drive.' He looked at her thoughtfully. 'When I came home from the war, and Ma told me what had happened to you, I wished I could comfort you. It must have been awful, losing your husband and child that way. I went to Schoolhill to see you, but your sister told me you'd gone away.'

Her stomach was churning, yet in a way she was glad that he knew. 'I couldn't stay in Aberdeen, not with everybody speaking about me.'

'I can understand that. It's queer, though, to think we've both been in Edinburgh so long and . . .'

'I didn't come here till years after that. Phoebe and I – that's my stepmother – we went to Dundee and got work in the mills, and we both got jobs in the office eventually.' She purposely didn't tell him of the deprivations they'd had to suffer while they lived in Jen Millar's room, and went on, 'We got a house in South Union Street, then I – married the boss's son.'

'Ah! I didn't like to ask if you'd married again.'

Hugh was sitting hunched up with his elbows on his knees, his eyes on the floor now, and she said, 'We're separated, as well. Would you like me to tell you what happened?'

His head came up slowly. 'Not tonight, not when we've just found each other again.'

There was something in his dark eyes that made her burst out, 'We can't start again, Hugh, we're both still married to somebody else.'

'I let Mary divorce me, though she'd been sleeping with other men. Couldn't you divorce him?'

'You don't understand, Hugh, and I'd better tell you. My brother Tommy came to see me, and the maid told Bertram I'd had a lover in when he was in Glasgow.'

'And he believed her?'

'He was sleeping with her, though I didn't know. He's wicked, and he put me out and kept my son from me.'

'Didn't you try to get him back?'

'Oh, God, Hugh, I tried and tried, but it was no use.'

'Couldn't your friends have helped you?'

She told him about Phoebe and Richard being in America at the time, about Roland Barclay refusing to let her talk to his wife. 'I wrote to Phoebe and Dorothy, but they never answered. Bertram's got them all thinking I'm the bad one. After I came here, I even went to see a solicitor about divorcing him, in case I could get Ricky back that way, but he told me I didn't stand a chance.'

Hugh rubbed his chin. 'Would it help if I went to Dundee with you and told him I knew Tommy was your brother?'

'It would likely make things worse. He'd say you were just another man I was carrying on with. I'll never be free of him, Hugh, and you'd better go away and forget about me.'

'Oh, Cissie, I could never forget you. I understand how you're placed, but I still want to come and see you. We can still be friends, can't we?'

'I'd be pleased to have you as my friend, Hugh, as long as you know that's all it can ever be.' She could tell by the way he was looking at her that he wanted more than friendship, but she couldn't risk it.

'I'd better go, it's getting late,' he said, after a short silence. 'Can I come to see you again tomorrow?'

'If you like.'

Letting him out at the shop door, she murmured, 'Hugh, I'm sorry if you thought . . .'

'No, Cissie, I didn't think anything, I only hoped, and I won't stop hoping.'

'You'll be wasting your time.'

'It won't be wasted if I can see you every night.' Giving her hand a quick squeeze, he walked away.

Had she been stupid? Cissie wondered, as she went back to the house. Should she have told him not to come back? If they saw each other every night he would likely want to kiss her, which would lead to something she wasn't ready for, might never be ready for.

Trying to sleep, she kept thinking of Hugh, of his rugged face, his wavy hair, his brown eyes, and she knew that she still felt something for him, more than something. It would be wonderful if he and Ricky could be with her as a family – but it could never be.

Cissie's heart accelerated the following evening when Hugh walked in, and it was beating much too quickly when she took him upstairs. She was about to tell him to sit down when he took a step towards her, and forgetting all that lay between them, she slid into his arms. 'Oh, Cissie,' he moaned.

His lips touching her brow, he held her tightly for some time before his mouth sought hers hungrily. The years fell away and it was as if they had never been apart, as if they were still the young boy and girl they had been the last time they kissed. But Cissie soon became aware that it was not the same, for Hugh was stirring up passions in her that she had never experienced as a young girl. She broke away from him breathlessly. 'We shouldn't be doing this, Hugh. You promised we'd just be friends.'

'Kissing friends,' he smiled.

She couldn't help smiling, too, but said, as if scolding him, 'Those were more than friendly kisses.'

'I could tell you liked them, though.'

His dear face so close, she couldn't hold out against him, and with a breathy sigh, she nestled against him again to return his 'more than friendly' kisses.

At last, he said, 'I shouldn't have promised anything. I

could never be just friends with you, I love you too much. Is there any chance that you still love me?'

His eyes, pleading desperately for the answer he wanted, made her abandon all pretence. 'I don't think I ever stopped loving you, Hugh, not deep down.'

'That's all I wanted to know, and I'll be quite happy just to see you for an hour every night.'

His smile, crinkling his face in the same old way, sent the same old tingles racing through her. 'You could come for your supper on Wednesdays, that's my early closing day, and we could have all day together on Sundays.'

He looked at her earnestly. 'Are you really sure? You've no doubts?

'I can't honestly say I've no doubts,' she admitted, 'but I'm nearly sure.'

He thumped down in one of the armchairs and pulled her on to his knee. 'We've a lot of lost time to catch up on.'

Over the next hour, they made up for the years they had been apart, keeping strictly to kissing, a little caressing and many words of endearment.

At last, Hugh said, 'Look at the time! I'll have to be off, but I'll be back tomorrow.'

Some twenty minutes elapsed before she locked the shop behind him and went back upstairs with his kisses still burning on her lips. She couldn't send him away now, she would die if she didn't see him again, and in any case, she didn't think he would let her go so easily a second time.

It was the following day before she remembered that he still didn't know everything, and as soon as she took him upstairs that evening, she told him about her life as a spinner, about her marriage to Bertram – omitting the months he had been a night-time monster – and more about Tommy's visit to her house and its dreadful after-effect.

'I wish to God I'd known Tommy had found you,' Hugh

burst out. 'I met him in a bar a while ago, and he didn't even know you'd been in trouble till I . . .'

'Was it you who told him?' Cissie was astonished. 'He said it was an Aberdeen man, but he never said it was you. If I'd only known.'

Hugh screwed up his nose. 'He likely hadn't wanted to tell you when he thought you were happy with your rich husband and your grand house.'

She smiled ruefully. 'As they say in the best melodramas, "Little did he know."'

Their nightly meetings deepened their love for each other even more, and on Sunday afternoons they walked hand in hand on their rambles round the docks, or to the Botanic Gardens, or Princes Street Gardens. If they felt more energetic, they climbed Calton Hill to see the Napoleonic War monument, or went up Arthur's Seat where they had a panoramic view of Edinburgh and its surrounding area. As far as Cissie was concerned, these outings made up for the short snatched hour which was all they had on other nights, but when, one Monday almost eight weeks after their reunion, Hugh became rather too passionate, she grew alarmed. If she let things go on like this, he would expect her to let him make love to her. 'Please stop, Hugh,' she murmured.

His voice thick, he said, 'I stopped once before when I shouldn't have listened to you.' Pausing, he looked at her contritely. 'No, my darling, I don't want to force you, I want you to come to me willingly.' He dropped his arms and turned away from her

'I'm sorry,' she said, miserably aware that she had hurt him deeply. 'I should have known this would happen, and I can't forget I'm still married to Bertram.'

'Would you go back to him if he asked you?'

'No, Hugh, I'd never go back to him, it's you I love. But can't you see how I feel about this?'

Whipping round, he took hold of her hands. 'I do see, my dearest one, and it doesn't matter a damn to me that we can't be married, as long as I know you love me.'

He looked at her pensively for a moment, then said, 'I've been doing a lot of thinking, Cissie, and I don't know how you'll feel about what I'm going to say, but I'm going to say it anyway. Isn't it stupid me going home every night to my lodgings when I could stay here? Now, I've said it and I'll leave you to think about it.'

He was halfway down the stairs before she got her breath back, and her heart was thumping when she went down to lock up behind him. Her own body had been set alight by his caresses, but she couldn't let any man make love to her again, not even Hugh.

She tossed and turned all night, and was still trying to make up her mind when the early dawn was sending red streaks through the sky and the gulls were screeching over something they had found in the street. She was a married woman, what would people say if she let him move in with her? But none of them knew her real circumstances, and they likely thought she was a widow. She tried to imagine Hugh living in her house, and quite liked the idea, but her mind boggled at thinking of him in her bed.

'I've been considering what you said,' she began, as soon as they went upstairs that night, 'and I suppose it is daft for you to be paying for lodgings when you could be . . .' She halted, but the joy dawning in his eyes made her hurry on. 'I've a spare room you can have.'

'A spare room?' he echoed, his voice hollow.

'I'm sorry, Hugh, I can't let you – not yet, anyway. I'll maybe tell you some day why I can't, once I've got over it properly. Just give me time.'

His disappointment was only too obvious, and his lop-sided smile nearly made her change her mind. 'I suppose sleeping under the same roof's a start,' he said, 'and I promise I won't take advantage of it, not unless you ask me.' His eyes twinkled suddenly. 'And I won't break that promise.'

'Thanks, Hugh,' she breathed.

'I'll tell my landlady tomorrow I'll be leaving at the end of the week, and I'll move in on Saturday afternoon, if that suits you? I haven't much to shift, just clothes and some odds and ends.'

When he was leaving on Thursday night, Hugh said, 'I won't see you tomorrow, Cissie. I promised I'd go for a few last drinks with my landlady's son. I used to pal around with him before, and he thinks I'm off my head giving up my freedom, as he puts it, for I didn't tell him . . .'

His shrug told Cissie that he was ashamed to let his friend know of her arrangement – he was maybe afraid that the man would laugh at him for agreeing to it – but she smiled encouragingly. 'Enjoy yourself, tomorrow, Hugh, and remember, I'll never stop you going out. There's no strings attached, you know.'

'I wish there were.'

The following night, Cissie took the opportunity of being alone to write up her books, which had fallen behind since she'd been spending most of her free time with Hugh, and felt annoyed when someone knocked at the shop door. The trilly whistle that followed wiped the frown from her face, and she ran down to let her brother in.

'You look pleased with yourself,' he greeted her. 'Don't tell me you've found yourself a man?'

'I'll tell you when we go up,' she laughed.

He was all smiles, too, when he heard how Hugh had come back into her life. 'I should have told you about him when I saw you in Dundee, but I thought . . . you looked happy enough.'

'It's all come right now, anyway. He's going to leave his lodgings tomorrow.'

Tommy's eyes danced. 'So you'll have somebody to share your bed at last? Good for you.'

'No, no, you've got it all wrong. I'm letting him lodge here, we won't be sleeping together.'

'Are you daft, woman? You surely don't expect him to sleep in a different room? That's asking a bit much of any man, especially when he loves you.'

'It's not that I don't want him, Tommy, I can't . . .'

He looked at her speculatively. 'There's more to this than you've told me. Why can't you let him sleep with you? Was it what Da did to you? But you married and had a son, so you must have got over that?'

She hesitated, wondering if she could possibly speak about the revolting things Bertram had done, then decided that she didn't need to go into great detail. It would be enough just to give her brother a general idea, and let his imagination fill in the rest.

A deep frown distorted his face when she told him about the teeth-marks and bruises Bertram had left on her, and when she came to a quavering halt, he burst out, 'I bet there's a lot more you're not telling me. I know what that kind of man can do to women, but you didn't have to put up with it, you should have reported him.'

'I should have told somebody, but I was too ashamed.'

'You'd nothing to be ashamed about! It was him that should have been ashamed. I've a good mind to go there and knock his teeth down his bloody throat.'

'No, Tommy, don't be silly! I only told you to let you see why I can't . . .'

'It's you that's being silly.' he interrupted. 'From what I saw of Hugh, he's a good man. He wouldn't do anything like that to you.'

'I don't think he would, it's just me. Maybe I'll forget my fears one day and let him . . .'

He chuckled when she stopped in embarrassment. 'If you're stuck for the right word, Cissie, I could give you a lovely four letter one.'

She couldn't help smiling. 'I've no doubt you could. You sailors could turn the air blue.'

'Aye, that we could – but not in ladies' company.'

'I'm glad to hear it.'

'Seriously, though, I'm pleased you and Hugh have got back together, but take my advice and don't dither too long, or you might lose him again. A man can only take so much, and if he's desperate, he might turn to somebody else. Now, can I come and see him tomorrow night, or would you rather have him all to yourself?'

'Stop teasing me. You're welcome to come.'

'Right, I'll leave you now, for I see you were busy.' He glanced at the ledger and the pile of invoices on the table as he stood up. 'See you tomorrow, then.'

After she'd locked up again, she sat down to carry on with her writing, but her mind wasn't on it. Was Tommy right? Would Hugh turn to another woman if she kept him in the spare room? Would she lose him again because of the fear her father had created in her, the fear which had increased three-fold with her husband's vile onslaughts?

Chapter Twenty-eight

❧

If Cissie had had her son with her, her happiness would have been complete. Since Hugh had come back into her life, her longing for Ricky had increased, and she sometimes dreamed of going to Panache with Hugh to ask Bertram to hand him over. In her dreams, it seemed that a quiet request would bring a quiet acquiescence, but when she woke up, she knew that Bertram would never agree. He would fight to the last stand, and her dreams were — only dreams!

As it was, Hugh helped by cooking what he brought in with him when he came home from work, and carried it down to eat with her in the store. After he washed up, he stayed in the shop with her until closing time, even serving when she was busy. After closing time, Hugh listened to the wireless and she caught up with her book-keeping, and when she laid down her pen, there came the best time of all, when he took her in his arms to say goodnight, his kisses so sweet that she had to tear herself away to go to bed. She even toyed with the idea of telling him he could sleep with her, and it was only the thought that her fear might end their heaven that held her back.

They had been living separately-together — the only way she could describe it — for some weeks before she sensed the change in him. At first, it was as if he had something on his mind that made him restless, but soon he couldn't settle at all, and when he began to pace the floor one night, she asked, 'What's bothering you, Hugh?'

'Cissie, my darling, you know what's bothering me. I can't go on like this, it's not natural. I'm getting scared to kiss you in case I forget my promise and lose my head.'

She had been giving some thought to this side of things over the past few days, recalling the warning her brother had given her. Also, she was as sure of Hugh's love for her now as she was of hers for him. 'Kiss me now,' she murmured, a little shyly.

Instead of trying to put into words how much she wanted him in spite of her fears, she let her passion tell him, and when his breathing quickened, she wouldn't allow him to draw away. 'Oh, Cissie,' he groaned, 'We'd better stop or I'll end up carrying you through to your bed.'

'Would that be so bad?' she whispered.

He jerked his head up from nuzzling her ear, hope shining like a beacon from his eyes. 'Do you mean — are you . . . ?'

'Just for tonight,' she cautioned, softly, afraid now that she would be unable to go through with it.

Ignoring her last three words, he swung her off her feet and carried her through to her bedroom, where he stood her up at the side of the bed and kissed her so fervently that her whole body quivered with apprehensive desire. When he started to unfasten her blouse, however, she felt herself shrinking away from him. 'I'm sorry, Hugh, I can't let you.'

He let her go abruptly. 'I know somebody must have made you frightened to make love, Cissie. Will you tell me?'

Thinking that he deserved to know at least part of the truth, and that she had to get it out of her system before she could ever act normally with him, she gulped, 'It was — Bertram.' She told Hugh even less than she had told Tommy, just enough to make him understand, because she had been so humiliated by some of the things Bertram had done that she couldn't bear to think of them.

When she ended, Hugh said nothing for a moment, making her pray that he wasn't disgusted at her for letting her husband treat her so brutally, and she was about to explain that she had had no choice when Hugh gave a long sigh.

'I'm glad you told me, my darling, but you don't have to be afraid of me, for I'd never hurt you. I'd best go to my own bed now, though.'

Even though her emotions were in shreds, she couldn't let him go without giving him some hope. She couldn't punish him for what other men had done to her. 'Maybe tomorrow?'

He patted her hand, 'Aye, maybe tomorrow, but only if you feel right about it.'

Many, many tomorrows were to pass, however, before she put her fears behind her.

*   *   *

When Hugh came home early one afternoon at the beginning of December, his grim face showed that something was far wrong.

'Some cartons of cigarettes have gone missing,' he told Cissie, 'and they think it's me.'

'They think you stole them?' She couldn't believe it.

'They know I live with a woman who runs a shop, and the boss accused me of giving them to you. He's sacked me.'

'Surely he can't do that without proof?'

'He's done it, and how can I prove I didn't steal them?'

The shop bell went, and by the time Cissie had finished serving, Hugh had gone upstairs. She longed to go to him, but guessed that he wanted to be alone. He didn't come down again before she closed the shop, not even with her supper, and when she went up, he was sitting by the fire, his head in his hands. She went over and gripped his shoulder. 'Have you no idea who's been stealing?'

'Not a clue.'

While she fried some bacon and eggs and set the table,

Cissie's brain was as busy as her hands, but she could think of nothing to help him, and she eventually told him to come and eat his supper.

'I couldn't eat anything,' he said gloomily.

'You'll have to eat it now it's made. I'm ready for it.'

He stood up reluctantly. 'I forgot to make anything for you. I'm sorry.'

'I survived,' she smiled, 'but only just.'

'Burnett said he's suspected for a while that somebody was stealing.' Hugh's mind was fully occupied with this. 'He's checking all his stock, and once he knows exactly what's been taken, he's going to report it to the police. They'll likely be round here in the morning, to see if you've a new supply of Woodbines. That's the last lot that disappeared.'

'Oh!' she exclaimed, looking at him in dismay. 'I got a delivery of Woodbines yesterday, and they'll likely think it's the stolen lot.'

'That's it, then.' He spread his hands wide in despair.

They looked at each other hopelessly, then she brightened. 'The driver would know I got them legitimately.'

'If he's the thief, he could swear blind he wasn't here yesterday.'

She sagged again. 'There must be something we can do.'

Their goodnight kiss was superficial, both afraid that, in this emotional turbulence, their passions might not remain suppressed, and neither of them slept for worrying.

Cissie had just set two plates of porridge on the table next morning when she let out a cry. 'I just remembered! I still have the delivery note for that Woodbines consignment.' She jumped up and delved through some papers lying on the sideboard. 'Yes, here it is!'

They studied it together, the scrawled signature easily distinguishable as W. Ross. 'He could have made it out himself,' Hugh said, uncertainly. 'He could have got hold of a spare pad of dockets, and this maybe hasn't gone through the firm's books at all. If he's been fiddling for a while, he'll be up to all the dodges.'

'At least it proves I didn't know he was giving me stolen goods,' Cissie reminded him.

'He could say we got somebody else to sign his name.'

Her face fell again. 'I can't understand it, though. Why would he give me stuff he's stolen? He knows I wouldn't pay cash, not when I've an account.'

'Maybe he just sells what he steals to his mates.'

'And maybe it's not him at all. Anyway, I'll show this delivery note to the police if they come.'

When it was time to open the shop, Cissie said, 'Come down with me, Hugh. You can tidy up the store, it'll be something for you to do to keep your mind off it.'

It was eleven o'clock exactly when a police sergeant came, frowning when he saw what Hugh was doing. 'You shouldn't be shifting any of that, Mr Phimister,' he admonished. 'I have to check what's there.'

Within an hour, Cissie's stock of cigarettes was lying untidily all over the place, several cartons being isolated in one corner as the sergeant checked them with his list of stolen goods. His polite manner vanished suddenly. 'We've got you, Phimister. They're all here.'

Overhearing, Cissie ran through. 'Hugh didn't steal any of that!' she cried, looking at the large pile that contrasted so eloquently with the other items scattered over the rest of the floor. 'I got the Woodbines two days ago, I can let you see the delivery note I got, and I've had some of the other cartons for weeks.'

The sergeant nodded seriously. 'Aye, it's been going on for a while apparently. You will have to accompany me to the station, Phimister, and a van will come this afternoon to collect the evidence.' Turning to Cissie, he warned, 'I've

321

got every box written down, Mrs Phimister, so you'd better not move any of them.'

'I'm not Mrs Phimister.' It was out before she thought, and she had to go on. 'It's Dickson. Hugh's just my lodger.'

'Oh, aye?' The two words held heavy disbelief. 'You'll be questioned later to see if you're implicated, Miss Dickson.'

'Mrs Dickson,' she corrected, automatically, then burst into tears as it dawned on her that it would probably make things look even blacker for Hugh. As far as the police were concerned, a man living openly with a married woman would be capable of anything – theft included.

When she was left alone, she was so upset that she put a notice in her window, 'Sorry, closed for personal reasons', and went upstairs to think. How could she prove to that obnoxious sergeant that Hugh was innocent? It didn't matter that they thought she was living in sin with him.

She agonised for the next thirty minutes but nothing came to her, and unable to bear the inactivity, she went down to the back shop, looking at the allegedly stolen property for several minutes. Gold Flake, Craven A, Capstan, Woodbines, Ardath, Senior Service – brands she always stocked, and she had taken in extra supplies in preparation for Christmas. She had paid for every last one of the cartons, except the Woodbines which wouldn't be due for payment until the end of the year.

Shaking her head, she turned to go back to her house, but something niggled at her now, something she should remember. She racked her brains for fully ten minutes before it came to her. Invoices! Not counting the last lot of Woodbines, she had invoices – and receipted accounts – for everything. Why hadn't she remembered, when the old filing cabinet she'd bought about a year ago was staring her in the face? Racing upstairs, she got out her purchase ledger and cash book and carried them downstairs, where she methodically found both invoice and account for every entry under the name of the company Hugh had worked for, going back some months.

Then she began the more time-consuming task of sorting out the boxes, checking code numbers and letters and putting the whole of each delivery together. It took her the best part of two hours, but at last she stood back. Instead of one large pile and a higgledy-piggledy mess, there was now a neat row of different heights of stacks, each with its corresponding invoice and receipt sitting on the top carton. Letting out a long sigh of triumphant satisfaction, she blessed the training she had received in Richard Dickson's office. If she'd been like some shopkeepers, she could have thrown out invoices and accounts once they were paid.

When the police van came for the 'evidence', she explained why the boxes had been shifted, but the young constable, a copy of the sergeant's list in his hand, looked flummoxed.

'They're all there,' she assured him, 'but now I can prove none of them were stolen.'

He scratched his head, then said, 'I'd better get Sergeant Binnie to come and see this.'

Several hours later, Hugh was sitting with Cissie on his knee. 'I'd have been a goner if it hadn't been for you. That sergeant asked me dozens of questions. Where was I born? Where were you born? What was your maiden name? Why did I leave Aberdeen? He was so sure I was guilty he nearly had a fit when the bobby told him what you'd done.'

She gave a delighted chuckle. 'I know. He came storming in ready to give me a right doing-down for moving the boxes, and he'd to change his tune when I checked over the receipts with him. I wish I'd remembered them before.'

'I'm thankful you remembered them at all,' Hugh smiled, kissing the lobe of her ear. 'The only dodgy thing was the Woodbines, but with you proving you bought the rest of the stuff, and having a delivery note for them, they let me go. I don't think they suspect Ross, but the sergeant on the desk said they've warned the firm to keep a sharper eye on their stocks, so I hope they catch whoever it is the next time he tries it.'

At half past nine the following morning, the manager of the wholesale tobacconist came to offer Hugh his job back. 'I'm sorry I was so hasty, but with you – um, living with a woman who sells cigarettes, you can understand why I jumped to the wrong conclusion.'

'I'm afraid I can't,' Hugh said, quietly, 'and you'll have to find another driver.'

Taken aback, Mr Burnett gripped his mouth then turned and stamped out. Hugh looked apologetically at Cissie. 'Don't worry, I'll look for another job. I couldn't have worked for him again, not after the way he treated me.'

'I wouldn't think so,' she said, indignantly, 'and there's no hurry for you to find another job. It's coming up for Christmas so I could be doing with help in the shop. It's a good while since I heard from Mrs Barbour, but the last time she wrote she said I should take on an assistant, so she'd be willing to pay you.'

'I can't sponge off an old woman, but I'll help you out till your busy time's past.'

When the post was delivered the following morning, Hugh took a quick glance through it. 'All invoices as far as I can see,' he observed, coming to the last one. 'No, this one's from Grangemouth. Mrs Barbour likely. You said you hadn't heard from her for a while.'

Cissie's smile vanished when she looked at the envelope. 'This isn't her writing. I hope nothing's wrong with her.'

'Oh, no!' she exclaimed, in a moment. 'She'd a stroke last month, and she died yesterday morning from another one. It was a neighbour that wrote. Oh, Hugh, the poor old soul. I should have gone to see her when I didn't hear from her for so long. Grangemouth's not far.'

He had taken the letter from her. 'She's to be buried in Rosebank Cemetery. Is that where her husband's buried?'

'I don't know, but her son's buried there.' She related the story of the troop train, then said, 'I'll have to go to the funeral on Saturday.'

'That's all right. I'll easily manage the shop on my own.'

'I'll only be about an hour, maybe less. She was so good to me, it's the least I can do for her.'

Something had occurred to Hugh now, but he could see that Cissie was too upset to discuss it. 'Go and make yourself a cup of tea,' he told her. 'You've had a nasty shock.'

Cissie was too taken up with her own sad thoughts to see that Hugh was also preoccupied, so she was surprised when he said, 'Cissie, have you thought what Mrs Barbour's death means to you?'

'I don't understand.'

'Had she any relations apart from her sister?'

'Just the son that was killed.'

'So the shop'll go to her sister.'

'Oh!' Cissie's eyes clouded. 'I see what you're getting at now. Her sister was an invalid. She'll likely sell it.'

'And the house,' Hugh reminded her.

'I suppose so.'

They looked at each other for a moment, then Hugh said, sadly, 'It's one thing after another, isn't it? First, the business with the cigarettes, now this.'

'We'll soon both be out of a job – and a home, and I'll never be able to have Ricky back now.'

Hating to see her so despondent, he said, 'Don't look

on the black side, my dearest. We'll still have each other, and we'll get by, whatever happens.'

She was not to be cheered. 'It'll be a poor Christmas with this hanging over our heads.'

Chapter Twenty-nine

❧❧

1929

The Christmas and New Year rush for gift boxes of chocolates and sweets, and presentation packs and tins of
cigarettes, kept Cissie and Hugh too busy to dwell on their
troubles – too busy to do anything except eat and sleep.
They had even given up their half days and Sundays to
comply with their customers' demands, and things did not
ease off until the third week of January.

'That's surely all the first-footing past now,' Cissie sighed
one night.

Hugh sat down and slackened his tie. 'I haven't had the
energy to give you a cuddle for ages.'

She perched on his knee and hugged him. 'I missed it.'

Fifteen minutes later, Hugh observed, 'We shouldn't
really complain about being busy. Whoever buys the shop's
going to be impressed by what we've taken in over the past
six weeks, though I thought you'd have heard something
by this time.'

'Maybe Mrs Barbour's sister's going to keep it, but I
wish we knew, one way or the other.'

Having seen that Hugh enjoyed his stint as her assistant,
Cissie persuaded him that she needed him permanently,
and insisted on paying him a wage out of her takings,
entering it into her cash book so that everything was above
board. They worked well together. Hugh had a good way
with the customers, and they took turns in time off for
meals. It was such a perfect arrangement, they almost forgot that it must come to an end.

*　　*　　*

One dreary, sleety morning in February, Hugh was having a quick look at the *Scottish Daily Express* while they had no customers, when he exclaimed, 'Good! They've caught that thief at last. That's a weight off my mind, for I've always wondered if they still suspected me.'

'Was it Ross?'

'No, and it's nobody you'd know. He was caught red-handed yesterday and admitted he'd been stealing for over a year.' Hugh fell silent again as he read the rest of the article, then he burst out, 'For God's sake!'

'What is it?' Cissie asked anxiously.

'Listen to this. "Last December, when the thefts were first discovered, it was suspected that the culprit was Hugh Phimister, another van driver with the same firm. It was thought that he was stealing the cigarettes to give to his common law wife, Cissie Dickson, nee McGregor, to sell in her small confectioner/tobacconist's shop in Duke Street, Leith. He was released from police custody when Mrs Dickson produced evidence that cleared him. Both parties, originally from Aberdeen, are reported to be relieved that the thief has been found." Why the hell did they drag that up after all this time? Nobody's been near us to ask how we felt, and whoever wrote this must have got it all from the police.'

'They must have been short of news, and it doesn't matter, does it? At least it says you were innocent. I just wish it didn't say I was your common law wife, though that's likely what everybody thinks I am.'

Hugh was still too angry to notice this. 'I'd like to get my hands on that reporter. I thought I'd heard the last of it when I walked out of the police station.'

Cissie was in bed before the dreadful thought occurred to her. Anybody who saw that article would know where she came from, where she lived. What if her father saw it? Her maiden name had been given, so he would know it was her. He'd make a beeline for the shop, and he might end up killing Hugh — like he had killed poor Jim Robertson — as well as her. She wondered if she should go through to tell him how afraid she was, but he'd been so tired when he went to bed it would be cruel to deprive him of the sleep he needed, and in any case, what could he do?

After going over and over it in her mind all night, she decided not to tell him at all, it would only worry him. She would keep on her guard for the next few days, and if her father hadn't come by then, she would know he hadn't read the newspaper, wherever he was.

Just after ten next morning, Cissie was making tea in the back shop when she heard a customer coming in. Hugh was at the counter, so she paid no attention to the mumbling voices until he called, 'Cissie, somebody wants to see you.'

'I'll be through in a minute,' she called back cheerfully, but, as she filled the teapot, she was gripped by a fear that made her break out in a sweat. Could it be her father? Hugh had never met him and wouldn't recognise him. Laying kettle and teapot down with hands that shook as if she had the palsy, she stood for a moment, panic-stricken, until common sense took over. Even if it were her father, what could he do in a place as public as this, where somebody could walk in at any minute?

Taking several deep breaths to compose herself, she went through, halting in the doorway in disbelieving delight then running forward and throwing her arms round her step-mother. 'Phoebe! Oh, Phoebe!'

'You'd better take them upstairs,' Hugh smiled.

'Oh, I'm sorry,' she said, wiping tears of happiness from her cheeks. 'I didn't notice you there as well, Richard.'

He gave a light laugh. 'I think I'll stay down here to let you talk to Phoebe on your own.'

Upstairs, the two women hugged rapturously again for a moment, then Phoebe said, 'I wouldn't have known where to find you if I hadn't seen a stupid article in yesterday's *Daily Express*. I didn't have time to read it till late last night, and I couldn't believe my eyes when I saw your name. I've been nearly sick with worry since we came back from America and found you'd disappeared.'

'But I wrote to you and you never answered.'

'There was a mountain of mail, but nothing from you.'

They looked at each other in puzzlement, then Phoebe burst out, 'I bet Bertram still has a key! I wouldn't put it past him to let himself in when we were away. He would recognise your writing if he'd been nosying through our letters, and he'd likely destroyed it.' Her nose wrinkled again. 'But I sent a cable to you telling you Richard had been taken ill in San Francisco, so you'd know we were held up.'

Cissie looked blank. 'It must have come after I left. Was it serious?'

'He had cancer. For a while, the doctors didn't think he would live. They pulled him through in the end, but it was a long, slow business and they couldn't promise that they'd cured it completely, so we will have to make the most of our time together,' she paused sadly, and Cissie could see just how much she loved this man.

'I was a bit put out you never wrote to ask how we were, but I can understand now. He wasn't fit to travel for a long time after he got out of hospital, and we've only been home for a few months. Anyway, when I told Richard last night you were in Leith, he said he'd take me to see you this morning and I hardly slept a wink.'

Cissie's smile was somewhat tremulous. 'Hugh was annoyed at that reporter, but I feel like writing to thank him now. If it hadn't been for him . . .'

'Cissie,' Phoebe interrupted, 'I want to know why you left Bertram. He said you'd found somebody else and walked out, but we knew you wouldn't have left Ricky.'

'It's the last thing I'd have done, but Bertram wouldn't let me have him. How is Ricky, Phoebe? Is he all right?'

330

'He's a wee darling. Not so wee now, he's three past.'

'Yes, I know. I used to pine for him, but I could hardly keep myself at first, let alone him. I went back to Dundee a few times, you know, though I just stood near the house to see him when Elma took him past in the pram, but at least I knew he was being well looked after. I often think about him, though I never say anything to Hugh.'

'You still haven't told me why you left Panache.'

It was more than an hour later when Richard went upstairs to find his wife with her arms round Cissie, who was weeping quietly. 'Should I have stayed in the shop?' he asked.

Phoebe shook her head. 'Come in. We've been having a heart to heart talk, and you'll not believe what this poor girl's been through. I'll tell you when we're going back in the car, for she's had enough just now.'

Standing up, Cissie swallowed hard then said, 'Sit down, Richard, and I'll make some dinner.'

While she prepared a meal, her stepmother said, 'I always said Bertram was a bad lot, and he still hardly speaks to me though he lets us take Ricky out for an hour on Sundays.'

'He won't remember me now,' Cissie said, sadly.

'It's a good thing he has Elma, for Bertram's out all day and doesn't bother with him much. I know how you must feel about her,' Phoebe went on gently, noticing the tightening of Cissie's face, 'but she's very good with Ricky. I'd say she loves him as much as Richard and I do.'

'It's not the same as having his own mother.'

Phoebe hesitated briefly. 'Do you want to have him back?'

'Oh, yes! You don't know how much I want to have him.'

'I wondered, seeing you've got Hugh now.'

Noticing that Richard had gripped his mouth as though

in disapproval, Cissie said, 'Hugh's my lodger. I don't sleep with him.'

Richard seemed relieved. 'I wouldn't blame you if you did, but I'm glad you don't.'

'I told him about Ricky, and if by some miracle I ever did manage to get him, I'm sure Hugh would be pleased for me.'

'Yes,' Richard put in, 'he was saying he wished you could be reunited with your son. He's a fine man, Cissie.'

'You don't have to tell me that.'

When lunch was ready, Cissie said, 'We'll have ours first, then I'll go down and let Hugh up.'

'Can't he eat with us?' Richard enquired.

'One of us has to mind the shop . . .' She broke off with a little giggle. 'What does it matter for one day, a day as special as this? I'll put a card in the window to say we'll be shut for one hour, and we can all sit down together.'

The meal over, Hugh ordered her to stay with her visitors. 'You'll have a lot to speak about. I'd just be in the way.'

Richard stood up with him. 'Something tells me I would be in the way, too, so if nobody minds, I'll go for a walk.'

Phoebe waited until he closed the door, then said, 'Why didn't you divorce Bertram, Cissie?'

'I tried to, but the solicitor I saw said I didn't stand a chance, for it was my word against Bertram's and Elma's.'

Phoebe shook her head. 'Richard's a respected business-man, and he would vouch for your character. You don't even sleep with Hugh, though I could see you loved him.'

'Bertram would swear blind I had, and he's just as well known in business as his father nowadays.'

'It's worth another try. Think about it, Cissie.'

'It wouldn't work.'

Her stepdaughter looked so downhearted that Phoebe decided to tell her some of the things she and Richard had done in America, and was pleased when Cissie brightened and started asking questions about the places they had visited. When that topic was exhausted, they reminisced about their time in the mill, and after a while, Cissie said, 'Do you ever hear anything about Jen?'

Phoebe's cheery face sobered. 'She died over a year ago.'

'Oh, poor Jen. She wasn't a bit well when I saw her. That was after Bertram – you know.'

'I wouldn't have known anything about it if I hadn't run into Johnny Keating one day.'

'Johnny Keating?' Cissie could still recall her anger on the day he ended their friendship.

'He's married now, with twins, and he said he'd been so worried about Jen after she had to stop work he'd made his wife, Babs, go to see her. As he said, "Jen was lying on her bed, just a rickle of bones." Anyway, Babs had got a doctor in, and she was in hospital visiting Jen when she died.'

Cissie gave a deep sigh. 'I'm glad she wasn't on her own at the end.'

'Johnny paid for her funeral,' Phoebe went on, 'so you see he wasn't as bad as you thought. Oh, I wish I'd gone to see her sometimes.'

'I only went when I'd nobody else to turn to.'

They sat in silence for a moment, thinking with affection of the woman who had taken them in when they were homeless, twice, in Cissie's case, then Phoebe said, 'We'd some laughs with her. Remember . . .'

The rest of the afternoon passed in more reminiscences, and they were astonished when Richard appeared just before six with a large bundle in his hands. 'I've bought fish and chips to save you having to cook again, Cissie,' he smiled.

'Oh,' she gasped, 'I forgot about supper.'

'I thought you might.'

At eight o'clock, Richard got to his feet. 'It's time we made tracks for home, Phoebe, my dear.'

'You'll come back to see us?' Cissie asked, anxiously.

'Every week,' Phoebe assured her.

'Could you make it on Wednesdays? That's our half-day and we'd both be free to enjoy your company.'

'Wednesdays it shall be,' laughed Richard.

The two women hugged each other again before they went out to the car, and when Cissie joined Hugh behind the counter, she sighed, 'This has been the best day of my life — apart from the day you walked in.' Then she remembered that she hadn't told Phoebe that Tam was no longer in prison. They'd had so much to talk about that it hadn't entered her head, and perhaps it was all for the best. It would only have alarmed her, and, in any case, he would have turned up yesterday or today if he had seen the newspaper article.

By the time they closed the shop, Cissie had more or less convinced herself that she had nothing more to fear on that account, and let her mind turn to what her stepmother had said. Sitting down beside Hugh, she said, 'Phoebe told me I should divorce Bertram.'

He looked at her in some surprise. 'That's funny. I was going to suggest that myself.'

She put forward the same argument against it that she had given Phoebe, but he put his arm round her and said, 'Once you were free of him, my darling, I could ask you to marry me, but it's up to you.'

'I'd do anything to be your wife, Hugh, but . . .'

'Anything but that?'

'You don't know what Bertram's like. He'd lie his head off and have everybody believing him. I went to see a solicitor before, and he wouldn't even take it on.'

'You could try again. You never know, Bertram might be wanting to marry somebody else himself by this time.'

'He'd divorce me if he was.'

'So your mind's made up?'

'I'm sorry, Hugh, dear.' The thought of standing in a

court listening to Bertram's version of Tommy's visit and seeing Elma sneering at her again, would be too much to bear. Besides, she would have no right to Ricky if she was no longer his father's wife.

Only five days after her reunion with her stepmother, Cissie had another surprise. Among the mail, there was one typed envelope addressed to her personally, and when she looked at the back, she said, 'It's from James Latimer, Mrs Barbour's solicitor, the one I went to about a divorce. Is this it?'

Hugh didn't have to ask what she meant. 'Open it and see,' he urged.

In a moment, she said, 'I've to go and see him as soon as I can. She must have left me a little something. That was really nice of her, for I never expected anything.'

'He doesn't say if her sister is selling the shop?'

'He'll likely tell me when I go, and he said as soon as I could, so I'd better go now.'

Less than an hour later, Cissie came back in a daze. 'Her sister had died, and she left everything to me. Oh, Hugh, my head's spinning. I can't believe the shop's really mine now, and the house.'

He grabbed her hand across the counter. 'I'm pleased for you, Cissie. She must have been very fond of you.'

'And I was fond of her, but I never dreamt ... Mr Latimer said we've to carry on like we've been doing, but all the profits'll come to us now.'

'To you,' he corrected, smiling.

'It's the same thing.'

'No, it's not, but I'm really happy for you, Cissie.'

'Don't let this spoil things between us. We're in this together, and it's as much yours as mine. Nothing's going to be any different.'

'As long as you don't think I'm after you for your money.'

'There won't be much money. We'll still take out the same in wages, only now we'll have a wee something in the bank.'

Phoebe and Richard were told the good news as soon as they came on Wednesday, the congratulations going on until Phoebe gave a loud exclamation. 'Oh! I nearly forgot, with all the excitement!' She rummaged in her handbag then handed Cissie an envelope. 'It's photographs I took of Ricky.'

Cissie wept as she studied the sturdy, fair-haired boy, his head to one side and his mischievous grin showing a tooth missing. 'Can I keep them?' she gulped at last.

'I took them for you,' Phoebe assured her. 'Isn't he a pet? He can be a wee monkey sometimes, too – I don't mean bad, though, just full of devilment. Now, I'm going to tell you something, so listen properly. The day after we were here, I went to Panache to try out a wee plan I had. I told Elma I wanted to take some snaps of Ricky, and after I was finished, I asked him to go and play in the garden. I could see she wasn't pleased, but what could she say?'

Richard smiled. 'Phoebe can get round anyone.'

She flashed him a warning glance and carried on, 'I looked her straight in the eye and asked her to describe the man she said you'd slept with. Well, that took the feet from her and she admitted it was all a lie. She didn't know I'd never met Tommy – if you remember, he left the night I went to Schoolhill – and she likely thought I'd recognise him from her description. But to get back to what I was telling you, she said she only did it because she'd been hoping to get Bertram to herself after he put you out, but he'd never had any time for her. Once her tongue was slackened, she told me he'd often stayed out all night, or took women home to sleep with him, and he'd treated her like dirt.'

'Serves her right,' Cissie muttered.

336

'She said she only stays on there for Ricky's sake, and I think she was glad to get everything off her chest at last. She's willing to testify now that she lied before, and that two beds were used, not one.'

'What difference will that make after all this time?'

'You're not listening,' Phoebe scolded. 'I said she was willing to *testify* to everything, in a court, and to tell about Bertram's women.'

'They wouldn't believe her, not when she's just a servant and he's what he is.'

'Oh, Cissie!' her stepmother exclaimed, in exasperation. 'Do you not understand what I'm getting at? You can call her and Richard as witnesses for you, and you'd get custody . . .'

'Oh!' Cissie's eyes widened. 'Do you really think so?'

'I'm nearly sure.'

'But Bertram said Ricky was his insurance . . .' She broke off, looking apologetically at Richard. 'I'm sorry. Maybe I shouldn't have, but I told him about the will you were going to make after Ricky was born and about your cancer. You didn't say not to, and it was out before I thought.'

'Ah!' Richard frowned reflectively. 'That explains a lot. Don't worry, Cissie. Knowing Bertram, he would probably have found out by some other means, fair or foul. He'll be planning to get his hands on Ricky's share.' He thought for a few seconds, then seemed to draw himself even more erect. 'If I guarantee that you will be given custody of the boy, will you go ahead?'

Taking no time to speculate on how Richard could promise such a thing, Cissie said, 'Yes, I will!'

Beaming, Phoebe burst out, 'Good for you! See a solicitor tomorrow and file for divorce on the grounds of Bertram's cruelty and adultery.'

'I'll go to Mr Latimer again,' Cissie smiled. 'He'll not refuse me this time.'

Hugh, who had said nothing so far, stepped forward to hug her. 'Oh, my darling, you don't know how pleased I am about this. We'll be married as soon as the divorce comes through and we'll be a ready-made family of three.'

Bertram had an unexpected visitor just before nine o'clock the following morning. Having had a late night, he was not in the best of tempers, and turned angrily when someone burst into the dining room while he was having breakfast. 'Oh, it's you, Father,' he said, trying to sound pleased.

Anxious to get this over as quickly as possible, Richard wasted no time. 'I have never made any bones about how I feel about you, Bertram. I have never trusted you, but I could hardly believe my ears when Phoebe told me what you had done to Cissie. I didn't think that even you could sink so low. And to tell me those lies about her . . .'

'I told the truth! Cissie did go away and leave Ricky.'

'Not willingly! And there was no other man involved.'

'She pretended he was her brother,' Bertram blustered, 'but Elma said . . .'

'Ah, yes! Elma! You made a mistake there. You turned her head with your attentions, you led her to believe that you loved her, and then, after she had served her purpose and had given you an excuse to get rid of Cissie, you turned your back on her.'

'I didn't turn my back on her. I made her Ricky's nanny.'

'She thought you would take her as your mistress, and you were fortunate that she loved your son so much, otherwise she would have exposed you then for the scoundrel you are. But she has now admitted everything to Phoebe, and Cissie is filing for divorce.'

After his initial gasp of shock, Bertram's wily brain got busy again. He'd be glad to wash his hands of his wife. He could sack Elma – the bitch deserved it for blabbing – and marry again to provide his son with another mother – a woman who wouldn't bat an eyelid if he siphoned off most of what his father would leave to Ricky. 'I'm sorry, Father,' he said, repentantly, 'I've made a hash of things, haven't I? But I promise you I'll . . .'

'Don't make any promises you have no intention of keeping. Cissie is to claim custody of her son, and I have arranged that Ricky's inheritance will be put into trust until he is twenty-one. Moreover, in case you think you can cheat the boy out of what is rightly his at some future time, I want you to – no, I insist that you leave Scotland as soon as you can.'

'Oh, Father! That's a bit much, isn't it? I still have two businesses to run.'

'From what I hear, your mill is on its last legs, and you can find a manager for the warehouse. I shall arrange that a set amount is paid into your bank every month.'

'So you've got it all worked out?' Bertram sneered. 'Where am I supposed to go?'

'To one of the dominions? I'll pay your fare of course.'

With dozens of creditors breathing down his neck, and a fifteen-year-old threatening to oppose him as father of her unborn child, Bertram grabbed his chance of escape. Heaving a resigned sigh, he muttered, 'I used to have a notion to go to Canada at one time. I suppose I could go there since you're determined to see the back of me.'

'I should have sent you abroad long before you married Cissie,' his father said, grimly. 'Now, I shall book your passage for – say in three months? That should give you time to find the right man for the warehouse, and to dispose of your mill and your house. And let me tell you now, once you have sailed, I trust that I will never see you again.'

With another sneering smile, Bertram said, 'You've never liked me, have you?'

'Not since you were old enough to manipulate your mother. One thing more, just in case you were thinking of coming home after I die, I'll add a clause to my will stipulating that on no account are you ever to be allowed to touch one penny of Ricky's inheritance.'

Turning smartly on his heel, Richard strode out, leaving Bertram utterly aghast. All his life, he had dreamt of being so rich he could act the playboy, get into high society and impress the elegant ladies he would meet abroad, and now he was being banished like a common criminal. His father had put the final nail in the coffin of his expectations.

Suddenly, with a shrug, he poured himself another cup of coffee. What the hell? He'd had a good innings, and his sins had caught up with him, but he would soon be setting off to a land where the poor became wealthy, where the unknown became famous. And he wouldn't be starting off penniless. He'd have more than enough to keep up a decent lifestyle. And if this divorce case was heard before he left, he'd go down smiling.

*   *   *

'Mr Latimer says there shouldn't be any problem about the divorce,' Cissie told Hugh, when she went home. 'He's going to write to Elma, to make sure she's willing to testify, but I'm scared Bertram'll fight it. You don't know how persuasive he can be. He could even talk her round to not testifying at all, so I'm not building up my hopes.'

'Don't be so pessimistic,' Hugh smiled. 'He must know when he's beaten.'

'He wouldn't give up, no matter what. He needs Ricky so he can get Richard's money. I wish Richard had left all his estate to Phoebe. People might think I only want custody of Ricky because he'll have money of his own some day.'

'Come here, my pet,' Hugh smiled, taking her in his arms. 'Anybody who knows you would never think that.'

Two days later, Cissie's mind was taken off the ifs and buts of the divorce case by the statement she received from the bank showing the balance in the account now in her

340

name. 'I didn't think it would be nearly as much as this,' she said, her face lighting up.

'How does it feel to be a rich woman?' Hugh teased.

'I haven't taken it in yet, but it's a good feeling, and it's not just mine, it's ours. Maybe we could have the shop painted. What do you think?'

'If the place is more attractive, it should attract more customers, but it's your decision.'

'No, I want us to make the decisions together.'

'Right, I'll go and see a painter after dinnertime.'

Hugh's plans were changed, however, because Tommy turned up in the late forenoon, and when he heard of Cissie's good fortune and learned what they were planning, he said, 'I've a few days to spare. Between us, we could do it for less than a quarter of what a painter would charge, eh, Hugh?'

'I suppose we could try.' Hugh did not appear to be so confident of their ability.

'I'll get ladders from the ship, and I could maybe get some of the crew to lend a hand. The more the merrier.'

Cissie, like Hugh, was not too keen on letting amateurs loose on the shop, but her brother swept all her objections aside. 'There's no need to spend more money than you need to. My God, Cissie, you're the jammy one. Your own shop! I'd never have thought you'd end up like this when I saw you that night down at the . . .' He stopped, scarlet-faced.

'It's all right, Tommy,' Cissie smiled, 'I've told Hugh about the night I nearly turned prostitute, and about the only man I picked up. I was jammy that night as well.'

The next few days were a nightmare to Cissie; men and ladders all over the place, customers ducking under them and having to lift tarpaulins to see what was on her counter. The smell of paint mingled with the smell of her candies and toffee, and most of her free minutes were spent making tea and washing cups, but at last it was done.

341

'I think we made a damned good job of it,' Tommy declared, surveying the pale yellow walls and the glistening white woodwork. 'What about the place in the back next?'

'No thanks,' Cissie laughed. 'I couldn't stand the smell of paint any longer. Maybe I'll get a new counter put in, with glass over the top to keep things from getting dusty.'

After the shop closed that night, Tommy told Cissie and Hugh that he was going to Archangel on his next trip. 'I was there once before, and God knows how the Ruskies stand the cold up there, for I felt like my best bits were frozen so solid they'd snap off any minute. What a disaster that would have been!'

Cissie looked embarrassed at this, but Hugh roared with laughter. 'Oh, Tommy, you're a tonic!'

'We were icebound for three months, and we were muffled up to the eyeballs in furs like Eskimos.'

Even Cissie laughed now, and he turned to her with his eyebrows raised. 'Is there any chance of a bed tonight?'

'No, Tommy,' she replied, blushing hotly because she knew he was really asking if she and Hugh were sleeping together.

Her brother shrugged. 'Remember what I told you. Hugh's not made of stone any more than me, are you, my friend?'

Hugh coloured now, and Cissie stepped in before he could agree or deny. 'Have you found yourself a girl yet?'

'I think so. Marion's the second mate's sister, so she knows how long us Merchant Navy boys have to be away. I met her when I spent a week at their house in Lowestoft, and I think she fancies me, too, but I'll have to wait and see what happens.'

'She won't be able to resist you,' Cissie joked.

'I hope not.'

He sounded so serious that she wished she hadn't teased him, but he was smiling again in the next instant. 'Well, there's nothing for it but go back to the old ship.'

When Hugh had seen Tommy out, he said, 'Why didn't you tell him you were divorcing Bertram?'

'You'll likely think I'm silly, but I thought I should wait till it was all cut and dried – if it ever is.'

After kissing her goodnight, he made to go to his own room, but turned at the door. 'If you don't get the divorce, Cissie, remember what Tommy said. I'm not made of stone.'

She knew that. She had felt his need against her on many occasions, but she still couldn't let him sleep with her. Of course, once they were married she would have to. At this thought, her insides gathered into a tight knot. Maybe she should withdraw her petition for divorce? But it was the only chance she had of getting Ricky back ... and she really did love Hugh.

Chapter Thirty

❧❧

Waiting for her divorce case to be heard, Cissie became so nervous that she wondered if she would be able to go through with it after all, and only the thought of Ricky stopped her from calling the whole thing off.

Hugh, however, had seen how tense she was and, one night before they separated to go to bed, he said, 'I'm going to strip the walls of the bedroom tomorrow night and we can decorate it ready for when Ricky comes.'

'We shouldn't count our chickens before they're hatched,' she murmured. 'I maybe won't get custody of him.'

'Richard's sure you will, and we won't have time to do it after you've been to court.'

Still not altogether convinced, she took time off the next day to choose wallpaper and curtain materials, and when the walls were stripped, Hugh began on the plastering, sanding and papering while Cissie was sewing.

When the room was finished, Cissie said, 'The carpet looks dingy against the fresh paint. I'd better get a new one.'

Hugh grinned. 'Anybody would think we were preparing for the Prince of Wales.'

'Do you think I'm making too much of a fuss?'

'Not a bit of it, my dearest, and I'm looking forward to having the boy here as much as you.'

The carpet bought, she decided to buy a new bedroom suite, too — nothing was too good for her son — and when the room was ready, she tried to see it through a child's eyes. 'Yes, Hugh, I think he'll like it,' she said, after a few moments. 'The blue in the carpet and the curtains makes it cheerier, though I thought it might look cold, and the flowers on the quilt match exactly. The wardrobe should be big enough to take all his clothes, even if he's got a suitcaseful. I think it's perfect.'

He gave her waist a squeeze. 'Aye, it is, so I'd better not use this room again.' Her patent shock made him go on, 'I'll sleep in the kitchen.'

She didn't want him to sleep in Ricky's bed, she didn't want him to be uncomfortable, and the only other solution was to . . . She couldn't take him to her bed, not yet. 'It won't be for long,' she murmured.

Next day, a letter came summoning her to 'compear before the Lords of Council and Session' in two weeks' time. 'I suppose compear is a legal word for appear,' she observed to Hugh, who was reading over her shoulder.

'Parliament House, Parliament Square? That's the building at the back of St Giles Cathedral. I remember seeing it once when I was having a walk when I first came to Edinburgh.'

'Oh, Hugh, I'm all shaky. I don't know what to expect, and what'll I do when I see Bertram?'

'Ignore him. He can't do anything to you now.'

Her dreams had been fully taken up with the happy prospect of having her son back, but on the night before the fateful day, she dreamt that she was alone with her father in a huge room, empty except for a bed. He was advancing towards her threateningly, and no matter how hard she tried to run, she couldn't move. Her feet seemed to be fixed to the floor, her arms tied to her sides, and she could only stand and watch as he came nearer and nearer until she could see the beads of sweat on his brow, the fire of lust in his glazed eyes, the wetness of his drooling lips.

'You didn't think you'd get away with having me locked up, did you?' he sneered, close to her now, and her mouth was so dry that she had no saliva to spit in his face. 'All the time I was in that place I was dreaming of this day,' he went on, his voice pulsing with passion, 'the day I could take my revenge on you. I'm going to kill you, Cissie, but not till I've had some pleasure from you.' His voice changed now, coaxing, 'Come to your Da, like a good lass.'

When his hands came up to take hold of her, desperation freed her arms and feet of their invisible fetters and she tried to shove him away, her whole body thrashing about wildly, but it was useless. At his touch, she screamed as loudly as she could, then struggled against the weight of his hand on her shoulder.

'Cissie! Stop it! It's Hugh.'

Sure that it was a trick, she still fought against her attacker until she was shaken rudely awake and looked up into Hugh's alarmed eyes.

'What's wrong, Cissie?' he cried. 'You frightened the life out of me with your shouting. You've just had a nightmare, but it sounded like you were fighting for your life.'

She drew in a deep, shuddering breath. 'I thought I was. Oh, Hugh, I didn't want you to know about it, but I have to tell you, no matter what you'll think of me.'

'Nothing'll change what I feel for you.'

She told him then how her father had raped her, but when Hugh realised that it had happened just after she had fled from his boyish attempt to make love to her, he groaned, 'It's all my fault. If I hadn't scared you that night . . .'

'No,' she burst out, 'I was scared long before that.' She explained that, as a small girl, she had listened to the sounds of her father's lust, and to the agonies her mother had suffered as a consequence. 'If I'd let you do what you wanted that night, everything would have been all right.'

'It wasn't your fault, either,' he murmured, drawing her even closer to him. 'So you married Jim Robertson because you were expecting your father's child?'

'Jim knew whose it was, that's why he married me. He

346

was a good man, Hugh, just wanting to give my baby a name, and he didn't deserve what happened to him.' In the merest whisper, she told him of her father's second drunken attempt at rape. 'It was whitewashed in the papers, but Jim tried to save . . .'

Hugh's mouth came down gently on hers. 'I know the rest. I could never believe you'd let that Jim touch you – Ma said he'd a hump on his back – that's what hurt me most. If only you'd told me about the baby, my darling, I'd have married you. I'd have said it was mine.'

'I didn't know what to do,' she gulped. 'I thought you'd be sickened at what I'd done.'

'But it wasn't your fault. Forget about it, my dear, and think of having your son back tomorrow.'

He cradled her in his arms for the rest of the night, and she could feel her fears – the fears her father and Bertram had instilled in her – diminish in the knowledge that Hugh would never inflict pain on her, would never force her to do anything she was unhappy about. She couldn't love him any more than she did, and she felt like telling him he could move into her bed for good, that she wouldn't be afraid if he made love to her, but she wanted their marriage to start off on the right foot.

In the morning, she remembered that she hadn't told Hugh what had happened in her nightmare, nor that her father was out of prison, but she kept silent. It would only alarm him, and maybe she had let it grow out of all proportion.

Next day, Richard drove Cissie and Phoebe to Parliament House, off Edinburgh's High Street. Hugh had wanted to go with them, but Cissie told him she would feel easier if he wasn't there. When they were shown into the waiting area, Elma was already sitting on a form a good bit away from the door, and Cissie averted her eyes hastily as she plumped down on the nearest seat, praying that Bertram would not turn up at all.

They had to wait for some time in the cold corridor, and when Cissie shivered – with apprehension as much as the low temperature – Phoebe gripped her hand. 'It'll soon be over.'

At last she was called, and ushered through to a small courtroom to find James Latimer waiting for her. 'They'll hear your testimony first and then the witnesses',' he told her. 'Just answer my questions slowly and clearly.'

She was told to take her place in the witness box, and on being asked to describe her life with her husband, she said she had been happy with him until after their son was born.

'What happened to change this?

Cissie's breath was coming in laboured gasps now, and she could hardly bear to get out what the man wanted her to say. 'My husband – started – doing things.'

'What kind of things?'

'Vile, horrible things, and punching me, and biting.' She gathered strength as she went on. 'My whole body was covered in marks and bruises.'

'Can anyone corroborate this?'

'No. There was nothing showing on my face – and I was too ashamed to let anybody know.'

'I see. Go on. What finally led you to leave him?'

She spoke now of her brother's unexpected visit, of Elma's vicious lie, of being denied entry to her home and access to her baby. When she came to the end, the tears were streaming down her cheeks, but when she was asked if she would like some time to recover, she shook her head.

Latimer then said, 'Did you make any attempts to gain admittance, or to remove your child from the house?'

After she had given an account of as much as she could remember, she was allowed to stand down, and she was so emotional that she lost track of what was going on, until she heard Bertram's voice and her head jerked up.

He was standing, erect as usual, and had obviously been

348

asked if the allegations she had made were true. 'Do I look the kind of man who would ill-treat his wife?'

'Is that a denial?' asked the man on the bench.

Bertram turned to him, smiling. 'Yes, sir, it is.'

Cissie's heart sank. He looked the perfect gentleman, how could anybody doubt him?

Latimer took up the questioning again. 'Did you love your wife, Mr Dickson?'

'Very much.'

If she hadn't known better, Cissie thought, she would have believed him herself, he sounded so earnest, and she felt like standing up and shouting, 'He's a liar!'

'Yet you believed the maid' – here the man consulted his notes – 'Elma Jackson, when she told you that your wife had slept with another man while you were away.'

'I didn't believe her at first,' Bertram said, looking suitably pained, 'but she was so insistent, I had to. Why would she lie about such a thing?'

'Why, indeed? Had your wife ever told you of her brother?'

'She said that her brother was lost at sea during the war. I did not know she had another brother.'

'Mrs Dickson has said that you refused to listen when she swore to you that the man who stayed the night in your house was indeed her brother. It seems strange that any man would take the word of a maid before that of his wife. Had you any previous indication that she was unfaithful?'

Waiting for another lie to trip with ease from the smiling lips, Cissie was astonished when Bertram glanced at her and then said, in a voice that rang round the small room, 'No, I had no reason to think so.'

'Then why would you not listen to her?'

'I was so shocked by what the maid told me, I was numb. It was as if I'd had all the wind knocked out of me.'

349

'Mrs Dickson called at your office the following day. Were you still in a state of shock?'

'Have you ever been told that your wife was unfaithful to you?' Bertram countered. 'If you had, you would know how it affects a man.'

'Fortunately, I have never been in that position. Thank you, Mr Dickson, you may stand down.'

Cissie kept her eyes away as Bertram walked past her. And when Elma was called, she wondered if the girl would keep her promise to Phoebe, or if Bertram had talked her out of it. He was so silver-tongued he could make anybody say anything he wanted.

'I told Mr Dickson that his wife hadn't said the man was her brother,' Elma was saying, 'and when he asked if I'd be willing to swear they only used one bed, I said yes.'

'They did not use only one bed?'

'No.'

'But why should you be willing to blacken Mrs Dickson's character in this way? Did you not like her?'

'I'd nothing against her, though it annoyed Cook and me to see her acting the lady when Bertram had told me she was once a spinner in his father's mill.' Elma coloured because she had inadvertently used his first name, and added, 'I slept with Mr Dickson the whole time his wife was in the maternity, and I thought he wanted her out of the way so him and me could . . .'

'Did he take you as his mistress after he sent Mrs Dickson away?'

'Not for long. We took Ricky away so Mrs Dickson wouldn't know where he was, and Mr Dickson slept with me the whole four weeks we were in Glasgow, but when we went back to his house, he told me I was a nanny now, and said I'd to sleep in the room next to Ricky. He treated me just like a servant again, and he took a lot of women home to spend the night with him. It was disgusting!'

'This made you very angry?'

'Yes, very angry and very hurt.'

Cissie held her breath. Was he trying to make Elma say she was only testifying against Bertram out of spite?

Elma looked sorrowfully at the presiding Lord of Session now. 'I did an awful thing, telling those lies, for I knew the man was Mrs Dickson's brother. They didn't sleep in the same bed, he was in one of the guest rooms, and that's the God's honest truth, I swear to you.'

Cissie was so overcome with relief at this that she did not hear the rest of Elma's testimony, nor Richard's calm statement that his son was not to be trusted and that his daughter-in-law was the only morally fit parent to have custody of the child. She was not aware of anything until the Lord of Session said loudly, 'Divorce granted, and custody of the child goes to the mother.'

Phoebe grabbed her arm and said, in an excited whisper, 'That's it, Cissie.'

'I won,' she said, in an awed whisper as they walked out of the courtroom.

Phoebe beamed at her. 'And you got custody of Ricky.'

Her legs giving way now that the ordeal was over, Cissie sat down on one of the forms in the corridor. 'I just can't believe it!' She looked at her stepmother for reassurance.

'It's true! Come on! Hugh'll have his nails bitten up to the elbows worrying about what's happened.'

Rising slowly, Cissie followed Phoebe to the door, but before she reached it, someone put a hand on her arm. 'Wait, Mrs Dickson.'

When she turned round and saw the face of the girl who had caused all her misery, a red mist swam before her eyes. 'Go away!' she said, brusquely. 'I've nothing to say to you!'

'I wanted to tell you how sorry I am for what I did, Mrs Dickson,' Elma pleaded, 'though I don't suppose you'll ever forgive me. I love Ricky, and I'm going to miss him, but I'm glad you're getting him back.'

'I wouldn't have lost him in the first place if it hadn't been for you,' Cissie snapped. 'It doesn't matter to me now that you'd been carrying on with my husband behind my back, but when I think of the torture I've been through since my son was kept from me, and what it must have done to him to lose his mother, I could kill you!' Realising that her voice had risen hysterically, she stopped, in an effort to gain control of herself.

'I tried to make it up to him,' Elma whispered.

The anguish in the girl's eyes made Cissie feel a touch of unexpected pity for her. It had not been entirely Elma's fault. 'Thank you for telling the truth today,' she said, stiffly, 'I only wish you had told it at the time.'

Waiting until Elma walked away and was well clear of her, she did not see Bertram coming up behind her and whirled round in alarm when he said, 'I congratulate you, Cissie, on getting the better of me at last. I never thought you would have it in you.'

Her hand flew to her chest at seeing him looking at her with his old, charming smile. What was he after?

'You'll be happy to know that I leave for Canada next week, so this is goodbye for ever, and I wish you good luck in the future.'

She was so dazed that she shook the hand he held out, and he walked away, swaggering a little as if he had been the successful one, not she. Phoebe came hurrying back. 'Oh, I'm sorry, Cissie. I should have made sure you were right behind me. What did Bertram want?'

'He said he was going to Canada next week. He even wished me luck in the future.'

'Wonders will never cease. But I saw Elma speaking to you, as well, and I couldn't get into the corridor because two of the Lords, or whatever they are, were blocking the doorway.'

'She apologised to me.'

'I hope you told her what you thought of her.'

'Yes, I couldn't help it, but I ended up feeling sorry for her. If Bertram hadn't turned her head . . .'

'She was as bad as he was,' Phoebe said, vehemently.

'I suppose she was.'

'Are you ready to go? Richard's waiting with the car.'

Outside, Cissie looked around her in the bright sunshine. 'It's like a different world to me now,' she told Phoebe. 'I only want one thing now – no, two things. To hug my son till he tells me to stop, and to marry Hugh.'

Holding the door of the car open, Richard said, 'Phoebe and I are going to collect Ricky this afternoon, so one of your wishes will be granted in a few hours, Cissie, but we can't do anything about the other one. That's up to Hugh.'

'He's applied for a marriage licence already, he was so sure I'd get the divorce.'

'We were all sure of that,' Phoebe laughed.

'Phoebe,' Cissie sounded uncertain now, 'do you think I'm wrong to marry Hugh? He'll be my third husband, and we're happy the way we are.'

Considering this for a moment, Phoebe said, 'Maybe you're happy, but I know Hugh's not. As for it being your third marriage, that's nothing. Some of the film stars I've read about have been married four or five times.'

Cissie had to laugh. 'This time'll be the last for me.'

Within ten minutes, she was dashing into the shop. 'Oh Hugh, they granted me the divorce and gave me custody of Ricky. They're sending me a copy of – what did you call it, Richard?'

'The Interlocutor of the Lord Ordinary. It's the verdict in writing.'

With his arm round his wife, he watched Hugh and Cissie dancing round the shop, then he said, 'This is such a happy occasion that I think we ought to go upstairs and celebrate with the wine I brought.'

Phoebe winked at Cissie. 'I told you we were all sure of the result.'

'Good idea, Richard,' Hugh said, locking the door. 'We may as well close for an hour.'

All four enjoyed the wine but ate very little of the salad Cissie had prepared first thing that morning, and she was too excited to care. That afternoon, waiting in the shop for Phoebe and Richard to bring her son from Dundee, she could feel her excitement increasing, and it was not until almost four o'clock that she was struck by a dreadful thought.

'What if Ricky doesn't want to come?'

Hugh laid his hand over hers. 'Phoebe says he wants to see his mother.'

'Maybe he won't like me. Maybe he . . .'

'He'll love you,' Hugh interrupted. 'Who wouldn't?'

'But he's being taken away from his home, from the person who's looked after him for as long as he'll remember. Elma said she loved him, and I'm sure he must love her. I'll be a stranger to him, and I won't be able to give him as much as Bertram did. He's likely got masses of expensive toys, and he'll miss that.'

'Richard said he's taking as many of Ricky's belongings in the car as he can.'

'After living in that great big house, what's he going to think of this place, Hugh?'

'If I know wee boys, the sight of all the sweeties'll win him round. We'll just have to give him time to adjust.'

'I'm glad Bertram's going to Canada. I was worried in case he'd want to come and see his son occasionally.'

Hugh kissed her ear. 'You've nothing to worry about now.'

Cissie wanted to believe him, and tried to put her doubts behind her, just as she tried to put aside the nagging fear that her father would appear and kill them all.

When Richard's car drew up outside the shop, Cissie was ready to take Ricky in her arms, but he jumped out and ran inside, looking in wonderment at the rows of bottles and the confectionery under the glass on the counters. At last, he turned to Cissie. 'Are you really my mother?'

'Yes,' she whispered, fighting back her tears yet timid of hugging him now the time had come. 'I'm really your mother.'

'Will you give me as many sweets as I want?'

'Too many wouldn't be good for you,' she said, gently, and Hugh added, 'You'll get some, sometimes, though.'

The violet eyes regarded him haughtily. 'Who are you?'

Disappointed at the turn the meeting was taking, Cissie said, 'He's going to be your Daddy.'

'I have a Daddy. I don't need two.'

Phoebe stepped in hastily. 'I'm hungry, how about you?'

The small boy contemplated for a moment, then pronounced, 'Yes I am. Where do we eat?'

'In the kitchen upstairs.' Leaving Hugh to serve, Cissie felt a little hurt that her son was holding Phoebe's hand as they went through the back shop.

'In the kitchen?' came the piping treble. 'Only servants eat in a kitchen.'

'We don't have any servants,' she explained, 'and you'll like eating in my kitchen. You'll see me filling the plates and you can help me to clear the table afterwards.'

'I don't have to do that at home,' the boy scowled.

'You don't have to do it here, either.' She was beginning to feel let down. 'Only if you want to.'

When they went into the room at the centre of the controversy, Ricky stood still and let his eyes sweep round. 'It isn't as big as ours.'

The three adults looked at each other apprehensively, then Richard said, 'Sit down, Ricky.'

'Will you be sitting down, too, Grandpa?'

'Yes, I'll sit next to you.'

'And Grandma Phoebe?'

'We're all sitting down,' she laughed.

355

When Cissie and Phoebe rose to clear the table and wash up, Ricky picked up the cruet set. 'Where does this go?'

He seemed to be quite happy to lay things past when Cissie told him where they should go, but when everything was tidy and Richard said, 'Phoebe and I had better be leaving now, Cissie,' he looked scared. 'How long do I have to stay here?'

Cissie's heart went out to him. 'What did Elma tell you?'

'She said I'd be living in Leith, but she didn't say when I'd be going home again.' His bottom lip was quivering now.

Phoebe pulled him on to her knee. 'You're not going back to Dundee, Ricky. You'll be living here with your mother.'

'For . . . ever?'

'Yes, for ever. You're a big boy now, and you won't be a cry-baby, will you?' He shook his head doubtfully, and she went on, 'You'll soon love this house as much as your old one, and we'll come to see you every Wednesday.'

'Promise?' It was a little squeak as he stood up.

'Cross my heart and hope to die.'

'Come down with me to wave goodbye to them.' Cissie held out her hand to her son, but he didn't take it.

As the car drew away, she could see that he was struggling to keep back his tears. 'I'll tell you what, Ricky. You can stay in the shop with me till Hugh has his supper, then I'll show you your room.'

Left alone with him, she said, 'Would you like to tidy up this counter? It's sweets for the children, and they like to rumble through everything to see what there is, so it's in a right muddle.'

He soon had it in order, but was still pretending to move things when Hugh returned. 'My goodness, what a difference you've made,' Hugh beamed. 'It hasn't been as tidy as this for a long time.'

'It's time for bed, Ricky,' Cissie told the boy.

When she took him into his room, she waited for him to say something, but what he said was not what she expected. 'I don't want to sleep here!' he declared. 'I want to go home!'

'This is your home now, Ricky,' she said, softly, and put her arms tentatively round his stiff little body. He did not push her away, as she had half feared, but neither did he turn to her. 'You'll get to like it,' she went on, trying to think of something to win him round. This was all going so differently from what she had imagined.

Noticing the boxes Richard had brought up, he brightened a little. 'Are all my toys in there?'

'As many as your Grandpa could pack in,' she assured him, 'and if you want anything that's not there, you can tell him next time he comes, and he'll get them for you.'

That seemed to satisfy him, and he pulled free to go and sit on the bed. 'Do I have to have a bath tonight?'

'Not if you don't want to. You must be tired, so I'll just give your face and hands a quick wash and we'll get on your night things.'

'I can put my pyjamas on by myself, but Elma fastened the buttons for me.'

In ten minutes, he was sitting up in bed and looking at her with his wide violet eyes. 'Where do you sleep? Elma was in the room next to me at home.'

Poor little mite, Cissie thought, he was missing his nanny already. 'The room next to you is the bathroom, but I'll be in the bedroom over the landing. I'll hear if you call to me, or you can come through if you're scared in the night.'

'I'm never scared,' he insisted, but she could see that he was afraid of being left alone in the strange room.

'I'll leave the light on.' He turned his head away when she kissed him, and she said, sadly, 'Goodnight, Ricky.'

Hugh came up at half past nine. 'Well, how did it go?'

'He's not happy here,' she gulped, standing up so that she could slide into his arms.

357

'He'll soon forget. It's been some day, how d'you feel?'

Her smile was wry. 'Like I've been pulled through a mangle backwards. I thought everything would be perfect once I got him back, but he's not . . .'

'It'll take time, Cissie.'

Giving him a kiss, she sighed, 'Oh, Hugh, I don't know what I'd do if I didn't have you, and – I don't want you to sleep in the kitchen again. I want you with me.'

'Are you sure?'

'I think so.' She gave a tremulous smile. 'That sounds silly, doesn't it? Yes, I'm sure.' Ricky's behaviour had unsettled her, and she needed the comfort of Hugh's arms around her, of his loving.

When they went to bed, she knew that he understood her reason for asking him, and he did nothing until she made the first move, then his tender caresses soothed her even more than she had expected. To begin with, he was rather wary of going any further, but her responses encouraged him and they consummated their love in perfect harmony.

In the morning, it was a very happy Hugh who went to the shop by himself so that Cissie could get to know her son better, and they spent most of the morning putting Ricky's clothes tidily into the wardrobe and tallboy, his toys and books on the shelves Hugh had put up for him. He did not say much for a start, then he began to chatter about Elma, what she used to say, what she had done, and Cissie wondered if he would ever forget. To her credit, she did not say a word against the girl, because it was only natural that he should speak about the nanny he had loved.

After lunch, they relieved Hugh for an hour, and as soon as he saw the children's section, Ricky cried, 'It's as bad as it was before I tidied it yesterday.'

'It gets like this every day,' Cissie told him, 'so you'll have a steady job.'

When Hugh came down, he said solemnly, 'A worker

358

needs to be paid.' Twisting a square of paper into a poke, he filled it with bright red sweets and handed it to the little boy.

'They're Cherry Lips,' he explained.

'Can I eat them now?'

'As long as they don't put you off your supper.'

A week passed with Ricky still showing no sign of thawing to Cissie, never once addressing her as 'Mummy' or 'Mother', not even by her name. He was more forthcoming with Hugh, talking quite animatedly to him on Wednesday afternoon after the shop was closed, and he ran to Richard and Phoebe when they arrived, climbing on his grandfather's knee to tell him about his 'job'.

'He's never going to accept me,' Cissie wailed to Phoebe, when the two men took the boy out for a walk. 'He's always speaking about Elma.'

'You're expecting too much. He's only four, and he must have got very attached to her. It'll take a while for him to settle down.'

'That's what Hugh says, but Ricky's friendlier with him than he is with me.'

So it carried on until the wedding, ten days after Ricky came to stay. Richard and Phoebe were witnesses and Ricky stood quietly, his eyes and ears taking everything in. After Hugh and Cissie were pronounced husband and wife, they all went outside, and as they stood briefly on the steps of the Registrar's building, Ricky looked up at Hugh. 'Are you my new Daddy now?'

'Yes, lad, I am.' Hugh's voice cracked as he bent down and lifted him up.

Ricky slid his arms round the man's neck. 'I like you lots better than my old Daddy. I hardly ever saw him.'

Cissie's eyes overflowed, and she held her handkerchief up to wipe away her tears. Her son had just acknowledged Hugh as his stepfather, but he was no closer to her, the woman who had borne him.

On Sunday, when they went out as a proper family for the first time, Ricky held Hugh's hand while they walked round the docks, and asked him anything he wanted to know. After some time, Cissie said, 'You'll maybe see your Uncle Tommy's ship here one of these days.'

'Have I got an Uncle?'

'He's my brother, and your mother's brother is always your uncle. You'll like him, he's good fun.'

'When will his ship be here?'

'I don't know.'

'You don't know very much.' Ricky turned to Hugh again.

'Don't let it get you down, darling,' Hugh told her later. 'He's just a wee lad. He doesn't know he's upsetting you.'

That night, she had another horrifying dream about her father, and woke in a cold sweat, thankful that she had not disturbed Hugh. Deciding that her nightmare was a result of being so troubled about her son, she said nothing to her husband in the morning. It was just something else that would take time to sort itself out.

Chapter Thirty-one

❖

Cissie had worried before Ricky started school that he might not mix with the other boys, but when he spoke of them there was no sign of condescension. In two weeks, he had lost his 'posh' accent and talked incessantly about the 'chums' he played with, and she was relieved that they had accepted him as one of them. If only he would accept her as his mother.

Hugh had scoffed at her suggestion that they should send him to a private school. 'He'll get as good an education at a council-run place.'

When she mentioned it to Richard, he had said, 'A private school didn't do Bertram much good', which was what finally decided her against it.

She was in the shop one afternoon when Ricky came in and addressed Hugh as if she were invisible. 'Daddy, my Uncle Tommy's a sailor, isn't he? Does he sleep in a hammock? Does he wear wide-legged trousers?'

Hugh burst out laughing. 'You'll have to ask him son. I'm only a landlubber.'

'What's a landlubber?'

Cissie stepped in as Hugh turned, still laughing, to serve a customer. 'Come and get your supper, Ricky.'

Running ahead of her, he said, 'Why don't you call it tea, Mummy, like Elma did? Or dinner, like my old Daddy had?'

'We used to call it . . .' she began, but halted as it dawned on her what he had said. He had actually called her 'Mummy'!

Trying to hide her joy, she started again. 'We always called it supper when I was a girl in Aberdeen.'

'It must just be in Dundee they get dinner, because all my chums call it supper, too.'

When his meal was finished, he said, 'Can I go down to the shop now, Mummy? Daddy said I could have a pennyworth of dolly mixtures after I finish my job.'

'You shouldn't be eating sweets when you've newly had your supper.' Cissie couldn't help reprimanding him, and hoped he wouldn't revert to being distant with her again.

'Daddy said I could.'

She couldn't let him off with this. She had to teach him what he could and couldn't do. 'Daddy should know better.'

He looked thoughtful for a moment, then said, 'Why should I not eat sweets after I've had my supper?'

'It would upset your stomach.'

'If I just took one or two . . .'

Cissie sighed. 'Only one or two, then.'

He gave a mischievous grin. 'That's what Daddy said you'd say. Can I go now, Mummy?'

So relieved that he was still calling her 'Mummy', Cissie gave him a small pat on the rear. 'For half an hour, that's all, but take Daddy's tray up first.' Hugh had insisted on eating his meals in the store, to let her attend to the boy.

Ricky came back carrying the tray very carefully. 'Daddy's going to give me a more than a pennyworth so I can share with my chums. They don't believe I live in a sweetie shop.'

When Ricky came upstairs again, he laid a small paper bag on the table. 'I just ate two, Mummy.'

Practically sure that he had eaten a lot more than two, her heart still swelled with love, and without thinking, she pulled him to her. After a second, his arms went round her neck, and he whispered into her ear, 'I love you, Mummy.'

Quite overcome, Cissie kissed his chubby, upturned face. 'I love you, too, Ricky.'

He pulled away. 'Daddy says we should love everybody, but I can't love people I don't like, can I?'

Richard had some welcome news when he and Phoebe arrived the following day. 'I had a cable from Bertram saying he has decided to settle in Montreal. It has taken him long enough, and I hope he gives up his licentious ways now and makes something of himself.'

'I wonder why he went to Canada so suddenly?' Cissie said.

'Ah!' Richard smiled self-consciously. 'I was quite surprised at that myself. He had never obeyed me before. I told him I'd make a clause in my will that he was never to get his hands on Ricky's inheritance, and I ordered him to leave Scotland.

'You asked him to go?'

'I ordered him, though I expected him to refuse. I think things were getting too hot for him in Dundee, his misdemeanours coming home to roost, and it suited him to leave, to emigrate and start again.'

Cissie's unease at the first mention of Bertram dissipated completely. 'Richard,' she breathed, 'you don't know what this means to me. I couldn't understand why he gave up so easily, and I've always been afraid he'd come and take Ricky away from me again.'

'Ricky is no longer any use to him. I've seen to that. Rest assured, Cissie, Bertram will not bother you again.'

Ricky couldn't understand why there were hardly any leaves on the ground. 'I used to scusshle through piles of them in the autumn at home,' he said one morning before he set off for school, his last word making Cissie wince.

'There aren't so many trees in Leith,' she reminded him.

'If I'm a good boy, will you and Daddy take me to the

docks again on Sunday? Maybe Uncle Tommy's boat'll be in.'

'It might be,' she smiled. 'He hasn't been here for a long time. All right, we'll go on Sunday if it's a fine day.'

Going to the door with him, she was conscious that a man was disappearing round the corner. His hair silvery-white, his back bowed, he was shuffling away at great speed as if he didn't want to be seen, and there was something about him that gave Cissie the shivers. 'Have you noticed an old man hanging about?' she asked Hugh. 'He's got a bent back and he doesn't lift his feet properly.'

'I've seen him once or twice. Who is he?'

'I hoped you'd know, for I didn't like the look of him. What if he's a thief?'

Hugh gave a reassuring grin. 'He's not likely to steal a lucky tattie off the counter.'

'No,' she chuckled, dismissing the man from her thoughts. 'Ricky was saying there used to be piles of leaves in the autumn at home, so he's still thinking of Panache as home.'

'Force of habit. He knows this is his home now.'

'I can't help being a bit touchy about it. He was asking if we'd take him to see the boats again on Sunday. He hopes we'll see Tommy.'

'Tommy's going to get the shock of his life when he sees him,' Hugh laughed.

Unfortunately for the small boy, the rain was streaming down his bedroom window when he looked out on the Sunday morning, and he went through disconsolately to Cissie and Hugh. 'We can't go out, Mummy, it's too wet.'

'Come in beside us,' Hugh said, making room for him, 'and we'll think what to do instead.'

The pyjama-clad little boy took a big leap into the bed. 'I love being beside you and Mummy,' he said, as he snuggled down between them. 'After we've had our breakfast, will you fix up my train set, Daddy? We haven't played with it for an awful long time.'

After breakfast, Hugh took out the big box, and he had only removed a few of the contents when someone knocked at the shop door. 'Can't we get one day . . .' he began, plaintively, but was stopped by a musical whistle.

'It's Tommy!' Cissie exclaimed, throwing her duster from her and running down the stairs.

'Uncle Tommy?' Ricky asked, his eyes wide with hope.

'Yes, Uncle Tommy,' Hugh laughed. 'We'd better put this lot back in the cupboard. You won't want to play with your trains now.'

His sister having told him nothing when she let him in, Tommy stopped in amazement at the sight of the little boy. 'It's not – it can't be . . .'

'It is!' Cissie cried. 'Come and say hello to your Uncle Tommy, Ricky.'

He seemed came forward shyly. 'Hello, Uncle Tommy.'

'Hello, son,' Tommy grinned, then, with a whoop of joy, he swept his nephew up in his arms. 'Well, well! This is some surprise, isn't it?'

'If it hadn't been raining, Uncle Tommy, we were going to go to the docks to look for your boat, but we didn't go and Daddy and I were going to play with my train set.'

Setting him down again, Tommy said, 'I wanted a train set when I was a boy, but I never got one. Can I play, too?'

Cissie smiled as the box was brought out again and her husband, son and brother squatted down on the mat to set up the track. The train set kept them amused until she told them that they would have to move to let her set the table for dinner, and not only the boy looked disappointed that they had to stop and dismantle it.

In the afternoon, Ricky hung on to every word Tommy was saying about the voyage he had just finished, asking an intelligent question every now and then, but not hogging the limelight. Then, unable to contain his curiosity any longer, he said, 'Uncle Tommy, do you sleep in a hammock when you're on your boat?'

'No, lad, I've got a wee room all to myself, with a built-in bed. I'll let you see her some time, she's a beauty.'

'Who's she?' Ricky looked puzzled.

'She? She's the ship.'

'How can you tell when a ship's a she, Uncle Tommy?'

'All ships are called she, Ricky.'

'Why? Is it because people can trust them? Elma used to say you couldn't trust men.'

Tommy shot a troubled glance at Cissie. 'I wouldn't be so sure about that. Maybe there's some men you can't trust, but not many. You can trust most men like you can trust . . .' he searched for a suitable comparison, '. . . like you can trust it always to rain on a Sunday if you want to go out.'

Ricky laughed delightedly. 'You're funny, Uncle Tommy.'

Tommy pulled a face to show he could be even funnier, and jumped up to execute a little dance, which made his nephew chortle with glee. 'Can you do the sailor's hornpipe?'

'No, I'd need bell-bottoms for that.'

'A bell bottom?'

Hugh let out a loud guffaw. 'It's what you were speaking about earlier on, remember? The wide-legged trousers that sailors wear.'

'But I thought Uncle Tommy was a sailor, and he doesn't have a bell bottom.'

'Oh, Ricky,' Cissie sighed. 'Give Uncle Tommy some peace.'

'No, it's all right,' her brother smiled. 'It's the Royal Navy that wear bell-bottoms, lad, and I'm in the Merchant Navy. I'll wear my uniform the next time I come.'

As Ricky opened his mouth to ask another question, Hugh said, 'That's enough now. It's time you were in bed.'

'Oh, Daddy, must I?'

'I'll come and say goodnight to you,' Tommy promised, and Ricky trotted off quite contentedly.

When her son was settled for the night, Cissie said, 'I suppose you want to know what's been happening?'

Her brother smiled. 'I gather there's been some kind of upheaval that ended happily?'

Tommy was amazed when he learned the full extent of the upheaval. 'Well, I'm tickled pink you've got Ricky back, and I'd better congratulate you on your marriage. If I'd known about it, I'd have bought you a wedding present. If all goes as planned, I might be getting married shortly myself.'

'Oh, Tommy!' Cissie cried. 'I'm pleased to hear that. Is it still the Marion you told us about?'

'Aye. I spent all my time in Lowestoft with her last time, that's why I didn't manage to come to see you, and we've been writing to each other. I'm going to pop the question when I go this time, and if she says yes, we'll get married after my next trip. We'll be in for a refit, so I'll have a month or so off.'

'Have you time to come back before you go to Lowestoft? Richard and Phoebe'll be here on Wednesday afternoon, and you could meet them if you wanted.'

'I'd love to meet them. Marion can wait till Thursday.'

Hugh stepped in here. 'You can't disappoint your girl if she's expecting you tomorrow.'

'I'll give her a call from a phone box in the morning. I want to meet Phoebe, and, anyway, I promised I'd let Ricky see me in uniform.'

On Wednesday afternoon, Tommy hit it off with Richard and Phoebe from the minute he shook hands with them, and they were soon talking as if they were old friends, Cissie and Hugh taking a back seat. When Ricky came home, he gave a cursory 'Hello' to his Grandpa and Grandma and rushed past them. 'Ooh, I didn't know you'd have gold stripes on your sleeves, Uncle Tommy, and gold buttons! Are you an officer?'

'First Officer McGregor, that's me! Next in importance to the Captain . . . Well, he thinks he's more important.' Tommy tapped his nose with his forefinger and winked. 'D'you want to try on my hat?' He picked it up from the side of his chair and held it out.

Ricky took it reverently, the gold braid round the peak and the gold anchor of the Merchant Navy badge making his eyes almost pop out of their sockets. When Tommy urged him to put it on, he lifted it as if it were a crown and let it down slowly on his head, laughing when it came to rest on his nose.

'It's just a wee bit big,' Tommy said, his eyes dancing as he pushed it up until his nephew could see.

'Can I keep it on till I go to bed?' Given permission, he retreated into a silent make-believe world, and the adults were free to talk without interruptions.

Phoebe and Richard left at nine, but it was after ten before Cissie saw Tommy out. 'I can see why you like her so much,' he smiled. 'She's a fine woman. But you were awful quiet, is there something on your mind?'

'I didn't like to say anything in front of Hugh, but it came into my head when you were speaking to Richard and Phoebe. I didn't tell you before, because I was worried sick about it, but Da's out of prison.'

'I thought he'd five or six years to do yet. How long's he been out?'

'Two years anyway.'

Tommy looked puzzled. 'Why would they let him out as early as that? And how did you know?'

'It was in the Stop Press one night. He was out on parole, and he was meant to report in and he hadn't. I don't really understand it, but the police were asking for information. I was terrified he'd come after me — and Phoebe, as well, he'd be mad at her for divorcing him — but he hasn't shown up at all, even after that article in the paper I told you about.'

Frowning, Tommy said, 'It beats me. They let him out years early and just allow him to disappear? They must have caught him again, Cissie, and they won't let him out on parole a second time. He'll have to serve his full sentence, maybe longer.'

'I never saw anything about them catching him, but maybe they have, and he could still look for me when he gets out. I'd half convinced myself he couldn't find me, but I've had nightmares about him, and I know he'd never give up.'

Looking pensive, Tommy said, 'Have you told Hugh?'

'I couldn't. Oh, Tommy, I wish I knew where he is.'

'They must have caught him, and he could have died in jail for all we know.'

Not aware that he was saying this to allay her fears, her eyes brightened. 'Do you think so?'

'It's not impossible. Who would they notify if he had?'

'Marie, I suppose.'

'Do you want me to find out? I could go to Aberdeen in the morning, and go straight to Lowestoft from there.'

'Would you? Oh, I hope he's dead. I know that's an awful thing to say, but it would solve everything.'

'I hope to God the filthy bugger has kicked the bucket, the world would be a better place without him. I'd better leave you and love you, as the saying goes, but I'll let you know how I get on at Schoolhill, and when I get back from Lowestoft, I'll come and tell you if I'm engaged or not.'

Chapter Thirty-two

❦❦

On the train to London, Tommy was recalling the six full days he had spent in Lowestoft with Marion Rowse, when they had taken advantage of the Indian summer to cement their fragmented courtship. On the third day he had asked her to marry him and he could scarcely believe, even now, that she had said yes.

He was still in a state of total bliss when he reached King's Cross, and boarded the express to Edinburgh, picturing Marion's dear face and wishing that he hadn't left her so soon. It was not until York was left behind that the memory of his visit to Aberdeen began to intrude. Determined not to let it spoil his happiness, he pushed it aside, but it kept resurfacing, the accompanying sense of impending doom growing stronger each time until he was forced to think about it.

Marie was pleased to see him, but her welcoming smile faded when he said, abruptly, 'Is Da back in prison?'

'Not as far as I know,' she muttered, warily.

'So he's still on the loose?'

'On the loose? You make it sound like he was an animal escaped from the zoo.'

'He is an animal. He didn't deserve to live.'

'Oh, you're callous, Tommy McGregor,' Marie stormed, 'and you needn't bother coming here again if you can't forgive him for something that happened when he was drunk and didn't know what he was doing.'

'He always knew what he was doing, even when he was drunk as a Lord.'

'I bet Cissie's put you up to this, and it was all her fault. He'd never have started drinking again if she hadn't made Phoebe leave him. That's what started it all.'

'But you don't know everything,' her brother said, softly. 'It was his own bairn he killed.'

'She told you the same story?' Marie sneered. 'That's why Phoebe turned against him, and all, and it's not true. Da wouldn't have raped Cissie, and he didn't mean to kill Jim or little James.'

'I wouldn't put anything past him, and he did rape her.'

'I don't believe it,' Marie cried, tossing her head. 'She just said that so nobody would know her lad wouldn't admit the bairn was his, then she cleared out and me and Pat were left to take all the sneers about us having a murderer for a father. Wilfie near dumped me, and all, till I made him see it wasn't Da's fault. So you needn't stick up for Cissie, and I'm telling you what I told the bobbies when they came asking. I don't know where he is, but I'm ready to make a home for him when he does come home. Now, you'd better get out of my house, Tommy, and don't bother coming back!'

Tommy had been going over and over it in his mind for hours, and as he left Waverley Station, he was certain that something awful was going to happen soon. Marie's resentment of Cissie had blinkered her, but knowing his father, he could imagine him coming out of prison hell-bent on revenge – on the person he blamed for putting him there – and Cissie was damned lucky he hadn't found her yet. Hugh should be told that she was in danger, and Richard Dickson warned to take care of Phoebe. Turning into Leith Walk, Tommy thought of going to the sweetshop, but decided to wait until morning, when there would be a better chance of catching his brother-in-law alone.

Passing a public house, he thought he may as well have a quick pint before going on board. It was hardly nine o'clock and a drink might help him get rid of the dread that was inside him. The place was thick with cigarette smoke, and he was practically deafened by the noise, but he didn't see a soul he knew, and he wasn't in the mood for company, anyway. He took his tankard over to a dim corner, and even his first mouthful of beer lifted his depression a little.

He was about to take another draught when his hand halted midway to his mouth, a prickle of fear running across his scalp. No, no, it couldn't be! From his dark vantage point, he watched the white-haired man shuffling unsteadily up to the bar, shoulders hunched even when he put his elbow on the counter. Laying his tankard down, Tommy kept his eyes fixed on the newcomer, stretching his neck for a sight of the man's face when he turned his head. Oh God, it was! His father was in Leith! He wasn't the swaggering Big Tam his son remembered, though. This was an old man, a man bowed down after nearly ten years in jail and more than two years on the run.

Tommy drew back abruptly when Tam staggered towards him, slopping beer on the floor. Luckily, three men moved to make a space beside them and he sat down with his back to his son. His slurred speech when he joined in the conversation confirmed Tommy's guess that he had been in several pubs before this, and he was in good fettle, laughing and joking with his companions. His son felt like dashing over to punch the moon-face to a pulp, but he had the sense to stay where he was.

Keeping his eye on the table in front, he was certain that it wasn't coincidence that his father was here in Leith. He must have found out where Cissie lived. Tommy tried to remember if he had told Marie about the shop and was positive he hadn't, so how could the evil sod know? Unless . . . Cissie had said there was a bit in the paper about Hugh and her when the police caught that thief – Phoebe had been able to track her down because of it – but that was months ago. If Tam had seen it, he'd have come to Leith long before this.

It was almost closing time when the old man stood up and reeled out, and Tommy, desperate to know where he was going, rose and followed him.

He had been sure his father would make for Duke Street, and was taken aback when he turned in the other direction. Having to go the same way himself, he followed a little way behind, shaking his head in disgust at the slow, erratic path the bowed man was weaving. At last, when they reached the quay, Tommy could stand it no longer. He had to know what his father was up to. Quickening his steps, he came up alongside Tam. 'Where do you think you're going?' he demanded, rashly. 'You're hardly able to stand up.'

Taken by surprise, Tam stumbled as he turned round, but managed to steady himself. 'Who the hell do you think you're speaking to?' he roared. 'Can't a man have a coupla drinks without some nosy bastard thinking he's drunk?' He peered at Tommy now. 'That's not a bobby's uniform you've got on, sonny boy, so just bugger off and leave me alone.'

Tommy contemplated leaving him in ignorance. More than sixteen years had passed since they stood face to face in the kitchen at Schoolhill, and his father obviously didn't connect him with that defiant fifteen-year-old boy. Yet . . . he wouldn't be so likely to open up to a stranger. 'Do you not recognise me?'

The old man's bleary eyes narrowed to slits in an effort to place the interfering stranger, but he couldn't focus them properly. 'No!' he declared. 'I bloody well don't! Who the fucking hell are you?'

At that moment, one of Tommy's crew – his second mate and future brother-in-law – passed on his way back to the ship. 'Hi, Tommy!' he called. 'Do you want me to wait for you?'

'No, Arthur, just carry on. I'll be a wee while yet.'

Tam's face had darkened as comprehension struck him. 'God Almighty!' he exclaimed. 'It's the bloody prodigal son! A damned naval officer now.'

Having realised that a man as drunk as Tam would not take kindly to more harsh words, Tommy tried to speak in a friendly manner. 'I could hardly believe it was you when I saw you in the pub.'

'Did you think I was still locked up? Not me, I've been out for ages, though maybe you didn't know it was your sister who got me put inside.'

Tommy saw red at this shambles of a man excusing himself for what he had done to his daughter. 'It was your own bloody fault you were in, not Cissie's.'

'I lost the best part of my life through that bitch,' Tam snarled, 'and I'm going to get her! I've watched her shop and I know her man goes out every Friday.'

His mouth drying up, Tommy muttered, 'How did you know she had a shop?'

Tam looked pleased with himself now. 'I came across an old paper under the mattress in a doss-house a month or so back, and there it was! Name and address and everything!'

Tommy dredged his brain for something to deter him, his blood curdling when he saw that his father's fingers were curled as though he were strangling someone.

'I've waited long enough,' Tam went on, 'and I'm all set for tomorrow.' He halted, a little unsure of himself. 'This is Thursday night, is it not? Aye, your sister's time's up. And you, you ponced up bugger, you're not man enough to stop me.'

Tommy saw now that his father's eyes were crazed. It was a waste of time arguing with a madman. He felt like wiping the stupid grin off the mottled face, but it would likely make things worse.

'I'll get Phoebe's address out of Cissie first,' Tam went

on, his tongue loosened by drink. 'And I'll do her next.'

It was a blessing his father hadn't seen Phoebe going into the shop on Wednesdays, Tommy thought, or maybe he had seen her and hadn't recognised the elegant woman as his ex-wife. 'They'd hang you this time.'

Tam gave a sneering laugh. 'I'd be happy to swing for the pair of them, whores that they are!'

This was too much for Tommy. 'You're off your bloody head, you drunken bugger!'

In the next instant, a massive fist shot out and caught him so unexpectedly on the side of the head that he went down as if he'd been poleaxed, and while he was still lying dazed on the ground, he heard a hoarse shout and a loud splash. Trying to get up, he realised, with dawning horror, that his father was nowhere to be seen. He must have fallen over the edge! Once on his feet, Tommy ran to look down into the water and was in time to see Tam's bloodied face break the surface and then go under again. Even after what had been said, even though he hated his father with all his being, Tommy's first thought – as it should be to any sailor when someone falls into the sea – was to dive in and attempt to rescue the drowning man.

He was still struggling in the narrow space between a ship and the wall of the dock, to get the limp body clear of the filthy water, when a welcome voice said, 'Turn him roon' so I can get a hold o' his arms.'

With the stranger's help, the unconscious Tam was hoisted on to the quay, but in spite of all the two men did to try to revive him, their efforts were in vain, and Tommy sat back hopelessly on his heels.

'He must have bashed his heid on the side o' the ship when he went ower,' the stranger observed, eyeing the deep cut on Tam's forehead. 'You cannae do nothing more for him. I'll tell you what, I'm in a bit o' a hurry, but I'll report it to the polis, and you'd better wait here wi' him so you can tell them what happened.'

'Thanks.'

Tommy's teeth were chattering now, and he stood up out of the pool of water which surrounded him, his senses dull. He had wanted his father dead, yet he had tried to save him; it didn't make sense. His head was still pounding from the blow Tam had struck, and when he put his hand to his temple, he wasn't surprised to find a lump the size of an egg, nor that it wasn't only water that was running down his cheek. Wiping his blood-stained fingers on the leg of his trousers, he looked down at the huge hole in his father's forehead, and his heart gave a sickening jolt.

What would the bobbies make of this?

Chapter Thirty-three

It was almost two o'clock in the morning when a thunderous knocking on the shop door catapulted the Phimisters out of a deep sleep, and Hugh still hadn't got his wits together when it was repeated. 'All right, all right, I'm coming.'

Before he unlocked the door, he called, 'Who is it?' and was astonished when someone answered, 'The Leith police.' It brought back memories of his childhood chums trying to say the old tongue-twister – 'The Leith Police dismisseth us' – three times quickly. When he opened the door and saw two men regarding him sternly, his smile faded.

It was the shorter man who spoke. 'I'm Inspector McVey and this is Sergeant Inglis. Does Cissie McGregor live here?'

Mystified, Hugh said, 'Yes, she's my wife, and our name's Phimister.'

'Does your wife have a brother called Thomas?'

'Tommy's her oldest brother. What's happened?'

'All in good time. May we come in?'

As Hugh took them into the store, Cissie came in by the back door. 'Who was it, Hugh?' She halted, her sleepy face filling with apprehension when she saw the two men.

'It's the police, and it's something to do with Tommy,' Hugh told her.

The Inspector took over. 'Mrs Phimister, was your brother here this evening?'

'We were half expecting him, but he didn't show up. What's wrong? Has something happened to him?'

'He is being questioned at the police station.'

'Questioned? What's he supposed to have done?'

'Was he on good terms with his father?'

Cissie's anxious glance at her husband was not lost on the Inspector. 'You'd better tell me if there was bad blood between them.'

'He hasn't seen my father since before the war — 1913 some time.' Thinking that it might be best to deny any knowledge of Tam being out, she added, 'I don't know what this is about, for my father's serving fifteen years in Peterhead.'

McVey shook his head. 'His sentence was reduced to ten after an appeal, and he was released on parole two years ago. He broke his parole, however, and disappeared. Didn't you know he was out?'

'No, and Tommy didn't, either.' She crossed her fingers as she told the deliberate lie.

'Are you sure about that? They were seen tonight in the same public house, and witnesses say they left together.'

Hugh put his arm round Cissie's shoulders. 'Tommy wouldn't have been drinking with his father.'

A brief look of triumph crossed McVey's face. 'So! They were not on good terms? I didn't say they had been drinking together, but they certainly went out together, and less than half an hour later, Thomas McGregor senior was drowned in the docks.'

Giving a small sigh, Cissie collapsed against her husband, who lifted her up and set her on the only chair available. 'Did you have to tell her like that?' he demanded, angrily, running to the sink to fill a cup with water.

'I had to make sure she wasn't in on it. McGregor swears it was an accident, but two of the crew on a nearby ship heard them having a heated argument, and there's no doubt they had a fight, for both of them had head wounds. It looks very bad for him.'

Kneeling down, Hugh forced some liquid through Cissie's white lips, and with a splutter, she came round.

378

'I'm sorry, Mrs Phimister,' the Inspector said, 'but you must understand my position. Now, if you're feeling up to it, I'll have to ask you some questions.'

Over the next thirty minutes, she told him why Tommy had left Aberdeen, why she had left Aberdeen, why her father had been in prison, what she had done since leaving Aberdeen. The one question she could not, dared not, answer was why her father had been in Leith. If she told the Inspector what she thought, it would make things much worse for Tommy.

When the questions came to an end, Hugh said, 'Would it be possible for me to see my brother-in-law?'

McVey's mouth pursed briefly. 'I don't see why not. Just for a few minutes.'

Hugh turned to Cissie when the two men left. 'One of us has to stay here for Ricky, and you're not fit to go, but will you be all right on your own? I could ask Betty next door to come and sit with you.'

'I don't want anybody else knowing about this,' Cissie whispered. 'I'll be all right. Get on your clothes and go to Tommy as quick as you can. He'll need some support.'

When he went out, she huddled over the black-out fire, shivering with shock as much as cold, to try to make sense of her confused thoughts. Was Tommy guilty? He'd hated their father, and suspecting Tam of wanting to harm her, it was quite possible that he could have lost his temper and pushed him into the water. The water of the docks. A faint memory stirred in her, of something she hadn't thought of, hadn't wanted to think of, since she was seven years old. When she had asked her mother where Da was taking the dead baby, Mam had said, 'He's going to throw it in the docks.'

And there had been two other dead babies born after that, she recalled, the last on the same night Mam died, and they had likely been thrown in the docks, too.

Her thoughts took a jump forward. What was it Mrs

379

Barbour had said once? Something about a higher power than us that shaped our destiny. Had that higher power guided Big Tam to the quayside in Leith? If so – she gave a hysterical giggle – it was a fitting end for him.

Hugh was horrified at how pale and distraught Tommy was when he was brought through from the cells wrapped in a dark grey blanket. Only a week ago, he had been bouncing with good humour; now he looked like a man on his way to the gallows, his sunken eyes filled with the deep despair of a man who recognises that his life is ebbing away. And maybe it was.

'You'll soon be out,' Hugh said, making a valiant effort to sound bright. 'They can't hold you long without charging you, and they can't do that when you're innocent.'

'They say I held him under the water,' Tommy muttered, his voice flat. 'Nobody saw what happened, though they've witnesses to say I went out of the pub with him. I only followed him out to see where he was going. We'd a few words and he hit me, and I was on the ground when I heard the splash.'

'Was nobody else about at the time?' Hugh urged.

'A man helped me to get him out, but he went to report it to the police and I never saw him again.'

'Surely they took his name and address before they let him walk out of the station?'

'He just phoned, and they say he hung up before they could ask him anything.'

'Can't you give them a description? Good God, Tommy, he might have seen what happened. Maybe he could clear you.'

'I'd never seen him before.'

'Think, Tommy! What did he look like?'

'I was in such a state I didn't pay any attention to him, but I think he was older than me, maybe fifty or so.'

'What was he wearing?'

Tommy shook his head. 'Something dark.'

'Was he a seaman?' Hugh persisted.

'I don't know. I've been over it a dozen times already, and I can't remember a thing about him.'

'Did he say anything to you?'

After thinking deeply for some moments, Tommy told him as much as he could recall of what the stranger had said. 'He'd a Glasgow accent.'

'A Glasgow accent? That's something, but not enough.'

'No.' The tiny fragment of hope left Tommy's eyes.

Hugh was frantically trying to think of something else to jog his memory when a sergeant appeared. 'Time's up.'

As Tommy got to his feet, he shrugged his shoulders. 'It's a bugger, Hugh.'

'Don't lose hope, man. Something's bound to turn up. I'll stick around for a while, just in case.'

Hugh went to sit in the front office, his heart as heavy as lead. It didn't look good, and he couldn't go home yet, for what could he tell Cissie?

About two minutes later, a burly man was brought in, drunk and incapable, and swearing at the poor constable who was doing his best to keep him upright. This was followed by the loud cursing of a woman who had been lifted for soliciting in the street, and it took some time for her to be charged and taken away. Hugh was grateful for the diversions; they made the time pass more quickly. The next customer, as he had begun to think of them, was a thief who kept denying that he had stolen anything – even when three bulging pocket books were found on him. Then the door burst open again as two policeman dragged in a couple of youths who had been arrested for fighting.

When at last quiet reigned again, Hugh looked across at the perspiring desk sergeant and remarked, with a smile, 'I see you're kept busy.'

The man ran a finger round his damp collar. 'You should

see us on Saturday nights. It's Paddy's Market in here.'

In the lull that followed, Hugh suddenly remembered the cryptic telegram Tommy had sent from Aberdeen. All it said was 'Still out', and when he had forced Cissie to explain, he'd been shocked to learn that she was living in fear of her father's revenge. His assurances that he would let no harm come to her had had no effect, so it was providential that the man was dead.

His wife's safety no longer in question, he had dozed off when a short stocky man came in and walked briskly up to the counter. 'I thought I'd better come and see you afore you charged an innocent man wi' murder.'

The Glasgow accent made Hugh's head snap up, his spirits soaring as the man went on: 'I saw that ould fella falling in the water last night.'

'Just a minute sir,' the desk sergeant said. 'You'll have to speak to Inspector McVey. He's in charge of the case.'

Hugh glanced at the clock as the man was taken away by a constable. Twenty-five past eight. It shouldn't be long now. He would have given his eye teeth to have heard what was being said in the interview room, but at least there was a good chance of Tommy being cleared.

'A rum business,' observed the desk sergeant, scratching his head with the end of his pencil. 'Why has it taken him so long to come forward if he saw what happened? And if he's the man who phoned reporting it, why didn't he give us his name and all the details at the time?'

Realising that they were rhetorical questions, Hugh said nothing, but it was a rum business, and he prayed that the man could convince McVey that Tommy had been innocent of causing his father's death.

Having ascertained the name and address of the witness, McVey got down to the meatier business of finding out how much he knew about the drowning. 'You say you saw exactly what happened, Mr O'Shaughnessy?'

'Aye, sir, I did. I was walking along the quay when I heard two men arguing. A right barney they was having, but I couldnae see much at first. Anyways, when I got a wee bit closer, I saw one o' them had on a uniform and the other man had white hair, a ould man, bent a bit.'

'Could you hear what they were quarrelling about?'

'Naw, but I'd say the ould fella was fighting drunk, and I sees him gi'e the young lad a thump on the side o' the heid, and down he goes, out for the count.'

'The younger man?'

'Aye, and the ould lad loses his balance, and he sways for a minute then staggers about a bit. He was awfae near the edge and I could see he was gonnae go in, but I wasnae near enough to stop him, and down he goes, between a cargo boat and the side o' the quay. Then the young lad comes round, and he gets to his feet canny like, for he'd got a right wallop, and he runs to the edge and looks down. I think he gets a shock seeing the ould man in the water, and he jumps in and tries to get him out.'

'He actually tried to save him? He didn't push his head under, or hold him down in any way?'

'I tell you! He was trying to get him out, and me being so close by this time, I ran to gi'e him a hand.'

McVey leaned back and tapped his pencil on the table. 'So between you, you fished him out? Did either of you try to resuscitate him, Mr O'Shaughnessy?'

'Resuss . . . Get him breathing again? Aye, we tried, but he was a goner. I couldnae say if he drowned or no', for he'd a helluva hole in his heid.'

Unwilling to relinquish a promising murder case, McVey asked, 'Did you see young McGregor hit his father at all?'

'His father, was it? That's how he'd been in such a state about him. Naw, he didnae hit his ould fella once. I'd say he banged his heid on the side o' that boat when he went in, for the young lad was still flat on his back.'

383

'Is there any chance that he had hit his father before you caught sight of them?'

'Naw, naw! He was well behind till he ran up and spoke to him, and it was the ould fella that was − aggressive. Aye, that yin was just looking for a fight.'

McVey stared at the table. 'Had you seen either of the men before?'

'I'd never clapped eyes on none o' them.'

'Two things puzzle me, Mr O'Shaughnessy. Why did you not give us this information when you telephoned, and what made you come and tell us now?'

The Glaswegian pulled a face. 'I'd better come clean. I didnae want to get involved. You see, I was gonnae to see a wumman, and she expects me at ten on the dot. She's a married wumman and I'm a married man, but we've had this thing going for years.' He stopped and eyed McVey apprehensively. 'This is just between me and you. You'll no' go and tell the wife?'

A slight smile crossed the Inspector's face. 'No, no, that will not be necessary. You were saying . . .'

'Aye, right! I was telling you I was gonnae see Mary, and her man's on night shift, see, so I've aye to leave early in the morning, and I was walking back to my ship when this man asks me if I've heard about the murder. "A murder?" I says, interested now, and he says, "Some lad pushed a ould fella intae the dock last night." "That wasnae a murder," I says. "He was blazing drunk and he fell in." Then I starts to think. If the polis is holding an innocent man, I says to myself, it's up to me to get him off. And here I am.'

'We'll have to check with your lady friend . . .'

'Mary? Oh, for God's sake, Inspector, her man'll kill her if he thinks she's taking up wi' somebody else.'

'You said her husband's a night-shift worker. He'll sleep during the day, and I'll tell my men to be quiet.'

'You're a jewel, Inspector. Is that the lot?'

384

'For the time being. I take it you'll testify for McGregor at the inquest?'

'We're here another week. I shoulda gone hame to see the wife, but ... you ken how it is. Will it be before that?'

'I should think so, and we do have the name of your ship.'

'Right, then, I'll testify for him. Poor bugger, he must have thought his days was numbered.'

'They likely would have been if it hadn't been for you.'

O'Shaughnessy leaned forward. 'D'you ken this, Inspector? My wife aye says I'm good for nothing and I wish she coulda heard what you said the now. Me, Patrick John O'Shaughnessy, actually saving somebody's neck. But it's just as well she'll no' hear about it, for she'd kick my arse out the door if she found out about me and Mary.'

McVey was grinning broadly as he told his sergeant to show Mr O'Shaughnessy out.

It was fully another hour before Tommy was taken through in his half-dried uniform and had the contents of his pockets returned to him. Hugh had finally succumbed to sleep by that time, and had to be shaken awake.

Rubbing his eyes and yawning, it took him a few seconds to remember where he was, and only Tommy's, 'Come on Hugh, I want to get away from here,' prodded him fully conscious. 'Was that the man ...' He broke off, stifling another yawn.

'I'll tell you going up the road.'

Before Hugh struggled to his feet, Tommy was outside, filling his lungs with the not-very-fresh misty air. 'God, I'm glad to be out,' he said, with deep feeling, when his brother-in-law joined him. 'I never want to see the inside of another police station as long as I live.'

Hugh nodded. 'They're not the best of places, I know that. You'd better come to Duke Street with me, and

Cissie'll give you some dry clothes. Now, what did that witness say?'

'McVey was laughing fit to burst when he came through to me. "I'm sorry, Mr McGregor," he said, "I know this is not a laughing matter, but that O'Shaughnessy would make the Pope laugh, though you wouldn't be walking out of here if it hadn't been for him." ' Tommy related as much as he could remember of what the Inspector had told him, ending by heaving a lengthy sigh. 'I wish I could find O'Shaughnessy to thank him. If he hadn't been walking along that . . .'

'Aye, you were damned lucky he'd a lady friend in Leith.'

'A wumman friend,' Tommy chuckled.

'Do you think your father was looking for Cissie?' Hugh wanted to know if Cissie's fears had been justified.

Tommy hesitated, then said, 'He was going to kill her.'

'What?' The blood drained from Hugh's face.

'He blamed her for him being put away, and he'd stored it up all these years. He was right off his head, and do you know this, Hugh? I was angry enough to kill him – I might have ended up shoving him in – but when I saw him in the water, I tried to save him. Does that make sense to you?'

'Tommy,' Hugh said, gently, 'I think you've had more than you can take tonight.'

'He had it all worked out. He'd been watching your shop for weeks . . .'

'The old white-haired man!' Hugh exclaimed.

'That was him. Just think, though. There was me trying to save him from drowning when it was best the thing that could have happened. It was an automatic reaction, but to the end of my days I'll be thankful I failed.'

Hugh fell silent, and after some time, Tommy said, 'I said nothing to the bobbies about what he meant to do to

386

Cissie, for it would have given me a prize motive for doing him in, and it's best she doesn't know.'

'I'll never breathe a word of it,' Hugh vowed, 'to Cissie or anybody else.'

Frantic with worry about Tommy, Cissie opened the shop at half past six as usual – she couldn't disappoint the men who came in for cigarettes before they went to work – but she went upstairs at eight to get Ricky ready for school. She hadn't had time to make porridge, and when he pulled a face as she gave him a boiled egg, her nerves were so on edge that she smacked his hand. 'Eat what's put in front of you, my lad.'

Head down, he lifted the bone egg-spoon and dug it into the bright yellow yolk. 'That's more like it,' she smiled, sorry now for being angry at him. It wasn't his fault she was so short-tempered.

When Hugh and Tommy walked in at ten to ten, her drawn face lit up, and Hugh said, 'Tommy's clothes are still damp. You'd better take him upstairs and give him something of mine to wear.'

After he changed, Tommy told his sister how he had seen Tam and followed him, but he glossed over the reason for their quarrel, and, although she suspected that it had been because of her, she didn't press him. 'He let fly with his fists when I told him off for being drunk, and the next thing I knew I was on the ground and he was in the water. The witness said he'd lost his balance. He'd a gash on his head, so it looked as if I'd clouted him one before I shoved him in, but I never touched him. I even tried to save him, God knows why, but the bobbies wouldn't believe me, not till the witness said he'd helped me to get him out.'

'I'm glad you tried,' Cissie said. 'At least you'll have nothing to reproach yourself for. It was his own fault for being so drunk. Drink's been the root of all his troubles.'

'Aye, I suppose there's something in that.' Tommy blew out his lips noisily. 'Well, the best thing now is to forget about it – or try to, anyway.'

Going out of the shop, he said, with his old exuberance, as if he had already put the trouble behind him, 'I nearly forgot to tell you. Me and Marion got engaged.'

'Oh, congratulations, Tommy!' Cissie cried, kissing him on the cheek.

'I'll bring her to Edinburgh for our honeymoon, so you can judge for yourself if I've made a good choice.'

'If she's half as good as Cissie, she's a good choice,' Hugh smiled, shaking hands with him.

'Maybe this next trip'll be my last. I've seen enough of the world and I feel like settling down.'

'High time,' Cissie grinned, as he went out.

Ricky came running in from school shortly afterwards, and she had no time to think until he'd had his dinner and gone out again. 'You should have been at the wholesalers today,' she reminded Hugh.

'It won't matter for one week.' It occurred to him that if Tommy had not seen his father the night before, he'd have gone out as usual and come back to find ... Shuddering, he drew his wife against him roughly. 'Cissie, I love you.'

The unexpectedness and warmth of his kiss surprised her. 'What brought that on?' she laughed.

'I mean it,' he said, earnestly.

Cissie had just washed the lunch dishes when Richard and Phoebe made an unexpected appearance, having read about Tam in the morning newspaper, and they were even more surprised when they learned about Tommy's arrest and release.

They had to stop talking about it when Ricky came home in the afternoon, but when the little boy went to bed, Richard said, 'I hope this doesn't shock you, Cissie, but I can't help being glad that your father is dead.'

'It doesn't shock me,' she burst out, 'I'm glad myself. He was an evil man when the drink was on him.'

Phoebe nodded vigorously. 'He was, Richard, he even . . .'

Her abrupt, embarrassed stop made Cissie realise what she had been about to say. 'It's all right, Phoebe. Hugh knows.' Turning to Richard, she explained, 'He killed his own baby.'

His eyes widened. 'He had raped you?'

'Phoebe promised never to tell anybody and I'm grateful to her for keeping her promise, but I told Tommy myself, and Hugh, so you may as well know.'

Richard laid his hand over hers. 'Thank you for taking me into your confidence, Cissie, and you have my word that it will never cross my lips. I know Phoebe's been worried about what he would do when he came out of prison, and she won't have to worry any longer. That's why I'm glad he's dead.'

Phoebe look at her husband in surprise. 'How did you know I was worried? I never said anything.'

'The workings of your mind are an open book to me, Phoebe, my dear,' he smiled, rising to his feet. 'Now, we must let these good people get to bed. They have been up since early morning, remember.'

Phoebe and Cissie both shed a few tears as the goodbyes were said, and Hugh insisted on going down to see their visitors off. 'It's been some day!' he remarked, when he joined his wife in their bedroom. 'I feel like I haven't slept for a week. How about you?'

Cissie heaved a long sigh. 'I feel like I've been turned inside out and back again, but I can stop worrying now. I was sure he was going to kill me.'

Hugh's heart did a sinking somersault, but he hastened to reassure her. 'No, my darling, you were imagining things.'

'I suppose I was, and it's all over now. I'll make us a cup of tea, then we can . . .'

'I don't want anything. I can hardly keep my eyes open.'

'I'll not bother, either.'

They had not been in bed long when Cissie said, softly, 'I've been thinking, Hugh. With the money we've got in the bank now, and what we'd get if we sell this place, we could buy a better shop, and a house with a big garden for Ricky and his little brother or sister to play in.'

Hugh's heavy eyelids shot up. 'Are you telling me . . . ?'

As his arms came round her, she snuggled against him. 'I meant to tell you today anyway, but – things put it out of my head. We'll make a new beginning, just you and me, and Ricky and . . .' She broke off laughing. 'We'll have to think of some boys' and girls' names.'

'Not right now, my dearest one,' Hugh murmured, with a purposeful gleam in his eyes.